Terror on the Bay

Charles Evans Jr.

Copyright © 2013 **Charles Evans Jr.**

All rights reserved.

ISBN: 0615865534

ISBN 13: 9780615865539

Library of Congress Control Number: 2013914829

LCCN Imprint Name: Cambridge, Md.

Best Wishes

Charlie

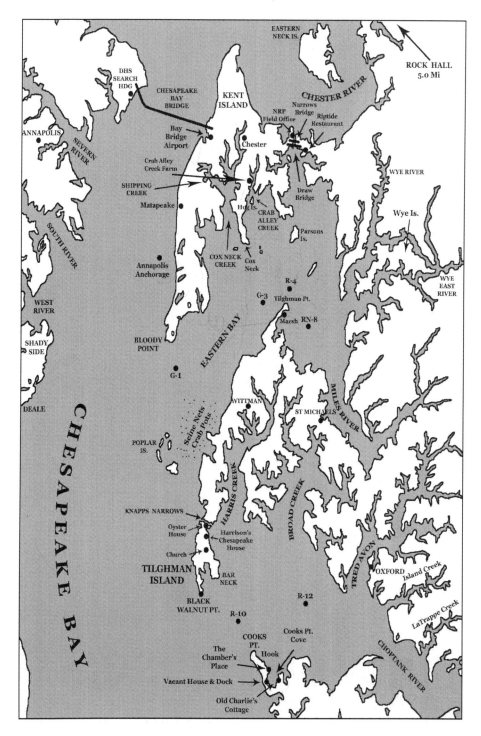

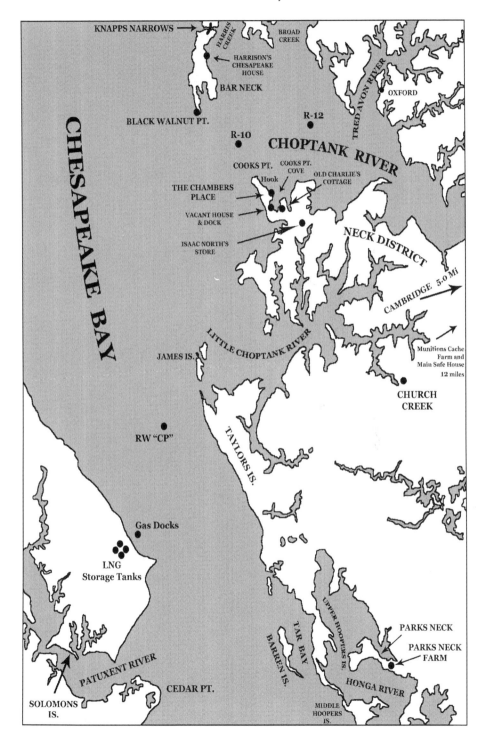

Dedication

This book is dedicated to the Chesapeake Bay Waterman and all those first responders, past, present, and future who have placed themselves in harm's way to help, save, or retrieve those in danger. It is further dedicated to all our soldiers who have died in our Country's service and to the Wounded Warriors who have returned home.

Acknowledgements

The writing of "Terror on the Bay" has been a journey of great joy. When I started I told my family and friends that it didn't matter if the book ever got published, it was the journey of researching and writing that brought such great pleasure and peace.

Along that road of travel there were many who gave of their time and expertise in editing, advising, and supporting my efforts; Judy Reveal for her editing - Kirk Eason, Paul Schurick, and Gail Romain for Beta Testing the book and for their encouragement, and Gail Romain for all of her support and editing, especially when I was discouraged with the process.

Illustrations by Artist: C. Keith Whitelock - Salisbury, Md.
Back Cover Photo by Griff Evans - Chester, Md.

Preface

We are ill prepared for the ferocity of a major jihadist's attack on American's homeland.

If you have ever wondered whether another terrorist attack of the magnitude of 9/11 could occur on American soil, this story will convince you that it can.

Chapter 1

The Intruder

It was a bitterly cold day in late February of 2010, as the *Miss Alice* plowed northward in the early morning light, the ice crackling and crunching under the weight of her bow. In her wake she left behind shattered ice crystals, rolling and undulating like a blanket of broken glass. The only sound Captain Pete Creighton heard was the steady rumble of the workboat's engines, as dark, oily smoke belched from her twin exhaust stacks.

Alone and at peace with the dawn of another day on the water, Pete steered *Miss Alice* toward the oyster grounds, which were just north of the Chesapeake Bay Bridge. The steaming coffee mug he held, which was old and dented, used to be his grandfather's. The heat from the metal mug warmed his cold hands. Through the dense fog ahead, the pilings and the structure of the Bay Bridge slowly began to emerge from the shadows of the dawn like a mirage, revealing the power and majesty of this Maryland Icon. As Pete passed under the bridge, the familiar voice of his childhood buddy and best friend, Mack North, abruptly broke the solitude of his trip to the outer edges of the bar.

"Hey, Pete. Where are you?"

Pete clicked the talk button on his mike and responded, "Just passing 'neath the bridge. Where are you?"

"I got started late, Pete, but I am not far behind you. I'll meet you where we decided, as soon as I can. Leave me a few of 'em oysters, you hear?"

"Fog's gotten thick around here, Mack. Keep an eye out for the bridge and those foreign freighters." Suddenly serious, Pete peered into the fog. "One of those container ships crept up on me from God knows where a little while ago just off Poplar Island. Ship damn near put me under with her wake - big as a mountain."

1

'Damn foreigners. No respect for us watermen,' thought Pete, as he put the microphone back in its cradle.

✳✳✳

As Mack neared the oyster bar, he slowed down his boat, the *Miss Patricia*, to trolling speed, looked around, and clicked the talk button. "Hey, Pete," Mack squawked into the microphone. "GPS says I'm getting close to the northeast bar marker, but this fog's thick as oyster stew. I can't see more than thirty feet off my bow."

Pete's voice came reassuringly back to him. "I'm anchored just off the bar marker. I think I hear you off my port side. Sounds like you're real close."

Mack peered into the gloom as a dim shape slowly emerged. He clicked the microphone. "Gotcha in my sight. OK with you if I come up and lay in the deeper water on your starboard side?"

"OK with me Mack. So far, I am doing pretty good in this shallower water."

✳✳✳

At the end of their first two hours of tonging and culling, Pete called Mack, "How you doing in that spot?"

"Not bad. Maybe four bushels so far. How about you, Pete?"

"Can't complain. Maybe six bushels, so far. But I am going to break for lunch, Mack. Louise fixed me a few slabs of scrapple, hash browns, and biscuits. Guess I'll heat 'em up on the stove, dry off while I eat, then get back to work. How about you?"

"I'm going to keep on tonging," Mack said, "cause at some point this calm's gonna change, the fog'll lift, and the wind'll start to blow. Besides, need to catch up to your six bushels before I give myself a break."

"In that case, maybe I'll keep on working too," Pete said.

"Yeah, sure," quipped Mack.

Once Pete had finished his lunch, he retrieved his dried gloves from the rack next to the stove, left the warmth of the cabin, went back on deck, and started right back tonging.

The National Oceanic and Atmospheric Administration had predicted fog from early morning until late morning. At about 11:30 a.m., as the wind began to pick up and the fog slowly started to recede, Pete stepped down from the gunwale and shouted across the water, "Hey, Mack, wind's starting to pick up. Think it's about time to head in?"

Barely hearing Pete's voice, Mack jumped down onto the deck and grabbed the microphone. "Couldn't really hear you, Pete. But, OK by me. It may take me a few minutes to cull this last batch and get her cleaned up before I can pull anchor."

Picking up his mike, Pete said, "Gotcha, Mack. It'll take me a few to do the same. Call me back when you're ready."

"Will do." Mack replaced the microphone, turned back to the board, and started to cull his last catch.

Knowing that Mack was slower than he was, Pete took his time cleaning up his board and putting his tongs back on top of the canopy. As he did so, standing on the wide gunwale along the side of the cabin, he heard the high-pitched sound of a boat's motor moving at a fast clip toward him. The sound echoed off of the water and through the fog. It seemed to be coming from his starboard side, where Mack's *Miss Patricia* was anchored. Holding onto the teak canopy handrail, Pete strained to listen, and as he did so, the noise grew stronger with each passing second.

Suddenly, Pete saw it. The thing sliced out of the dense fog, brushing perilously close to Mack's anchor line and throwing a huge wake as she knifed through the water. 'Must be moving damn near forty knots,' Pete thought.

Pete watched in horror. Mack, concentrating on cleaning his deck, hadn't seen her coming. At the last second before she cut in front of him, Mack saw the intruder bearing directly down on him. Mack quickly grabbed onto the canopy strut and held on for dear life. The wake slammed into the starboard side of the *Miss Patricia*. The boat healed over almost twenty degrees.

Mack strained to stay upright. "Holy Shit! What the hell was that?" he blurted out.

Pete stood helplessly by as Mack slipped and fell to the deck. Mack regained his footing, stood up and turned around to stare at the intruder that had just bolted out of the fog.

Luckily, Pete had heard the boat coming as it breached the fog. He now found himself staring straight at her. She was a Bay-built dead rise, with an acutely flared bow - typical of the early Hooper's Island-built workboats. The hull was all white. Even the bottom paint was white. She seemed to be about forty feet long with a beam of around fourteen feet. She plowed through the oyster grounds, knifing through the water like a coast guard cutter.

Pete stared at the fast-approaching boat and realized that she had no numbers or stickers on her bow, no equipment on her decks, and no name on her stern. However, she had enough antennas - he counted six - to match the communications needs of a coast guard patrol boat. More strangely, no one was on deck. The only thing he had seen was the outline of a man standing in the cabin at the helm, his attention focused on a large GPS screen whose electric-blue hue reflected on the man's shadowy foreign facial features. As the boat flashed by him, Pete was sure he had seen an assault rifle slung over the captain's chair.

Pete jumped down from the gunwale and grabbed the microphone, but before he could punch the talk button Mack's voice pummeled his ear.

"God Almighty. Pete, did you see that?"

Pete keyed the microphone. "Damn right I saw the bastard. Shit. I was listening to what I thought was a boat moving toward us fast. Then, the son of a bitch launched straight for us! You OK, Mack? Didn't swipe you, did he?"

"No, Pete. But the bastard damn near knocked me overboard. Almost took my anchor line with him! Did you get a good look at it? Cause I didn't. It just happened too damn fast."

"I saw it real good," Pete muttered. "She had no name or numbers on her Mack, but I'd recognize that hull anywhere."

As his boat rolled back and forth with the residual aftershocks of the intruder's wake, Mack called out, "Reckless son of a bitch!"

Pete went back to shoveling his catch against the starboard stern boards, shaking his head and grumbling about the stupidity and arrogance of such people. He checked the bilge and restarted the engine. Pete went forward to haul in the anchor. He reached for the microphone and said, "Hey, Mack. You ready to head back?"

"Yep. Just give me a minute to check my bilge." Mack started up his engine. "Hey, Pete. Switch over to our channel." To lessen the likelihood of others overhearing their conversation at times like this, they always used channel seventy-eight in this part of the middle Bay because it was rarely monitored.

As the two headed back to the Oyster House, the banter back-and-forth was contentious. While Pete was determined to chase after the intruder, Mack, though mad as hell, was able to cool Pete down and convince him that it would be too dangerous to run off half-cocked in this fog, especially if that really was an assault rifle hanging off of the captain's chair. Besides, there was no way they would be able to catch up to a boat moving at forty knots.

On the way back to Tilghman, a fellow waterman named Bill Collins, who had by chance overheard their conversations before they switched to channel number seventy-eight, hailed Captain Pete on channel number sixteen. "Hey, Pete. You guys aren't the only ones who've had a run-in with that bastard. He ran right in front of me a week ago and damn near ran over my cousin George's boat the week before. Sure hope someone catches up with him and settles the score."

"Thanks, Bill. Glad to know we aren't the only ones with a grudge."

As they approached the entrance to Knapp's Narrows, Pete switched back to channel number 78, summing up his frustration and anger by saying, "Mack, I am so pissed with that damn guy. The bastard needs a lesson in respect and seamanship. But what really worries me is what that guy is up to. You don't run the Bay without a name or boat numbers, unless you're hiding something."

"Your right, Pete. Something is very wrong with this."

Just before they arrived at the Oyster House to unload their catch, Pete said, "Mack don't know how you feel about it, but I don't think we should share today's goings-on with anyone else, including family. We need to try to figure it out on our own. If this turns out to be some illegal activity, like drugs or such, I don't want to risk harm to anyone else by sharing it with them."

"Since we probably won't be able to get out tomorrow 'cause of the gale winds they're calling for, I'll stop by your place in the morning after I return from my errands in town," Mack said. Pete nodded in agreement. "See you in the morning, Mack."

That night, Pete tossed and turned. His mind was overactive from the day's encounter. He got up at 12:30 a.m. and tiptoed quietly into the kitchen to grab a glass of juice from the fridge. He sat at the old Formica breakfast table recalling the events of the day, trying to figure out where the hell that boat had come from. He returned to bed an hour later with no answers. Unable to sleep, he got up at 4:30 a.m., checked the weather, and realized that Mack's prediction had been right. Twenty-five-knot winds would keep them off the water for at least that day. Given the rake of her bow, her long flowing lines, and the fact that he had never seen her anywhere around Tilghman Island, Pete's initial thought was that the intruder had to be harbored somewhere south of them - maybe Taylor's, Hooper's, or Deal Island. He also thought she might be harbored across the Bay on the western shore. However, with that Hooper's Island flared bow and those beautiful lines, her origins were clearly rooted somewhere in or near those Eastern Shore Islands.

'So, if I'm right,,' Pete thought. 'If we want to find out who owns her and what they were doing barreling through our oyster grounds, we got to go out and look for her. As soon as Mack comes over, we'll put our heads together and figure it out. Just like in the old Hardy Boys books we used to read on summer days. Just like old times. Mack and me, skipping school and running off on an adventure or an investigation of sorts.' Pete chuckled to himself. 'Imagine that, at our age!'

Outside, truck tires rolled over the gravel in Pete's driveway and came to a grinding halt, drawing his attention back to the present. He looked out the window to see Mack jump down from the cab.

"Hey, Pete. Where are ya?" Mack called out as he slammed the door shut.

"Back in the kitchen, Mack."

Mack opened the back door as Pete, sitting at the kitchen table, continued to pour over an old chart of the Hooper Straights. Grinning, with an un-characteristic lilt to his voice, Mack said, "What you lookin' for? A place to hide from Louise?"

Pete's tone was solemn. "No. I'm looking for someone else's hiding place."

"You're serious, aren't you?" Mack pulled up a chair next to Pete and cast his eyes on the spot on the chart where Pete's finger rested.

"Damn right, I'm serious. I want to know who that bastard was and why he was cutting through our water at forty knots in thick fog, paying no mind to anyone. I know that bum's up to no good."

"OK. So, how we goin' to find him? And, more importantly, what we goin' to do with him if we do?" Mack said.

Pete leaned back from the table, turned to face Mack, and said, "First, we are goin' to give him a real good lickin,' then turn him over to the authorities - that is, assuming he's still able to walk. Mack, remember when we snuck off from Mrs. Jackson's eighth-grade class? As I recall, we rode bikes clear down to Black Walnut Point to find out if that nasty old Mr. Mudge was actually makin' booze in his corn crib."

"Yeah," said Mack. "And I remember the whippin' we both got from our fathers that afternoon when we got back. You lookin' for a whippin' when Louise finds out you're playing hooky 'stead of makin' a livin'?"

"Come on, Mack. Aren't you curious 'bout what that boat was doing there without no markings?"

"Sure I'm curious, but why chase after a ghost?"

Leaning forward with his elbows on the table, Pete said, "Cause that guy's up to no good and this is our Bay." The more Pete thought about it, the angrier he got. "Or did you forget that?"

"I didn't forget Pete, but my Beth's one strong women - stronger even than my old man was, and she's got a mighty temper. Don't need no whippin" from her or Louise."

Pete grinned and thought about how Mack's old lady sure was one tough gal. "But, Mack, we ain't been on an adventure for a long time, my friend. Ain't it about time we launched our second childhoods?" Pete looked at Mack and thought about what a pair of sixty-five-year-old men could do, or more importantly what they could no longer do. Here they were with lean yet crooked frames, leathery hands, wrinkled faces, and skin like tree bark. Both men wore the thousands of rough days they had spent on the water, but they were stronger than most men in their thirties. They sure looked like two shriveled-up and waterlogged old men rather than two eighth graders about to go on a new adventure.

"Damn you, Pete. You always get my ass in trouble." But Mack found himself smiling at the thought of a new adventure. After a moment of silence, he looked across the table at Pete. "So, what's the plan?"

Pete looked around to be sure they were alone, then he leaned in closer to Mack and began to share the plan he'd been working on - a plan that would take them on a dark journey into a world of treachery and danger they could never have imagined.

Chapter 2

The Search

Mack met Pete at his dock early the next morning. The wind was blowing up from the south across Tilghman Island, carrying a steady rain that churned the waters, turning them a frothy brown.

"Pete, it's starting to rain awful hard, and lightning's coming up the Bay. With the way this storm's picking up, I am against going by water to look for that boat."

Pete could barely see ten feet in front of him. No one in their right mind would go out on the Bay in this mess. "You're right Mack. Let's just take my truck, drive down to Church Creek, and start looking around."

"OK with me," Mack said. "But what if someone we know sees us? What's our excuse for being down there?"

Pete shrugged. "Let's just say we're out looking for a used crab boat for Mike to use come spring."

"You mean my Mike?"

"Yeah," said Pete. "Why?"

"Cause my boy's trying to get away from the water - not get more involved in it. Mike's been doing more carpentry work than anything else. Says he's looking for a real career, not a dead-end waterman's life." The admission that his son was turning away from the family business sat heavy on his heart. It was hard for Mack to think that the family tradition of working on the water might end with him. The bitterness and pain came through in Mack's voice.

"Mack, those guys down below Cambridge don't even know Mike. They'll never know the difference."

"Maybe," said Mack. "But the story you've concocted seems pretty weak to me."

"You worry more than a preacher, you know that?"

"Yeah, and sometimes my worryin' has kept us both out of trouble, including jail. Remember when you wanted to steal that case of beer off the dock at Tilghman Market so's you'd have a damn good time after the prom with…what was her name? That girl from Whitman - Dana?"

"Lay off it," Pete said.

"By the way, there wasn't enough beer on the whole Eastern Shore to get her to come 'round to liking you!" Mack laughed.

"All right, then you come up with a better idea," Pete grumbled.

After a long period of quiet tension, Mack finally broke the silence. "I'll go along with you this time, Pete, but not one word to Mike - or anyone else, for that matter. And if someone gets suspicious, we back off and back off fast, OK?"

"OK."

They climbed into Pete's Ford-F 350 and headed for Cambridge. Just south of the Choptank River, they turned onto Route 16 and drove southwest to Church Creek. They spent the next few hours poking around the many creeks between the town of Church Creek and Taylor's Island. They searched the county docks where watermen usually tied up, but finally they decided that the boat they were looking for was most likely docked on private property. They spent the rest of their time driving down private lanes and back roads, peering through the rain-drenched windshield and trying to find the proverbial needle in a haystack.

Finally, Mack looked at his watch. Shifting uncomfortably in his seat, he said in disgust, "Nothing, Pete. Absolutely nothing. We've been at this for hours. She's not around here, as far I can see."

"So, what do you want to do?" Pete said.

"How about calling it quits for the day," Mack answered.

Pete sighed in resignation. "Well, OK, but unless we're serious about this, we'll never find out what's really going on."

On their drive back, they stopped at the local store in Church Creek to get a soda and asked the store clerk if he knew of any boat that had been rebuilt there in the last few months. The young boy scratched his chin and said, "Only one I know of is a big old forty-footer that has been redone, but nobody seems to know where she was worked on or who owns her. Boat's been seen off of Hooper's Island. Evidentially, she's captained by a foreigner who's pissed off some of the local watermen, including my own dad, by cutting across their wakes too close to their sterns. Seems the guy has no idea what he's doing."

"Is that all you know about her?"

"Well, I know that several of the local watermen say that she has lots of antennas on her and that they have picked up foreign chatter when they have been near her, as though they are calling someone to let them know about the waterman's boats they had come across. But that's about it. Oh, one other thing. They say that one waterman saw guns onboard her, including what looked like an assault rifle."

"Thanks, young man."

"Sure, but why'd you ask?

"We've seen her too and are trying to check her out."

"Well, as my dad says, with foreigners and guns onboard, he's going to steer clear of her. Says life's too short to meddle in someone else's business. Tough enough makin' a living on the water these days, let alone fooling with some foreigners with guns."

"Your dad is probable right. Anyway, thanks again for the information."

Back in the truck, Mack and Pete talked about what they had heard. They agreed to continue their search during the oyster season, when the weather prevented them from tonging. They also decided that if they didn't find the boat before the season ended, they would keep on looking until they mutually agreed to give up. Normally, a long-term commitment of time was not their style, but in this case they feared that something was seriously amiss.

✳✳✳

The season was progressing without incident. Then, toward the end of March they heard that someone out of Hoopersville in Somerset County had experienced a similar run-in off of Barren Island. The story was that a smaller Hoopers' Island-style boat with no name or registration numbers on it had cut through a gill-net area. It had happened at dusk - just as the watermen were attaching a new section of net to the last pole. The rumor was that the boat had swerved to starboard just before it clipped the poll and sideswiped their small net boat. One man was knocked overboard, but he managed to climb back in. Pete heard this from his son, Bo. When he told Mack, Mack immediately called his brother Walt, who lived on Hooper's Island, to see if he'd heard the same story. Walt confirmed the story; the guy who was knocked overboard was a close friend. His friend told him that the idiot driving the boat was a foreigner who didn't seem to know what he was doing. The guy appeared to be focused solely on his GPS screen, never once looking up from it until the last second - just before he hit the pole. Because he got a real good look at the guy, when he got back he called Maryland's Department of Natural Resources to tell them what had happen. DNR, however, said that without a boat name or registration number they were at a loss to do anything except keep an eye out for any undocumented vessel in those waters.

***

By the end of May, Pete and Mack had not received or uncovered any additional information on the rogue boat. Their interest was waning, so they made a pact to quit if they hadn't found the boat by mid-June. Crabbing and fishing charters would be in full swing by then, and there really was little time for them to be looking for some ghost ship that had probably already left their area of the Bay.

One day in early June, they decided to do some backtracking, taking one more shot at the Neck District west of Cambridge. On the way, they stopped by the old Isaac North Store for a soda and a late-afternoon sandwich. Isaac North's Store had been a fixture and local conversation pit for almost fifty years. One corner of the store had a couple of benches and ladder-backed chairs with ratty cushions arranged around a 1940s vintage potbellied stove. Retired farmers, watermen, and day laborers gathered there every day to eat, swap stories, and tell lies.

After getting their sandwiches, Pete took a seat on one of the benches. Mack claimed the other end of it, facing two older gentlemen in coveralls and plaid checkered shirts. The two local men acknowledged Pete and Mack with a nod. The old-timers chattered about the goings-on at the old Chambers Farm on Cooks Point. The local pair were complaining about some strange activities across the Cove from where their friend, Old Charlie French, lived.

From what they could gather, it seemed that Old Charlie regularly suffered from insomnia, often getting out of bed at odd hours of the night and going into his kitchen for a glass of milk. Then he'd go sit in his weathered fabric chair on the enclosed front porch. There, he would sip his milk and watch the ducks feed in the shallow waters next to his dock until he was ready to fall asleep again.

During an early morning insomnia session the previous May, it seemed that Old Charlie had noticed a bunch of folks tying up to the Chambers dock in cigarette-type boats at about 10:30 p.m. and leaving at about 3:30 a.m. Charlie also observed that they didn't use any running lights, and they seemed to sneak in and out of the Cove at no more than a couple of knots, as if trying to avoid being seen. The boats didn't have the usual flashy decals and vivid colors of the typical cigarette boat. Instead, they were battleship gray and they had a dull and inconspicuous finish.

One of the men also remembered Charlie mentioning having seen boat repair work going on just past the Chambers dock, on the land between the big barn and the Manor House. Most of the work, he claimed, was being done between 11:00 p.m. and 3:00 a.m. Over the past month, he'd seen a bunch of men working on two dry-docked boats. The halogen light at the corner of the Chambers barn cast sufficient light to see the boats that were being renovated. It wasn't strong enough, however, to identify the workers themselves.

After overhearing this conversation, Mack couldn't hold back any longer. "Gentlemen, since my friend and I are poking around to find a crab boat for my son, you think maybe they're fixing up an old crab boat over there?"

The older of the two shook his head. "No way. According to Charlie, these boats are over forty feet long with short canopies. They're built for speed. No room for crab pots on top. He says they ain't even got trotline rigs on the gunwales. Says they look more like charter boats."

Pete shifted on the bench to face them more directly and asked, "Why do you think they're doing the work at night?"

"Don't know," said the older of the two. "Either 'cause they don't want nobody seein' what they're doing or they employ illegal's - Mexicans and the like. Charlie says, from looking at them through field glasses, he's sure they're foreigners 'cause they're so small and built slight - nothing like a typical Eastern Shoreman's build."

The two old guys, tired of talking, got up from their seats, said good-bye, walked to the front of the store, dropped their trash into the big can next to the counter, waved good-bye, and stepped outside.

Pete and Mack traded knowing glances and then they did the same.

Once back in the truck, Pete felt re-energized. He'd just about given up, but here they had stumbled on this vital information by chance. "I think we're on to something, Mack. What about you?"

"Whole thing sounds fishy, Pete. We need to plan a trip to the Chambers farm to see what's up. I feel it in my gut; something's really wrong about this."

"How's this Thursday night, the tenth, look to you?"

"Works for me. Want to take my truck this time?" Mack asked.

Pete thought about it for a moment. "No. We're going by boat. That way, they're less likely to see us, and if by chance they do, we can always fake early-morning trot lining to throw them off. Since Cook's Point Cove is a hotbed for big crabs, it should make a believable story."

"Then you better put that trot-line rig back on your boat before we go," Mack said. "Otherwise, they'll know we're lying."

✳✳✳

On Thursday afternoon, Pete picked up an old trotline rig from his storage shed behind his house and drove down the short distance to Tilghman's Knapp's Narrows, where he kept his boat. He climbed aboard and bolted the rig into the set of plugged holes he had used when *Miss Alice* had served as a crabbing boat. To make sure he looked legitimate, he also grabbed two trotlines and a bunch of baskets out of the truck and hauled them onboard. No one would doubt his intent to crab now.

Back at the house, Pete mulled over the chart that showed the Choptank River and Cooks Point. He knew that entering this shallow cove under the cover of night would be a tricky maneuver. Luckily, that night the sky would be overcast and high tide would be at just about 1 a.m. Based on the tide table and the NOAA chart, this meant that he and Mack had only about three-and-a-half feet of water under them. With the *Miss Alice* drawing exactly two-and-a-half feet, they would be cutting it very close.

Pete thought, 'If I stay just off the sandbar at the outside hook of the point, the water there is six to seven feet deep. The question is whether we can see enough from that spot to make it worth the risk. What the heck? No guts, no glory.'

Pete collected his gear, binoculars, cooler, and thermos, and loaded them onto the bed of the truck. After an early supper, he set the alarm and made his bed on the couch so that he wouldn't wake up Louise when he rose to pick up Mack.

At 11:00 p.m. the alarm went off. Pete pulled the blanket back, pivoted off the couch, and headed into the kitchen to light the burner under the coffee pot. Ten minutes later, he was sitting in his truck by Mack's back door, sipping his coffee and waiting.

A few minutes later, the screen door slammed shut and out came Mack. He dumped his stuff into the truck's bed, opened the door, slid in, and grunted, "Morning."

"Morning," said Pete.

They set off in silence for the *Miss Alice*. At the dock, Pete started the engine while Mack untied the lines and cast off. Not another word passed between them. As Pete moved out of the Narrows and into the Choptank River, heading toward Buoy R-12, he finally said, "Get a good sleep, Mack, or are you still asleep?"

Mack grumbled back, "Yep."

Pete chuckled, "Yep, you got a good sleep? Or yep, you're still asleep?"

Mack remained silent, opening his thermos and pouring a cup of steaming coffee.

At Buoy R-12, Pete cut his running lights and all the electronics. He set a direct southern course of 170 degrees, which in four miles would bring them to their destination at the end of the channel, just opposite the outside hook of Cooks Point. There, they'd anchor and begin their surveillance.

All of Pete's calculations assumed that old Charlie French was correct that the cigarette boats with their folks aboard usually arrived at the Chambers dock between 10:30 p.m. and 11:00 p.m. before leaving at 3:30 a.m. If they arrived later or left much earlier, they might be confronted and Pete would have to haul anchor quickly and resort to their crabbin' story.

Two miles from the hook, Pete slowed the *Miss Alice* to trolling speed, hooked up Mack's small handheld Garmin to his transducer, and checked the water depths. When he reached the five-foot mark at the end of the channel, he signaled Mack to lower the anchor by hand, avoiding any unnecessary noise. Pete put *Miss Alice* in reverse and set the anchor in the mud so that the stern was in no more than seven feet of water.

Knowing that sound traveled quickly across calm waters, Pete and Mack kept their voices to a whisper as they began to discuss where they would focus their binoculars and how they would get each other's attention if one of them saw something of interest. For the first time since arriving at the designated spot, they took a serious look across the water to the Chambers dock.

Sleek cigarette boats lay on each side of the dock, silhouetted against the shoreline some three hundred yards away. As Charlie had described, both of the boats were battleship gray with no identifying marks. Through the binoculars, the boats appeared to be some thirty-six to thirty-eight feet long, with about nine-foot beams. Mack calculated that if the workers came by boat and were kept down below, each boat would be capable of hauling about ten men below and maybe four on deck. The boats blended in so well with the water and the shoreline that it was easy to see how at night nothing would detect them except for the sharp eyes of an insomniac like Old Charlie.

At about 11:55 p.m. they began their surveillance in earnest. While Pete was responsible for checking out the area from the dock to the Manor House on the right, Mack was to observe from the dock to the barn on the left. Since the wind was coming from the northwest, both men hunkered down on the port side to get the best possible view.

Two men walked onto the dock. Each took up a position next to one of the cigarette boats that were tied-up. Both men appeared to have weapons slung over their shoulders. They too were scanning the waters across the Cove and along the far shoreline. Pete saw nothing near the Chambers manor house - no lights and no people. Mack, on the other hand, began to make out the vague outline of two large boats in cradles, sitting up on land and being worked on by a team of men. A bright beam of light shone down from the barn's corner floodlight.

Mack turned and whispered, "Just like Old Charlie said."

"Yep," Pete agreed, focusing his attention toward the boats as well.

The vigil continued. Several times during the next two hours, Pete had to remind Mack to keep his head down. Mack had a tendency to stick his binoculars too high over the gunwale. It would not be good if light reflected off of them, drawing the guards' attention.

Other than some welding activities going on between the dry docked boats and the barn itself, few changes occurred during their watch. The acetylene torch welding started to escalate, and sparks began flying in all directions. The pattern of the sparks and the large space between them indicated that at least two torches were being used to work on two separate items. Unfortunately, though, the distance between Pete's boat and the Chambers dock made it impossible to determine exactly what kind of work was being done on the two boats.

At 2:30 a.m. Mack looked at his watch and said in a low voice, "Pete, don't seem like we're going to learn any more tonight. I vote we go back home before they stop work and leave the dock. No sense getting caught, especially when we won't learn any more by staying later."

"I agree, Mack. Let's haul anchor and head back."

On the way back to Tilghman Island, just north of R-12, Pete said, "I think I got an idea how to get closer so's we can see what's up."

Mack looked inquisitively. "How you plan on doing that?"

Before Pete could get out another word out, one of the gray cigarette boats roared up on their starboard side almost thirty feet from *Miss Alice*. Out in the darkness, like a muzzle flash, a three-million-candle-powered beam of light blanketed the *Miss Alice*. All the while, the gray boat continued to clip along at over forty knots. The intense beam of the searchlight swept smoothly from *Miss Alice*'s stern to her bow. Then it clicked off. Not wanting to be identified as a boat manned by foreigners, the gray boat immediately turned hard right and sped up the Choptank River toward Cambridge.

"Damn, Pete. That was close. Scared the shit out of me, just like that intruder on the oyster bar did!"

Though surprised, Pete maintained his calm. "At least they didn't ram us." To himself, he thought, 'Thank the Lord I turned my running lights back on and had the trotline rig mounted and a bunch of crab baskets stacked at the stern for effect.' Then he said, "Given how fast they were running and the short burst of light they threw on us, I don't think they figured we were a threat. They probably thought we were night poaching."

"Probably so," Mack agreed. "But they did get a good look at the boat's name and the two of us. So, now that they've seen us at this early hour, and they know this is the *Miss Alice* -How do you propose we come back and get even closer?"

"Doesn't change my plans at all, Mack. In fact, it may even help. If we come back in late afternoon tomorrow and actually crab the Cove on the high tide in some three feet of water, they will think this is our spot for legal crabbin' and for night poaching. By doing so, we will accomplish two things: one, they will think we aren't aware of their activities, and two, we'll have established our nighttime alibi. Obviously, those guys have some type of around-the-clock security on the property. So, they'll see us legitimately working the Cove, and they'll think nothing of it."

"Sounds good," Mack agreed.

"Just before dark," Pete continued, "We'll anchor right off the dock that's down at the end of the Cove by that vacant house. At night, from there, we can get a good view of the barn and the boats they're working on. Once we stop crabbin' we can put over the folding rowboat I use for hunting ponds. With our catch in it, we can head over to the vacant house's dock. Tomorrow morning, we'll have to drop off my refrigerated truck so we'll have both a place to put the crabs and a place to catch a nap. At 11:00 p.m., under the cover of darkness, we'll row the boat back to the *Miss Alice* and commence our surveillance."

"Let's see, Pete, so's I understand it. We drop off the refrigerated truck in the morning, drive back to Tilghman Island, and then take *Miss Alice* down to Cook's Point to crab the Cove. Then, after crabbin', we leave *Miss Alice* anchored off the end of the dock, go to shore, eat supper, sleep, and then wake up at 11:00 p.m. At that time, we re-board *Miss Alice* to start snooping again. Then I guess, after the cigarette boats leave at 3:30 a.m. we haul anchor and go home. Next day, we go back down to retrieve your refrigerated truck, right?"

"Yep. That's how I see it," Pete said.

"Pete, you're crazy! That plan won't fool them one darn bit," Mack said.

"Why not?"

"Well, it just won't. They'll know we're spying on them."

"No they won't. They'll just see us as watermen trying to make a living. My guess is, since they saw us last night being cautious, soon as they see we've anchored and returned to shore, they'll board *Miss Alice* early tonight to look her over. If I were one of them, I'd want to be sure we really were crabbing and not hiding onboard. Once they check *Miss Alice* out and find that we're really here to crab, they'll never expect us to return in the rowboat after dark."

Mack shook his head and grimaced. "Pete, these guys are foreigners with military bearing. They carry automatic weapons and they do their work at night, when darkness shrouds their activities."

"Mack, believe me. I know how these guys think. It will be OK, I promise."

Mack didn't immediately answer, needing time to digest Pete's plan before responding. "Look, I'll go along with you this time. But, at the first sign of any trouble, you've got to agree, we run for cover and get the hell out of there. Clearly, these guys are for real, Pete. Guys don't carry AK-47s around to hunt deer. I just plain don't trust them."

"OK," Pete agreed, happy that he'd finally convinced his friend. "But I know this will work." 'It'd better work, he thought, or they'd be dead meat.' He had no doubt that the stakes were high, given what he'd already seen.

On Friday morning, as agreed, Pete drove his refrigerated truck to the parking area adjacent to the vacant Cook's Point house, where they would anchor *Miss Alice* later that night. Mack followed Pete down. As soon as Pete locked up his truck, he hopped into Mack's truck. On their way out, they decided, to drive down the lane to the Chambers Farm to check out the perimeter security.

The road was chained off with two big stainless steel padlocks. Pete hopped out to test whether the locks were actually secure. As he reached for the chain, Pete heard a vehicle coming down the lane. It was coming fast. With dust flying, a six-wheel crew cab emerged, all of a sudden, from around the bend. The truck came to a screeching halt a few feet from the chain. Two medium-height men with swarthy complexions and big muscles jumped out and walked toward the gate.

The darker of the two spoke in broken English, "What are you doing here?"

"My buddy," Pete said, pointing back at Mack, who was just then climbing out of his truck, "and I are out looking for a place to lease for hunting season next year."

As Mack walked toward Pete, he noticed that both men were dressed in khaki pants, black T-shirts, and wide dark brown belts with black quick-draw holsters secured to them. As far as he could tell, their pistols were nine-millimeter Glocks - the same kind that Mack carried in his truck. Both men had closely cropped hair, and they moved with military bearing. One of the guards moved up to the chain and announced, "This place is already leased."

"You just farming it, or hunting it too?" Pete asked conversationally, keeping an eye on the guns.

"No. We lease whole place," he replied, pointing to the sign nailed to the chain's post that said, "No trespassing."

"You are trespassing." The guard waved his hand back in the direction of the main road, and said, "Must leave!"

Mack came up beside his friend. "Problem, Pete?"

"Looks like the place is already taken, Mack."

Clearly wanting them to leave, the guard again pointed back down the lane and raised his voice, saying, "You leave. Now!"

The clicking sound was unmistakable; the second guard had slipped his nine-millimeter Glock out of its open-ended holster and lowered the weapon, pointing it straight at the ground. Startled, Mack backed up a few steps and for a split second he saw a glitter of light reflected from above. He looked up and noticed the source of the light: the shiny lenses of two camouflaged cameras affixed to the pine trees overhead. His awareness of the cameras did not go unnoticed by the guards.

With a hatchet-like chop of his arm, the first guard said, "Leave Now!"

Pete shrugged his shoulders and held up both hands in resignation. He turned, grabbed Mack by the elbow, and started back toward the truck. They climbed inside the truck. Mack put the truck into gear and slowly rumbled down the lane toward the public road. They looked in both the rear and side mirrors, catching a glimpse of the lead guard speaking into a handheld mike.

"Probably reporting what happened," Pete mumbled.

Mack let out a long whistle. "Pete, that was really scary! That level of security and those types of characters on the payroll does not bode well. Whatever is going on here is way beyond us. I think we need to call the sheriff."

"Calm down, Mack," Pete said. "Yeah, it looks serious. But if they lease the property they have the absolute right to secure it."

Mack let out a loud groan of frustration. "Come on, Pete! Those guys aren't off-duty rent-a-cops with nightsticks. They're foreigners carrying nine-millimeter Glocks!"

"I agree. It looks a little suspicious, but before we contact the authorities we need to know more. By tonight, we'll have a better idea of what they're up to. Then we can decide what to do."

Mack threw up his hands and stared at Pete. "A little suspicious isn't how I would describe what just happened. They meant business back there. I am telling you, we're playing with fire, Pete."

"Look, Mack, if we jump the gun on this thing, we may end up being the laughing stock of the Eastern Shore. Who knows? It could be our own government that's messing around over at the Chambers place. Could be a CIA deal - a mock something or other. Who knows?"

Mack looked sullen. "I'm not going this afternoon, and that's it!"

"Well, at least think on it. No need to make a decision 'til after lunch. Speakin' of lunch, want to try North's Store again?"

Mack's spirits seemed to brighten at the mention of food. "Sure, why not? That sandwich yesterday was pretty darn good."

A few minutes later, they pulled up to North's Store to order takeout.

On the way back to Tilghman Island, Pete and Mack ate their lunch in silence, listening to country music on the satellite radio. Neither of them spoke until they'd gotten to St. Michael's.

"Pete, I still don't want to go, but I'm not going to let you go alone."

"Thanks, Mack. I promise it will be OK. We'll get as much info as we can and then bug out of there. Once we're back home, we can decide what we want to do, if anything."

Seemingly satisfied, Mack nodded in agreement. "So, what time do you want to arrive back at Twin Point Cove?"

"Well, we'll be at our dock in twenty minutes. If we leave at noon we'll be able to crab from, say, one o'clock to five. Then we can leave the *Miss Alice*, grab dinner and a little sleep, and return to her by eleven tonight."

Chapter 3

The Rogue Resurfaces

It was 1 p.m. when the *Miss Alice* arrived back at Twin Point Cove, opposite the vacant house on the Point. Pete and Mack set about crabbing. They hauled the baited trotline out of the cooler and tied it to two concrete anchor blocks. While Pete positioned the boat, Mack prepared to drop the blocks and the buoy overboard before playing out the trotline.

Pete looked over his shoulder from the boat's mid-station and hollered over the sound of the engine's exhaust, "Drop 'em, Mack."

Mack dropped the blocks and started playing out 1,200 feet of baited line. As Pete steered the boat into the wind, Mack, for the first time, looked over to see what was going on at the Chambers dock. He saw that no boats were tied-up there, but the welding near the two workboats and the barn was going on full blast. There still appeared to be two separate welding locations underway.

Miss Alice moved forward and Mack played out the line behind her. As the boat slowly moved into the wind, the land that rose from the barn to the Manor House obscured Pete's line of sight to the Chambers place. After all the line had played out and tightened at the far end of the line, Mack repeated the same task of dropping another set of anchor blocks and a buoy. He then shouted back to Pete, "Done."

At last, Pete started to turn *Miss Alice* around, slowly steering her back to the first buoy. Mack joined Pete at the mid-station, grabbed his coffee out of its gunwale holder, and told Pete what he'd seen as he played out the crab line. "Except for the welding that's still going on, I didn't see anyone working on the boats. There are no cigarette boats at the dock, and no one's walkin' around the property. Maybe as we work the

Cove we'll see more, but my guess is that most of the work, as Charlie says, occurs at night."

For the rest of that afternoon, Pete and Mack worked back and forth along the trotline, catching crabs. By five o'clock, they'd managed to harvest close to five bushels. Since nothing new had occurred at the Chambers property, except for the welding and the late arrival of a large self-powered boatlift that was now parked next to the barn, they decided to call it quits.

Pete made sure the trotline was re-baited and put back in the cooler, and he left the cabin unlocked. Having set *Miss Alice*'s anchor, they unfolded the hunting dinghy, put her over the side, loaded their crabs, and climbed aboard. By putting the dinghy overboard on the side facing the Chambers dock, they made their leaving, as obvious as possible. As they rode the short distance to the vacant house's dock, Mack said, "I bet they'll come over in the early evening and board *Miss Alice* to check her out."

"I strung some pieces of four-pound test line across the cooler box, the engine box, and the cabin door, using a tiny bit of gum to secure them. If they check her out, we'll know they came aboard."

"Smart thinking, Pete. But if they do, how do we know they won't mess with the engine and disable her so we can't start her up? If they do that, we'll be sitting ducks."

Pete had already thought this out. "First thing we'll do when we come back tonight is check out all the fishing lines and then be sure they haven't messed with the engine."

Mack still looked worried. "Maybe we should have brought our guns."

"Sure. That's all we need! If we got in trouble and pulled out shotguns, you think we could compete with their firepower? No way, my friend. It's better that we're unarmed and perceived as being just plain old dumb waterman who *bend* the rules at night."

After they'd loaded the crabs into the truck, they headed up the road to Cambridge to grab dinner at Dayton's Restaurant, a popular local eatery. After dinner, they returned to Twin Point Cove, parked the truck, set a small clock that Mack kept in his truck for 11 p.m., locked the doors, and reclined back in the seats. It was just shy of 7:15 p.m. when both of them fell soundly asleep.

At 11:00 p.m. the alarm woke them from their deep sleeps. Without conversation, they gathered their gear, climbed out of the truck, locked it, and quietly made their way back to the dock. Crawling along the rough planks, Mack nearly forgot about the severity of the situation. He felt like laughing at himself and Pete, a pair of old farts crawling along like children about to pull off a Halloween prank on an unsuspecting neighbor. The trouble was, this wasn't some innocent prank. Rather, this was two cocky watermen skating on thin ice.

From their vantage point on the dock, they saw that the two cigarette boats were back and the activity around the dry-docked boats was going full steam. The welding had ceased and the two forklifts were being maneuvered around the boats.

At the end of the dock, Pete and Mack climbed down into the dingy with their gear and quietly paddled to the starboard side of Miss Alice. As Pete slid on his belly up and over the gunwale, he looked for the fine filament he'd attached to the boat's engine box. It was no longer there. His eyes moved to the deck, where he saw the piece of line lying next to the engine box.

Pete thought to himself, *Damn them!* They'd opened it, but at least they hadn't seen the line he'd attached.

Mack followed close behind Pete. They folded and stowed the collapsible dinghy. Pete put his finger to his lips, nudged Mack's elbow, and pointed to the line lying on the deck. Pete gestured that they should both crouch down. He motioned toward the cooler, indicating that Mack should check it out. Still crouched down, Pete moved to the cabin door to inspect it. After Mack checked the cooler, he crawled over to Pete and whispered, "They opened up the cooler but didn't mess with the trotline."

"They also opened the cabin door, but nothing seems to be out of place or removed," Pete whispered.

Mack looked as concerned as ever. "I'll start checking out Chambers."

Pete took out his small red-filtered flashlight. "I'm going to see if I can quietly lift up the engine box and see what's up there." Pete slowly moved to the box, lifted it, and looked inside. Seeing that there was nothing wrong with the engine, Pete crawled over next to Mack on the port side and began scanning the Chambers place. While in a far better viewing spot than he had been in the night before, the next two hours revealed few changes in activities across the way.

The forklifts lowered what appeared to be large stainless steel gas tanks into each boat's hole. The hammering and power drills droned on, and new antennas and radar domes, which were identical to the larger boat's array of equipment, were affixed to the top of the smaller boat's cabin. At about 1:15 a.m. two more guards appeared on the dock, along with two tall men who seemed out of scale with the smaller and more compact guards.

It was clear from the way they carried themselves and from the deference that the guards showed them that the two larger men were certainly not workers but managers. They walked to the end of the dock and stared out into the darkness toward Buoy R-12. Less than two minutes later, one of the new guards joined them at the end of the dock. Using a handheld spotlight and holding a walkie-talkie, he sent three short bursts of light out into the darkness toward R-12. A corresponding three-burst signal returned from the darkness, just off the hook of Cook's Point.

Five minutes later, the hull of a third gray-colored cigarette boat that was much smaller than the others emerged from the darkness and slowly approached the end of the dock. A guard stepped forward to secure the lines from that boat. Once the boat was secured, the guard backed off and returned to stand with the other three guards on the dock.

Raised voices softly rolled across the quiet waters. With this boat's arrival, Pete and Mack could tell that the atmosphere had become electric and the intensity had ratcheted up. A large man with military bearing stepped off of the boat, providing further reason for this change of attitude. This new arrival was clearly in charge. Both unarmed men on the dock greeted him with short, precise bows and crisp salutes. The man in charge now turned to one of the two men, who greeted him and gestured for him to lead the way. As they departed, others gathered and saluted him at the end of the dock, but no handshakes ensued. He and his entourage disappeared behind the dense shrubs and trees that lined the path leading to the barn and the Manor House.

Pete and Mack followed the progress of the small group, as a lantern cast eerie shadows on their path. As they headed up the narrow walkway toward the barn areas, the group approached the boats. Mack saw the boatlift begin to move toward the large boat. He elbowed Pete. "Lift's moving."

"Uh-huh," replied Pete.

They determined that the new man was getting a guided tour of the workboats and the staging area. Within ten minutes, the entourage thinned out and the lantern light moved toward the Manor House.

As soon as the lantern disappeared into the Manor House, the boatlift moved into place next to the larger of the two boats. Workers scrambled around the boat as the lift moved from stern to bow and the wide straps were secured underneath her. As the lift hoisted the boat up into the air, Pete and Mack got their first good look at her bottom. It was all white paint. As the lift turned and started to head behind the barn, the stern came into view. There was no name on her stern.

In an excited but controlled voice, Pete said to Mack, "That's her! That's the intruder."

"You sure it's her, Pete?"

"Mack, I'm damn sure!" Pete gripped his friend's arm. "I'd recognize that Hooper's Island flair and shape anywhere."

"Why do you think they're taking her behind the barn?"

"Damned if I know," said Pete. "Maybe they have more work to do on her back there."

"Could be," replied Mack.

Twenty minutes after the big boat disappeared behind the barn, the lift returned and picked up the smaller boat. Here again, only white paint covered her bottom. She had no name on her stern and she too had the Hooper's Island flair, though it was nowhere near as pronounced as it was with the bigger boat.

They also noticed that this boat's twin props were clearly four-blade stainless steel speed props. In contrast, the bigger boat's props seemed to have been standard three-blade brass. As before, once it was on the lift the boat disappeared out of sight behind the barn. By 2:30 a.m. the activities seemed to have subsided into silence.

Fifteen minutes later, the site workers began to gather in small quiet groups on the dock. One by one, they climbed back onboard their assigned boats as one of the guards checked each name off on what appeared to be a clipboard. As the last man boarded the boats, the light reappeared at the Manor House side door. Two minutes later, the two heavily armed guards, the two tall men, and the new man, who clearly was the boss, reappeared at the foot of the dock. At that moment, as though with the wave of a maestro's baton, one of the guards raised his hand and all three of the boats' engines came alive. In spite of the enormous horsepower that had just sprung to life, the sound was as muffled as a kitten's purr.

Pete thought, *Boy, they spent a lot of bucks on those sound suppression mufflers.* As the boats backed away from the dock, the boss's smaller boat took its place at the back of the pack of three. The flotilla began to slowly creep out of the Cove. Simultaneously, the barn halogen light and the lights in the Manor House went out.

Pete whispered, "Shows over, Mack. Let's get ready to haul anchor. Before we do, though, let's wait to hear their engines crank up off the Point. Last thing I want is for them to see us following 'em."

A minute later, Pete looked out toward R-12 and heard the boats rev up as they cleared the hook of Cook's Point. Pete started up the *Miss Alice* and motioned for Mack to pull anchor. As they passed the hook, he pushed the throttle up to 2,800 rpm's. Pete could see the larger of the three cigarette boats moving up the Choptank toward Cambridge, with the mid-sized cigarette boat following closely in its wake. Looking for the boss's boat, Pete further scanned the river, but he only saw the two boats heading to Cambridge. He turned to look toward the town of Oxford. Seeing nothing there, Pete settled down into his captain's chair. As he did so, he noticed the white line of a boat's wake directly out in front. It was heading toward the old Nelson place at the tip of Black Walnut Point.

"Hey Mack, would you put the night goggles on that wake straight ahead and see if you think it's the boss's boat?"

Mack picked up the night goggles and strained to find a wake ahead in the darkness.

"Got it."

"Well?"

"Can't tell yet, but it sure is moving fast and has a low profile," Mack said. "If it's going to the Nelson dock, we'll pass it on our way and get a better look then."

Ten minutes later, as they passed off the end of Black Walnut Point, they saw that the boat they'd been looking for was being tied up at Nelson's dock.

"Wow," Pete said. "These guys, whoever they are, must be renting the Nelson's place too. This is no small operation, Mack. Something big is being planned. Ain't got a clue what, but it's big, Mack - something real big!"

"Yeah, I told you so, Pete. This ain't, as you said, slightly suspicious. This is a big-time deal. Don't it scare the hell out of you too?"

"Yeah, it scares me too Mack—a whole lot."

Miss Gale continued to head up toward the Miles River to the entrance to Knapp's Narrows.

Tired from a long two days, Mack and Pete docked *Miss Alice* at her berth at Knapp's Narrows, and then they headed to their respective homes.

"Mack, we need to think about today and talk on it tomorrow morning on our way back to get my truck."

"Sure," Mack said, as he dropped Pete off at his house. "What time do you want to go back down?"

"What about nine-thirty?" Pete asked. "So's I can tend to *Miss Alice* first?"

"Fine with me. See you in the morning," Mack said.

✳✳✳

The next day, they headed back to Cook's Point Cove in Cambridge to retrieve Pete's truck. Halfway to Cambridge Pete, finally, said, "So, what do you think is going on?"

"I don't know, but it ain't good. All that work going on at night, extra fuel tanks, special speed props, the boss-man arriving, and those guys bowing down to him - I just don't know."

"Pete, what do you think happened to those two workboats?"

"My guess is that they launched them from the Chamber's big boat ramp on the Bayside."

"But that ramp hasn't been used in years. It's in horrible shape. There's no way they could launch from there."

"Mack, given the number of carpenters they had doing woodworking and the welders they have, they could've easily fixed that ramp up in no time."

"I guess there's nothing more we can do but keep our eyes and ears open in case something else turns up."

"You're probably right, Mack, but I want to check out who's renting the old Nelson place. The guy who's obviously in charge looked to me like a foreigner with military training, and he's up to no good. I'm now absolutely convinced that whatever has been going on at the Chambers place is not CIA and has nothing to do with our government. Also, one more thing I might do is call my son Bo and see if he's seen anything on Hooper's Island. Since these boats were built on Hooper's Island, Bo may know something."

"Since his divorce, I thought you and Bo weren't talking anymore."

"We talk every once in a while. It's just that since my grandson Donnie died in Iraq, my relationship with Bo has been pretty strained. He blames me for encouraging Donnie to become a marine. Of course, the loss of Donnie led to even more problems with my daughter-in-law. Seems it caused her to get all messed up, and she eventually ran off with that guy from Chesapeake Beach."

"Pete, you can't blame yourself for Donnie's death or for Bo's divorce, and it's not fair for Bo to blame you either. It was Donnie's decision and Bo ought to be damn proud of how he fought—Bronze Star and all that," said Mack.

"Well, it is what it is, Mack. Unless Bo changes his mind, we'll continue going our separate ways. At least Wes is at home, and thank God he's said he's not planning to enlist after school."

"Yeah, at least you all still got Wes. Lots of parents don't have anyone left after these damn wars." Sensing that Pete wanted to move on from this difficult topic—not that the next one would be less difficult—Mack said, "Pete, when does your sister's boy, Brady, come down?"

"Well, let's see, his Mom Judy says his last physical therapy session at Walter Reed is next Monday, so he'll probably be arriving a day or two after that - about the fifteenth of June, I think. You know Brady says the rumor is that they will be closing Walter Reed next year 'cause the place is in such bad shape it's not worth fixing."

"Yeah, I heard that too—seems a real shame." Mack hung his head then looked up and took a deep breath.

"You know Pete, you all are too much, you and Louise, taking on that young man, as troubled as he is."

"Mack, he's got problems, all right, but I feel so bad for Judy. She has had such a tough year with Brady and the loss of Pat. With Brady's battlefield injuries, the hospital's screw-ups, and then the loss of his father, who he idolized, they need all the help we can give 'em."

"Pete, did they ever figure out what actually caused your brother-in-law's death?"

"Doctors say it was the pneumonia coupled with his lung cancer that finally got him," replied Pete.

"Man. What a shame, Judy losing him."

"Damn shame, is right," said Pete.

"Pete, don't you think it's a little too much for you guys to be taking him on this summer?"

"We're Judy's only family, so Louise and I are going to do our damnedest to help 'em out. Unfortunately, Judy says, in addition to his recent drug dependency to relieve the pain from the shrapnel that's still in his neck, he's now off on some Islamic religious kick, meeting with some group of Muslims in Baltimore. Hard to figure him rubbin' elbows with Muslims, since they were the ones he was fightin' and trying to kill in Afghanistan. Go figure."

"Maybe with some help from all of us, we can get him back on his feet. He needs to be working with me on charters, with you on crabbin', and with Mike on trot lining and carpentry. Maybe through hard work, fresh air, and early rising, he'll find some joy and peace."

"For both your sake and his, I sure hope so."

For the rest of the trip, the two friends changed the subject to the new proposed DNR regulations that they and most of the watermen thought would ultimately run them out of business. While the issues surrounding these regulations had been on the back burner for the past few months, DNR's recommendations would be forthcoming in July, and the watermen knew that they needed to be ready to respond to the State's proposals with a strong and united front. Because of the differences in the fisheries in various parts of the Bay, to date unity among the waterman had yet to be achieved. During the drive, Mack worked hard to convince Pete that he needed to lead the effort to unify the various factions and negotiate a compromise. If the State could get what it wanted without killing the seafood industry (the harvesters, growers, processors, and the distributors) then the Bay and the State would be well served.

Pete promised he'd think about it, but only if there was no dissension between them and the two watermen's associations unanimously agreed to have Pete head it up. Mack said, "OK, Pete. I'll work on it and get back to you."

When Pete and Mack arrived at Pete's truck, they decided to walk out to the pier to see if anything was going on at the Chambers Farm. As they stood at the end, the Chambers place looked like a ghost town—no boats, no people, and no noise.

When they got back to their trucks, Pete said, "Mack, on our way back let's go to Chambers Lane and see what's up."

"Sorry, Pete, but I'm not interested in another meeting with those two guys."

"Bet you a buck they're gone, along with the security cameras."

Without a reply, Mack followed Pete's truck down the lane. They turned around in the last driveway, got out, and walked the rest of the way to the fence. While it was still locked, there was only one padlock - not two. There were no guards, and sure enough the security cameras were missing.

"Pete, I owe you a beer"

"No way. I want the buck. I got enough beer."

✳✳✳

A couple of days later, after a successful day of crabbin' and after readying his pots for the next day, Mack stopped by Pete's back porch. He told Pete he'd been talking to Mike, who was all set to take on Brady as a helper. Mike had just come off of a big marine job, but he had several smaller jobs in the pipeline. Mike thought Brady could learn a lot on these jobs, and hopefully Brady would help him out in the process.

Pete shared with Mack what he had pulled together for Brady: two detailed pamphlets on the basics of crabbin' and sport fishing on the Bay. He had also written a list of the duties that Brady would have to perform for crabbing and first-mating on the *Miss Alice*. Pete asked Mack to look at the list to see if he'd missed anything.

After reading the list, Mack said, "Looks fine to me. By the way, were you able to find out who's renting the Nelson place?"

"Sort of," said Pete. "Seems some company out of New York City has leased it until the end of July. The rental agent in Easton says they've never met the tenants and that communications have all been by e-mail and FedEx. The agent also said that the renters demanded that the contract exclude random visits by the agent to check on the property. She also mentioned that they have twenty-four-hour security at the entrance to the place. Other than that, she didn't know anything else."

"Pete, did you ever get ahold of Bo?"

"Yeah. Damn. I forgot to tell you. Bo says six months ago two tall guys who looked and talked like they were from the Middle East came by the old Hooper's Island packing plant asking about charter fishing-type boats for sale. Some old fellow Bo knows, whose health is failing and whose been forced to retire, mentioned to them that he had both of his boats up for sale. Evidently, both needed lots of work, so the basic repairs were done at Hooper's Island. Then they took them somewhere up the Bay to be finished. He didn't know where."

"What did Bo say about the flair of those boats' bows?"

"He said they were old-style Hooper's Island flairs, just like we saw."

Getting up from the porch seat, Pete said, "Want to come with me? I got to go down to the dock to ready *Miss Alice* for a group coming to fish with me in the morning. It's the old Phillips Construction guys out of Pittsburgh. They're coming for four days this time - great bunch, and good tippers too. By the way, Wes is coming up from Hooper's tonight and staying with Louise and me. He's going to be first mate 'til Brady gets here."

"Sounds good, Pete. Thanks for the offer, but I got to head back to the house to finish up Beth's *To-Do* list. Better I do her list than some darn list you'd hook me into doing on the *Miss Alice*."

"Now I wouldn't do that to you, would I?" Pete chuckled.

"Damn straight you would!"

"Oh, before I forget, Mike, you and me, if you also want Brady on your boat, will need to sit down and figure out exactly how we're going to split Brady's time between us."

"That's fine with me, Pete."

"Mike called me the other day and told me he could use him for three days a week. I can use him mainly on Saturdays and Sundays for my charters," Pete said.

"And I can probably use him one day a week," said Mack.

"Good. That leaves him with one day a week for himself. I think that'll work out just fine."

Chapter 4

The Enemy Emerges

Having slipped across the border into Arizona eighteen months earlier, Abed Muhsi-Sami was constantly on the move, zigzagging across the country, and never stopping. As he traveled to the East Coast, Abed, though constantly aware of his surroundings, felt quite secure in the four prearranged safe houses located along the route. Guarded by fellow Taliban-trained soldiers, each of these way stations was well hidden in relatively mid-sized rural communities. Thus, feeling safe and secure, Abed was able to spend long hours on his computer and international cell phone, communicating with mission headquarters in the Northern Highlands Region of the Hindu Kush Mountains of Pakistan. Marching across America and staying in safe houses, Abed was able to meet with his regional cell commanders to discuss and plan future operations.

Abed was the Islamic Brotherhood's best hope for another 9/11. As Osama Bin Laden's top foreign-country operative, he was the man Bin Laden had entrusted with carrying out a series of devastating attacks on American soil. Trained in the Pakistani mountains as a terrorist and expert in explosives, Abed was physically imposing. He was a superb military strategist who was clever and ruthless. His life's work was to carry out the Brotherhood's war against America.

The safe houses that Abed used were located roughly an hour outside of major cities. They were close to relay cell towers and strategically placed along the country's network of cross-country bus systems. The buses allowed Abed to travel in relative anonymity in places where the police presence, if any, was usually limited to the larger stations. After weaving his way across country for four weeks, he finally arrived at his destination: Cambridge, Maryland.

In addition to the large farmhouse on the Choptank River north of Cambridge, which would serve as a regional headquarters, Security Chief, Salah Mohamed, had secured three other safe houses. These other houses provided Abed with the flexibility to move easily from one to another in case anyone, particularly the authorities, got suspicious of him or his team's activities.

Two of the houses were located in separate low-income areas of the city, where foreign workers from Mexico, El Salvador, Nicarguara, and other Central and South American countries resided. The third safe house, like his headquarters farm, was located in an isolated setting along a deep-water creek west of Cambridge, where it had direct access to the Choptank River. This particular three-hundred-acre farm was used as a staging and storage area. They rented it from a local man, under the pretense that it would be used for waterfowl hunting and fishing. As with all of their refuges, they leased this farm and the headquarters farm through a New York City-based LLC shell. The refuges had been set up eighteen months earlier for the purpose of providing Abed and his team with multiple locations from which to launch their terrorist activities. As with the three additional farms that were used for staging and operations - one in the Neck District of Cambridge, the Chambers place; one on Crab Alley Creek near Kent Narrows; and the other at the southern end of Tilghman Island, The Nelson Farm - all documentation and correspondence was handled through Federal Express and e-mail. Again, all of these rental contracts forbade the owner or his agents from visiting. Each location was under twenty-four-hour security.

For the past eighteen months, Abed's right-hand man, Salah, had been recruiting loyal Islamic fundamentalists to aid them in various aspects of the mission, including filling security positions and helping find local undocumented foreigners with the types of skills needed to implement The Plan. Carpenters, welders, and electricians had been the main focus of his search. By limiting his recruitment for the non-security trained jobs to illegal immigrants, Salah had enhanced the operation's security; as undocumented aliens, there were no records to verify their existence. Should some of them prove to be unreliable or incompetent and warrant being disposed of, the chances were strong that they'd never be reported as missing.

The Islamic fundamentalist network across the country was both broad and deep in terms of skill sets, yet Salah found most of his young fundamentalist recruits through an Islamic temp agency that he had set up eighteen months earlier in Salisbury, Maryland. Through this agency, Salah's nephew, Haamid Jagir, and his sister, Maya, had already recruited ten highly trained security personnel, as well as eighteen skilled workers: electricians, carpenters, and mechanics. They were also working on a plan to befriend a young, disenfranchised ex-marine named Brady Wilson, who had been referred to them by friends in Baltimore. They were drawn to his carpentry skills, his underwater military demolition expertise, his local Eastern Shore of Maryland connections, and his general knowledge of the Bay. Haamid believed that this young man might make an excellent unwitting member of the terrorist team. Salah charged both Haamid and Maya with approaching him. If they liked him, then Salah would meet him to evaluate his potential.

✳✳✳

The day Brady arrived at Pete and Louise's home it was immediately obvious to them that Brady was both physically and mentally fragile. When he came into the house, Louise showed him to his room, got him a piece of her four-layer chocolate cake, and told him, after he settled in, to come on down for lunch.

Twenty minutes later, Brady came down from his room and announced, "Aunt Louise, thanks so much for the offer of lunch, but I'm not really hungry. Since I need some shorts and T-shirts for work, I think I'll drive to Salisbury and check out the mall."

"Will you be back in time for dinner, Brady?" she asked.

He paused as he opened the front door to leave. "Yes ma'am. I'll be back to see Uncle Pete when he returns from fishing around four-thirty."

Though Brady hadn't been back on the Eastern Shore since just before the beginning of his two tours in Afghanistan, he had no trouble finding his way to Salisbury. After passing the Mall, which he had used as an excuse, he headed to the temp agency. Thanks to his Islamic contacts in Baltimore, who had provided him with directions to the temp agency, he arrived there at about one o'clock.

Brady's Islamic friends in Baltimore, unbeknownst to him, had contacted the temp agency in Salisbury about Brady's possible arrival that week. The agency's director, Abdul Mulani, came out to the visitor's desk and greeted Brady. After welcoming Brady, Abdul gave him a tour of the offices and some written materials on the agency's programs and offerings.

At the end of the tour, Abdul introduced Brady to two of the agency's young professionals, Haamid Jagir, and his sister, Maya. Through their mutual Baltimore friends, Abdul had been made aware of Brady's military background, his disdain for

The Walter Reed Medical Center's treatment of his injuries, and his negative feelings about the marine corps' abandonment of the families of his buddies who had died in Afghanistan.

Brady pulled no punches when it came to describing his negative feelings about the way his country had treated him and his fellow marines. As a result, Abdul was convinced that Brady might be a real asset to Salah and his Team. Being a member of Abed's inner circle and knowing about Salah's recruitment program, Abdul had shared the situation and his thoughts with Haamid, Salah's nephew, and the Team's chief personnel recruiter.

As Haamid and Maya sat and chatted with Brady in the lobby of the agency, it became clear to Haamid that Brady was not only disillusioned, but also very angry with both the marine corps and his country. Clearly, Brady felt disenfranchised and abandoned. The level of commitment and sense of brotherhood that he had seen among his Islamic friends in Baltimore - things he felt were missing in his own life - also fascinated Brady.

As the three continued to chat, Brady and Haamid struck up an immediate friendship. As their conversation continued, Brady also found himself drawn to Maya's intelligence and beauty. Brady was mesmerized by her electric blue eyes, which were set against the almond color of her skin and the long, flowing, silk-like, black hair that framed her face. Brady was clearly smitten with Maya.

Engrossed in their conversations at five minutes before three o'clock, Maya realized it was almost time for their afternoon call to prayer. She apologized for cutting their meeting short, but said that they should continue their discussions at another time. Brady looked at his watch and said, "No problem. I also have to go. I need to get back on Tilghman Island in time to meet my uncle for dinner."

Having traded cell phone numbers, they agreed to meet later in the week. Then they said their good-byes and parted company.

As Brady walked toward the front door, he stole one last look over his shoulder at Maya. Walking back to her office, she too turned her head to catch a last glimpse of him. Grinning sheepishly to hide their mutual attraction as they made eye contact, they turned and went their separate ways.

When Brady arrived at Tilghman Island, Louise informed him that his Uncle Pete was at the dock cleaning fish for his charter party. Louise also relayed that his cousin, Wes, had returned to Hooper Island and would be back the next day for his second day as Pete's first mate. Brady headed down to *Miss Alice's* slip. As he approached the dock, Brady called out, "Hey, Uncle Pete. How are you? What can I do to help?"

Pete replied, "Hey, Brady. How am I? Well, better for seeing you, young man. Welcome to Tilghman!" As Brady jumped onboard, Pete extended his meat cleaver of a hand to shake Brady's. Then he wrapped his arm around him and gave a bear hug. "Good to have you home, Brady."

Smiling from such a warm welcome, Brady moved to the pile of fish in the baskets at the stern of the boat. "Uncle Pete, hand me a knife so's I can clean some of these fish."

Pete handed him a fillet knife, and they both got to work in earnest, each quietly vying with the other to see who could clean the most fish in the least amount of time. Staying focused on the task at hand, they didn't bother talking until the last fish had been cleaned and they had counted up their score.

"Damn, Brady. You beat me! Where did you learn to use a knife that fast? Afghanistan?"

Brady, in a serious voice, responded, "Knives over there were for killing, Uncle Pete - not for filleting."

Pete winced. "Sorry. Bad choice of words on my part, Brady."

"No problem. I was just stating the facts."

They packed the catch with crushed ice in wax-covered cardboard shipping boxes and hauled them up on the dock. As they turned to start scrubbing and hosing *Miss Alice* down, the charter party returned, picked up the boxes of filleted fish and handed Pete the fish-cleaning fee and a large tip.

Mr. Phillips, head of the Pittsburg construction company that bore his name, said, "Thanks, Pete. Great day. See you at six-thirty tomorrow."

Pete replied, "Thanks, guys. You all sure pulled 'em in today! See you in the morning." Before Pete started to scrub the cutting boards, he slapped a twenty-dollar bill in Brady's hand. "That's for helping clean those fish."

Brady tried to hand it back. "No, Uncle Pete. I just wanted to help."

"You keep it, son. You earned it."

As the two finished the cleanup and re-rigged the rods for the next day's charter, Pete said, "So, how's your mom doing? Last time we talked, she seemed real down."

"Well, Uncle Pete, she is down—very down." Brady's expression revealed his pain. "Dad's death was the hardest thing she's ever had to deal with. I guess my troubles at Walter Reed and my difficult re-entry into civilian life hasn't helped either."

"Well, hopefully being with us this summer and workin' the Bay will be a healthy change. We all want you to know that we appreciate your two tours in Afghanistan. While I'll never truly know what it was like, I do know it must have been very hard, and it must have taken an enormous amount of courage to wake up every day, not knowing if the next day would ever come."

"Thanks for your kind words, Uncle Pete. You don't know how much they're appreciated." Wanting to change the topic, Brady asked, "So, what's the plan for me, Uncle Pete?"

"Well, tomorrow Mike, Mack, you, and I will grab breakfast together at the Tilghman Store and go over the proposed schedule. In the meantime, I've collected some information about charter fishing and crabbing on the Bay that may be helpful."

"Thanks, Uncle Pete," said Brady. "I'm sure they'll be helpful. Don't forget, I did spend a bunch of summers down here during my junior high years as a first mate and trot-liner, so hopefully it will all come back to me quickly."

"Geez, I'd forgotten all about that. What's it been—eight years or so?"

"I guess."

"Wow, age is gettin' to me, Brady. My mind's gone plumb south."

Early the next morning at breakfast, the four men met to finalize a work schedule for Brady. From Tuesday through Thursday, he would work with Mike on two carpentry jobs in Royal Oak, which was just west of Salisbury. On Fridays, he would alternate with Mike on trot lining and with Mack on hauling crab pots. On weekends, Brady would work on fishing charters with Pete.

Today, Friday the eighteenth of June, Wes would mate for Pete. The next day, Saturday the nineteenth, Brady was going to start working the weekend with the Phillips Party. After his breakfast meeting, Brady, knowing that starting tomorrow he would enjoy little flexibility in his schedule, decided to call Maya to see if she and Haamid could meet with him, as they had talked about earlier.

As Brady dialed Maya's cell phone, his heart beat accelerated. Clearly, he was developing feelings for her that were beyond his control. "Hey, Maya. It's Brady."

"Hi, Brady. How are you?"

"I'm great - Thanks. I start work tomorrow, but I have some free time today and I wondered if you guys would like to get together again?"

"Well, that would be great. Unfortunately, Haamid is tied up in meetings until four o'clock this afternoon, but I could meet you for lunch and he could join us later. Would that work for you?"

"Yeah, that works for me. Where do you want to meet?"

"How about here at my office. Then we can decide on a lunch spot."

"OK," said Brady. "I'll be there about noon."

"Great Brady. See you then."

After parking in front of the agency office, Brady reached into his glove compartment for his hairbrush and the aftershave he kept there. He brushed his hair, splashed on some aftershave, and straightened his shirt and sweater. Then he got out of his truck and walked to the agency's front door. As soon as he asked for Maya at the visitor's desk, she emerged from the adjacent office area, as though she had been watching for his arrival through the office's glass door. Her beautiful smile and gorgeous eyes captured his heart once more.

"Hi, Brady," she called out. Before he could respond, she wrapped her arms around him and gave him a long hug. Holding his face in her hands, she kissed him on each cheek, backed away, and gently repeated, "Hi, Brady."

Taken aback by the warmth of her greeting, Brady responded with a quick hug of his own and mumbled, "Hi. Uh, are you ready to go?"

"Sure," she replied. "I've picked out a place close by, if you like Mexican food?"

"Sounds great." Brady opened the truck's passenger door for Maya.

As they drove the half-mile to the restaurant, they chatted about the weather and how they were both looking forward to the summer. After ordering and trying not to focus on her looks, Brady asked Maya what she and Haamid actually did at the temp agency.

Maya paused for a moment before responding. "Well, we coordinate things at the agency."

"What kinds of things?"

"We find jobs for our clients. Companies and organizations come to us to find Muslim part-time employees. We act sort of like any temp agency."

"So, there are enough part-time jobs here on the Eastern Shore to warrant the two of you doing this?" Brady asked.

"Well, we actually are part of a network of Islamic Agencies across the country that share a common database to provide services countrywide, not just locally."

Brady said, "That sounds cool!"

"It is. We get to meet lots of interesting people from all across the country."

Brady was curious because Salisbury was a fairly small Eastern Shore town, yet this group had found jobs for people around the country. "So, what kind of jobs do you guys actually fill?"

"Jobs for carpenters, electricians, plumbers, laborers, and computer techs - those sorts of things." Cupping his hand to the side of his mouth so that no one would hear, Brady leaned over toward her and asked in a kidding tone, "And terrorists?"

Maya, in a quiet yet firm voice, said, "Well sometimes we do supply our Brothers in the field with uniquely qualified personnel who are not readily available."

Stunned, Brady leaned closer and whispered, "You're kidding, right?"

"No. I'm not kidding, Brady," Maya continued in a serious tone. "You know from your Islamic friends in Baltimore that The Koran requires that we support our Islamic

Brothers on the front lines. Sometimes they need personnel with skills that only we can provide."

Brady was surprised by her intensity and the determination in her voice. He leaned back in his chair and pondered her frightening words, words that suddenly recalled all of the fear and chaos of Afghanistan. While looking straight into her eyes, Brady saw before him, in a flashback, all that he and his marine buddies had endured at the hands of Islamic fundamentalists.

Maya reached for his hand. "Are you all right, Brady?"

It took Brady a moment to recover. "Yeah, sure."

But he wasn't all right. Suddenly, Brady was struck by the enormity of the dilemma he had found himself in. A wounded warrior who had suffered at the hands of Islamic extremists, he was also a man drawn to the sense of family that the Islamic community offered. Brady felt the excruciating pain of conflicting emotions. Considering his growing feelings for Maya, he found himself disoriented and confused.

Sensing his uneasiness, Maya again reached across the table and gently squeezed his hand. "Brady, we need to talk in private. Let's settle up and go."

Brady nodded in agreement and asked for the check. On their way back to the agency, Maya asked him to pull off the road into a vacant lot next to the highway. When he turned the engine off, Maya moved over next to him.

She gazed into his eyes. "I know deep down that you agree with us, Brady. From everything that you've told our friends in Baltimore, you too are committed to the formation of a better world order - an order that respects each of us as a child of Allah. And we, all of us, are in this holy war together. The truth is, if this country had not imposed its democracy and Christianity on the people of Afghanistan, Iran, and Iraq, you would never have had to go to Afghanistan and your buddies would still be alive today." Moving even closer to Brady, Maya took his face in her hands again, looked him straight in the eye, and said, "Brady, since the first moment I saw you, I felt a sense of déjà vu. I felt like I was revisiting a love story of the past that never came to full fruition. I know it sounds crazy to you since we just met, but I care for you. I so want you to be part of our Brotherhood Family and a part of my life."

"Maya, this is all so fast. I just don't know. I'm confused. I need time to think. I just need some time to think." Brady started up the truck and drove in silence back to the agency.

Though she too was silent, Maya cuddled closely with Brady, resting her head on his shoulder. Once they were back at the agency, Maya tried to convince him to come in and talk to her and Haamid. But Brady repeated that he needed time alone to think about their talk.

He put his arms around her and said, "I'll call you on Monday." Backing away, she turned and briskly walked to the agency's front door. Just as she opened the door, she blew a kiss back to Brady and mouthed, "Miss you."

That evening, as Brady lay in bed, he glanced at the book on his bedside table. It was called *The Soldier*. It was a true story about an American soldier's battlefield experiences in Afghanistan. A friend had given it to him, but he was reluctant to read it. He had read less than two chapters since beginning the book some six weeks earlier. Brady found that when he read it, he often experienced nightmares or restless sleep, yet he was drawn to its honesty and its similarities to his own battlefield experiences. As he picked up the book to read a few more pages before falling asleep, Brady couldn't help but think about the decision he needed to make. Where did his loyalties lie? This was going to be a fitful night.

Chapter 5
Fishing with the Phillips's Party

At three-thirty on Saturday morning, Brady abruptly sat up in a wet sweat, breathing heavily. He tried to shake off the screams of his fellow marines as mortar rounds descended on their bunker. Reaching for what he thought was his weapon, he knocked his glass of water onto the bedside table. He grabbed the towel from his duffel bag, picked up the empty glass, and soaked up the water from the floor. Realizing where he was, he flopped back onto his bed and tried to regain some level of composure.

For the next thirty minutes, Brady lay flat on the bed clutching his pillow. He concentrated on clearing his mind of the screams and fear that gripped him whenever these nightmares returned. His post-traumatic stress syndrome was in full control. Knowing there was no way for him to get back to sleep, he got up, took a shower, got dressed for fishing, and crept downstairs to fix some cereal and coffee. As he descended the back stairs to the kitchen, he saw that the lights were on. As he reached the last step and entered the kitchen, he heard his Uncle Pete say, "Good morning, Brady."

"Hey. Good morning, Uncle Pete. You're up early."

"Maybe a little, but Mr. Phillips likes to get his employees out on the water before the fish are awake. He hates to miss that first bite. And you, Brady—you're also up early?"

"Yeah. I had those recurring bad dreams again and couldn't get back to sleep."

"Sorry to hear that. That's got to be very tough."

"It's OK, Uncle Pete. You just learn to live with it."

Fixing some cereal and juice, they sat down to wait for the coffee to brew.

"You know, Brady, I'm a pretty good listener. If there's ever anything bothering you, don't hesitate to let me know. I know I'll never be as good of a listener as your dad was, but I'm here if you need me."

"Thanks, Uncle Pete. I promise if something is bugging me and I need to talk, I'll take you up on your offer."

"Good," said Pete.

The coffee finished brewing and Pete filled cups for both of them. Sitting across from each other, Pete began to talk to Brady about his fishing plan for the Phillips's party. Pete also shared some of the quirks of the members of Mr. Phillips's group. "Old man Phillips always wants to take his own fish off the hook," he said. "Although half the time he ends up losing them overboard or putting the hook in himself." He also told Brady about Mr. Phillips's young office manager, Michelle. "Whether it's a sunny day or not," he said, "she thinks nothing of climbing up on top of the canopy, removing the top for her bathing suit, and sunning herself half-nude."

Hearing that, Brady said, "I think I can handle the Michelle thing, but I'm not sure about Mr. Phillips unhooking his own fish."

Pete, putting his hand on Brady's shoulder, replied, "I bet you'll be able to handle both."

On Saturday, June 19, 2010 at 6:45 a.m. on the dot, the Phillips's party climbed aboard *Miss Alice* and headed out to the Diamonds, one of Jack Phillips's favorite spots. It was a place where Captain Pete had always had pretty good luck. On the way out, Brady introduced himself to the party of six, paying special attention to Mr. Phillips and of course to Michelle. Brady checked the plane-in boards, the rods for correct drag, and the umbrella rigs. As usual, Pete had prepared everything when he came in late on Friday, but as he always preached - *"double-check everything just to be sure."*

For the first three hours, the fishing was fast and furious. At least two lines were in the process of reeling in fish at all times. Sometimes they were reeling in as many as four lines at once. So, Brady found himself constantly pulling fish onboard, measuring them, throwing back most of them, and putting the big ones into the fish box. Trying to keep six lines straight and untangled was quite a feat, especially since two of the people fishing were new to the sport and were constantly getting tangled up with each other. While it was the mate's job to take fish off of the hook, he was mighty thankful that old man Phillips was taking care of his own.

By10:30 a.m. the pace slowed down considerably. Pete had Brady pull all the lines in so that he could head down to the Gas Docks on the western shore to try their luck there. After pulling in the lines and stowing the rods in their holders, Brady took a short break to check out the lunch his Aunt Louise had packed for him. Since everyone in the party had gotten up early, they too were hungry. They started to chow down on the fruit and other goodies in their bags, saving the sandwiches and fried chicken for later.

Although Brady had briefly introduced himself to everyone when they had first come aboard, he did not recall all of their names, with the exception of Mr. Phillips and Michelle. While it was the custom for the first mate to tend strictly to himself and the work at hand, leaving communication with the clients up to the captain, Brady found himself wanting to know the story on one guy who wore a desert fatigue hat with a fifth marine corps patch sewn onto the brim.

Since Mr. Phillips was up in the cabin talking to Pete, Brady introduced himself to the fellow with the hat.

"Hi. I'm Brady," he said. "Sorry I didn't catch your name when you first came onboard."

"I'm Dan Howard, Maryland Regional Manager for Mr. Phillips."

"Glad to meet you. I couldn't help but notice your hat and the Blue Diamond patch."

"Please, call me Dan. Yeah, I can't seem to go anywhere without it—even to bed. My wife says it seems to be permanently sewn to my bald spot."

"How long did you serve?"

"Before I joined Phillips I was with the fifth marines for eight years. I served in Iraq, Iran, and at the end mainly in Afghanistan, west of Kandahar."

Giving a high-fi, Brady exclaimed, "Semper-Fi. I served two tours with the first marine division, third Battalion—the Black Diamonds. We were in the Sangin District along the Helmn River just north of Deh Shu."

"Nasty place to be," said Dan.

"Yeah," he said, "but being in Kandahar Province, you were in the thick of it too."

Leaning against the gunwale and arching his back, Dan looked up and said, "Tough times, but they were worth it just to know the men I served with." Then he paused, "I lost a lot of buddies to those bastards." After some silence, he said, "So, Brady, how are you doing back in the real world?"

"Well, I had some problems with my recovery at Walter Reed. Doctors put me through hell with some meds that I got by mistake and with two botched surgeries on my neck. Other than that and some recurring nightmares, I guess I'm OK. How about you?"

Taking a swig on his bottled water, Dan said, "I am OK too. My wounds were minor. I had some shrapnel in my leg but the real problem I continue to have is my thoughts about my lost buddies and the anger I harbor for the Taliban."

"So, how do you deal with that anger?" asked Brady.

"First thing, I support my fellow marines through the USO and the Wounded Warrior Program. Second, I back legislators that will make sure those bastards stay put and don't come to our shores. We don't need another 9/11." Pointing to Brady and then to himself, Dan said, "As only we know, those bastards are bound and determined to bury us here, as well as over there. We can't let them succeed!"

"Yeah, you're right," Brady said. "But how do we keep them from coming here?"

"We make sure we elect the right leaders, secure our boarders, and stay vigilant."

Changing the subject before Brady could ask any more questions, Dan said, "So, where are we going?"

"We're going down to the Gas Docks on the western shore. It's just below the Calvert Cliffs Nuclear Power Plant."

"Good spot?"

"Oh Yeah. Because of the Docks' huge superstructure, which sits a couple thousand yards off shore, the fish like to congregate around all of the Docks' pilings. The natural gas plant's warm water discharge, just like the Calvert Cliff Nuclear Power Plant's discharge several miles north of the Docks, is right there. The warm water seems to attract lots of fish. Unfortunately, because of homeland security issues after 9/11, there is a five-hundred-yard restricted area around the docks so that private boats can no longer get close to the pilings. Fishing outside the restricted area is still good for trolling or live-lining, but the best fishing still remains around the pilings themselves."

"See what I mean, Brady. Islamic extremists aren't only trying to obliterate us. They're also trying to obliterate our fishing."

Smiling, Brady said, "Yeah but you'll get your fish today, regardless. I promise."

The *Miss Alice* arrived at the Gas Docks just before 11:30 a.m. Pete began to troll with all six lines out. But for the next hour not a single fish was hooked - not even a bite. Dan looked over at Brady and said, "Hey Brady, when marines promise, they deliver. Don't they?"

"Don't worry, Dan. We'll deliver."

Pete called Brady up to the cabin. "Brady, we need to change from trolling to live-lining, so start to rig up the spinning rods. In the meantime, I'm going to move south of the Docks and get everyone to catch more spot. I got some spot in the live well, but they're not very lively, so I think we'll need a few more."

"OK, Uncle Pete."

Drifting south of Cove Point, just inside Buoy G-77, Pete gave everyone a double-bottom rigged line with razor clams as bait. Pretty soon, everyone began pulling in Norfolk Spot and some small croakers. As fast as Brady and Pete unhooked and reset the lines, the rods started to bend again. The dance of unhooking and baiting continued. After they placed about forty small fish into the live well, mixing them with the ones from the previous day, Pete called for a halt to this frenzy. "OK, everyone," he said. "Let's pull in the lines so we can go back to the Docks for some rockfish."

Pete knew that by live-lining **they** would stand a better chance of catching big rockfish. Because of his long-time special relationship with Jack Phillips, he decided to anchor two hundred feet off of the Docks, instead of the required five hundred yards. While some said that Homeland Security monitored the five-hundred-yard restricted area, Pete didn't believe that. From time to time, he had seen DNR or coast guard vessels around the Gas Docks Area enforcing the five-hundred-yard regulation, but he had never seen any Homeland Security Patrol Boats. As far as he could determine, there are no cameras on the Dock's superstructure to keep track of activities around the Docks. Besides, he and lots of other captains had breached the restricted area before without any consequences.

On their short trip back to the Gas Docks from Cove Point, Pete called Brady into the cabin to tell him about his plan to go inside the restricted area.

Brady said, "Uncle Pete, I understand, but what if they catch you inside. Will they fine you, take the boat, or take your license?"

"I don't know, Brady, but my guess is that they'll just levy a fine if they catch me."

"It's your call, Captain Pete."

Fifteen minutes later, arriving back at the Docks, Pete said, "Let's get set to anchor, Brady."

Brady went up to the bow to unhook the anchor clip and turned to look back at Pete for his signal to drop her. After slowly moving around the Docks to see what the fish finder could pick up, Pete put her into neutral and called up to Brady to drop anchor. Then he put *Miss Alice* into reverse to set the anchor. Pete looked at the fish finder to see what was below them, and he found numerous *hits* on the screen.

"Brady, let's bait-up and cast off in the direction of the pilings."

Within two minutes of the first cast, Michelle got a good hit. Then old man Phillips got a fish on. Then Dan got one. This happened all around the boat until all six lines had fish on them.

Brady thought, *Man this is going to be a mess. There are going to be more tangled lines than Medusa's hair.*

Michelle shrieked, "I got a big one."

Dan chuckled and mumbled, "I bet you do!"

Brady moved beside Michelle to help her pull in what turned out to be a thirty-nine-inch rockfish. While Michelle was bright, pretty, and full of life, as many times as she had gone fishing, she still had no clue how to hold a rod or unhook her fish. Instead of leaving some slack in the line, she kept the line taught. When Brady finally flipped the fish off, the hook flew back and snagged him in the arm, impaling him just below the elbow.

Brady turned to Michelle and jokingly said, "It's OK, Michelle. You can lower the rod now. You've already landed me." Blood seeped out of Brady's arm where the hook remained embedded.

Michelle screamed, "Oh, I'm so sorry, Brady. Are you OK?"

"Sure. No sweat," said Brady, cutting the line where it attached to the hook and grabbing a clean cloth from the top of the engine. Using his teeth and his free hand, he tied the cloth around his bleeding arm. Then, without skipping a beat, he helped bring in the other four fish. He measured them and threw three overboard, but he kept Mr. Phillips's fish, which measured just over thirty-seven inches. As he re-set the lines and dropped them over, Pete came out with a set of needle-nose pliers. He then got Brady to sit on the engine box and surveyed the damaged arm.

"Not too bad, Brady. Hold on to the edge of the engine box and I'll work this hook out."

Luckily, the hook's barb had broken off when the fish had hit the gunwale, so it was easy to remove with a simple twist of Pete's wrist. This caused only a minor tear in the skin. Keeping quiet, a slight grimace formed on Brady's face. Pete returned to the cabin and brought out a first-aid kit. Handing it to Michelle, he said, "You do the honors, Michelle."

Michelle quickly found ointment and a patch that was two inches long and two inches wide. Brady compressed the cloth over the injury until she was ready to apply the ointment and the patch.

Actually, Brady thought, she had remained surprisingly calm when she was helping him. In fact, she had done a very good job fixing him up. All along, she continued to whisper to him, "Brady, I am so sorry. It was so dumb of me. I'm so sorry."

Brady reached for her hand, held it gently, and said, "It's OK, Michelle. It's fine now. Thanks for all of your help. I'm OK. I promise."

The fish continued to attack the lines for the next two hours, and Brady's deck dance never stopped.

At about 3:00 p.m. the fish stopped biting and the tide went slack. More importantly, the boat had reached its limit of rockfish. Since there was no limit on spot, Pete announced to everyone that they could go back to Cove Point to catch more spot if they wanted to, or they could go in. Mr. Philips spoke up. "Let's go in, Pete. I'd like someone to look at Brady's arm."

"Absolutely, Mr. Phillips. We'll head in right now."

After putting all of the rods away, Brady went into the cabin and said, "Uncle Pete, I don't need anyone to look at my arm. It's fine."

"That's fine with me if you really feel it's all right, but let's at least make sure Mr. Phillips thinks you're fine. He feels responsible and he doesn't want you to get an infection, OK?"

"OK, Uncle Pete. I'll play along."

On the way back to the dock, most of the party dove into their late lunch. Until then, there hadn't been any slack time to actually eat the lunches that Louise had prepared. Brady retreated to the dining table and the benches in the cabin to finish his sandwich and two pieces of fried chicken. Shortly thereafter, Dan came in and sat across from Brady.

"So, how's the arm?"

"It's OK," said Brady. "It stings a little, but that's all."

"Did Florence Nightingale do a good job?"

"Yeah, actually she did. She surprised me."

"She's a good soul. She's a little ditzy but she's a good gal. We couldn't operate without her. She is the glue that holds the place together."

"As long as you don't give her a fishing rod in the office!"

"Yeah, that's a fact."

The men sat there, quietly munching on their sandwiches and peering out the window at the dark green, almost black hue of the water.

"Great day, Brady. You delivered, as promised."

"Yeah, Captain Pete's the best. I thought we'd find them, but you never know." Picking up where they'd left off that morning, Brady asked Dan, "You think we'll ever see another 9/11 here?"

"I sure do - and not just one. I was attached to our G-2 intelligence group. As you may know, our G-2 guys in Afghanistan were constantly coming across Pakistani communications that indicated multiple future plots on US soil."

"Yeah, our G-2 also intercepted lots of chatter, but our guys just sort of blew it off. They'd been hearing about it for two years, but nothing was actually happening."

"Well, Brady, our guys took it pretty seriously and passed it up the chain. Who knows? I'd bet my pension on it happening. I don't know when it will happen. But I'd guess it will be sometime soon."

Once he was back at the dock, Mr. Phillips announced that he was taking his group up to Easton for dinner. He asked Pete to hold the fish until the next day, since they would not be back to the dock before dinner.

The next day, Sunday, June 20, 2010, the Phillips party gathered again at 6:45 a.m. and boarded the *Miss Alice* for the final day of fishing. As Brady helped Mr. Phillips onboard, Jack asked Brady, "You get someone to look at that arm of yours?"

"I sure did, Mr. Phillips. I had the EMT at the firehouse take a look, and he says Michelle did a perfect butterfly-tape job. Thanks to her, it looked fine to him."

"Well, I'm glad to hear it. If you don't want to end up hooked again, though, I'd stay clear of her today." Overhearing the conversation, Michelle blurted out, "Mr. Phillips, that's an awful thing to say!"

Chuckling, Joe Phillips responded, "Come on, Michelle, you're always looking to hook a good man."

Putting his hand on her shoulder, Brady said, "Michelle, I'll keep unhooking your fish just as long as you keep bringing 'em in. And thanks again for the great nursing job. The EMT said it was very professional."

Pressing her side into Brady, Michelle wrinkled her nose and whispered to Brady, "Next time I hook you, I promise it won't hurt."

Brady stepped back some and he whispered, "You're a flirt, Michelle, and you're very good at it too."

"Thanks, Brady," she said. "I'll take that as a compliment."

"Enough of this chatter," said Pete. "Let's cast off, Brady."

"Gotcha, Captain." Brady turned to unhook the stern line and then walked up to the bow and released that line too. Stepping down from the gunwale, Brady went into the cabin to get Pete to fill him in on where they were going and what he wanted him to do. "Uncle Pete, what's the plan?"

"First, we'll go back to the Gas Docks. If that doesn't work, we'll go to the Stone Rocks and see what's going on there."

"Are we going to go for spot on the way?"

"Yeah, I think I'll try off Cook's Point." Pete headed out of Knapp's Narrows and into the mouth of the Choptank River. They pulled in some sixteen spot between Cooks Point and Buoy R-10. Then they headed down to the Gas Docks.

A breeze blew out of the southwest at five knots. The sun grew stronger by the minute, and the ride to the Docks was both smooth and uneventful. Again, Dan and Brady swapped stories about their Afghan Tours. Michelle wrapped her arm around the port canopy strut for support. Leaning toward the two, she listened intently to their conversations. Every so often, she asked questions about the stories that they were telling - stories. about firefights and friends they'd lost.

Pete called out from the cabin door, "Got a minute, Brady?"

"Yes, sir." Brady excused himself and entered the cabin. "Yeah, Uncle Pete."

"Need to get the rods out and remind everyone how to fish with live lines. We'll be at the Docks in short order."

"Yes, sir."

Brady returned to the deck and began preparing the rods and the Phillips party for the live-lining that they were going to be doing - setting anchor and fishing for large rockfish with live spot on the ends of their hooks.

For the next four hours, the fishing was fantastic. By 12:30 p.m. the Phillips party had limited out on rockfish. Pete headed up to the Stone Rocks to try their luck at croakers, which he'd heard an hour ago were running large up there.

After they anchored and Brady got all of the lines over the side, Pete sat at the dinette and began to eat Louise's tasty lunch. Between pulling in lots of croakers, the others also took bites of their sandwiches and chicken.

True to form and wishing to improve on her already bronze tan, Michelle climbed up onto the canopy, spread out a beach towel, and loosened her bathing suit top. Instead of lying on her front, she lay on her back and removed her top completely. Since they were used to her lack of modesty, the others in the Philips party paid little attention to her. Between baiting lines and removing fish, however, Brady stole glances in Michelle's direction, and he wasn't disappointed by what he saw.

Their success with fishing continued through the afternoon. Arriving back at the dock at 3:30 p.m., Brady and Pete cleaned the fish while the Phillips party returned to the Tilghman Hotel to gather their belongings. At 4:30 p.m. they came back to collect the ice-packed boxes of cleaned fish. Mr. Phillips thanked both Pete and Brady for a great three days. He handed Pete an envelope, and he gave Brady three hundred dollars as a tip. Brady thanked him and gave Dan a high-fi. "Thanks for sharing your experiences and advice," Dan.

"Thanks for listening. Any time you want to talk, just call me."

"Will do. Be sure to come back this summer, Dan. You guys were a hoot, but don't forget to bring Michelle, OK?"

"OK. I think I get the picture, Brady."

Brady hopped up onto the dock, faced Michelle, and thanked her again for tending to his injury. Michelle gave Brady a warm hug. As she handed him her business card, she said, "Call me sometime. I'll come down here for dinner, if you want me to."

"I'd like that, Michelle," said Brady. "I'll give you a call."

After parting, Brady walked back home as Pete finalized some paperwork. Then he closed up the cabin. Back at his uncle's place, Brady took a long hot shower before returning downstairs for dinner with Pete and Louise.

At the table, Pete said, "So, tomorrow's your day off. How are you going to spend it?"

"I don't know, Uncle Pete," said Brady. "Maybe I'll go to Salisbury for the day."

"Tuesdays and Wednesdays are with Mike on those carpentry jobs, right?"

"Yep."

"To save time, you might want to give Mike a call and maybe stay at his place tomorrow night. I know he'd be glad to put you up."

"Might be a good idea, Uncle Pete. I'll give him a call on his cell phone tomorrow."

Brady finished his dinner, thanked his aunt for the meal, and said he was going for an early evening walk to work out the kinks in his injured neck. The screen door's taught spring snapped back with a loud bang. Just outside the door, Brady stood motionlessly listening to the spring's sound as it slowly evaporated into the night. A light breeze rustled the maple tree leaves, gently soothing Brady's suntanned face. As he stood on the porch steps, he took a deep breath and soaked in the sunset palette of purple, orange, and blue.

Brady moved off the porch steps and started his walk to Dogwood Harbor, where the last three remaining Tilghman Island Skipjacks were moored. At this time of day, the harbor was a place of peace and quiet. Brady walked around the harbor and sat on an old, weathered wooden bench, enjoying the final moments of a brilliant sunset.

In this historic and peaceful setting, surrounded by an assortment of workboats and the skipjacks from the 1900s, he let his mind run through the last two weeks of events:

his arrival on Tilghman, his meeting with Haamid and Maya, his recent discussions with Maya, his talks with Dan Howard, and the conflict he was experiencing. Clearly, Brady knew he was at a crossroads. He was attracted to Maya, yet he rejected her politics of terrorism. He was finding comfort in the sense of purpose in his work on the water, yet he was reluctant at this time to embrace it as a long-term profession.

Many questions cluttered his thoughts. What was actually going on with Maya and Haamid? Why had they befriended him? Did they have ulterior motives? Could they really be involved in providing trained terrorists to third-party organizations? If so, what was the endgame?

As the sun slipped below the horizon and early evening brought a salty breeze and a symphony of slapping halyards, Brady came to the conclusion that he just didn't know enough. He had to learn more - much more - before he could make any decisions. Brady promised himself that he would call Dan soon to get his advice on the situation.

Chapter 6

The Job Offer

On his walk back to the house, Brady dialed Maya's cell phone. On the fourth ring, she picked up and said, "Hello."

"Maya, it's Brady."

Her voice rose as she responded, "Hey, Brady. How are you?"

"Great. Thanks. If it suits you and Haamid, I thought I'd come down tomorrow to see you guys."

"Sure," she said. "Do you want to have lunch?"

"Yeah, that works for me. What about eleven-thirty?"

"That's fine. Let's meet at my office, OK?"

"Ok. See you then."

As he walked back to his Uncle's place, Brady flipped the phone cover shut, stuffed it in his pants pocket, and took a deep breath of the soothing night air. Brady said goodnight to Louise and Pete, and then he headed to his room. He sat on the side of his bed and took a small pad and pencil from the nightstand. He began to make a list of questions he would ask when he met with Haamid and Maya the next day. As he started to think about that coming meeting, he came to the conclusion that the manner in which he would ask the questions would be as important as the questions themselves. He began to scribble down his thoughts: *How can I help you? Obviously, you all have some thoughts in mind? What do you believe I can bring to the table?* The thoughts kept coming and he kept writing them down.

✳✳✳

As Brady stepped through the temp agency's entrance door, he saw Maya there waiting for him. She came up, threw her arms around him, and gave him a warm embrace.

"How are you, Brady."

Slightly blushing, Brady replied, "Fine. Thanks. Good to see you."

As Brady backed away, he saw Haamid walking up behind Maya.

"Hey, Brady," said Haamid. "How are you?"

"Great, Haamid. How about you?"

Shaking hands, Haamid said, "Doing well. Thanks."

"Where are we going to lunch?"

"How about a different place? "There is a small restaurant downtown on the river where we can sit outside," said Maya.

"Sounds great to me."

As they stepped out on the restaurant deck, Haamid asked the waitress if they could sit at the far end of the deck, where they would be away from the other patrons. She said, "Sure. Whatever you wish." She then placed them at a table at the river's edge.

After ordering their lunch Haamid asked Brady, "So what's going on at Tilghman?"

"Well, I just finished a very successful three-day fishing party with some longtime customers of my Uncle Pete's."

"Where did you all go?"

"We fished the Stone Rocks, the Diamonds, and the Gas Docks—places south of Tilghman that you've probably never heard of."

"Well, I don't know of the other two, but I do know where the Gas Docks are."

Huh, thought Brady. *I wonder how he knows the Docks?*

"You ever fish around Kent Narrows or Bloody Point?" Haamid asked.

"Not this season, but I have before. Why do you ask?"

"Well, we have some potential demolition and repair jobs both there and at the Gas Docks," said Haamid.

"Really," said Brady. "What kind of jobs are they?"

"We've been asked by US Maritime, a new startup company who's just getting into the marine demolition business, to find them some skilled labor for projects they expect to be awarded fairly soon. One job is at Kent Narrows and the other one is at the Gas Docks."

Smiling, Brady said, "Sounds like a job for someone who likes fishing."

"Exactly," replied Maya. "That's why we thought you might be perfect. Some of the tasks involve shuttling supplies and workers to and from the sites by boat, along with some under water demolition work, which we understand you are qualified for."

"I'm flattered you guys have thought of me, but I couldn't do it full-time. I'd also have to know more about the demolition work to decide if I was comfortable with it or not."

Haamid said, "I think the client is only looking for someone for two days a week. As far as the demolition work is concerned, if you're interested I'll have you talk to Salah, since he is the one who is the most knowledgeable about US Maritime's needs and the job qualifications.

"Isn't Salah Mohamed your uncle?"

"Good of you to remember. Yes he is, Brady. What about our trying to meet with him after lunch?"

"Works for me."

"I'll check with him right now." Haamid got up from the table, walked to the far corner of the deck, made his call, and then returned to the table. "It's all set. We can meet him later in his office at two-thirty."

"Good," said Brady. For the rest of the lunch, the three bantered back and forth about inane subjects, such as weather, sports, and recent movies.

$$***$$

Salah was waiting for them at the front desk when they arrived back at the agency. After introducing himself to Brady, Salah escorted the three of them back to his office. Maya closed the office door and sat down next to Brady, across from Salah and Haamid.

"Brady, I understand that Haamid has told you a little bit about our client, US Maritime. It's a new startup marine construction company that has asked us to help them fill some slots on their Chesapeake Bay Team. This week, they expect to get awarded two jobs that involve the demolition and reconstruction of marine structures."

"You're referring to Kent Narrows and the Gas Docks?" asked Brady.

The normally mild-mannered Salah immediately became stone-faced. In an accusatory voice, he asked, "Where did you hear that?"

"Haamid mentioned those sites during lunch."

Turning abruptly to Haamid, Salah focused his wrath on his nephew like a sniper using telescopic crosshairs. In an angry tone Salah said, "That was a flagrant breach of your oath, Haamid. Severe consequences will follow." Allowing no response from Haamid, Salah regained his composure and turned back to Brady. "Brady, the project I am speaking of is subject to a confidentiality agreement between us, US Maritime, and Homeland Security. It requires a security clearance for anyone in a field position on this project. I apologize for subjecting you to my reprimand of Haamid, but his breach was egregious, and it could jeopardize the security of the operation."

"Why would demolition and reconstruction be of any concern to Homeland Security?" asked Brady.

"The Gas Docks house liquid natural gas. Homeland Security deems them to be a potential terrorist target, and the same is true with the Narrows Bridge, which is a crucial evacuation link between the mainland and the Eastern Shore. I think it's overkill, but that's a requirement of the contract. Now, let's get back to this particular job. First, U. S. Maritime is looking for someone who is knowledgeable of the middle Bay Area. They need someone who is proficient at operating large Bay dead rise boats and has expertise in underwater demolitions. Do you fit the bill?"

"Yes, sir," said Brady. "But as I told Haamid, I only have two days a week available, and I have no idea what the pay is or what the level of risk is."

"The client confidentiality agreement provides no benefits and like the waterman's world, they pay in cash at the end of each day. The daily rate for this position is $1,500. It's a substantial amount, but it's appropriate, given the risk of diving at night."

"Why would I be diving at night?"

"Since the two areas are well traveled during the day, the thought is to try to do as much of the work when traffic is not an issue."

Brady responded, "Certainly avoiding other boats and vehicular traffic makes sense, but underwater night work is very dangerous. It demands excellent coordination with an experienced surface crew. I wouldn't touch that kind of work without a high level of comfort in my surface crew."

"Good point, Brady. I'll get back to you on that."

"Thanks. The pay's fine, Salah, but I'd want to know more about the dive team, the surface crew, and the equipment before I'd consider signing on. Do you know exactly what the actual tasks are? Is it only explosives rigging, or does it also include detonation itself?"

"It's only a rigging job. They evidently have their own detonation team."

"So, where do we go from here?"

"Well, I'll check on your questions and probably have you meet with the project manager so you can discuss it with him directly."

"Sounds good to me. I'll just wait to hear back from you."

"Good, I'll call you after I have talked to US Maritime."

Brady stood up to leave and said, "I want to thank you, Haamid and Maya, for thinking about me and considering me for the job. It sounds interesting and it would certainly use my expertise."

As Salah rose to shake Brady's hand, he turned to Haamid and asked him to remain. After exiting the office, Brady turned to Maya and said, "God, I hope I didn't do anything that will cause Haamid any problem. He didn't tell me those locations were confidential."

"Haamid knew the rules and I think it just slipped out by mistake. But, Salah was not pleased. In fact, I haven't seen him that angry in a long time."

Brady could understand that their first job with US Maritime was an important stepping-stone to more jobs with them in the future, but he was beginning to wonder about all the secrecy when the job seemed to be a simple demolition and reconstruction project. Brady sensed that something was askew. A frown came over his face as he left the building.

Maya and Brady walked outside to say good-bye. "Brady, you sure seem preoccupied. You seem detached. It's like you are somewhere else."

"I do?"

"Yes, you do," said Maya, "and it worries me."

"Maya, I'm fine," said Brady. "I just got a lot of stuff on my mind."

Maya reached out for Brady. As she placed her hands on his arms, she said, "Is there something wrong with the job offer or with me personally?"

"No, Maya. Things just seem to be going faster than I had expected. So, I need some time to think about this job offer and about us."

Maya hugged Brady, backed away, and said, "I understand, Brady. We'll talk as soon as Salah has answers to your questions. I care for you, Brady, and I only want the best for you." There was a pause. "I hope the job works out. It would be wonderful to see more of you."

"Thanks, Maya. I'll be in touch."

On his way back to Cambridge, Brady got a call from Salah.

"Brady, I have talked to the project manager for US Maritime. Unfortunately, he's in California for the next two weeks, but he asked me to relay the following to you. They want you to be the captain of the dive team. They confirmed that their own due diligence proved that the proposed surface team members are also very skilled divers—people you can count on in an emergency. Your tasks will be limited to setting and wiring, in sequence, the demolition charges on predesignated, deteriorated, and obsolete pilings. If because of fast running tides or strong winds you need an extra hand, one of the experienced surface crew can assist you. The surface crew, as I mentioned, will be comprised of skilled divers. One is an explosives expert, and the other is an underwater rescue expert who will be responsible for all of the equipment, such as air tanks, the lifelines, and the emergency air hose and compressor. This coming Thursday, the twenty-fourth, assuming you can start then, you will get the opportunity to meet the two team members when you go out to recon the pilings at both sites. If possible before you start full-time on Thursday, Abed would like you to meet me at the dock in Cambridge on the afternoon of Wednesday the twenty-third, so you can get familiar with the first boat and perhaps take it out for a short trial run."

"Sorry, but did you say the first boat? Is there more than one boat?"

"Yes, we have two boats, Brady. The second one is a backup. We have it in case we have a mechanical failure on the first boat. However, the second boat is on the Honga River, near Hooper Island. We will show you that one later in the week."

"Oh, OK."

"So, have I answered all of your questions satisfactorily?"

"I think so."

"Do you want the job, Brady?"

"Yes," said Brady, "but I still reserve the right to go back on this offer if, after meeting them, I don't think the surface crew is capable of doing their job."

"Fair enough. Then I will see you at two o'clock on Wednesday at the dock. I will e-mail you directions to the dock, but don't forget that all of this is highly confidential and no one is to know where these boats are moored."

"OK. I understand. It's s not the first time I've dealt with security. It was a way of life in Afghanistan. See you on Wednesday, Salah." Hanging up, Brady then dialed Mike to inform him about the job offer and his decision to accept it. Adhering to the confidentiality agreement, however, he did not share the boat's location or the fact that there were two of them.

Before the call to Mike connected, Brady hit the cancel button. Was this fair to Mike and Pete to back out of a job he had accepted first? Would he be letting Mike and his family down? As he redialed Mike, Brady vowed to turn down the US Maritime job if he gathered from Mike that it would pose a burden on him.

The call went through. "Mike. Hey. It's Brady."

"Hey, Brady. How are you?"

"Great. Thanks. Listen, Mike, I wanted to call you to tell you about a job offer I just got. If I accept it, it would mean I couldn't work on Royal Oak. Please understand, if taking this job puts you in jeopardy or in any way causes you a problem, I won't accept it."

"So, Brady, what type of job is it?"

"Well, it's working for a new company called US Maritime on some piling and bulkhead demolition work. Since it requires captaining a boat and diving, the pay is excellent. I feel bad calling you on this after I committed to you, Mike, but the money is excellent and will allow me to help my mom out of some of the debt she incurred after Dad's death."

"Look, Brady, I want you to do what's best for you. I can certainly manage alone. In fact, I have a young carpenter apprentice bugging me to bring him onboard, so that would work out fine. Sounds to me like you should grab that job. Don't think another thought about it."

"Mike, I can easily work tomorrow and a half-day on Wednesday if that would help. They don't need me onboard until Wednesday at about 2 p.m."

"Actually, that would work out great, since the other guy won't be available until Thursday."

"Mike, you're the best! I'm glad you understand. More importantly, I'm glad this works for you also."

"I'll miss working with you, Brady, but this sounds like too good of a deal for you to pass up."

"Thanks, Mike," said Brady. "What time do you want me tomorrow?"

"About 6:30 a.m. at the Royal Oak site. I will e-mail you directions later today."

"Great. See you tomorrow."

Brady arrived back at Pete's at about 5:00 p.m. He walked into the house to find it empty. There was a note on the kitchen table telling him that Pete was down at the dock and Aunt Louise was off at the beauty parlor in St. Michael's. Knowing that Pete probably had some chore for him on the Miss Alice, Brady went upstairs to his room and changed into shorts and an old work shirt. He left the house and headed down to the dock. As he reached the boat, he saw Uncle Pete working on some teak trim in the cabin. He jumped aboard and shouted over the electric sander that Pete was using, "Hey, Uncle Pete. What's up?"

"Hi, Brady. I'm just trying to improve Miss Alice's looks for the new customers coming on Friday. I need to impress them so they'll come back again."

"Uncle Pete, it's the fish and your smile that will bring 'em back—not some piece of teak trim."

"Well maybe, but every little bit helps. Oh, by the way, I got a call from Jack Phillips and he's coming back for another three-day weekend after the Fourth of July. He said to tell you Michelle sends her best and to remind you about some dinner you promised her."

"Huh," said Brady. "I'm not really sure I promised her dinner, but I wouldn't mind that at all."

"Say, Brady, would you grab some of that fine sandpaper and smooth the rough edges off of this trim?"

"Sure, Uncle Pete."

After about five minutes of sanding in the quiet, Brady spoke up. "Uncle Pete, I called Mike today to get his OK about my accepting a Tuesday-through-Thursday job with US Maritime. I'll be doing marine demolition and diving work on a couple of jobs they've just been awarded."

"Exactly what kind of work, Brady?"

"Well, they tell me I will be captaining a forty-foot dead rise for them and doing underwater explosives work like the work I did in the service. The only difference is that I'll get paid $1,500 a day instead of pennies a day."

"Wow. That's quite a chunk of change. You're serious about this?"

"I sure am, Uncle Pete. You think I'm wrong to do it?"

Pete stopped what he was doing and put his sander down. He pursed his lips, as thoughts rumbled through his mind. "No. You're not necessarily wrong, as long as it's OK with Mike."

"Mike says its OK with him. I'm going to work for him tomorrow and a half day on Wednesday. His new apprentice comes onboard on Thursday. Uncle Pete, I sense you have reservations."

"Yeah, Brady, I do. What do you know about this US Maritime?"

"Not much. They are a new firm and they are getting assistance with hiring from a Salisbury Islamic temp agency that is run by Middle Easterners who are friends of some people I know in Baltimore."

"An Islamic temp agency, huh." Then it hit Pete. "What kind of boat will you be using?"

"It's a forty-foot Bay- built dead rise. It's just recently been renovated and re-powered. I understand that she has a new custom-built Cummins six-hundred-horsepower diesel. I haven't seen it yet, but I will on Wednesday afternoon."

Pete knotted his brow but decided not to discuss the boat any further. He just said, "Take some pictures of her on your phone on Wednesday, Brady. I'd like to see what she looks like. She may have a name I recognize."

"Don't know her name, Uncle Pete, but I'll find out for you."

"Know where she's moored?" asked Pete.

"Don't know that either, Uncle Pete," said Brady, "but right now, she's somewhere down the Bay."

"Sounds like a good deal to me, Brady. Hope it works out well for you."

"You still sound a little skeptical, Uncle Pete."

"No, I'm not skeptical, Brady," said Pete. "Just curious."

After a restless night that was punctuated by nightmares about Afghanistan, Brady got up at 5:00 a.m. sharp. He took a quick shower, grabbed a bowl of cereal, and quietly walked out the kitchen door to his truck. His cell phone marked the date as Tuesday June 24, 2010. It was another beautiful Eastern Shore day.

On the way to Royal Oak to meet Mike, Brady mulled over his concerns about the secrecy surrounding the US Maritime job. Until he knew more about the specific tasks he'd be asked to undertake, though, he would keep his thoughts to himself.

Working with Mike on the renovation job at Royal Oak was a pleasant break from the worries he was experiencing. Mike was a terrific carpenter and Brady enjoyed working with wood again. At the end of the day, when they boxed the tools and cleaned up the porch they were renovating, Mike and Brady said they'd see each other the next day. They parted and went their separate ways.

When Brady got back to Tilghman, he went straight to the dock to see if he could help Pete with the teak trim. Arriving at the dock, he found Pete hard at work on the interior teak. Pete's friend Mack was staining the exterior canopy's ceiling slats.

"Hey, Captain Mack," said Brady. "I see Uncle Pete's got you working too."

"Hi Brady. Yeah. Anything for an old friend in need."

"Uncle Pete's not in need; he just likes to have an old friend to talk with."

"Yeah, you're right. I've been so tied up with crabbin' that Pete and I haven't had much of a chance to sit and bitch over a beer or two. Luckily, I got some extra help onboard for the next two days. Hopefully Pete and I can catch up."

"That's good, Captain Mack. Uncle Pete, what can I help you with?"

"Hey, Brady. Well a little more sanding in here would help."

"Gotcha. I'll be right there." Brady picked up some 220-grit sandpaper and began to give a final sanding to the teak inside the cabin.

Once Mack had finished the first coat on the canopy slats, he entered the cabin. Following behind Brady, he wiped the finely sanded wood with a soft cloth and then began to apply the first coat of varnish. With all three of them crowded in the cabin, Pete announced that he was going on deck to start working on Miss Alice's bright work.

"Wow," said Mack, "I can't wait to see those new customers. You haven't been this fussy since you landed old man Phillips as a customer twenty years ago."

"Maybe," said Pete. "But in these times, another good client like Phillips would sure help."

"Amen to that," said Mack.

At about 6:30 p.m., when Mack had finished the cabin's first coat, Pete came in from the bow and said, "What do you say we put the brushes down, call it quits for the day, and go to my porch for a beer?"

"Sounds good to us," said Mack.

"Uncle Pete, you and Mack go ahead now," said Brady. "I'll come up after I clean up the mess you all made."

"You don't mind, Brady?"

"No, Uncle Pete. I'll see you on the porch in a little while."

"You're a good man, Brady. Thanks. We'll just go ahead and do that," said Mack.

✳✳✳

When Brady got to the house, he pulled a beer from the fridge and walked out onto the porch. As he came through the kitchen door, he heard Pete say to Mack, "Sounds like our boat, doesn't it?" Seeing Brady step onto the porch, Mack nodded but he didn't answer Pete.

As he pulled up a chair, Brady said, "So, what's new, Captain Mack?"

"Not much, Brady. I am sitting here trying to convince your Uncle Pete to get the two dissident waterman's associations together and run for president of a combined waterman's group, but it's like pulling teeth."

"I agree. Uncle Pete would make a great peacemaker and a fierce leader when it comes to gettin' the state back on track. There's a need for positive change in Maryland's seafood industry. There are too damn many regulations and there's too much politics in the Bay's management, especially with the Feds trying to run everything."

"You can say that again," said Mack, taking a swig from his beer. "Hey, Brady, I hear you got a new job."

"Yeah," said Brady. "Well, I think so. I got a few things to work out before I make a final decision."

"Pete says you'll be captaining a newly renovated Bay boat."

"That's what they tell me, Captain Mack, but I won't see for myself until tomorrow afternoon."

"Well, let us know what she's like. You know, take some pictures and all."

"Uncle Pete asked me to do the same. You guys think you may know the boat?" Brady asked, pausing. "Was that the boat you mentioned when I came onto the porch?"

"Not sure, Brady. Mack and I are just curious about it."

"How so, Uncle Pete?"

Pete looked at Mack and then continued. "Well, Brady, Mack and I have seen what we believe is a rogue forty-foot Bay boat that we believe is up to no good."

"What kind of boat, Uncle Pete?" Brady asked, putting his beer down and leaning forward.

"It's a re-powered Hooper's Island dead rise that was secretly renovated in Dorchester County. We believe it's presently tied up at a private dock on the Choptank River."

Pete paused. Brady's back stiffened. "Go on," said Brady.

"Well, Mack and I have spied on their renovation efforts, which have only been done in the dead of night on privately leased lands. We've seen their extreme security measures, including guards with heavy weapons. The boat we saw damn near ran over Mack one foggy day in February, and we've been lookin' for her ever since."

"Have you talked to anyone about her, like DNR or the coast guard?"

"No. We've kept what we know to ourselves until we can gather more information about her."

"So, what do you think is going on?"

"We don't really know, Brady. What we do know is that they are a sizable organization that has leased at least two large farms on the water, both of which are heavily guarded. This group is clearly military-trained. They have a strict chain of command, and they conduct their activities totally under cover. They are all from the Middle East."

Now, if that doesn't sound like a group of terrorists, I don't know what does," said Mack.

Brady thought, 'What's this all about? What the hell's going on? Could this be related to my job offer?'

Chapter 7

Discovery at Kent Narrows

Brady left Royal Oak at 2:00 p.m. on Wednesday, June 23, 2010. He arrived at the Chambers Farm, where he was to meet Salah and the surface dive crew and familiarize himself with the boat. After Salah briefly introduced the crew, Carlos and Smitty, and had a short chat about the afternoon's plan, he walked to the stern and began texting from his PDA. On his own, Brady walked around the boat to get the lay of the land.

The engine was a huge Cummins six-hundred-horsepower marine diesel with a trolling clutch and noise-suppression mufflers. There was a mid-station two thirds of the way back from the bow. It had a full set of electronics secured in a large canopy-mounted weatherproof box. Brady turned and briefly interrupted Salah's texting, asking him if he had a key to the electronics box and keys to the cabin, lockers, doors, and hatches. Salah told him that a duplicate set was being made and they would give it to him once the actual work began. In the meantime, he told Brady he would open the locks he needed access to with his own personal set of keys. He then opened the large mid-station canopy electronics cabinet. Stacked into two rows were a GPS plotter, two VHF radios, a small separate radar screen, an underwater sonar side-scanner, a depth finder, and a military type, olive-drab radio with foreign nomenclature on it. Each screen had a U-shaped reflector guard over it to avoid being viewed by anyone other than the mid-station operator or someone standing directly behind him.

While curious, Brady refrained from asking Salah questions about the array of electronics—especially the olive-drab military style radio—for fear of sounding too inquisitive. He did not want to raise any red flags if he could help it. The display of electronics in the cabin and at the mid-station explained the six-antenna overkill extended above the cabin's canopy. Brady returned to the steerage cabin and inspected the duplicate set of electronics mounted on the cabin bulkhead just above the steering wheel. Here again, there was a military-style radio nestled on the right side of the panel.

The steerage cabin was equipped with a chart table, a dining table with benches, and the captain's chair with storage underneath. Under a pale-gray tarp was a bank of six heavy-duty interconnected marine batteries, diving equipment, a large military-type generator, and a compressor. The generator and the compressor both had side-mounted exhaust stacks.

The interior forward cabin itself was sparse. It had an inordinate amount of large-keyed storage lockers and two narrow bunk beds. Behind the set of steps that led down into the forward cabin, there was a secured wooden door that was three feet wide and three feet tall. It appeared to lead farther below deck.

Upon returning to the steerage cabin, Brady asked Salah, "What are the lockers below for?"

"Nothing right now, but they are lead-lined to store explosive primer caps and wiring for the demolition work," said Salah.

"And what about the locker behind the stairs?"

"That's where we have installed a large extra fuel tank."

"Do you have a key to that?"

"Not on me right now, but I'll get a duplicate made."

Brady sat in the captain's chair and familiarized himself with the myriad of gauges and electronics spread out before him. He began to check out the GPS route and set the waypoints to the Kent Narrows Bridge.

As Salah climbed back onto the dock, he turned toward Brady and said, "I'll meet you back here at the dock for a debriefing at about 7:00 p.m."

Brady said, "It'll probably be between seven and seven-thirty before I get back, depending on how long the run actually takes."

"OK," said Salah. "If there are any problems, call me on my cell."

"Yes, sir. Will do."

Brady turned to Carlos and Smitty and ordered them to cast off for their run up the Bay. Brady checked his watch and noted that his departure time from the Chambers dock was 2:45 p.m. Instead of using the autopilot, he steered her manually to get a feel for how she handled. Brady set the Garmin screen to the Kent Narrows Route. Cautiously, he put the big boat into gear. After clearing Cook's Point, he pushed the throttle up to 2,600 rpms, which produced a speed of twenty-eight knots. Because the gear ratio had been adjusted to provide a sustained cruising speed of thirty-six knots with a maximum top speed of forty-three knots, the boat got up on plane in a matter of seconds. Under her original power train, it would have taken a minute and a half.

Brady marveled at the way she cut through the water effortlessly and quietly, due to her sound suppression mufflers. She handled like a dream. It felt more like the PT boats he had been on in the Afghan rivers. Brady settled her in at thirty-six knots and proceeded to the mid-station to check out the canopy-mounted GPS and radio systems.

Brady ran through a radio check of all three units, including the olive- drab colored military radio. The sister radio to the olive-drab one was a handheld unit that Salah kept on his webbed desert belt. Wishing to let Salah know how well the boat was handling, Brady activated the military radio mike, "Boat to Base." Salah responded, "Base here." As he started to explain how things were going, Salah immediately told Brady that he was not to use this military channel for anything other than dire emergencies. Salah told Brady not to call again and that he'd see him later. Then he abruptly terminated the call.

Brady replaced the microphone and muttered under his breath, "Bastards sure are clippy. All work and no play." Taking a deep breath, he said to himself, "Too damn intense for me."

On their way up the Bay, Brady began to talk to Carlos and Smitty about their demolition and surface-rescue experience. Carlos was a Nicaraguan. He had been recently involved in demolition work surrounding the expansion of the Panama Canal. The Islamic Agency had recruited him. Smitty, on the other hand, had been recruited directly through Salah. Mainly stationed in the Mediterranean, he'd been a Sea Bee for some twenty years. Both of them were knowledgeable. Based upon their answers to his questions, Brady felt that they were proficient in surface procedures, communications, and underwater rescue. This gave Brady the level of confidence he needed to feel comfortable diving at night in the dark, murky waters of the Bay.

Not wanting to push the engine too hard, Brady pulled back on the throttle and set the boat between twenty-eight and thirty knots, arriving at Kent Narrows in less than one hour. As he entered the multiple-buoyed area just outside of the jetty, Brady dropped to below the required six-knot speed. He turned on the side-scan sonar screen and prepared to punch the man-overboard button (MOB) into the GPS so that he could record the exact location as he arrived at the first in-water bridge piling on the east side of the Narrows. By doing so, he would record on the route the exact spot where he was to anchor the next evening. On a notepad, he recorded the exact depth on the east side of that piling and any side-scan sonar images that reflected the piling shape below the surface.

Brady made a note that when he started to head back to the Chambers place he would also record the depth on the west side of that same piling. He reasoned that if the depths were about the same, anchoring on the east side would provide more cover for the operation. The piling would block much of the view from any boat traversing the Narrows, since boats normally went under the bridge in the middle section, which was three pilings to the west of the piling that was to be demolished.

Upon arriving at the east side of the piling, Brady noted that the depth as fifteen feet, and he punched the MOB button. The GPS screen immediately recorded the MOB location with its coordinates. Brady continued north to the cluster of restaurants on the east side of the Narrows. to better understand the lay of the land.

It was about 5:15 p.m. when he pulled alongside one of the restaurants that had a sprawling outdoor patio bar. It was loaded with muscled-up young men with bikini-clad women hanging off of their arms. He also noticed that numerous bar security personnel were keeping an eye on the crowd and the raft of boats docked alongside the restaurant's bulkhead. Smitty and Carlos gawked at the festivities taking place on the patio, and they asked Brady if they could dock there for a beer or two. Brady quickly reminded them that they were there to work—not party. They could always drive up to this bar on their own time, but not on US Maritime's time.

As Brady turned the boat around to head back to the bridge for another depth-sounding and side-scan sonar reading on the west side of the piling, a hotshot in a big Donzi, rafted up on the outside of the bulkhead, shouted to Brady, "Hey, Mr. Waterman, there's no name on your boat. Is that 'cause you can't spell?" Joining his girl and some friends in a collective roar of laughter, the guy gave Brady a half-assed salute. Then he turned and went back to drinking his beer.

While Brady wanted to drive his boat straight at the loudmouth's Donzi, throwing her into reverse just shy of hitting the guy's boat, Brady opted, smartly, to just wave at the guy, smile, and continue south to the bridge. Once at the piling, Brady did another side-scan sonar reading. As on the east side of the piling, it revealed what appeared to be about a two-foot wide concrete ledge some ten feet below the surface. It ran all the way along the base of the piling. It was a good ledge to set the explosives on, since it was low enough to destroy the piling base yet high enough from the bottom to achieve a secondary shock wave for maximum effectiveness.

Just as Brady recorded the depth and side-scan images, his cell phone rang. It was Salah. "Brady, before you finish and head back, I want you to check out the passage from Kent Narrows to coordinates 76°-17'-30 sec. West and 38°-56'-10 sec. North. It's a dock on a small farm we've leased. US Maritime may want to keep the boat there to lessen the fuel costs between the Chambers Farm and the Narrows. We'll talk about what you find when you return."

Before Brady could respond, the line went dead. Again, Brady thought, *Man these guys sure are short on social skills.*

He punched in the coordinates that he had been given. Then he pressed the "Go To" button. The new route appeared on the screen to guide them to the new location. Setting the new course, Brady told the crew where he was heading, but for security reasons he did not tell them why. The boat left Kent Narrows and moved into Prospect Bay. Because of the shallow waters around Parson's Island, even though the GPS indicated a path between Narrows Point and Parsons Island, Brady decided to go south of Parson's past Buoy G-1. Then he headed north to enter Crab Alley Bay from that point. Once in Crab Alley Bay, Brady steered a magnetic course of approximately 340 degrees north until he intersected with the screen's GPS route at Buoy G-3. At that point, he entered a narrow channel with eight- to eleven-foot depths that led up Crab Alley Creek to the small farm and dock that Salah had leased on Cox Neck. Brady arrived at the coordinates, tied up the boat, and told the crew to stay onboard as he checked out the small dock and its pilings. It seemed to him that the eight-foot depth at the dock was sufficient for the boat. He could tell from the watermarks on the pilings that the tide changes there were no more than two feet. That would leave him at least six feet of depth, which was more than enough. Brady's curiosity got the better of him, so he walked to the end of the dock that faced the land and looked down the gravel lane to the two-story white farmhouse that was set back one hundred yards from Cox Neck Road. Unbeknownst to Brady, this property had been under lease for the last eighteen months, and Salah's security men regularly visited it at night to be sure that no one was using the house or the dock. To monitor any comings and goings, they had placed trip cameras at strategic spots along the entrance road, at the cottage, near the barn area, and at the dock. So far, the only sign of life that the cameras had recorded was a small boat carrying three teenage boys, who tied up at the dock, secretly drank a six-pack of beer, and then left an hour later.

Just before walking back to the boat, Brady, remembering Mack's request, took his cell phone out and quickly snapped a few pictures of the boat, making sure that the crew could not see what he was doing.

Jumping back on the boat, Brady turned on the running lights and ordered Carlos and Smitty to cast off. As he worked his way south using the GPS calculator, he estimated the time it would take to go from the Narrows to the dock on Crab Alley Creek. At a standard speed of twenty knots, it would take about half an hour to cover the eight-mile distance. Checking his watch, it was now about 6:15 p.m., which meant that he could be back at the Chambers dock in less than an hour if he ran at a sustained cruise speed of thirty-five knots.

After telling the crew that they were heading back, he set the throttle at 3,600 rpms, which produced somewhere between thirty-five to thirty-six knots. Again, Brady was amazed at the power and smoothness of the boat as she plowed her way back to Cooks Point.

At 7:25 p.m. Brady pulled up to the Chambers dock, where Salah met him with two armed guards. Salah jumped down into the boat and asked Brady to join him in the cabin. Salah closed the door, and while Carlos and Smitty went about cleaning the boat, Salah and Brady reviewed the Narrows trip.

"Brady, show me the Kent Narrows Route you took, and show me where you did your depth calculations."

Reserving the captain's chair for Salah, Brady turned to the GPS and walked Salah through the entire route, showing him his handwritten notes on the depths at the base of the pilings and the side-scan sonar graphs, which showed the two-foot wide ledge where he recommended placing the charges. He also showed Salah the route to the dock on Crab Alley Creek and explained why he had gone south around Parsons Island to avoid the shallow depths.

"Brady, you made the right decision to come under Parsons before you went into the creek, but I worry about the amount of time it took you."

"Since it was my first time going into Crab Alley Creek, I was only doing twenty knots. Flat-out, I can certainly run that eight miles in half the time, if that's what's needed."

"That's exactly what we will need."

"OK. We'll do that tomorrow on her nighttime run."

"Good," said Salah. "So, tell me how she ran?"

"She was perfect. Whoever refurbished her and put the new engine and electronics on her sure knew what they were doing. She's as sweet of a boat as I've ever been on."

"Excellent." Turning from the GPS screen to face Brady and sitting up straight in the captain's chair, Salah said, "Brady, I am pleased with everything but your use of the emergency radio. Do not...I repeat, do not use it unless you are in an emergency situation and in grave danger."

"Yes, sir."

"I also expect you to monitor the coast guard channel and both the NRP and Homeland Security channels at all times. And, I expect you to turn the handheld VHF unit to the weather channel and have the weather alert button turned on."

"Yes, sir," Brady responded. Yet after agreeing to do so, he couldn't help but wonder why Salah needed him to constantly monitor those channels, unless he was concerned about the coast guard monitoring his boat's comings and goings.

Brady knew about the new AIS-B radio systems that were now available for smaller vessels. These VHF radio units had small GPS-type screens that identified similarly equipped ships nearby. Like radar, they showed the ship's name, location, heading, and speed. Brady thought, *Why wouldn't Salah have these onboard?* He reminded himself to mention this to Salah when he was hopefully in a better mood. Salah handed Brady an envelope containing his payment for working for half a day. He asked, "Any questions?"

Brady put the envelope in his shirt pocket and thanked Salah for paying him.

"Yes, sir," said Brady. "Just one question. Will you be putting a name on the boat?"

"We've got a carver from Hooper's Island doing one now."

"Good, 'cause some hot shot at the Kent Narrows Bridge gave me a rash of crap about her having no name because I couldn't spell."

Salah nodded and then said, "That it?"

"Yes, sir."

Without another word, Salah opened the cabin door, exited, and climbed up onto the dock. Turning to face Brady, who had followed him out to the stern, Salah said, "See you here at seven-thirty tomorrow evening. I will be joining you on tomorrow night's run. Be prepared to dive tomorrow night and to scout out that two-foot shelf around the Narrows pilings. Once we finish our work at the Narrows, we will secure the boat at the Crab Alley Creek dock. Maya will meet us there and drive you back to the Chamber's place to retrieve your truck."

"That works for me," replied Brady.

"You can release your crew now and the guard will escort them out."

"Yes, sir."

"After you secure the boat for the night, the guard at the end of the pier will follow you out through the security gate at the end of the lane. Any questions?"

"No, I think I understand your instructions clearly."

With a stone face, Salah said, "You must be sure, Brady. You cannot just think you understand."

"Yes, sir," said Brady. "I am sure."

"Good."

Salah handed his keys to Brady and told him to give them to the guard after he locked everything up. He then turned, walked to the end of the pier, gave the guard some instructions, and left.

Brady asked Carlos and Smitty to attach a spring line and place four big bumpers over the boat's dockside. He then told them that he would see them the following night at 7:30 p.m. Both of the men hopped up on the dock and left with the security guard.

Brady returned to the cabin to be sure that all of the electronics were off and that the surge protector was on in case of an overnight storm. He also checked the generator and compressor, starting each to be sure that they were running smoothly, had ample fuel and oil, and were putting out the required amps and air flow. His years in the marines had trained him well, so that now double-checks were a way of life. On the battlefield, lives depended on well-maintained and operable equipment. He figured it was no different here on this job.

After checking the diving masks, air bottles, and regulators, he decided to take one more look at the extra fuel cell under the steps that led down to the forward berth. He lifted up the hinged stairs and secured them onto an overhead hook. He found the wooden hatch's key, unlocked it, and secured it to yet another overhead hook. On a hunch, he tapped on the fuel tank, which was now exposed. To his surprise, he received a hollow echo. The tank was empty. He also noted that there was no tank vent or fire suppression system in the tank compartment. These were safety issues that he felt Salah should have addressed.

Stopping to think about what he was really looking at, Brady realized that this could not be a fuel cell, as he'd been told. It was a chamber of some kind. 'But what kind of chamber is it, and what is its purpose?' Fearing that this boat's mission was more clandestine than a security-cloaked commercial demolition job, Brady sat on the lower forward birth and tried to imagine what was really going on. 'Was US Maritime a legitimate company with actual contracts with the state? Was there really a confidentiality agreement between US Maritime, Homeland Security, and the state? Why was security so tight? Why was there so much secrecy, since once the work commenced next week, everyone would know about the demolition and reconstruction work? Were Abed, Salah, Haamid, and Maya actually who they claimed to be, or were they really foreign combatants seeking to wreak havoc on Maryland and the Bay?'

As he sat on the bunk, not a single answer to these questions came to him. It was as though the dots just weren't connecting. There were too many unknowns and too few answers. So, how could he come to any conclusion? Finally, he decided that there definitely were more answers, but they would have to reveal themselves in their own good time. He had no real control. All he could do was remain vigilant and await the answers as they surfaced.

Brady heard the guard's footsteps on the dock. "Are you ready, captain?"

Brady shouted up from the forward cabin, "Yes. I'll be up in a few minutes. I just have to lock the cabin and secure some of the equipment." Brady quickly relocked the wooden hatch, unhooked the steps, and secured them back into place.

Exiting the cabin, Brady locked the cabin door, checked the dock lines again, and jumped up onto the pier. As he approached the guard, he handed him Salah's set of keys, said good-bye, and walked up the hill to his truck.

Chapter 8

The Rogue is Revealed

At 8:30 p.m. Thursday the twenty-fourth, Brady exited the security gates and started driving down Cook's Point Road. He waved to the security guard as the guard secured the gate behind him.

Another workday was over and his first half-a-day's pay, $750, was in his pocket—not bad for a guy who had been earning miserly military pay in his last full-time job. It was also nice to no longer be on call 24/7 and to have some free time.

When Brady got back to his Uncle Pete's house, it was after 10 p.m. and everyone was sound asleep. Only the rear porch light was on. Brady tiptoed into the house, made a cold-cut sandwich, and headed upstairs to bed.

The next morning, Brady awoke at 6:30 a.m. to the sound of Pete downstairs cooking up a storm. Brady wandered down to the first floor, where he found Pete shuffling pots and pans around like a drummer. With great abandon, Pete was banging pots on the counter, on the stove, and in the sink.

"What are you doing, Uncle Pete," said Brady. "It sounds like Ringo Starr is in here practicing for a concert?"

"Oh. Hi, Brady," said Pete. "I'm just working on making some of my famous corn chowder. We're going to have it onboard this weekend for the new fishing party."

Brady took a deep breath and enjoyed the savory scents that caressed his nose. "Don't know how it will taste, Uncle Pete, but it sure smells good."

"I promise it'll taste even better than it smells."

"Looking forward to it," replied Brady. "Where you heading today, Uncle Pete?"

"Going to go and put the finishing touches on the teak and do the bright-work. Also, I need to check all the rods. Later, I'm going over to the store for a few umbrella rigs and weights."

"Since I don't have to be down in Cambridge 'til later this afternoon, I'm glad to lend a hand," said Brady.

"Great! Where are you going in Cambridge?"

"Well, it's actually Cooks Point, which is at the end of the Neck District."

Suddenly, electricity charged the kitchen air as Pete stiffened at the mention of Cook's Point. Drawing a deep breath, Pete turned to Brady and looked him straight in the eye. In an elevated and quivering voice that Brady had never heard from his Uncle before, he said, "Brady, we need to talk."

"Sure, Uncle Pete. What's wrong?"

"Let's go onto the porch. I don't want Louise to hear us." Pete turned the burners down on the two chowder pots, put the tops on them, set the stove alarm for forty minutes, and directed Brady onto the porch by placing his hand on his shoulder.

"Brady, when Mack and I talked with you yesterday, you said you'd get some photos of that boat and check out her name."

"I did. "

"So, what's the story?"

"The boat doesn't have a name yet, but a stern plate is being made by a decoy carver they hired from Hoopers' Island. They also have him doing one for their smaller boat." Brady pulled out his cell phone and scrolled to the pictures he had taken of the boat when it had been moored in Crab Alley Creek. He turned the screen toward Pete and slowly clicked through the three shots he'd taken.

Pete's mouth dropped and in an excited voice he said, "That's her. Damn. That's the rogue boat!"

Stunned, Brady said," Are you sure, Uncle Pete?"

"No question Brady," said Pete. "That's her."

Then they went silent.

Brady was the first of speak. "If that's her, Uncle Pete, we got a mess on our hands."

"Yeah, we do. More importantly, what are we going to do about it?"

In a disheartened voice, Brady said, "I don't know, Uncle Pete. I got to think about this."

"Look, sit tight. I got to call Mack and have him come right over."

Pete went back into the kitchen and called Mack. "Get your ass over here. I think I've found the rogue!"

Less than three minutes later, Mack burst onto Pete's porch and said, "So, tell me what the hell's going on."

"Look at these, Mack," said Pete. "Brady, show him your photos."

Mack flipped through Brady's pictures several times.

"So, what do you think, Mack?"

"Oh my God! That's her. God. That's really her, Pete."

Mack turned to Brady and asked, "Brady, where is she?"

"Right now she's down at Cooks Point. We're taking her up to Kent Narrows this evening."

"We? Who are we?" Mack demanded.

"Hold on, Captain Mack. Don't shoot me. I'm only the messenger."

"Sorry Brady, you just don't know how pissed off I am about that damn boat."

Brady looked at Pete for some direction.

"Brady, as I told you the other day, Mack was almost rammed by this boat, so he's rightfully angry at its captain—not at you."

"I know that, Uncle Pete. It's just that I'm under a confidentiality agreement, and if they find out I'm talking about my job, I'll lose it. More importantly, if these guys are as bad as you all think they might be, I could be a target for their wrath. Uncle Pete, they're armed and deadly serious about whatever it is they are doing." Suddenly, Brady was not sure about what he had gotten himself into.

"Brady, I'm not going to tell you what to do, but whatever they're planning, it sure doesn't appear to be in our best interest."

"I know that." Pausing to gather his wits, Brady continued. "What I need from you and Captain Mack is a promise not to share this with anyone—absolutely no one—and that includes wives and family. My military experience tells me my life could be in danger."

"I promise not to say a word," said Mack.

"Me too," said Pete. "The last thing we want is for you to be in any kind of trouble."

"OK, here's what I have been told. US Maritime has some kind of a contract with the state to demolish and rebuild pilings at the Kent Narrows Bridge. As I understand it, they're under contract for another two pilings at the Gas Docks. Tonight, I'm going up to Kent Narrows with their head of security to dive on those pilings. Mainly I'm going to see how and where to set the charges. On Monday the twenty-eighth, I'll be going to the Gas Docks to check those pilings out, and on the twenty-ninth at 9:00 p.m., like in the Narrows, I will again be diving at night at the Gas Docks. Sometime this week, with the help of their security chief, I will be putting together the explosives, the detonation caps, and the chain-link wiring harnesses. I won't actually be doing the detonations. They have someone else set to do that. Well, that's about it."

Mack spoke up first. "Why are you diving at night?"

"Captain Mack, according to the head of security, they want to do the demolition at night, which is when both the boat and the road traffic will be minimal."

"Yeah, I can understand that," said Mack, "but maybe the real reason is to avoid being seen setting the charges. This doesn't sound right to me."

"I agree with you, Captain Mack. That's one of the things that really worries me," said Brady.

"It should worry all of us," said Mack.

Pete joined the conversation. "What else worries you, Brady?"

"I'm concerned about a whole bunch of things, Uncle Pete. I'm concerned about their military bearing, their military fire arms, the fact that they are all foreigners, the sophisticated military communications system they have onboard the boat with some six canopy-mounted antennas, and the new fuel tank that, as it turns out, really isn't a fuel tank. And, those are just a few of my concerns."

"What fuel tank?" asked Pete.

"I discovered a large stainless steel tank just below deck. The access door to it was locked, but I found a key on the chain of keys that the guard provided me. Oddly enough, the access seems to be solely from the forward bunk area. I didn't see any access from the deck, and it doesn't have any fume vent or gas fill-port on deck. Hopefully, I will be able to investigate it further."

Trading knowing looks with Mack, Pete said, "Sound familiar, Mack?"

"Sure does, Pete."

Leaning forward in his chair, Brady said, "OK, gentlemen, what is this really all about?"

Taking a deep breath, Pete began to share their story about the boat with no name. He started with the encounter they had on the water on that cold day in February, when the rogue boat almost crashed into Mack. Pete took Brady through the hunt for her from February through June. He told him about the surveillance they did at Cook's Point and the investigations he performed on the various pieces of property that the foreigners seemed to control. He discussed their encounter with the armed guards, their seeing the stainless tanks being installed, and their final decision not to further pursue the hunt unless new information surfaced concerning the whereabouts of the boat.

As Pete rolled out the story, Mack added colorful commentary to the narrative, describing the anger, fear, and frustration they had experienced throughout the five-month search.

When he finished, Pete said, "That's it Brady. That's the secret we've kept between us until now." Pete leaned back in the wicker chair and breathed a sigh of relief. He felt relieved to have finally told someone else about his and Mack's quest for the rogue boat and their thoughts about her purpose.

Brady took it all in without any interruption. At the end of Pete's story, he said, "We need to do something and we need to do it soon. Whatever their ultimate plan is, my guess is that it's no more than a week away from being implemented. I don't know about you all, but I've seen terrorist activities in Afghanistan, and this seems to follow the same pattern. It smells like there's an attack coming, but I don't think the Narrows Bridge is the only focus. I believe it could be an attempt to sidetrack the authorities. I think it might be a way to perhaps delay first responders to the site of an even bigger attack. In Afghanistan, we almost always saw attacks on smaller villages just prior to a major assault on a much larger target or on one of our key strongholds. These smaller attacks were always a diversionary tactic to prevent a successful response to the larger attack."

"God, Brady, you really think that's what's going on here?" said Mack.

"I not only think that's the case, Captain Mack, but if it's the last thing I do, I'm going to find out." Shifting in his chair, Brady said, "Starting now, all of us need to treat this as if they are planning an act of terrorism."

"So, what's that mean?" said Pete.

Brady leaned forward and spoke in a low voice. "Well, first of all, to ensure my own safety, I have to be on high alert. I have to make sure that nothing I do will raise suspicions about my loyalty. Traditionally, as these attacks get closer to being implemented, the terrorists get nervous and hyper about security. Several days prior to an actual attack, it's not unusual for the team's inner circle to do away with those on the team who are not the actual implementers on the day of the attack. They simply get rid of those who are no longer needed. By doing so, it greatly reduces the risk of security breaches."

"How does that work?" asked Mack.

"Captain Mack, suppose your team included unskilled laborers or people working in trades that were no longer needed. To reduce the chances of a security breach, wouldn't you do away with them?"

"Yeah," he said. "Thinking like a terrorist, I guess I would."

The porch became dead quiet. One could almost smell the fear emanating from Pete.

"Brady, you said they didn't need you to actually detonate the explosion because they have someone else to do that. Does that mean that you are expendable after you place the charges?"

"Yes, Uncle Pete. It means exactly that, and that's why I need to be very careful and alert.

"You should be alert 24/7."said Pete.

Feeling less comfortable than he had just minutes earlier, Pete said, "OK, so where do we go from here?"

Brady looked at his watch. "I will be heading back to Cook's Point this afternoon to prepare the boat for our evening dive. After the dive, I will come back here probably sometime after midnight. Unless something happens on my trip tonight, I will wait until the morning to bring you up to date on the dive and any new information I might obtain. For now, I suggest we all just go about our business as usual—at least until we know enough to decide how to proceed."

"Friday, I will be helping put the demolition charges together. That will probably take all day. I should return to the house by about seven that evening."

"You don't know where this will take place?"

"No, Captain Mack. They haven't told me. Why don't we meet here at seven-thirty Friday night to discuss whatever new information I've been able to gather? In the mean-time, we don't say a word to anyone, OK?"

"OK. Whatever you say. By the way Brady why don't you just call me Mack? You've earned that."

"Thanks Mack. Your vote of confidence is very much appreciated. These next few days are not going to be easy."

"See you all tomorrow night," said Mack, opening the porch door to leave.

"See you then, Mack," Pete answered.

"See you tomorrow, Mack," Brady added.

✳✳✳

After breakfast Pete and Brady walked down to the *Miss Alice*, climbed aboard, and quietly set about finishing the teak and bright work on her. For the next three hours, the two men worked in silence. When they'd finished cleaning up *Miss Alice*, she looked like a bride ready for her wedding. She glistened in the morning sun as a light breeze slapped her sturdy sides with small blue-green waves. Brady and Pete put away their stain and brushes, hopped up on the dock, and turned to face *Miss Alice*, admiring her classic beauty.

"Thanks, Brady, for all your help. She certainly looks ready for Saturday's guests."

"Uncle Pete, between her makeover and your corn chowder, these people will be hooked forever."

"I sure hope so. I better get going to the store for those rigs and weights. Want to grab lunch there?"

"Thanks, Uncle Pete, but I need to be on my way to Cambridge to prep the boat for tonight's dive. Have a great day, and I'll see you for an update at breakfast tomorrow."

"Watch your back, Brady. If you feel like they're worried about you or your loyalty, get the hell out of there, call me, and we'll go straight to the police."

"I promise I will, Uncle Pete."

"OK. I'll see you tomorrow morning," said Pete. On his way to the store, Pete thought to himself, *After all that he's been through, Brady finally seems to be making real progress in getting his mental and physical balance back. Thank God.*

Chapter 9

The Speed Trial

After grabbing lunch at North's Store in the Neck District, Brady arrived at the security gate to the Chambers Farm. Before letting Brady pass, the guard called Salah to verify Brady's early arrival. After a few seconds, the guard handed Brady his cell phone.

"Brady?"

"Yes, sir."

"It's only two-thirty. How come you're so early?"

"I want to have plenty of time to check out the diving gear, compressor, and generator, and I want to take the boat out for a short run to test her top speed. Since I haven't opened her up full-throttle for a sustained run, I thought I ought to do so before tonight."

"OK, Brady, but don't run up toward Tilghman or up the Choptank. Take her down toward Taylor's Island. There are fewer boats down there. I don't want her being seen by anyone doing her top speed, OK?"

"Yes, sir."

The phone went dead and Brady handed it back to the guard. Brady followed the guard, parked, and walked over to the guard's jeep. "You got the keys?"

Without a word, the guard fished a set of keys out of his pocket and handed them to Brady. The guard then headed back to his post at the entrance gate. Brady walked down to the boat. He hopped onto the boat, unhooked the cabin door, and set his dive suit, goggles, extra shirt, and nose clip on the Captain's chair. He then flipped on the two large banks of batteries to check out their voltage levels. The bank of batteries that were hooked up to the compressor and the generators were registering a full charge. The bank of batteries, for the boat itself, was showing about seven-eighths of a full charge. Brady had expected a drop in this battery bank, since they had previously run the boat for about four-and-a-half hours, which drew down some of that charge. Brady thought, 'After this afternoon's run, I'll check that battery bank again to be sure it's fully charged.'

Rather than turning on the air conditioning, Brady opened up all of the operable cabin windows, the cabin door, and the forward hatch to capture the cooling breeze. With the battery switches turned on, Brady turned on the full array of electronics, except for the olive green military radio. He monitored weather channel number three for the latest update concerning that evening's run up the Bay. To be sure all were in working order, he then turned on the large Garmin GPS, as well as the small handheld GPS and radar.

Satisfied that all of the electronics were working correctly, Brady checked to see whether a guard was on the dock. He scanned the entire dock but saw no one. He went into the forward cabin, lifted the cabin stairs, and secured them on their hooks. He searched the keys that the guard had just given him to find the one that fit the wooden hatch in front of the large extra stainless steel tank. Brady found a key that looked like it might fit, so he inserted it into the lock. The lock opened.

"Damn. Not bad for a first try, if I do say so myself," he muttered. He lifted up the wooden hatch and snapped it to the hook above. Before him was a very large stainless steel tank that was about three feet high, four feet wide, and six to seven feet long. Brady crawled into the hold next to the tank to investigate further. As before, when he rapped on the tank's side it echoed the sound of his own knuckles back to him. It was empty. 'Huh. I thought this was supposed to be full of fuel,' he said to himself. 'There is no opening for a wire for a fuel-level indicator. There is no vent for fumes and no stack for filling the tank. That's not right,' he mumbled. As he ran his hand along the top of the tank, where there was a three-inch space between the tank and the deck above, he felt a gasket and a metal lid that had a screw-down watertight wheel on top of it.

Talking to himself Brady said, "No way this is made to hold fuel. It's constructed more like a water tank with a submarine-type access hatch." As he brushed his hand along the underside of the deck above the tank's metal hatch, Brady felt what seemed to be another wooden hatch that was three feet in diameter in the underside of the floor above. Sitting hunched over on the boat's bottom planks between its sturdy wooden ribs, Brady tried to calculate exactly where the circular wooden hatch was located in the steerage cabin above. He determined that it had to be in the dining area of the cabin.

Brady crawled out of this space below the deck, secured the wooden hatch again, locked it, and replaced the forward cabin stairs. Returning to the large steerage cabin that held the captain's station, chart table, dining table, and benches, Brady stood there and estimated that the three-foot circular hatch was located directly under the forward dining bench. "But how do you get to it?" he asked himself. Getting down on his hands and knees, Brady searched along the pedestal base of the dining table. He also searched around the benches and the bulkhead behind the forward bench.

Brady noticed a slight separation between the cabin floor and the forward bench. He decided to remove the table and its pedestal from its metal base. He put them aside and on a hunch lifted up the forward bench, which easily came up with the assistance of two hydraulic pistons. As the forward bench rose, it swung back toward the dining bench in the rear, revealing the wooden hatch that was three feet in diameter, which Brady had located when he had been sitting directly below this spot. Brady removed the wooden hatch and there it was: the large fuel tank with its pressure-sealed circular hatch.

Brady spun the hatch's wheel lock until the watertight seal broke and the hatch could actually be lifted up. The open hatch revealed a stainless steel tank bottom that had a double gasket seal running the full seven-foot length of the tank itself. Brady also discovered that there were four hydraulic cylinders located inside the tank. Each one of them was at one of the four corners of the tank's floor. Clearly, these were electrically operated hydraulic levers that would open and close the floor of the tank. At the bow end of the tank was a one-horsepower submersible trash-type pump. At the end of the tank, its two-inch drainage tube ran up the inside. From what he could tell, it merged with the boat's main bilge pump's exterior port. Just above the tank, affixed to the bulkhead and hidden behind the forward dining bench when it was seated in place, there was an electrical panel that had several switches and a disconnect plunger. One switch had a red bulb light and was labeled, "Flood tank." Another one had a green bulb light that was labeled, "Empty tank." The plunger was marked, "Interior disconnect." Just inside the tank on the bow panel, there was also a waterproof rocker switch and a waterproof plug labeled, "Communications." Next to it was a four-way waterproof switch labeled, "Open," "Closed," "Flood," and "Empty." Having been part of nighttime raids launched from submarines off of the coast of Iran, Brady recognized that the tank had all of the earmarks of a diver's underwater launch. It had the same kind of recovery system that Navy SEALs on US naval vessels typically used.

Suddenly, Brady heard voices on the dock. He quickly closed the metal hatch, spun the wheel lock, shut the wooden hatch, lifted the bench back into position, and replaced the pedestal and dining table. Moving quickly to the chart table, Brady started to appear to be busily working, moving various maps back and forth across the table's surface.

"Hey, Brady."

Brady popped his head up from the chart table and turned to see Maya standing on the dock.

"Hey, Maya. Come onboard."

As Maya started to step off of the dock, Brady reached up and lifted her down onto the deck. Putting her arms around Brady, she pulled him to her. Pressing herself against him, she kissed him on the cheek and said, "I've missed you, Brady, more than I can say."

Flattered by her passionate greeting yet not convinced of the honesty of either her feelings or of his own, Brady said, "I've missed you too, Maya. What are you doing here?"

"I'm subbing for Carlos tonight, and I thought I'd come early to check out the boat. Unfortunately, Carlos has come up sick and they want me to take his place."

Surprised, Brady asked, "Are you a qualified diver?"

"Yes I am," she replied. "I'm a very good one."

Feeling somewhat broadsided, Brady asked, "Have you ever done surface support and rescue?"

"Yes, Brady." Annoyed, Maya continued. "I wouldn't be here unless I were capable - especially when it comes to backing you up."

"Sorry, Maya, but with all due respect, I don't know your capabilities. However, I have talked with Carlos and I believe I know his. I certainly believe that he's qualified."

"Brady, I've been a dive technician for over eight years. I was deployed in Iran with the government as an underwater specialist for four of those eight years. I promise you, I know how to keep an air supply line open. I know how to deal with the bends and how to fix and maintain pumps, generators, and compressors in both normal and emergency situations. I promise that I can and will cover your back."

"I hear you, Maya, but I've been in tough situations before, in which the surface crew was responsible for saving my life. That's the kind of backup I need and expect here."

"Brady, I have been part of a surface crew that has saved lives. Trust me, I can do this. If I couldn't, I promise I wouldn't be on your team. You mean too much to me for me to be lying about my credentials. Besides, my uncle would certainly never put my life in jeopardy."

Folding his arms in front of his chest and then dropping them and swinging them to each side as if to say, "Let's stop this," Brady said, "OK, Maya - enough of this. I believe you and most importantly, I trust you."

Maya said, "Thank you, Brady. Thanks for trusting me."

"Now that that's put to bed, let's go over the plans for tonight's dive. We'll bring Smitty up to date when he arrives this evening."

From 3:30 p.m. to 4:30 p.m. Brady and Maya sat at the dining table and reviewed the route to Kent Narrows, the dive depths, water temperature, free-dive safety, the diving tanks, valves, and various emergency equipment procedures. After reviewing the dive plan, Maya moved over to the dining bench next to Brady. Laying her head on his shoulder, she said, "Brady, what's going on? You seem so distant."

"Nothing's wrong, Maya. I am just trying to do two jobs. I am helping my uncle with his fishing parties, which take all weekends and some evenings, and I'm also trying to do the best job possible for US Maritime. My Uncle Pete's pretty demanding, but your Uncle Salah is one tough guy to work for. He expects me to perform, but he doesn't share everything with me. He tends to keep his cards close to the vest."

"He does, but that's just his style. Don't forget that he heads up our security."

"When you say security, do you mean for the agency, US Maritime, or for some other organization that he's a part of?"

"He heads up the agency's security Brady, and under our contract to US Maritime, he heads up security on this particular demolition job."

Shifting his right leg underneath him, Brady turned to face Maya. "Maya, why would you need security for the agency?"

"Our offices are in a questionable neighborhood, Brady. We need to protect our building and our employee files." Uncomfortably with her hesitancy in responding, Brady said, "You said you worked for the government in Iran. Was it our government or Iran's?"

"Iran's, Brady," she said. "Don't forget, I'm a Muslim."

"I understand that, Maya, but I must admit, I don't understand the hatred that Muslim extremists feel toward Christians and especially toward Americans."

"I thought after your experiences in Afghanistan and at Walter Reed, you were against your government's leaders. I thought you were angry with their poor handling of the thousands of other wounded warriors?"

"Yeah, I am," said Brady, "but as time goes by, I am beginning to see just how bad the Muslim extremists really are. Of course I'm angry with my country, but I'm more angry with the extremists who seem to kill for the joy of it and who have taken so many of my buddies from me and from their families."

Laying her head back on his shoulder and reaching around to rub his neck, Maya said, "Let's forget politics for now and just enjoy our time together, OK?"

"OK."

Maya hugged Brady. He responded in kind. After embracing for a minute and feeling very awkward about his feelings for Maya, Brady leaned back and said, "Maya, we should not be doing this on US Maritime time. Right now, we need to take the boat out for a speed trial before dinner and Salah's arrival at seven-thirty."

"You really need to do that?"

"Yeah," said Brady. "I told Salah that I would check out the boat's top speed to be sure she can do what we think she's capable of. He said to go ahead."

Brady moved away from Maya and flipped on the circuit breakers for the radar screen, the large Garmin GPS, and the VHF radios, one of which he set to the NRP channel. He set the second VHF radio to the coast guard channel. Brady was able to receive these secure channels and the two Homeland Security channels because Salah had obtained the appropriate chips from his DC operatives, who had stolen them from each organization's repair shops. Clearly, Abed's reach was far and wide. No organization seemed to be safe from his team's ability to penetrate it and obtain any supposedly secure information or equipment.

After pulling up the GPS map in a size that showed the portion of the Bay from the Choptank River to Solomon's Island on the western shore, Brady started the engine and called Maya to cast off all lines.

Within five minutes, the boat had reached Buoy R-12, which was just north of Cooks Point. From there, Brady set a course to Buoy R-10, from which he would start his first speed run of five miles to Buoy G-3, which was four miles west of Mills Point.

The second run would be a little longer. It was seven miles from Buoy G-3 to Buoy RW-CP, which was two miles west of the north end of Taylors Island. Brady calculated that the two southern runs and their returns would be enough to give him a good feeling for the boat's speed and capability, as well as the engine's reliability.

Maya stood next to Brady with her arm draped over his shoulder and her right side pressed up against him. He started the first run to Buoy G -3. Slowly, he pushed the throttle forward: 2,500 rpms and twenty-four knots; 2,600 rpms and twenty-eight knots; 3,400 rpms and thirty-six knots; and finally 3,900 rpms and forty-three knots.

She was flying.

The wake behind her was as thin and straight as a contrail, and the waves she cast off were long with razor-sharp crowns. She sliced through the water like a knife through butter.

"Man, she is fast and smooth. Whoever re-powered her sure knew what they were doing," said Brady, speaking above the noise of the engine. "Maya, this thing is just like a navy PBR."

"What's a PBR?"

"It's a River Patrol Boat—the kind we used in the Gulf. It's similar to the ones we used in Vietnam, but it's much faster. Wow, she's as smooth as silk."

To test her turning ability, Brady did a 180-degree turn, but her speed dropped only by five knots. "This is cool," said Brady. "This handles exactly like a PBR. It's fast, agile, and quiet. The only differences are that this is eight feet longer, four feet wider, and a lot faster. Of course, it also lacks the fifty-caliber machine guns and torpedoes."

On the second run to Buoy RW-CP, Brady let Maya take the wheel so that she could experience the power and agility of the boat. As Maya approached Janes Island, about halfway along the second run, Brady noticed a Natural Resource Police boat coming out of the Little Choptank River on its way north. Brady grabbed the wheel and said, "I got her, Maya." He switched places with Maya and knocked the boat back down to 2,500 rpms, or about twenty-four knots. As he did so, he looked back over his left shoulder. The NRP whaler turned around and started following him. As the NRP boat approached, they hit the siren and lights. With a hand gesture, the boat's captain indicated that Brady needed to pull up and stop. He complied. As the whaler came up alongside them, Maya, with an ample amount of cleavage showing, bent down and flipped over four large bumpers. As she did so, she said, "Hey, officers."

"Good afternoon, ma'am."

"Captain, can we see your registration, please?"

"Yes sir," said Brady.

Brady reached up to the overhead storage locker and retrieved the registration envelope that Salah had given him. He handed it over the side to the officer. As the officer read the registration, he said, "It says here that the boat's owned by an LLC in New York City. Is that right?"

"Yes, sir," said Brady. "It is."

"Are you the owner of the LLC?"

"No sir. I'm just the captain."

"Captain? Is this boat for charter?"

"No, sir. She's just a Bay workboat."

"I don't see any gear onboard - no pots or trot line."

"She's just recently been renovated and repowered, so that equipment ain't on-board yet."

"What about her name? I don't see one on her bow or stern."

"We have a guy coming tomorrow to deliver a stern plate with her name on it."

"I see."

During this exchange, Maya sat on the gunwale, holding onto the canopy strut while dangling one leg over the gunwale, which she used to hook over the side of the whaler. While the two boats gently bobbed together, rising and falling with the whaler's movement, it caused her shorts to ride up and down. This was not lost to the officers. The younger one's eyes were glued to her every movement.

"Any reason to pull me over?" asked Brady.

"No, not really. We were just interested in her speed. She sure was clipping along."

"Yes, sir. She's a fast one. She has a six-hundred-horsepower cat under the box. In fact, I was taking her out for a trial run to see how she'd do."

"Well, from what we saw she seems to be doing just fine. What's she top out at?"

"Somewhere between forty-three and forty-six knots."

"No kidding? That fast?"

"Yes, sir."

Flipping two of the bumpers back onto Brady's boat, the NRP captain said, "You all be careful. That's a lot of speed in this crowded part of the Bay."

"We'll take her easy. I promise."

"OK, captain. You all have a good day."

"Yes, sir," said Brady. "Will do."

"Take care, guys," said Maya, as she leaned over and hauled in the other two bumpers. The NRP whaler slowly turned away and moved off.

Brady looked at Maya, winked, and said, "Thanks, Maya."

"Why? What for?"

"What for? Come on, Maya, if you'd bent over one more time, their eyes would've fallen into the water. Your diversion was terrific."

"So you noticed, huh?"

"Yeah, I noticed."

Maya moved to the mid-station helm where Brady was standing and gave him one of her full-body hugs. Gently pushing her away, Brady said, "OK, enough of that. We have a job to do."

Brady put the boat into gear, pushed her up to almost forty-five knots, maintaining the course he'd been on to Buoy RW-CP. Reaching RW-CP, Brady slowed the boat down and checked her vital signs: oil pressure, battery charge, fuel gauge, and water temperature. Satisfied with the readings, he turned her on autopilot and set her on the reversed course back to Buoy R-12.

"Brady, are we going someplace for an early dinner?"

"Sure. Do you have a suggestion?"

"How about that place on the water in Cambridge. What's it called?"

"The Sandbar?"

"Is that OK with you?"

"Sure. That's great."

At Buoy R-12, Brady turned off the autopilot and headed straight into Cooks Point Cove. When they arrived at the dock, two security guards were waiting for them. They helped Maya tie up the boat. One of the guards handed two two-by-five wooden stern plaques to Brady. He told Brady that Salah's men had delivered them while he was out on his run. The guard then handed Brady an envelope from Salah. It contained a note telling Brady which plaque to use on the boat and which one to store under the forward bunk. The envelope also included four stainless steel base plates that were to be glued to the stern to secure the plaque. An epoxy glue gun and the bolts for the bases were also included. All that Brady needed to do now was to follow Salah's instructions. He had to glue the base plates on the stern, wait one hour until the glue dried, and then affix the stern plaque by placing the holes in the plaque over the base plate bolts. He then had to put on the washers and thread on the nuts. Then she'd be ready to go.

Brady measured the correct distances for the base plates, and then he affixed them to the stern. He hopped up onto the dock and handed the keys to the guard. With Maya sitting next to him in the truck, he followed one of the guard's jeeps out to the security gate. It was about 5:40 p.m. when the guard closed the gate behind them. They arrived at the restaurant at about 6:00 p.m.

After ordering, Brady said, "I guess we did all right with those NRP guys. They seemed satisfied with the registration and with our explanations of why we had no crabbing equipment onboard."

"I think so, Brady. I'm just glad they didn't go below and see all of the diving gear and compressor. Questions about those would have been far more difficult to answer."

"Thank goodness we'll have a name on the boat for tonight's trip. I must admit, I really felt awkward and exposed when that guy at the Narrows Bar yelled at me about having a no-name boat because watermen can't spell. That guy really pissed me off. I think I got him good, though, when I just simply smiled and waved. He wasn't expecting that. By the way, Maya, you sure handled those NRP guys well. You were quite the distraction."

"Anything for the cause," she said.

As they began to eat their food, silence set in. Poking away at his salad, Brady picked up his fork. Pointing it in the air for emphasis, he said, "So, what really is the cause, Maya? Is this US Maritime job legit or just a front for something else?"

"Brady, why are you so concerned about this?"

"I am not sure. There just seems to be so much secrecy surrounding what should be two very simple demolition jobs. I just can't help but wonder."

"You're right, Brady. It is simple. US Maritime is a new client for us. They are anxious to do everything right so that these jobs with the state go well. The state has demanded confidentiality and they don't want any publicity because of the public's concern about the state's reduction in local highway funding, especially for the Eastern Shore. The Department of Transportation believes that these two jobs are priority projects, but they also know that the public wants to see visible road improvements, such as traffic signals and extra lanes. They don't want unseen infrastructure work, such as the replacement of pilings."

"OK," said Brady. "I understand that but when Route 50 closes at the Kent Narrows Bridge and the Gas Docks are closed to new shipments for two months or more, the public will know it then."

"You're right, Brady, but that will be after the fact, and the public's ire will be far less for the administration to have to deal with."

"I'm sure you're right, Maya, but my experiences in Afghanistan have taught me to question everything - even the motives of people I trust."

"Even me?" asked Maya.

"No, Maya, not you," said Brady. "But I do wonder about Salah. I've been suspicious ever since he jumped all over your brother for telling me about the Narrows and the Gas Docks. The military operating format you all use in place of a civilian approach also concerns me."

"That's typical, Brady. Almost everyone in the marine building and demolition business is an ex-military Seabee type. In fact, most construction jobs on land also have a high percentage of military-trained personnel. Don't forget, Brady, my job is to place workers all across the country in construction jobs, and we specifically look for ex-military people because they are disciplined, dependable, knowledgeable, and hardworking. Look at yourself, Brady; you're the poster boy for that very kind of worker."

"I guess you're right, but your uncle seems focused on secrecy instead of the job at hand."

"He's ex-military and he still thinks he's a major in the Pakistan Special Forces."

"I hear you, Maya, but I'm not fully convinced."

In a serious voice, Maya said, "Your views, Brady, are yours. It makes little difference to us, as long as you follow the rules and do your job."

Frustrated by her criticism and sharp tongue, Brady said, "Maya, I don't need this job or the lack of respect that seems to come with it. I'm here to do my job and collect my check. If I don't follow instructions or if I do something wrong, I want to know about it. But I don't intend to be someone else's whipping boy just because he's off his meds or isn't getting enough."

"Brady, I promise you neither one of those conditions is what sets Salah off. My uncle's never taken even so much as a prescription drug in his life."

"Well maybe that's the problem."

"As for women, he has dozens of women constantly after him all the time."

"Look, Maya, I don't know what the problem is, but he better back off or I'll just walk."

"Brady, do you mind if I say something to him about your concerns?"

"No. Not at all," said Brady. "But don't piss him off. I'd hate to see him really mad, and I don't want to lose this job."

"I won't," said Maya. "And you're right. You don't want to see him really mad. It's not a pretty sight."

Chapter 10

Night Run to Kent Narrows

During the twenty-minute drive back to Cooks Point, Maya wrapped her arms around Brady's right arm and nestled into his side. Except for the country music on the truck's radio, no sounds but her breathing reached his ears. It was a peaceful trip back to Cooks Point. They did not engage in any sort of conflict, and no bad words passed between them. Everything was just quiet.

When they arrived at the Chambers security gate, Salah was pulling up right behind them in his dark green Hummer. The guard checked out both vehicles and ushered each of them through the gate.

After pulling into the parking area next to the barn, Brady and Maya hopped out of the truck and greeted Salah and Smitty. As they walked toward the dock, Brady asked Salah how Carlos was. Salah brushed off the question. He said that he had some kind of flu and would be out of commission for a while. "Maya will be taking Carlos's place until he returns," said Salah.

"That's what I heard from Maya. It would have been nice if someone had let me know earlier."

"No need," said Salah. "Maya's more than qualified."

Shaking his head, Brady walked onto the dock and muttered to himself, "It's my safety we're talking about, and that does matter."

Maya walked next to Brady on the way to the boat and whispered, "I thought you didn't want to piss him off?"

"I changed my mind," said Brady.

Hopping down into the boat, Brady didn't turn to help Maya onboard. He figured that if she were capable of rescue diving, she should be able to board without his help.

95

Salah grabbed the keys from the guard and stepped down from the dock. He handed the keys to Brady and said, "Before we move out, I want you to give me a rundown on the trip and your dive plan."

"Yes, sir."

"Also, how's your fuel?"

"She's down about a quarter of a tank, so I plan to pull into Oxford and fill her up."

"We're not going to do that. We have a Ford 350 pickup in the barn up there. It's got a two hundred-gallon tank in the truck bed. We'll use that to fill up the boat. You're not to stop at any gas dock or public place, no matter what. We'll fuel her up when we return later tonight."

Brady didn't respond to Salah's clipped statement. Instead of responding, he went about checking the batteries, the electronics, and the engine's oil. He then asked Maya to check out the dive gear.

"I just did that before dinner, Brady."

"Doesn't matter, Maya. Do it again."

"Right," she tersely replied.

When Brady was satisfied that the boat was ready to shove off, he went into the cabin and removed the boat plaque that Salah had wanted to put on the stern board. For the first time, he looked at the boat's name and the homeport designation: *Miss Gale. Rock Hall, Maryland.* Taking the plaque and the four stainless steel nuts, Brady leaned over the stern, checked the glue on the base plates to be sure that it had cured, and he mounted the plaque on the four bolts. He put on the washers and threaded the nuts on tightly. 'Glad to finally have a name on her,' he thought.

Walking back to the cabin, Brady said, "I'm ready to give the briefing now." For the next forty minutes, as the sun slipped below the horizon and the dark of night descended, Brady brought Salah up to date on the boat's readiness, the speed trial, and their encounter with the NRP just off of Janes Island.

In response to the NRP visit, Salah simply said, "Good they didn't come onboard and see the dive gear and the communications bank."

"Yeah," said Brady. "Well, if it hadn't been for Maya's keeping their attention focused on her, they might very well have boarded us."

With the briefing having been completed at 8:45 p.m., dark skies and only a sliver of the moon was visible through the thick evening clouds as Brady fired up the *Miss Gale* and ordered Smitty and Maya to cast off. As Brady put the *Miss Gale* into reverse and swung clear from the dock, he flipped both the running lights and the cabin lights off. He also lowered the brightness on the GPS screen and turned the VHF radio volumes down to the lowest possible audible range.

***

From across the way, old man Charlie, using his binoculars, peered out from his sun room at the Chambers dock, taking in all of the goings-on and noting the time of their boat's departure. It'd been the first time he'd seen a boat back at the Chambers dock since mid-May, when the late-night boat renovation ruckus was in full swing. In fact, the boat he was looking at, *Miss Gale*, sure looked like the big boat they'd been working on near the barn. And that foreign guy on the boat certainly looked like one of the two management types that he'd seen meeting the boss after he arrived in the third cigarette boat that evening. Charlie thought to himself, 'It's odd that they mounted a stern name-plaque, rather than having the name painted on. Also, it's odd as hell that they were heading out without any lights on. Tomorrow, I'll have to let my friends at NRP know what I've seen. Maybe they can make some sense out of it.'

As they set off for Buoy R-12, Salah took up a position next to and just behind Brady. From this location he could both see the GPS and talk to Brady as he steered *Miss Gale* north to Kent Narrows. The plan had been for Brady to hug the shoreline as close as possible to avoid the shipping channels and coast guard patrols in the middle of the Bay. While this was good for maintaining a low profile and blending in with the shore-line, it did pose depth-clearance problems that were potentially dangerous in these shallow waters. Also, this shoreline course forced *Miss Gale* to ride through innumerable crab pot fields in the pitch-black night. Luckily, the sliver of moonlight reflected on the water and highlighted the colorful paint on the crap floats. To make sure they didn't get caught up in the crab pot lines, Brady had Maya sit up on the bow, straddling the anchor so that she could give Brady hand signals as to where the pots were and whether to turn left or right to avoid them. This spotter technique, which was similar to the Navy's RPB Bow Rider Program for spotting mines and enemy boats, proved to be very effective, especially around the pots off of Poplar Island and the mainland areas around Tilghman and Whitman. Prior to setting off, Brady had failed to adequately calculate the effect of darkness on his ability to spot the pots. While Salah said nothing to him about this mistake, Brady was disappointed in himself, and he knew that Salah would broach it later.

Very little conversation occurred between Salah and Brady on their way to the Narrows. It was obvious to Brady that Salah was just as irritated with him, as he was with Salah. This was not a good thing.

As *Miss Gale* reached the outer buoys of Kent Narrows, Brady pulled back on the throttle and put her in neutral. When the following wave caught up to her stern, he then eased her back up to the six-mph speed limit as he passed the western jetty and headed to the bridge before him.

As they approached the bridge, Brady steered *Miss Gale* to starboard and settled her on the east side of the targeted piling. He called for Smitty to drop anchor. Then he backed the boat up to hook the anchor in the muddy bottom. As soon as she caught, Brady told Smitty to tie off the anchor rope. With no other boats around, they got out the fishing gear and bait, all of which would be the cover-up excuse for being there at the piling if someone were to come by and check them out. Brady and Smitty then got out the three dive tanks and readied them. Since Brady was the only one diving and Maya was his backup, they both stripped down to their bathing suits and pulled on their wetsuits. Maya then rolled up her neoprene pants and pulled a beach cover-up over her suit so that if anyone came by they would not notice her wetsuit. Brady, on the other hand, donned his flippers and mask.

The divers were both responsible for their own tanks and regulators. Unless an emergency occurred, Brady would be the only diver overboard. So, Maya set her tank and the extra one under a small tarp so that they would be within easy reach if they were needed in a hurry.

Brady strapped on his tank, adjusted the mask and regulator, picked up the under-water light, and eased himself overboard. No one said a word as he slid over the side. The only communication between Brady, Salah, and his crew was a thumbs-up sign just before he slipped below the surface.

The murky, cool, silt-filled water washed over Brady as he submerged below the surface. Because the Bay waters were in such poor condition even with the light on, Brady could barely see four feet in front of himself. He slowly swam to the piling, the condition of which was fairly good. There was little visible deterioration. Dropping down the side of the piling, Brady quickly found the two-foot ledge that had shown up on the side-scan sonar. There was no question that this was where the explosives should be placed.

Why does this piling need to be demolished, he thought. *The thing looks to be in damn good shape to me.* There was a venturi effect at the Kent Narrows resulting from Eastern Bay and The Chester River converging at this restricted connection. As a result, the tides ran fast and strong. Experiencing the pull of the tide, Brady had to keep his flippers in constant motion to stay next to the piling. Brady swam completely around the piling to make sure that the two-foot ledge was consistent in its depth and shape. Based on the strong tide, Brady determined that he would need to place piton-type anchors on the shelf all around the concrete piling to secure the bandolier charges so that they wouldn't drift off of the ledge. Some twenty minutes into his dive, Brady was preparing to surface when he heard a sharp *shoot* as two fishing lines with two to three ounce weights sliced through the water around him like bullets shot from above.

This was not a good sign. It meant that someone was nearing the *Miss Gale* and the crew was being forced to initiate the agreed-upon alibi about going fishing. Knowing that he only had another thirty minutes left in his tank before the five-minute reserve activated, Brady swam to the anchor rope off of the bow, wrapped his legs around the rope to avoid the pull of the tide, and awaited the all-clear signal from above.

The dive plan had included a strategy for handling this eventuality. When the fishing lines were cast overboard, it meant that someone was approaching the dive boat. With an all-clear sign from above, the fishing lines would be pulled in and the engine would simultaneously be started. This was done in case Brady could not see the lines being pulled in and the engine sound was the only audible indicator that everything was clear.

While Brady was clinging to the anchor rope to stay stationary under the boat, he heard metallic noises coming from the bottom of the boat. Brady pulled a small nylon line out of his wetsuit's front pocket, tied it to a metal ring on his belt, and secured the other end to the anchor rope. Swimming under the boat to the stainless doors, whose topside he'd seen earlier that day, he observed the thick black rubber gaskets that edged the doors and formed a watertight closure where the doors met in the middle. Treading water under the doors, he again heard what sounded like someone moving around in the fuel tank above.

Then it hit him. Salah had hidden there to avoid being seen by whoever approached the *Miss Gale*. Treading water, Brady thought, *Of course Salah wouldn't have wanted anyone to see him. It's enough for them to see Maya. Although she's beautiful, she certainly doesn't look American. If they'd seen two foreigners onboard, it would have heightened their curiosity. Using the fuel tank was a smart move.*

Brady swam back to the anchor rope. He untied the umbilical cord he had tied between the anchor line and his belt, and he placed it back in his pocket.

There were twenty minutes left on his regulator. When would this mystery person leave so that he could surface? . Then he saw it: one of the lines had a small rockfish on it and was slowly being reeled in. As a joke, the devil in Brady was tempted to unhook the fish, jerk hard on the line, and then let it go, but. he opted for a more cautious approach. He just yanked hard on the line and then released it. Whoever was up there reeled it in fast so as not to lose the prize.

Fifteen more minutes went by, and there was no sign of the lines being pulled in. In fact, the line that had the fish on it returned with a loud *shoot*, as the weight and rig dove to the bottom only three feet from Brady. *Wow. That was a little close*, he thought.

Five minutes later, the reserve kicked in. *There's not much time before I need to surface,* thought Brady.

Two minutes into his reserve, the lines were finally pulled up and the *Miss Gale* came to life with her engine turning over at about 1,100 rpms. At that same moment, Brady heard more sounds from inside the stainless steel tank, as Salah extricated himself from the fuel cell. Brady quickly swam to the starboard side of the *Miss Gale* and surfaced. With the boat between himself and the Narrows, Brady's exit from the water was not likely to be seen by anyone. Smitty helped Brady over the gunwale and onto the deck. Regaining his balance, Brady pulled off his neoprene suit and squared away his flippers, light, tank, and regulator. He looked around; neither Maya nor Salah were on deck.

Brady asked Smitty, "So, what caused you all to fake the fishing?"

"I'll let Salah explain it to you."

"Ok," said Brady. "But where is he?"

Before Smitty could answer, Brady turned to see Maya, who had shed her wetsuit and cover-up, and Salah emerging from the cabin. Salah's normally crisp pants were wrinkled and tiny metal filings could be seen smeared across his back and seat. It was a clear indication that he had been lying on his back in the fuel cell, which was new but had not yet been scrubbed.

Salah said, "How was it, Brady?"

"Just as I expected," said Brady. "And as the side-scan indicated, the two-foot-wide collar goes all the way around the two pilings. Because of the strength of the tide, I believe we need to secure the bandoliers with clips and piton-type concrete anchors. It will require another dive to place and anchor those pitons and clips—probably a fifty-minute underwater job. To secure those bandoliers, I will need at least fifty clips and fifty two-foot long stainless steel wires with snaps at each end."

"I'll have those for you tomorrow at the place where we'll be making up the charges."

"Great."

Not wishing to ask Salah about tomorrow's location and knowing that he would probably get an answer that was less than truthful, Brady opted to wait until Salah was ready to reveal the location to him. As usual, he would learn this information all in Salah's good time.

Brady called out to Smitty to pull anchor as he set the GPS on the reverse course back to Cooks Point. Brady made a mental note to deviate from that course on the way back. He wanted to avoid the crab pots and seine nets, since the earlier moonlight had now given way to a pitch-black sky. Gently edging *Miss Gale* around the north end of the piling, Brady put her on course, passing a small eighteen-foot Seahawk with two men onboard who were fishing off of the west side of the bridge. As they approached the Seahawk, Smitty motioned to Salah and Brady to hit the deck.

Maya and Smitty waved at the men in the Seahawk, and they waved back. Brady and Salah remained flat on the deck until *Miss Gale* was well south of the jetty and out of the sight of the smaller boat. Salah then got up from the deck and went into the cabin. Brady stood up and resumed his place at the helm.

"OK. What was that all about, Maya?" said Brady.

"Just after you went over the side, that Seahawk back there pulled up alongside to see what we were fishing for. They were curious about a charter boat fishing at night. Salah thinks they were nosing around for other reasons."

"Like what?"

"I don't know."

"Do you think they were spying on us?"

"No, I don't but I must admit that when it comes to security issues, Salah is almost always right. He thinks they were very questionable."

"Is it OK if I ask him why he thinks they approached the boat."

"Sure," said Maya. "But he may not tell you."

"No harm in asking," said Brady.

Salah took up his earlier position right behind Brady, as Brady shoved the throttle up to 2,800 rpms. Settling into the captain's chair, Brady turned toward Salah and told him that on the way back, because of the lack of moonlight, he was going to go around both the seine nets and the crab pots off of Popular Island.

Salah said, "OK."

Then Brady said, "Maya says you think the guys in the Seahawk were more than just curious fishermen."

"I was in the head when they came alongside Brady, so I didn't actually get to see them, but Maya says they were toned-up men in their early thirty's with crew cuts, NRP olive drab-type pants, and heavy black steel-tipped boots. I don't know too many civilians who would wear military pants and boots when they are fishing at night, do you?"

"Actually no - unless they just came off duty and decided to go fishing before going home. In fact, there is a small NRP office on the west side of Kent Narrows, just north of the bridge. They may have come from there."

"I don't doubt that they were really fishing Brady, but their approaching our boat and asking probing questions was typical of police work—even off-duty police work."

"Perhaps," said Brady. "But if they were serious, wouldn't they have announced who they really were and asked for the boat's registration?"

"Maybe," said Salah. "But I just don't trust them. When you return to place the pitons and anchor the bandoliers next week, just keep your eyes out for them."

"Will do. But if I see them, what do you want me to do?"

"Just leave that up to Maya. She'll take care of them."

While Brady didn't necessarily like the sound of that, he let it go and returned to concentrate on following the GPS and monitoring the radios.

Just before reaching Popular Island, Brady turned *Miss Gale* west to avoid the gill nets and crab pots. Once they were past the entrance to Knapp's Narrows, Brady resumed the GPS route back to Cooks Point. As *Miss Gale* arrived at the Cove, Brady turned on the running lights so that the guards on the Chambers dock could prepare for her arrival.

Smitty and Maya tied up the boat. Just before stepping on the dock, Salah told Brady that he'd meet him in front of the Cambridge Wal-Mart when he was finished. He would be driving his green Hummer.

Brady closed down all of the electronics, secured the cabin, and asked one of the guards to bring the gas truck down to the dock so that Smitty could fill up the boat's tank. Once the boat was filled and the boat's lines had been checked again, Smitty asked, "On your way to Tilghman, will you drop Maya and me off at the Wal-Mart in Cambridge?" Salah said he would meet us there after he finished a few errands."

"Yeah, I know he mentioned that just before he left. I'll be glad to do it. No problem."

Maya, who had finished washing-down the boat, packed the rockfish in a small cooler filled with ice to take back home.

Brady looked over the boat one last time. He hopped up on the dock, took the cooler for Maya, and gave her a hand.

"Thanks, Brady."

"Sure thing," said Brady. On the ride back to Cambridge, Maya sat next to Brady. Using the excuse of there being a crowded front bench, she cuddled up next to Brady again. Brady pulled up in front of the Wal-Mart and parked in an open space a few feet from Salah's Hummer. The three of them hopped out and walked over to the Hummer. Salah rolled his window down and handed Brady a folded-over note. "Here's your pay and the directions to an intersection where I will meet you tomorrow at 8:00 a.m."

"Thanks," said Brady. "I'll see you there. How long do you think it will take to get everything ready?"

"I'd say I should be able to drive you back to your truck at about 4:00 p.m. Oh and by the way, bring your lunch with you."

"Will do."

After saying good-bye, Maya and Smitty got into the Hummer and Brady walked back to his truck. Brady was tired and he almost fell asleep at the wheel as he passed through St. Michael's on his way home. Luckily, he yanked the wheel to the left, just barely avoiding tumbling into the drainage ditch on the north side of the road.

"Wow. That was close! You can't afford to buy a new truck or a new life, stupid. Stay awake!" he said to himself.

As he pulled up to Pete's house, he quietly exited the truck, opened the porch screen door, and tiptoed up to his room. It was a quarter to 12:00 a.m. when he finally turned off the bedside table lamp, shut his eyes, and once more drifted off into a shallow sleep that was often permeated with the sounds of gunfire and the familiar screams of his wounded friends.

Chapter 11

The Munitions Cache

At 6:30 a.m. the alarm went off and Brady bolted out of bed, rubbed the sleep from his eyes, and launched himself toward the bathroom. At 7:00 a.m. Brady walked down to the kitchen to join Pete for some coffee, grits, and ham.

Brady shared the events of the previous day with Pete. He told him about the two guys in the small boat that had come alongside *Miss Gale*, and he said that he believed that they might have been off-duty DNR police. Pete and Brady both agreed that the potential act of treachery was approaching more rapidly than they had believed possible. Before he left for the designated intersection to meet Salah after breakfast, he and Pete confirmed their after-dinner meeting with Mack that evening.

Using the directions in Salah's note, Brady drove toward the rural intersection northwest of Cambridge. As he drove, Brady noticed a small 300 Series black BMW following him at a safe distance. With blackout window screens, the car had started following him when he had turned right onto the Easton bypass. To be sure he was not imagining it, Brady pulled off of Route 50 north of Trappe, Maryland, to fill his truck. Pulling into the first set of pumps, he saw the BMW back into one of the empty parking spaces in front of the adjacent convenience store, providing the driver with a clear view of Brady's truck and a straight shot back out onto the highway. Brady locked up the truck and walked to the convenience store in the hopes of seeing the driver of the BMW through the lightly tinted driver's window, but he had no such luck. The driver's window was still too dark to make out any facial features, other than the heavy beard and the crooked nose of the driver.

Remembering Salah's statement about bringing his own lunch, Brady grabbed a six-inch Italian sub, chips, and a coke to put in the small fabric cooler he had in the truck. In the store, Brady kept an eye on the BMW to see if anyone would exit the car and come into the store. Unfortunately, the mysterious BMW driver did not want to be seen, especially by him.

As soon as Brady got back into his truck and started to drive south on Route 50 toward Cambridge, the BMW took up its surveillance from a safe distance. Ten minutes later, as Brady approached the designated intersection and pulled off onto the shoulder, the BMW came barreling up behind him. One of Salah's security men emerged from the front passenger side, came up, tapped on Brady's window, and gestured for him to get out. As Brady stepped out and started to close his door, the security guard grabbed his keys. Before Brady could even object, the guard hopped into the driver's seat, locked the door, and started the truck. Stunned, Brady watched his truck speed off down the intersection's crossroad. Brady yelled at the top of his lungs, "Hey! Come back here, you bastard. What the fuck's going on?" After driving for about two hundred yards, the driver stopped Brady's truck, locked it, got out, and climbed into the 300 Series BMW that had been following him.

Before he could say another word, a second large black BMW pulled up in front of Brady, and Salah quickly stepped out of the backseat.

"Don't worry, Brady. It's all part of the security precautions we're required to initiate. At the end of the day, your truck will be waiting for you right where it is now. You are to come with me. The other car will follow and cover our rear."

As soon as they sat in the backseat of the big car, which was a 750 LI Series BMW, Salah handed Brady a pair of wrap-around blackout glasses that were like the glasses that flight instructors use while training student pilots for their instrument rating. "Sorry, but this is a US Maritime contract requirement. They're hyper about security."

For the next twenty minutes, the car proceeded along what seemed to Brady to be a very poorly paved, uneven backcountry road that occasional turned into gravel. Barreling ahead as though on a mission of great importance, the car never seemed to slow to accommodate the changing surface conditions.

Not a word passed between Salah and Brady for the entire trip. Although unseen, Brady could hear the rustling of paper and the obvious flipping of pages. It was clear to Brady that Salah was totally immersed in reading some report or brief. As quickly as this trip had begun, it came to an end with an abrupt sideways skid on a loose gravel surface. The minute the car shuddered to a halt, Salah told Brady that he could remove his blackout glasses. Adjusting to the first light he had experienced in twenty minutes, Brady began to take in the scene around him. The BMW was parked in front of a very large red barn. A multi-dormered brick manor house stood a short distance away. Though somewhat rundown, it was clear to Brady that the estate dated back to the early 1800s.

Over the years, it had clearly fallen on hard times. Off in the distance in front of the house were the headwaters of a river. It was most likely the upper Choptank. Brady determined this based on the time of day, the angle of the sun, and the weather report's prediction of northeast winds.

Brady climbed out of the 750 LI and immediately began to notice the heavy level of security at the property. Dressed in farm clothes, overalls, blue jeans, T-shirts, and checkered short-sleeved shirts, all the guards had AK-47s slung over their shoulders with the barrels pointed at the ground. From a distance or from the air, none of these men and women would appear to be anything other than farmers or laborers. Salah was clearly attempting to cover up the operation that was taking place at the site.

Salah motioned for Brady to follow him into the red barn. Adjusting to the overall low light level inside and the long rows of tables lit by low-hung incandescent lights, Brady realized he was where he would remain for the balance of the day, packing, wiring, and piling explosives into four-foot-long bandoliers that each had prewired sequence connectors.

Seeing Brady walk in, Maya left her station at the head of the tables and came over to say hello. Brady started to give her a hug, but she just extended her hand to shake his. Brady thought that this greeting was very strange. As she shook his hand, she also winked and nodded her head toward a small group of men to her right. When Brady looked over, he saw Abed holding court in the center of the small group. Realizing that she did not want Abed to notice anything other than a professional relationship, Brady shook her hand and said, "So, what do you want me to do?"

Maya said, "Well, I've just started laying out the components on the tables. The two men at the end of the last table will be packing the explosives; only you and I will be wiring the charges. Salah doesn't trust anyone else with that job."

"So, how many charges will we be making?" asked Brady.

"We will need twenty for each of the Narrows Bridge's side-by-side pilings, and another thirty for the drawbridge pilings."

"The drawbridge? When was that added to the contract?"

"Just yesterday."

"How can we demolish both bridges when the drawbridge is to act as the traffic alternative to the Narrows Bridge?"

"I don't know that answer, Brady," said Maya. "I just do as I'm told."

"That's all well and good, Maya, but until I understand more clearly what the program is, I'm not going to set additional charges on the drawbridge pilings."

"If you want to ask Salah that question, go ahead. I'm not going to question his protocol. Brady, please don't ask him until we are finished at the end of the day. I don't want there to be any confusion or diversions while we're handling the explosives, OK?"

"OK. Fair enough."

Maya and Brady began to discuss the best and safest process for wiring and packaging the explosives. Maya produced two sheets of paper that included a drawing describing the wiring procedure that US Maritime recommended. It was written on scruffy, old brown paper in a very stylized English script. The drawing was not computerized and the narrative was handwritten instead of typed; this seemed less than professional to Brady.

After Maya laid out the brown sheets, she moved to the other end of the tables, asking two assistants to bring more materials from the storage area.

While she talked to them, Brady turned over the paper and held it up to the lights hanging overhead. As he did so, it became evident that the paper was bonded with the light engravings of an Arabic seal. As Maya started to turn back to Brady, he quickly flipped the paper back over and placed it right side up on the table. Maya didn't detect his Houdini-type move.

"They're bringing more materials out for us," said Maya. "What do you think about the drawings and US Maritime's recommended procedures?'

"They look good to me," said Brady. "My only concern is with the waterproofing of the proposed connections. The tape and the insulator wrapping are fine, but we need to encase these connections in Marine Goop. Goop will provide a durable waterproof seal that is flexible and won't crack."

"So, where do we get this Goop?"

"You can get it at any hardware or home improvement store."

"How much will we need?"

"I'd say certainly at least two cases. My guess is that we'll use half to a third of a tube on each connection - maybe more."

"OK," said Maya. "I'll tell Salah to send someone to get it right away."

"Why can't the two guys at the end of the tables do that, since it'll be a while before we are ready to provide them with bandoleers for packing?"

"Brady, one of them doesn't speak English and neither one of them has a driver's license."

"So what good are they?"

"They do manual labor just fine, and they can also provide security when needed."

"Are they military-trained?"

"Yes, but why are you so interested in them?"

"I'm not, Maya. I'm just skeptical of their ability to properly pack the bandoliers."

"Not to worry, Brady. They are capable and loyal men who have explosives experience. Jamil speaks some broken English, and he is also a dive expert. Believe me, we can trust them."

Maya got up and found Salah in the northeast corner of the building meeting with Abed and his security team. She relayed Brady's concern. Then, at Salah's request, she asked one of his security men, who spoke fluent English and was in civilian clothes, to go get the Goop.

Just before 9:30 a.m. Maya and Brady began to package the C-4 explosives into strips of wired-cakes. They wired each cake to the next and then placed them in a fine plastic mesh insulator-type wrapping, using plastic ties to secure them at each end. Each bandoleer string was four feet long and contained four, nine-inch by four-and-a-half-inch C-4 cakes.

The work was both tedious and exacting. Each cake's wire needed to be stripped, twisted, and then carefully matched to the next corresponding cake's wire. One in-line wiring mistake when the bandoleers were finally connected to the detonator would result in a short circuit. That would be all she wrote.

At 12:15 p.m. Salah walked by and announced the lunch break. Maya slumped back into her chair and took a deep breath. She finally felt relaxed. This work was mentally wearing and it required great concentration. She was constantly concerned about messing up the wiring.

Maya excused herself, saying she was having lunch with Salah to work on a list of potential new hires.

Brady took his small cooler out from under the worktable, unwrapped his turkey sub, and began eating. About halfway through lunch, he got up to go to the bathroom, which was at the far corner of the barn, where Salah and Abed had had their meeting earlier with their security team. Not knowing exactly where the bathroom door was, Brady poked around a couple of storage areas back in the corner of the building. As he did so, he came upon a large storage area in a shed that was attached to the barn. The fifteen-by-twenty-foot room he found himself in was stacked with wooden crates that had thick steel straps wrapped around them and two-by-four wooden braces along both their width and their length. There were at least thirty crates in this small space. Upon further investigation, he saw foreign language writings and markings on each of them. Basically, there were four different types of boxes. Two had Slavic-style writings and the others had Arabic-style writings. Two boxes inscribed with a different language were the largest of the thirty crates. These two were almost twice the size of the other boxes. Brady took out a pen and the piece of notepaper that had the directions to the intersection that Salah had given him. He began to copy down the writings and numbers on each of the four kinds of boxes. Knowing all too well what ammo and weapons boxes looked like, he was sure that the largest boxes contained field weapons and the two smaller ones contained ammo. Based on the size and dimensions of the two larger boxes, he guessed that one was for RPGs and one for mortars. He had seen similar crates in Afghanistan, where his patrol had uncovered a large cache of Russian weapons in a cave in the mountains of Kabal.

After making some notes, Brady closed the door and turned to his left to continue his search for the bathroom. Three doors down from the weapons room, he finally found the bathroom door. Brady closed the stall door and sat on the toilet. He took a minute to clear the cobwebs from his mind and contemplate what he had just uncovered: hidden weapons. They were weapons for urban fighting. They were weapons made for destroying both personnel and structures. As he took the notes out of the pocket of his pants and studied the numbers, it came back to him. The Slavic-style language was Russian. "RPG-29-Vampir" referred to a Russian-made RPG. The corresponding ammo boxes, which were marked "PG-29V," were both personnel and thermobolic rounds, which were used for piercing armor and steel plates. He also had in his notes a reference to one box that was marked, "Eighty-two millimeter." This box was the biggest of them all, and he guessed that it was most likely a portable field mortar.

The Arabic nomenclature was more difficult to decipher, but the large boxes had "TBG-32-Hahim" stamped on them. The corresponding shell boxes had "TBG-32V" on some and "PH" on others. Brady thought, *I bet the PH stands for 'phosphorous rounds,' and the others are thermobolic penetrating rounds. When I get home tonight - if I get home tonight - I'll go online to see exactly what each of these really is.*

Brady put his notes away and left the bathroom. As he walked out into the main barn area, Abed and two of his guards were just reaching the weapon's shed door. They stopped and waited until Brady was well past the door before they entered the shed.

That was close - too close, thought Brady. He returned to the worktable and finished eating his sub sandwich. Maya joined him a few minutes later. Again, they began to assemble more bandoliers. Brady and Maya chatted about when to go back to check out the drawbridge and place the piton anchors. After they checked their calendars, Monday the twenty-eighth appeared to be the best day. So, they decided to meet at Cooks Point at 8:30 a.m. on Monday.

As they were about halfway through making up the bandoliers for both bridges, the security man who had gone to get the Goop came back and placed the two cases of it on the table in front of Maya. Nodding, he went back to the group of security guards near where Brady had discovered the weapon's shed.

"Brady," said Maya. "Why don't you put the 'Goop' on the connections, and I'll continue to do the bandolier wiring."

"That's OK by me."

Brady moved down the line of tables about midway between Maya and the packers, who stood at the end of the assembly line. Brady began to cover each connection with Marine Goop, making sure that the wiring, electrical tape, and connector wrapping were all covered completely so that no water could penetrate through to the wire itself. Because the 'Goop' was so thick, it took time to cure. Brady told Maya that the packers should not start to bundle the bandoliers until the 'Goop' had hardened.

A little after four o'clock, Maya and Brady finished all of the bandoliers, and the packers spent the next thirty minutes carefully placing the strings of bandoliers in a circular pattern in used crab baskets. Once packed, the basket lids were locked in place and then further secured with half-inch plastic ties so that one could tell if the lids had been tampered with before the explosives team actually put them to use.

As Brady and Maya watched the packing of the explosives, they cleaned up the wire clippings, tape, and excess 'Goop'. They then placed all of it in heavy-mil contractor bags, which the security guards then took outside and placed in one of the pickups for transfer to the county dump. No stone was left unturned when it came to covering their tracks.

Maya told Brady that until they were needed the crab baskets would be kept under lock and key in a small, refrigerated seafood truck that was parked behind the barn.

After cleaning up, Brady said good-bye to Maya and reconfirmed their meeting at Cook's Point on Monday, June 28, 2010 at 8:30 a.m. From there, they would go to Kent Narrows. Under the guise of fishing again, Brady would dive to secure the pitons on the pilings. For the first time, he would check out the drawbridge pilings and secure pitons to them as well.

Brady asked, "Will Smitty be with you, Maya?"

"Yeah, Smitty will join us for the trip."

"What about Carlos? Has he recovered yet?"

"No. In fact, they sent him to Baltimore to recover from what they now have diagnosed as Rocky Mountain spotted fever and some form of encephalitis."

"Sorry to hear that. If you talk to him, please send him my best."

"Will do. See you on Monday, Brady." Maya touched his elbow and gave him it gentle squeeze.

"See you then," said Brady.

Brady turned and spotted Salah near the large barn doors. He walked over and stood there waiting for Salah to finish his conversation with one of the security guards who had been packing the crab baskets. When they were finished, Salah said, "What can I do for you, Brady?"

"Well, I was just told today that the drawbridge pilings next to the Narrows Bridge are also to be demolished. I thought that bridge was going to be placed in service to handle the excess traffic when the Narrows Bridge goes under renovation."

"I did too, Brady, but. the state decided to kill two birds with one stone and do both bridges at the same time. Their answer to the traffic issue is to undertake a major public awareness campaign to redirect people north around Aberdeen and send them down Route 301 to Route 50. I think it's going to be a real mess, but they're the client and they know what is best."

"I also think it's crazy but I guess they're in the driver's seat," said Brady.

"They are, Brady. We complained but it did no good. We also need to follow their orders or someone else will replace us."

"That's just plain stupid."

"You're right. It is stupid."

"Well, I guess I'll see you next Tuesday, the twenty-ninth. Maya and I are going up to the drawbridge on Monday the twenty-eighth to check it out and to set piton anchors around all of the pilings."

"Good. If you're ready, I will have a guard take us back to your truck."

"Thanks. I am ready to go," said Brady.

As Brady climbed into the BMW ahead of Salah, he noticed a small, refrigerated pickup truck behind the barn that had "Miller Seafood" painted on its side. Salah gave Brady the blackout glasses and told him to put them on. Salah took the front passenger seat, so Brady got in the backseat by himself. As with his early-morning trip out to the farm, the ride back was again made in silence. Blindfolded, Brady closed his eyes and reviewed the day's events. He promised himself that he would call Dan Howard to get his take on the situation, especially on the munitions cache.

Once back at Brady's truck, Salah told Brady that he could remove the glasses. He bid Brady good afternoon and Brady got into his truck. It was about 6:00 p.m. by the time Brady returned to Pete's home.

As usual, Brady went directly down to the dock to see if he could help Pete prepare for the new client who had booked the entire weekend with him. When Brady arrived at the dock, Pete was nowhere to be found. Seeing that the boat needed to be washed-down after the recent storm and heavy winds, Brady uncoiled the hose on the dock, jumped onboard, and set about cleaning up *Miss Alice*. At about 6:45 p.m. he finished cleaning and headed back to the house.

Just as Brady got to the screen porch door, he heard Pete coming up the gravel driveway. Seeing a bunch of tackle and new life preservers in the truck bed, Brady went over to the truck to help Pete unload his wares. "Hey, Uncle Pete. Can I give you a hand?"

"That'd be great."

They pulled everything out of the truck bed and laid each item on the porch so that Pete could rig up the new rods and mark the life preservers with *Miss Alice's* name. Ever since the *Lora-Anne* went down off Janes Island in the big winter storm of 2002 with unmarked life preservers onboard, this had become a standard procedure for Pete. Because the *Lora-Anne's* vests were old and had no boat name on them, when the search party found them washed up on Janes Island, everyone thought that they had been thrown away or blown up on the shore from the storm. Without a name on them, no one knew whom they belonged to. Sadly, had they known they were from the *Lora-Anne,* they would have searched the island and probably found old man Jones before he died of exposure, lying there on the aft deck of his half-sunken workboat.

Brady finished his task and turned to Pete. "Between spit-polishing your boat and all this new stuff, you better get a bunch of re-bookings from this new client, Uncle Pete."

"Sure hope so. From what I understand, the president of this company has been fishing out of Chesapeake Beach for years, and he finally gave up on the captain he was using. Not only because he couldn't find enough fish, but also because his boat and equipment were old and in poor shape. We may not find him enough fish, Brady, but he sure won't complain about *Miss Alice* or my equipment."

"Yeah, Uncle Pete. Only Aunt Louise can complain about your equipment."

"Thanks, Brady. Just wait 'til you're in your midsixties and see just how well your equipment works."

With a chuckle, Brady replied, "Yeah, you're probably right, Uncle Pete. It may happen even sooner, if I keep living on this female-deserted island for much longer."

"Maybe," said Pete. "But when Phillips Construction returns after the Fourth of July and you take Michelle to dinner, who knows? You may experience a rebirth. Of course, you could borrow my can of WD-40, if you want. Seems to help me."

"Uncle Pete, you're as horny as ever, you know that?"

"Yep, and I'll never change. Remember, I'm a Waterman."

"No mistaking that," Brady said under his breath. "By the way, Uncle Pete, I washed down *Miss Alice* when I got in. She was in need of it, due to the rain and all."

"Thanks, Brady. I owe you one."

"Don't think so, Uncle Pete. I owe you and Aunt Louise big time. After all you've done for me and Mom, I owe you big-time - that's for sure."

"You're family, Brady. It's just that simple."

"Family or not, I can still thank you all."

"And, we appreciate it, Brady - we really do."

As they entered the kitchen, the smell of pot roast filled the air. "Pot roast?" asked Pete.

Louise replied, "Sure is. Hey, Brady. How was your day?"

"In two words, it was tedious and frustrating. We spent the whole day making up charges for some bridgework that US Maritime is doing with the state."

"Isn't that dangerous?"

"Not really. As long as the blasting cap wires are covered, the stuff's pretty harmless on its own. Put it this way, it's not near as dangerous as fishing with Uncle Pete."

"Is that so?" said Uncle Pete.

"Yes, sir. That's so," replied Brady.

After a delicious dinner and lots of talk about the upcoming Fourth of July celebration that the volunteer fire company would be putting on, Pete and Brady thanked Louise and then went out onto the porch.

At 7:30 p.m. on the dot, Mack arrived and came to the porch door. Pete ushered him in and then they each grabbed a beer out of the porch cooler, cracked them open, and settled in for Brady's recounting of his day. For the next hour, Brady walked Pete and Mack through his day, highlighting the day's security measures, the work that he and Maya had done, and his discovery of the weapon's cache. While Pete and Mack interrupted for some clarification a few times during Brady's story, it wasn't until Brady finished that the floodgates of anger and disbelief opened up.

Pounding his fist on the arm of the chair and turning to face Pete, Mack said, "What the hell is going on? Those bastards are planning to bring us to our knees, Pete. The sons of bitches damn near killed me last February, and I ain't going to give them a second chance."

"Oh yeah? So, how are you going to stop them from doing something - something that you don't even know what it is?'

"Well, we know it's the Kent Narrows bridges and maybe even the Gas Docks."

"OK. I'll give you that but look, Mack. It's got to be way more than just those two targets. This plan is too sophisticated. It's too broad in scope and it involves too many people to only involve pilings. This is much more involved than that, I guarantee you."

"I agree with both of you, so let's try to figure it out," said Brady. "Let me show you a chart I've worked up to try and understand just what they could be up to." Getting up from his chair, Brady said, "Hold on a minute. I'm going upstairs to my room to get it. I'll be right back."

After a few minutes, Brady returned to the porch with a roll of brown crab-table paper and unrolled it before them on the porch table. "When I've had the time, I've been working on this a little each night before I go to bed. This may be somewhat confusing, but let me explain. On the left is the timetable starting with your encounter with the rogue boat in February. Then it goes through your search for her between March and May. It ends over here on the right in early June, when you all found not only the rogue boat, but also the similar but smaller boat."

"Next are the four properties that have been leased by a New York City LLC: the Chambers Farm at Cooks Point, the Nelson's place at Black Walnut Point, the Crab Alley Creek Farm on Cox Neck, and" - Brady began making a note of the new munitions-cache farm on the crab paper - "the farm where I was today on the Choptank River somewhere north of Cambridge. There are probably several other properties that we don't even know about that they also lease—places where they have living quarters and a command post. Then I have listed here on the right the key characteristics of the people involved. With the exception of Smitty and myself, they are all foreigners of the Islamic faith who have connections to people in Salisbury, Baltimore, and perhaps other American cities. Below these is a list of the boats' renovations, including sophisticated electronics, major repowering, lockers for explosives, and secret compartments to release and recover divers."

Pointing to the chart, Brady continued: "Here next to the renovations list are some of the elements of secrecy and the extraordinary security measures they have instituted, including a significant weapons cache. Finally, there is a list of the unexplained. Why do they want to demolish both bridges? What are the unknown whereabouts of Carlos? There are no visible signs of US Maritime workers or managers. Anyway, that's a rough draft of the events, the issues, and the unknowns. What are your thoughts?"

After a long silence, Mack said, "While we may not know the ultimate objectives or targets, these guys are definitely getting ready to attack one or more Chesapeake Bay icons: the Gas Docks, The Bay Bridge, the Inner Harbor of Baltimore, or maybe even the Naval Academy. Who knows?"

"You're right, Mack," said Brady. "While we've thought about those places for some time, we haven't really expressed it until now. We still aren't any further along in finding out what's really going on than we were a month ago. So where do we go from here?"

"Mack," said Pete. "What do you think about Brady pushing Salah for a meeting with US Maritime concerning the drawbridge? If they flatly deny him access to US Maritime, that may indicate that US Maritime is just a hoax and not a real company."

"Pete, I think that that would place Brady in a tough position. That approach would make them think he didn't trust them. I don't like that approach at all; it's too risky."

"Uncle Pete, I agree with Mack. That's too dangerous. I need to be sure they continue to trust me." After a long pause, Brady continued. "Uncle Pete, I think you need to go to your DNR friends and tell them about what we know. Only tell them what we absolutely know is true, though - nothing speculative. I don't think you need to necessarily share with them our assumptions. Let them draw their own conclusions."

Pete said, "Don't you think that may be premature?"

"I don't think so, Uncle Pete. If we don't start to get them up to speed now, it may be too late for them to react once we uncover the real targets. We can't even be sure the bridge pilings are the initial targets until we actually place the explosives there. Suppose the real targets are all those restaurants at Kent Narrows or the Naval Academy in Annapolis."

It was a while before anyone spoke.

After internally reaching a conclusion, Pete finally said, "Look, even though we've been waiting all this time since the rogue boat crossed Mack's bow, we still need more information. When I go to DNR, I want to be sure I know what the hell I'm talking about."

In his typical blustery way, Mack slammed his fist on his thigh and said, "Pete, I believe you should go now!"

"Hold up, Captain Mack. Maybe Uncle Pete's right. On second thought, I vote we wait 'til I've gone to the Gas Docks and spent more time with these guys. I need to scope this thing out a little more."

"You think waiting a little longer is best, even though these guys are close to pulling off this attack as soon as next week?" asked Mack. "After all, next Monday is Independence Day. They'd love nothing better than to hit us on the Fourth of July, when everyone is celebrating."

Not wishing to step on anyone's toes, Brady said, "I vote that we wait 'til after my Gas Dock trip, since it's only four days away. What do y'all say?"

"I'll go along with that," said Pete.

"Me too, I guess," said Mack, once again going with the flow.

"That's it then. We'll wait 'til after the Gas Dock trip."

Mack got up. "I guess I'll head home now. I've got some early-morning crabbin' to do with Mike."

"Night, Captain Mack," said Brady. "I'm heading to bed too. Night, Uncle Pete. See you in the morning."

"Night, Brady. See you at six o'clock."

The porch door shut behind Mack as he walked to his truck. Pete told Brady that he'd make coffee for the morning. Brady thanked him and headed upstairs. Brady went into the bathroom, brushed his teeth, washed his face, and dried off. Sitting on his bed, he then dialed Dan Howard's number.

After four rings, a voice said, "Hello."

"Dan, is that you?"

"Yeah. Who's this?"

"Brady Wilson."

"Hey, Brady. How's it going?"

"Pretty good. But, I need to talk to you about some things that are going on down here - things that have me really worried."

"What's up?"

"Remember when we talked on the *Miss Alice* about keeping terrorists from coming here?"

"Yeah, I sure do."

"Well, they're here, Dan, and I'm right in the middle of it."

"You're kidding me?"

"I wish I were. Last week, I began a new job helping a start-up company do some piling demolition work. As it turns out, I believe the company is really a terrorist cell that is planning multiple attacks on the Bay."

"You're shittin' me?"

"No, Dan. I am not. This is for real."

"Have you gone to the authorities?"

"No. Not yet."

"Huh. Why not?"

"It's complicated, Dan. I'd rather talk in person than over the phone. Plus, I don't trust the security of my cell phone."

"OK. How about our meeting tomorrow? I am traveling in the Baltimore area, so I could come down in the evening and meet in either Easton or St. Michael's."

"That will work. I'm fishing with Uncle Pete tomorrow, and I should be back by about 4:00 p.m. or 4:30 p.m. After cleaning up the boat, I could be in St. Michael's by, say, 6:30 p.m."

"Where should we meet?"

"You know the Shore Pub on Main Street?"

"The one where all the watermen hang out?"

"Yeah, that's the one."

"Sure, that works for me."

"I can't tell you how much I appreciate your meeting with me, Dan. Here I thought I had gotten a really good-paying job and maybe even a new career path. Then boom! All of a sudden, like in Afghanistan, I find myself once again back in harm's way with no way out."

"Brady, we'll figure it out. You'll be OK."

"God, I hope so."

"See you tomorrow, Brady."

"Yep. See you then. Thanks again, Dan. You don't know how much I appreciate it."

"Look, Brady. We're marines. We take care of our own. See you tomorrow evening."

"OK, Dan." Brady hung up and lay back on the bed. Finally, at about 10:30 p.m. he fell soundly asleep.

Chapter 12

The Pieces Start to Fit Together. Saturday, June 26

At 5:00 a.m. Brady woke to the shrill sound of his old alarm clock. Pulling the covers over his head, he tried to go back to sleep. Within a few minutes, though, the alarm on his cell phone went off. It always took a second alarm to force him to finally wake up. He threw the covers off. His feet hit the floor and he cradled his face as he wiped the sand from his eyes.

Mechanically, Brady showered, shaved, and got dressed. Since this weekend they were hosting a new client, Brady put on his best shorts and his Columbia fishing shirt, which had "Miss Alice" embroidered across the pocket. This was hopefully a big customer for Uncle Pete. So, Brady felt he had to be at his best.

Brady expected to find Pete wrapped around a hot mug of coffee, eating cereal at the kitchen table. Instead, he found a note from his uncle under the saltshaker: "Brady, can you go to the store and get four twenty-pound bags of ice and two eighteen packs of regular and light beer? Your choice. Let me know if this fifty dollars covers it or not. Meet you at the boat. Uncle Pete."

Brady stuffed the note into his pocket and drove off to the store. He picked up the items on the list, plus a bacon-and-egg biscuit and a black coffee. Then he drove down to the pier and unloaded the beer and ice.

Pete was not onboard, but Brady saw him two piers down, talking with another charter boat captain named Bob Moore, whose advice Pete highly respected. Brady stowed the beer and ice. Then he went into the cabin to inventory the lunchboxes that Louise had prepared. *Wow*, he thought to himself as he rummaged through the contents of one box. *In addition to Pete's corn chowder, these guys have a special treat—apples, turkey sandwiches, shrimp salad, chips, Smith Island cakes, and the best fried chicken anybody could ever hope for. Man, Pete's sure puttin' on the dog.*

Pete walked up to the boat and said, "So, what do you think, Brady. Everything looking OK?"

"Sure does, Uncle Pete," said Brady. "Good enough for the Queen of England."

Pete grinned. "Good. I just talked to Captain Billy and he says that the word out of Chesapeake Beach is that the Gas Docks are full of good-sized rock. He live-lined down there yesterday and had his limit in two hours."

"Well, let's hope we do that well. If we do, what will we fish for next?"

"I've fixed up a bunch of bottom rigs, and I have several buckets of razor clams. I figure we'd go up off the mouth of Harris Creek, where the big croakers have been plentiful."

"That ought to keep 'em busy."

"I hope so," he said. "But first, we got to get 'em rockfish."

At six-thirty, Brady had finished all of the necessary preparations. Like clockwork, two large SUVs pulled up to the dock. The first to emerge from the SUVs was Mr. Duncan, a larger-than-life figure whose military bearing and all-encompassing smile were both disarming and magnetic.

Extending his meat-cleaver-sized hand, Mr. Duncan said, "Good morning, Captain Pete. Jack Duncan."

"Morning, Mr. Duncan. Welcome to the *Miss Alice*. This is my nephew and first mate, Brady Wilson."

After shaking Mr. Duncan's hand, Brady hopped up onto the dock to greet the other six guests, all of whom were key employees of Duncan Electric. Four of the six were young men between the ages of twenty-five and thirty-five, and the two women were somewhere in their mid-fifties. It was obvious that the young men were excited to be going fishing, while the women, who he thought had taken very good care of themselves over the years, were somewhat reluctant. Shaking hands with the women in the group, Brady thought about how they, like the Phillips Company, sure hired pretty women. Clearly, the two women were in key company positions, given the respectful way that the other men referred to them.

Brady helped the ladies onboard. Then he gathered everyone together to explain where the life vests were and how to put them on. He ran through the protocol for hooking the fish when they hit and how to reel them in. After a few questions about how big the fish were and how many fish each person could keep, Brady settled them in. At Pete's command, he cast off the *Miss Alice*.

With Mr. Duncan standing next to him in the cabin, Captain Pete departed Knapp's Narrows and headed out to the Gas Docks.

The day was a beauty. The sky was robin's-egg blue, which resulted in the same blue cast to the waters of the Bay. Little rain had occurred within the last week, so the clarity of the water was good. There was little silt to turn it that dirty brown color that always followed a bad storm. The winds were coming out of the southwest at about five knots. The waves were less than a foot high, so the ride to the Gas Docks was smooth and swift.

Brady found it interesting to listen in on the guests' conversations as he went about preparing the rods and bait. He learned that Duncan Electric was doing a major job for the State of Maryland. They had been contracted by the state to upgrade the traffic signalization on the east and west approaches, as well as the suspension sections of the Chesapeake Bay Bridge. Mr. Duncan's chief field manager, Mike Fisher, was telling the others in his party about a satellite system that tracked the comings and goings of big commercial ships on the Bay. He said that it was housed in a private shipping company's headquarters in Baltimore. The system was mainly geared to managing port dockage issues and stevedore work schedules. However, this surveillance system was also used by the state to help them monitor shipping activities on the Bay. In addition, Mike Fisher said that the camera systems for the bridge and the approach ramps were ill equipped to create effective surveillance. He also shared the fact that he had been told that the response capabilities of the Maryland Department of Transportation and State Police to any major incident on the bridge were inadequate. Mike said that he had stated his concerns to Maryland's DOT staff, but he had received assurances from them that the security systems were state-of-the-art and they could respond to any major disaster immediately and effectively. Mike said that he was pursuing this further in hopes of expanding their contract to include a new bridge surveillance and monitoring system.

Mike continued to share with his team the specifics of the security procedures they had been instructed to follow. Most of the procedures dealt with how to evacuate the bridge in the event of a major issue, especially if the signalization system that they were working on went down.

While Brady listened, he continued performing his duties as first mate. He didn't catch all of the conversation, but he got enough information to make him feel even more concerned about the state's ability to detect terrorist activities on the Bay and to respond in a timely manner.

Captain Pete called out to Brady to come into the cabin, where he and Mr. Duncan were going over the day's fishing plans. He pointed to a spot on the map and said, "First, we'll go down to the Gas Docks to do some live-lining with the Norfolk Spot that I have in the live well. Then, if you all haven't reached your limit of rockfish, we'll head up to *The Diamonds*. Brady, are you sure we're ready with all of the equipment?"

Brady responded, "Yes, sir. We're ready to go."

∗∗∗

After anchoring off of the restricted area of the Gas Docks, Brady set about baiting all of the lines and monitoring each rod as the live bait gently pulled on the taught monofilament. Within half an hour, they had landed four keepers and thrown back three smaller rockfish. The action was terrific and it was all Brady could do to keep up with the constant strikes that they were getting. The Duncan Team was ecstatic with the action, laughing and joking with each other about who would catch the most and the biggest fish. Brady saw firsthand how competitive this party was, and he helped fuel the fire by cheering them on.

While the pace was brisk, Brady forced himself to take a deep breath and concentrate on slowing his heart rate down, just as he'd been told at Walter Reed when he'd found himself in a hyper mode. It always seemed to work and this time was no exception. Brady held onto the canopy strut and gazed off toward the horizon. Looking across to the western shore, he noticed that four of the natural-gas storage tank tops were visible from where the *Miss Alice* was anchored. *Pretty sight*, he thought. *The crowns of those tanks look like they're resting on the tops of the pine trees in front of them - like four domes of stationary spaceships with antennas and red strobe lights protruding from their roofs.* He smiled.

"Brady, is something wrong?"

Pete's question pulled Brady out of his stupor.

"Nothing's wrong, Uncle Pete."

"Well then, get back to pulling in those fish. You got four lines with fish on right now!"

Pete's response and the tone of his voice indicated his aggravation with Brady's daydreaming.

"Sorry, Uncle Pete. I won't let it happen again."

Brady scrambled for the guest's rods and pulled in all four fish. As Brady was re-baiting the lines, Mr. Duncan turned to him and said, "Good job, young man; that was great action. I've never had this good of a trip in all my life."

122

"Thanks, Mr. Duncan. You're right. We're having a darn good day!"

After lunch, they experienced a lull in the action. Pete decided to move up to *The Diamonds* to see what they could find there. While the fish finder showed lots of fish, the slack tide kept the fish deep and stationary. At about 2:00 p.m. the action picked up and they reached their limit of two fish per person by 2:30 p.m.

After the last fish was tossed into the ice locker, Pete announced that they could either move up to Harris Creek to fish for perch and croakers or head back in.

Mr. Duncan asked his team what they wanted to do. The overwhelming response was that they wanted to head back in. They all figured that by the time they retrieved their cleaned fish at the dock, it would be close to 4:00 p.m. With dinner at the hotel at 5:30, they needed some sleep before rising again to fish on Sunday.

Arriving back at the dock, Mr. Duncan and his group thanked Pete and Brady. They gathered their belongings and headed to their hotel for the evening. When the boat was cleaned up and ready for the next day's trip, Pete and Brady parted ways. Pete went directly home and Brady, unbeknownst to Pete, headed up to St. Michael's to meet with Dan.

✳✳✳

Brady parked behind the pub in St. Michaels and walked down the alley to Main Street. As he turned the corner, he spotted Dan standing on the steps to the bar's front door. In the background, music from the jukebox drifted through the bar's open windows and out onto the sidewalk.

"Hey, Brady," called Dan, spotting Brady clearing the corner of the alley.

"Hey, Dan. Great to see you."

The two men high-fived, embraced, and patted each other on the back.

"Want to sit at the bar?"

"Sure," said Dan. "If we need more privacy, we can always move into the dining area."

"That's OK with me."

There were two empty stools at the left end of the bar, next to the wall separating the dining room from the bar.

"So, tell me what's going on," said Dan.

"This will take some time, Dan."

"I've got plenty of it, Brady."

Brady started with Pete and Mack's search for the rogue boat. Over the next hour he took Dan through the chronology of the last five months, culminating with the plan to go to the Gas Docks on Tuesday. During Brady's retelling of the story, Dan seldom interrupted. When he did, it was only to get clarification. When Brady had finished telling the story, he asked Dan what he thought.

Dan responded, "Man you're lucky to be alive. Depending on how your trip goes to Kent Narrows and the Gas Docks, I'd say you'll be dead by the end of Tuesday. They won't have any need for you after that."

"You really believe that?"

"No," said Dan. "I know that! You're on your way to the grave, my friend."

Brady took a deep breath, turned toward Dan, and said, "Dead or not, I've got to do something about this. I can't let these guys succeed. I've made up my mind. I've got to stop them." Brady paused. "I'm just not sure how to do it. That's why I need your help figuring out how to keep them from executing their plan."

The intensity of their discussion had drawn the interest of two men sitting on stools at the window seats behind them. With his eyes, Dan signaled Brady that people were listening to them. Curiously, Brady turned slightly to his right to get a better look at them.

Crap, he thought as he turned back to Dan and grabbed a pencil from the highball glass next to the cash register in front of them. He wrote a note on his cocktail napkin: "Those are two of the guards from the barn where we prepped the explosives."

Knowing that the men at the bar might have recognized them, the two men turned to face out of the window behind them. Slowly, they put their jackets on, shoved down the rest of their crab cakes, and quietly slipped out of the dining room door.

Brady scrunched up his note to Dan and said, "Shit. What do you think they heard?"

"I don't know how long they were listening, but based on how quickly they left, my guess is that they heard something. If I were them, I would have wanted to be sure you hadn't recognized us, and the quicker we left the Pub, the better off we'd be."

"Now I've done it."

"I doubt it, Brady. While they might have heard something and recognized you when you turned toward them, I doubt they heard very much, especially since I only noticed them looking over here a minute before I nodded to you."

"God, I hope you're right."

"Can we have another round, miss?" Dan asked.

"Sure. Same for both?" The waitress asked.

"Yep," they replied in unison.

Sipping on the new beer, Dan said, "You got a choice, Brady. Either you go to the police now or you stick with your plan to find out exactly what the targets are. Then, you go to the police. When you finally do go to the police, you need to be sure that you've got documentation that's believable."

"That's what I've actually been trying to do for the past month: get solid evidence and discover the actual targets."

" I'd say you've been right on Brady, especially since you're still here and not floating in the Choptank."

"Thanks for the vote of confidence."

"You're welcome. Just stay below the radar, Brady."

"Sure," he said. "Just like I did tonight with those two behind us."

"Don't worry about that. I think they were more concerned with you recognizing them. I bet that guy - what's his name, Salah - would cut their throats if he knew they were eating at a bar. That's a Muslim no-no, especially when there's an active operation underway."

Brady turned toward Dan and said, "Look, Dan, could you do some checking with your friends in Naval Intelligence and see if they know anything about this cell? I need to know as much as I can before setting those pitons and going to the Gas Docks."

"Not to worry. I've already planned to call navy intelligence and Langley tomorrow."

"Are those guys on duty on Sundays?"

"They're always on duty, Brady. They don't have nine-to-five jobs. For them, it's 24/7."

"Want to grab some dinner, Dan?"

"No, but thanks. I need to get back to Baltimore and call the kids before they go to bed. You know, parenting duties. How about you?"

"I think I'll just stay here at the bar and get a hamburger before I head back."

Dan got his wallet out. Pushing Dan's wallet away, Brady said, "No way. You're in my backyard and after you've come all the way down here to see me, this is my treat."

Dan stood up, put his hand on Brady's shoulder, and said, "Thanks, Brady. Next time, it's my turn. Keep up the good work and lay low. I'll call you tomorrow."

"Thanks again, Dan. You've helped me crystallized my thinking and that's a good thing."

"Glad I've helped. Talk to you tomorrow." Dan left the pub by the front door. Brady picked up the bar menu and ordered his burger.

Chapter 13

The Truth About US Maritime. Sunday, June 27

On Sunday morning, Pete and Brady gathered in the kitchen with Louise. While she didn't normally fix Pete's breakfast because he got up so early, this morning she did. She had to be at the church early because she and some of the other ladies in the women's auxiliary were cooking for an afternoon celebration of the minister's birthday. Scrapple, ham, eggs, biscuits, and gravy greeted them at the table, along with black coffee and a side of grits with butter and cinnamon.

"Aunt Louise, this ought to stick to my ribs 'til lunch. Thanks so much for the vittles. They're delicious."

"You're welcome, Brady. If it weren't for you thanking me, I'd never know if it was good or not."

Pete looked up with a sheepish grin and said, "Sorry, Louise. You know I love your cooking. It's just hard to wake up early and get the cobwebs out before I have one of your terrific meals. It's delicious. Thank you."

"Apology accepted," said Louise, flipping two eggs over easy for Brady.

When they had finished, Brady and Pete got up, placed their dishes in the sink, hugged Louise, and thanked her profusely for such a great early-morning treat. Too anxious to just wait for Dan's call, Brady excused himself and went to his room to check in with Dan. Dan's line was busy, so he planned to call him after fishing.

Fifteen minutes later, Pete and Brady boarded the boat. Each of them went quietly about his task of readying the *Miss Alice* for the day ahead. At six-thirty sharp, Mr. Duncan and his party arrived at the dock, greeted Pete and Brady, and hopped aboard.

"Cast her off," said Pete.

"You got it, captain," answered Brady, as he cast off the final stern line. Brady returned to his task of preparing the rods for trolling off of Janes Island, just south of the Choptank River.

Pete called Mr. Duncan to the cabin to share with him the weather report, which was projecting high winds and rain starting at 2:00 p.m. Pete told Mr. Duncan that he thought they'd be OK until about 12:30 p.m. or so. Then, he said, they'd probably have to pick up and head back to Tilghman.

Duncan said, "Captain Pete it's your call; whatever you think we need to do we'll do it."

"OK then, we'll first troll off of Janes Island. Then later in the morning, as the front approaches, we'll move up the Bay."

"Sounds good to me, Captain Pete."

"Great. Then that's the plan."

Pete was not only a terrific fisherman and boat captain; he was also a darn fine businessman and psychologist. He knew that if he asked his client to participate in the planning of the day ahead and if he shared any concerns with him, such as concerns about the weather, they'd be vested in the day's fishing. This, Pete knew, would help guarantee return trips, even if the fishing were mediocre.

At about 11:30 a.m. the skies started to cloud over. What had been white and billowy cumulus clouds began to change into a palette of light and dark grays. The wind picked up and at about 12:30 p.m. they could see rain moving up the Bay from just south of Solomon's Island off in the distance.

Captain Pete asked everyone to pull in their lines, and he directed Brady to secure the planning boards and tackle.

The fishing had been so good that Pete had not been forced to move north of the Janes Island area. So, they had a slightly longer run home than he'd expected. Once Pete got underway, he pushed *Miss Alice* up to 2,800 rpms to outrun the rain. Pete arrived at the dock about a half an hour before the rain. Everyone quickly put on their rain gear and stepped off of the boat. Each person thanked Pete and Brady for two great days of fishing. Mr. Duncan and his employees were ecstatic with their two days on the Bay. Mr. Duncan was very generous with his tips, and he told Pete he'd call him on Monday to schedule another trip in July.

Pete was thrilled. After the Duncan party left, he told Brady, "See, all of the hard work of getting *Miss Alice* tuned up was worth it."

"It certainly didn't hurt, Uncle Pete, but it was essential that you put them on the fish the way you did and that you have an obviously good relationship with Mr. Duncan."

"Well, I guess those factors didn't hurt either."

Rather than finishing cleaning the boat as the heavy rain approached, Pete decided to head back home, clean up, and then returned at about four o'clock, when the rain was projected to move off to the north. He preferred to tackle the clean-up after the rain had passed.

By four o'clock, the rain stopped and Pete and Brady returned to the *Miss Alice* to ready her for the next guests who were scheduled for the weekend following the Fourth of July.

While working on the boat, Brady got a call from Maya saying that she had gotten the required number of pitons and clips and she was scheduling their run-up to the Kent Narrows at 6:00 a.m., rather than 8:00 a.m., which was the time that they had previously agreed upon.

Brady asked her, "Why so early?"

Maya responded, "Because the earlier we get the job done, the less likely we are to be seen by the many folks who regularly travel the Narrows from morning 'til late afternoon."

"OK. No problem," said Brady. "Who will be joining us? Carlos and Smitty?"

"No. Carlos is still in the Baltimore hospital, and he probably won't return to work until late July. But, one of the guys who helped bundle the C-4 bricks - a guy named Jamil - will be coming along."

"The other day you said both the guys bundling the explosives were trained divers, but you said that only one of them spoke broken English and the other one didn't speak any English at all. How will that work if someone comes along side the boat while I'm below securing the pitons?"

"Brady, don't worry. I'll do the talking. It will be OK. I promise."

"Sure hope so. I'll meet you at 6:00 a.m. at the Chamber's dock."

"No. Meet me at the Crab Alley Creek dock. That's where *Miss Gale* is now moored."

"OK. Crab Alley Creek it is. See you at 6:00." Brady closed his phone cover and resumed his cleaning.

"Hey, Brady. Are those St. Michael's girls chasing after you?"

"No, Uncle Pete. Last night was just a bunch of us guys talking about sports. There were not many women in there last night. Besides, most of them were a lot older."

"So, what's wrong with that?"

"Come on, Uncle Pete. You think I should be messing around with women twice my age?"

"I guess not, Brady, but you might want to keep those phone numbers in case times get tough."

"Tell you what, Uncle Pete, I'll keep the numbers and auction them off at the Fourth of July celebration at the firehouse, and. I'll tell them it was your idea."

"Huh," said Pete. "Do that and both of us will be thrown out on our ears."

"Yeah, probably so, Uncle Pete," said Brady. "Probably so."

They stopped their sparring and finished cleaning up and preparing for the fishing they would be doing the following weekend. At 5:30 p.m. Pete and Brady quit and returned home to get an early dinner before Mack was to arrive at 7:00 p.m. for their next meeting about the rogue boat.

As he was about to go downstairs for dinner, Brady's phone rang. It was Dan calling to report his latest findings.

✳✳✳

At 7:00 p.m. Mack knocked on Pete's porch door. Brady opened the kitchen door and stepped out onto the porch.

"Hey, Mack. What's good with you?"

"Not much, son. What's the latest news on these guys of yours?"

"Hold up, Mack. They're not my guys!"

Before Mack could respond, Pete stepped onto the porch to join the discussion. Overhearing Mack, he said, "Brady, Mack doesn't mean they're your friends. He's only referring to them as the group that you work with."

"Yeah, Brady. Why are you so touchy?" said Mack.

"Look, both of you have been on the sidelines of this game while I've been in on every play. It may seem like a game to you all, but to me it's Afghanistan all over again."

There was complete silence.

Pete opened up the cooler and got out two beers. He gave one to Mack and handed the other one to Brady, who said, "No thanks, Uncle Pete." Pete cracked open the can he'd gotten out for Brady and took a seat next to Mack.

Brady paced back and forth in front of the two men. After a minute, he grabbed another chair, pulled it up in front of them, and started to tell it like it was.

"I talked to Dan last night in St. Michael's, and I just had another conversation with him before I came downstairs."

"You mean the same Dan who works with Phillip's Construction?"

"Yeah, that's him."

"Why have you been talking to him?"

"Well, Dan is an ex-marine. He was attached to G-2 Naval Intelligence in Afghanistan. He is very savvy about both the Intelligence Community and Al Qaeda."

"OK. So?" said Pete.

"Since yesterday, he's had some contact with friends at both the Pentagon and Langley. He's confirmed that US Maritime does not exist." Brady paused so that the importance of his statement would sink in. "Evidentially, Naval Intelligence has been on alert for a cell in Maryland that's planning a waterborne attack. He's convinced that it's the same group I'm working with."

"Holy shit, Pete. What have we gotten into?" said Mack.

Pete gave Mack an exasperated look and turned to Brady. "Brady, is Dan sure it's the same group?"

"Yeah, Uncle Pete. He's sure."

"Has he alerted anyone?"

"No."

"So, is he going to?"

"Since I'm caught in the middle of this, he said it's my decision, but I better decide soon or he won't have any other choice but to alert Naval Intelligence and Homeland Security."

"By when, Brady?"

"By Wednesday the thirtieth, Mack." "That doesn't leave you much time," said Pete.

"No. It sure doesn't, especially since I need documentation to prove it."

"What are you going to do?"

"I have two choices. I can go to the police now or go to Kent Narrows tomorrow, then to the Gas Docks on Tuesday and then contact them. The idea here would be to see if I could get the exact locations of the targets and their timetables. I need to have some believable documentation to prove it."

"How can we help, Brady?" Said Pete.

Mack chimed in, "Yeah, what can we do?"

"The first thing, Mack, is that you and Uncle Pete need to continue to keep this between us and no one else. We can't go to NRP or the state police. When the time is right, I'll do that myself. I don't want you all to do anything else. What you've done so far has been incredibly helpful. If it weren't for your inquisitiveness, tenacity, and belief that something very wrong was afoot, we would still be just bumping along in our everyday lives, unaware and unable to do anything about the coming attacks. The baton has been handed to me and it's my job to finish this race."

Pete sat back in his chair and thought to himself, *Brady sure is a chip off the old block— no doubt about that. His dad was a Vietnam Veteran who not only distinguished himself on the battlefield, but also in his community back home. This boy seems to be just like him: quiet, strong, and in control. I didn't see that in him at first, but he sure seems to be on track now.*

Mack put a hand on Pete's shoulder, "You OK, Pete?"

Pete was jarred back to the present. "Yeah, Mack. I'm fine. I'm just thinking."

"You're right, Brady. From now on, this is your mission and yours alone. We just want to be there when and if you need us," said Pete.

"Thanks. I appreciate that," Uncle Pete.

"There's a good chance that they will want to keep me close to them and under surveillance. Therefore, we need some way to communicate if I get into trouble. Instead of using cell phones, which are easy to trace, in my truck I have two palm-sized marine corps radios and a charger, which I used in Afghanistan. Luckily, my captain told me that I could keep them when I left. They're Motorola radios and they have two secure bands that were specifically reserved for special ops. I will have to charge them and test them to see if they're still operable. These radios rely on a satellite system to bounce the signals. This was necessary to provide continuous communications in the mountains of Afghanistan. The only issue might be the military's ability to listen in on our conversations. Since we won't use them unless I'm in real trouble, that won't make any difference at that point."

"Look, we've all had a rough day, and I for one need some sleep before my meeting with Maya at 6:00 a.m. I'll be going to the Crab Alley Creek Farm, and I will leave from there to go over to the Narrows. I'll probably return about 5:00 p.m. or 6:00 p.m. Before I leave in the morning, I will have charged the radios. I will leave one on the kitchen table with instructions on how to use the special ops bands. Tomorrow night, we can meet here again at 7:00 p.m. so that I can give you all another update. OK?"

"OK," said Pete.

"Yeah, that's OK with me too," said Mack, once again going with the flow.

"Well, gentlemen, wish me well. The next three days are going to be very interesting."

Mack got up, shook Brady's hand, and said, "Good luck, son."

"Thanks, Mack."

Mack left the porch, walked out to his truck, and headed home.

Pete also stood up, embraced Brady, and said, "Godspeed, Brady. Your dad sure would be proud of you."

"I don't know about that, Uncle Pete. I'm just trying to do the right thing," said Brady. "Night."

"Night," Pete replied.

Chapter 14

Six Days Left. Monday, June 28

Waking at 4:30 a.m., Brady dressed and quietly exited the house. He grabbed two bacon-and-egg sandwiches at the Tilghman Store and headed north to meet Maya. He crossed the Kent Narrows Bridge, turned off of Route 50, and headed down the Old Cox Neck Road to the small farm off of Crab Alley Creek. Turning left onto the farm's driveway, he drove toward the dock. On his way, Brady noticed the Miller Seafood truck he'd seen at the big farm north of Cambridge. The truck was tucked back into the far corner of the tractor shed that was attached to the farm's main barn. *It makes sense that the crab baskets with the C-4 bandoliers curled up in them would be here,* Brady thought. *They'd be used at the Kent Narrows Bridges.* Brady also noticed two black Hummers wedged into the same shed between a large four-wheel #9430 John Deere Tractor and a #9570-STS John Deere Combine. *They sure don't want anyone to see these,* he thought.

As Brady drove past the barn, he looked into the rearview mirror and noticed a security guard stepping out of the shed with an AK-47 slung over his shoulder. The man raised a handheld radio to his mouth, obviously notifying dock security of Brady's arrival.

Brady placed his truck alongside a camouflage Hummer that was parked behind a bank of thick pine trees at the end of a hedgerow that separated two of the farm's fields. He locked his truck and got out a fifteen-foot tether rope with easy release clips at each end. He had made it to secure himself to the piling in case the tides were running too strong. Walking down to the dock, he noticed that two additional security cameras had been placed on the dock. Along with the original cameras, this would provide a 360-degree view of the dock and its surroundings.

Maya, Smitty, and Jamil were checking out the dive gear as Brady approached. They were so engrossed in their work that it wasn't until Brady actually jumped onboard that they finally saw him. Almost in unison, all three of them said, "Hi, Brady." Brady gave Maya a friendly hug and then shook Jamil's and Smitty's hands.

"Is the equipment OK?" he asked.

"Yeah. Everything is in order," said Maya.

"Can you put this new regulator on my tank, Smitty? I didn't like the airflow the last time I dove. The airflow wasn't smooth. It came in fits and starts," said Brady.

"Sure, I'll put it on," said Smitty, grabbing Brady's tank, a wrench set, and the new regulator. Brady watched as Smitty, with a dexterity that clearly came from having a lot of practice, removed the old regulator and replaced it with a new one. Smitty seated the new value, recharged the tank, and declared that the regulator was working just fine. As a backup, Brady checked the valve and pressure himself.

"Thanks, Smitty. Good job. It usually takes me three tries before I can seat it properly."

"When you get as much practice as I have, it's like tying your shoes."

"Speaking of that, Smitty, your laces are loose."

Looking down and then back up, Smitty produced a broad grin and said, "You got me on that one, Brady. I forgot I was wearing crocs."

Patting Smitty on the back, Brady said, "Yep. I got you good."

Maya went into the cabin and got her folder. "All right, boys, come on in. We need to go over our plans."

Brady, Jamil, and Smitty walked in and took seats at the dining table across from Maya. Maya walked the three men through the schedule. First, they would set the pins on the west side and then go around to the east side of the Kent Narrows Bridge. Once they completed this, they would move over to the drawbridge and follow the same procedure. As on their last dive at Kent Narrows, Smitty, Maya, and Jamil would fish, if need be, from the boat. This would be a diversionary tactic. They would know to come to the surface when all three lines were pulled up and the boat's engine started. Also, if any trouble were to occur at the surface, they would drop one crab cage over the side. The signal that everything was clear would come when the crab cage and all three fishing lines were pulled up and the engine was started. If for any reason Brady's air supply were to run out, he was to pull on a fish line five times to notify them. In this scenario, they would lower another mask and a bottle with a regulator to Brady as an emergency measure.

When the briefing was over, Brady checked the bilge, turned on the engine box blower to clear any fumes, waited two minutes, and then started the engine. Clearing the dock, Brady set all of the radios to the correct frequencies for monitoring, and he moved down the creek toward Parsons Island.

Maya went below and began to pull out pitons bags from the small lockers in the forward cabin. Each bag contained five pitons and clips—just the right amount to open at one time underwater. The bags were hooked onto two large steel rings that would attach to straps on Brady's wetsuit. This provided him the easy access to them that he needed.

As Brady approach the pilings at the Kent Narrows Bridge, Maya placed the two large rings in an empty crab basket on the starboard side of the boat just in front of the mid-station. Smitty and Jamil pulled down three rods from the overhead canopy rack and baited each with razor clams from a two-gallon bucket. They'd placed a wet rag over this to keep the clams cool.

Brady moved the boat just north of the GPS marker. He lowered and secured the anchor so that the *Miss Gale* drifted directly over the marker. He then went into the forward cabin and pulled on his wetsuit. Emerging from the cabin, Brady put on both of his flippers and the air tank. With little effort, he slipped over the side. Maya handed him the waterproof electric drill, a hammer, some quickset marine 'Goop', and the tether.

"Brady, you've got forty minutes to rig both pilings before we move over to the drawbridge. Don't rush, but be sure to keep your eye on your dive watch. We don't want you running out of air."

"I'll be fine, Maya. You guys catch some decent-sized fish, and try not to hook me."

"Will do."

With a thumbs-up sign, Brady descended below the surface and swam off to the pilings, where he began to drill the necessary starter holes around both the east and west pilings. Maya and the deck crew cast their bait off of the port side of *Miss Gale* so that anyone passing through the Narrows would see them fishing.

Brady developed a smooth yet rapid rhythm of drilling and filling - the dentists' way of describing their workdays. Each starter hole was just large enough to hold the piton upright as Brady pounded it in, applied the quickset Marine Goop, and fastened on the stainless steel clips. As the work moved along, Brady realized that he could not finish the job in forty minutes. He would need another twenty minutes to complete both piers. With about twenty more pitons to go, Brady surfaced on the starboard side and gently rapped on the haul.

Maya placed her fishing rod in a gunwale holder and moved across the boat to talk to Brady.

"I need another tank. Everything OK up here?"

"Yeah. A few boats passed. They acknowledged us with a wave and then moved on. Hand me your tank and I'll be right back with a new one." Maya returned and handed over the new tank.

Brady said, "Thanks. I'll be up in about another twenty to thirty minutes."

"We'll be waiting."

Brady rolled over and dove for the pilings. He secured all of the pitons and clips around both of the pilings. He checked them all one more time to be sure that the quickset filler had hardened. As he pulled on each piton, there was no give. Feeling good about the job he'd just completed, he turned and surfaced. As he broke the surface, he was immediately aware that something was wrong. The deck lights were on and he heard male voices that weren't Jamil's or Smitty's. Brady had another twenty minutes of air, but he figured that he was well hidden by the boat's profile, unless the men were to decide to come onboard and Maya were to actually let them do so. Brady continued to tread water, focusing his attention on the conversation between Maya and the two men. They had obviously pulled up alongside to ask questions.

"Would you please show us your registration? I don't see the state fishing sticker displayed anywhere. If you would, please get that out for me also." It was the Natural Resource Police. Luckily, after the last time they had been approached off of Janes Island, Brady had told Maya that he always kept the registration and fishing stickers for each boat in an envelope at the back of the pedestal drawer under the captain's seat.

Maya said, "Just a minute. I'll get it out of the cabin."

"By the way, young lady, that fishing sticker you're getting out is supposed to be next to your boat registration number at the opposite end of the boat sticker."

Turning to face the two NRP police, Maya give them a coy look, stretched her arms out, and squeezing her hands together below her waist. This move accentuated her cleavage, lessening the impact of their rebuke.

"Sorry about that, guys. I'll do that when we dock, OK?"

"OK," said one of the officers.

As she turned back to enter the cabin, this same officer said, "So, where is the *Miss Gale* docked?"

Brady froze. 'Shit. They either suspect something or they just want to continue a conversation so that they can gawk at Maya.'

"She moves around the Bay a lot, so she really doesn't have a permanent berth," said Maya.

Brady thought, *That's not a good answer. They'll see on the registration that she does have a home port.*

Maya returned and handed the registration and sticker over the side to the tall officer in the NRP whaler.

"Huh. It says here, ma'am, that the homeport for *Miss Gale* is Rock Hall, Maryland. This also says that she's a commercial charter boat. Are you the regular captain?"

"No. Smitty here is running her today since we're not on charter. The charter captain took the day off and we decided to just go out for a day of fun."

"Since you're the captain, Smitty, I'd like your permission to board her to check on your coast guard safety equipment."

"Sure," said Smitty. "Come onboard."

Jesus, thought Brady. *I hope to God they stored my empty tank and Maya's tank. I wonder if they still have the compressor out of sight? Shit. This could be it.*

Brady's thought trailed off as he reset his mouthpiece and dove under the boat to hide.

Up on top, the NRP officer asked Smitty to show him the fire extinguishers, flare guns, VHF, and life jackets—all of the coast guard's required equipment. Satisfied that the boat met all of the regulations, the officer asked, "How come you all come all the way down here from Rock Hall when the fishing's been so good up there?"

Smitty stuttered for a second, not knowing exactly how to respond.

Maya quickly interrupted, "Smitty's kind of shy about this, officer. He likes it down here because of the bars along the Narrows. See, Smitty's got an eye for the girls. He doesn't cheat, mind you. He only likes to look at them and dance. If his wife knew about it, though, she'd kill him."

Catching on, Smitty said, "Come on, Maya. You like those bars too. There are lots of guys with fancy boats and gold chains."

"OK, Smitty. I like them too. I guess choosing this spot is not all your fault."

The NRP officer chuckled. "I agree. Those bars do have a lively crowd, but so do the ones in Rock Hall, and I think the fishing's better up there."

Getting into it now, Smitty said, "Yeah, but that's in my own backyard and this ain't."

To cut short the officers inquisitiveness, Maya asked, "So, where are you stationed?"

"Right over there," said the tall officer. He pointed to the small DNR office just north of the boat ramp on the east side of the Narrows.

Knowing he'd seen the boat and both Smitty and Maya last week, Ken, the senior NRP officer who'd remained on the whaler watching the discourse between his partner and Maya, spoke up. "You remember me from last Friday evening when my partner, Marty, and I'd just gone off duty and saw you all fishing out here?"

"Was that you?"

"Yeah. It sure was."

"Sorry. I didn't recognize you. With that uniform on it makes things so different, and it was kind of dark that night." Bending down to look into the whaler, Maya said, "Now that I can see your face in the deck lights, you're right. You are the same guy. So, where's your partner?"

"Right behind you on your boat."

Caught off guard and feeling really stupid, Maya turned toward Marty and said, "Damn. You are the same two guys."

"Yeah. The same two guys."

Wanting to quickly gloss over her faux pas, Maya said, "If you guys weren't on duty, I'd hand you a fishing rod and a beer. You'd probably have better luck than we have."

"Thanks for the offer," said Ken, "but we've got another call to respond to up near Eastern Neck. You ready, Marty?"

"Yeah, as soon as I check out the extinguishers." Marty asked where they were and Smitty showed him the three extinguishers. One was on deck next to the engine box and two were in the cabin. As he walked Marty into the cabin area, Marty noticed the smell of gas. He asked Smitty where he thought it was coming from. Thinking a lot faster than he had a minute ago, Smitty responded, "The blower in the engine compartment hasn't been working. Each time before we start her, we have to pull up the engine cover and let fresh air clear out the fumes. Must be the diesel fumes you smell."

"No. I don't think so. It smells like gas to me."

"Well, the only thing we have onboard is diesel."

Knowing full well that he smelled gas but needing to get to their next call, Marty shrugged his shoulders and went back on deck.

"You all set, Marty?" Ken asked.

"Yeah. All of their equipment checks out."

"Good. Hop onboard and let's get going."

Calling out to Maya, Ken said, "Remember to affix that fishing stamp like I told you."

"Will do officer. I promise."

"Good."

"Oh, by the way, do you have a card on you?'

"Sure," Ken said, handing her his card.

Trying to cover their tracks for when they moved to the drawbridge, Maya asked, "What's it like fishing along the drawbridge pilings?"

"Not bad," said Ken. Actually, with the tide rippin' like it is, it should be pretty good."

"We may try there later. OK with you, Smitty?"

"OK by me."

Marty jumped back aboard the whaler and both men turned toward Smitty and Maya. As with the NRP officers she had encountered on the Speed Run off of Janes Island, Maya bent over to help push them off, making sure to use her arms to press her breasts together in a very seductive matter. The move was not lost on Ken and Marty. Both men smiled. Almost in unison, they said, "Take care."

"You too," said Maya, flashing her best smile and grabbing the canopy strut as though it were a dance pole. Maya just couldn't help herself; she was a real flirt. She took great pleasure in seeing men react to her.

As soon as the whaler was back up on plane and heading north into the Chester River, Marty told Ken about the gas smell. They both thought the *Miss Gale* was not what she was purported to be. They had no clue, though, about what she really was. They would file a report on her being suspicious, but their captain would probably dismiss it as an unfounded theory and nothing more.

Once the Whaler had cleared the Narrows, Maya cut the deck lights, turned the engine on, and began to pull in the fishing lines. A minute later, Brady broke the surface. With a hand from Smitty, he swung his legs overboard and climbed onto the deck. Jamil, who had kept himself scarce during the NRP conversations by staying back in the forward cabin, came out and grabbed Brady's tank. He then took it into the forward cabin and stowed it under the port bunk.

"What happened, Maya?" Brady asked.

"Two NRP officers came alongside - the same ones who were fishing the night Salah was with us. They asked lots of questions and were curious that we had come all the way down here when fishing up around Rock Hall has been so good. I convinced them that it was 'cause Smitty and I also like to visit the bars over there, pointing to the three bars and restaurants just off the bow. They boarded us to check out our coast guard requirements, then they re-boarded the whaler and moved off into the Chester River."

"Do you think they were satisfied with your explanations and with the boat?"

"Yeah, but I must say they sure were curious. I wouldn't doubt they shared their concerns with their superiors," said Maya. She then redirected the conversation by saying, "Brady, let's get you a new tank and move over to the drawbridge."

"OK."

Smitty set the *Miss Gale* into the wind, pulled up the anchor, and moved her some forty feet northeast. He drifted back so that they were directly opposite the drawbridge pilings. Then he yanked the line to set the anchor. Brady, in silence, put the new tank on his back, checked the regulator, gave them a thumbs-up, sat on the gunwale, held his mask to his face, and rolled over into the dark. He immediately resurfaced. Maya bent over the edge of the boat and handed Brady two steel rings that held the piton bags and several tubes of the fast-set Goop. As before, Brady felt weighted down but strong enough to carry these things to the pilings.

After forty-five minutes, Brady had completed placing and cementing the pitons. He began, however, to feel lightheaded and short of breath. He checked his regulator and realized that he had actually run out of air a minute and a half earlier. Brady tried to fight the complacency and urge to go to sleep that comes with a lack of oxygen. He knew what was happening to him, but he found himself helpless to take the appropriate action. The last thing he remembered was seeing an explosion of bubbles above him as Maya hit the water and dove down fifteen feet to retrieve him.

Listless and unconscious, Brady was of no help to Maya. She wrapped her arms under his and began to kick her flippers, propelling them both up toward the light. As she broke the surface, Smitty reached down and grabbed Brady's shoulders, lifting him up onto the deck. Smitty removed Brady's mask, regulator, and tank and began to apply CPR. Jamil helped Maya get onboard and then stowed the tanks and gear into the forward cabin.

For the next few minutes, Maya and Smitty alternatively performed chest compressions. Brady finally spit out a small amount of water, choked, and opened his eyes.

Catching his breath, Brady said, "What happened? Last thing I remember was seeing the regulator gage on empty."

"Well, that's exactly what happened," said Smitty. "If it hadn't been for Maya, you would have ended up as fish food."

Brady tried to sit up, but Maya grabbed Jamil's knapsack, put it under Brady's head, and pressed on his shoulders so that he couldn't rise. Jamil handed a small oxygen bottle to Maya. She hooked the tubing over his ears and inserted the cannula into Brady's nose.

"This will help, Brady. Just stay put and let the oxygen do its job. That was a close one, and it wasn't your fault. We should have been monitoring our watches. We should've realized that your air was running out."

Still groggy, Brady said, "Not your fault. It's my responsibility to monitor my own tank - not yours."

Smitty pulled anchor and navigated the boat back to Crab Alley Creek. On the way back, Brady started to recover. By the time they reached the dock, he seemed to have returned to normal. Maya helped Brady secure the *Miss Gale* to the Crab Alley Creek dock pilings. Smitty and Jamil cleaned up the boat. Both of them then hopped up onto the dock and headed back to the Hummer. Brady checked the engine oil and bilge. Then he locked up the cabin. He stepped up on the dock, gave Maya a quick hug, and said he'd see her the next day at Cooks Point.

"Are you OK to drive back?" she asked.

"Yeah. I still have a splitting headache, but with a little rest I'll be as good as new."

"OK, but call me if there's any change. Tomorrow's going to be a busy day of diving. Maybe we'll do the dive together, and Smitty and Jamil can handle the deck work."

"Well, let's wait 'til tomorrow to decide about that. I'll be fine by then."

"OK. Take care of yourself, Brady."

"You too," said Brady. He hopped into his truck and headed back home to take some medicine for his headache and try to get a late-afternoon nap.

Maya took Smitty and Jamil up to the Cox Neck Farm house and dropped them off with one of the security guards who would drive them back to the Chambers place. Maya went into the farmhouse to check in with the head security officer. Five minutes later, she emerged from the farmhouse, got back into her Hummer, and headed for Abad's security meeting at the staging and storage farm, just north of Cambridge.

Seven Hummers were hidden in the equipment shed behind the two combines and three six-wheeled John Deere tractors that were parked in the shed. Each Hummer had just enough room between it and the farm machinery in front of it to squeeze past and depart on short notice. The Hummers were covered with brown twenty-by-thirty-foot tarps so that they could not be seen from the air. Salah had made excellent preparations for this meeting. Every one of Abed's senior team was there, so security was extremely tight. Security guards were stationed at various places throughout the farm: at the dock, along the entrance road, around the barn housing the munitions cache, in the equipment shed, and surrounding the farmhouse. Each guard was so well concealed by local vegetation and grass that even Maya could not tell where they were located. As Maya approached the back door of the farmhouse, a security guard stepped out from behind the large Nandina bush that flanked the left side of the back door and completely surprised her. The second Maya saw him emerge from behind the bush with Nandina plant materials woven into his helmet and flak vest, she assumed a defensive karate position. She reached for the hammerless .38 Special revolver that was tucked in her belt behind her back. Just before crouching to aim at this man, she realized it was one of her own.

"Damn it, Miguel. You scared the shit out of me!"

"Sorry, Miss Maya. I didn't mean to."

"Well, you did a damn good job of it."

Taking in a deep breath and exhaling to gain some level of composure, Maya said, "Actually, your cover was excellent, Miguel. But next time, if it's your own team, announce yourself before you pop out, OK?"

"Yes, ma'am," he said, opening the door for Maya. Then he resumed his position behind the Nandina bush. Miguel was proud of himself. Maya hadn't noticed him, even though she had been only four feet away. Maybe it was good that he had scared her. If she told Salah about how well he had been hidden, this might help Salah evaluate him. After all, he had been told that he might be up for a promotion to the inner circle, which consisted of bodyguards who were charged with Abed's personal safety.

✳✳✳

The farmhouse dining room had been converted into a conference room. It was thirty feet by twenty-two feet, and it could host a seated meeting at the dining room table of some sixteen to twenty people, not including the ten to twelve people who could be seated along the walls. The windows had been covered with interior louvered shutters and heavy dark-fabric draperies hung over them. Lighting was provided by top hats set in the ten-foot-high ceiling and by two large ceiling-mounted fanlights that were centered over the table.

Small six-by-four-inch plain paper pads and pencils were arranged in front of each conference table seat, but none were placed on the ten sidewall chairs that were saved for Abed's security guards. Three ice-water pitchers and plastic glasses were evenly space along the conference table. Abed sat at the head of the table facing the kitchen and its large swinging service door. Salah was seated to Abed's right. Haamid, his personnel and logistics manager, was seated to his left. All of the other seats were occupied by Abed's communications director, Kaleem Kahn, along with Kaleem's communications team of three people; Abed's weapons expert, Omar Safi, and Omar's two weapons technicians; two helicopter pilots, Chief Pilot Bashir Aman, and First Officer, Haron

Khail, and the Pilot's crew chief, and Abed's demolitions expert, Raffi, and Raffi's assistant, Jamil.

Maya quickly took the one open seat left at the table. Haamid had saved it for her. Maya apologized for being late.

"Sorry, Abed. We just got back to the dock."

Focusing his dark and penetrating eyes on her, Abed said, "No excuses, Maya. This operation must and will be run by the second hand of the clock. Turning in his seat to individually address everyone in the room with direct eye contact, Abed said, "No one is to be early or late. You must be exactly on time for each task you are to perform. At our next meeting, each of you will be given a Navy SEAL watch that's accurate to the hundredth of a second. So, there are no excuses. An excuse means that you have failed. If you fail, the consequences will be permanent. Is that understood?"

In unison, all sixteen people at the table and the inner circle of security guards seated along the wall said, "Yes, sir."

"Now we'll get down to business. Salah, please explain the administrative procedures we will be following today."

Salah coughed, cleared his throat, and began to explain. "Those with note pads and pencils in front of them are the only ones allowed to make notes. Each person must initial any pages they write or scribble on. At the end of the meeting, you are all to hand these pages back to Haamid for safekeeping. None of you are allowed to take these notes with you. The notes are merely a means to an end. Write something down and you will be better prepared to remember the point you have noted. For security reasons, there is no written agenda. Either Abed or I will explain it all to you. At the end of the meeting, everyone except for the senior team will be excused. Those remaining will stay for an additional meeting. I expect this meeting to last about two hours. There will be no bathroom breaks or for that matter any other kind of break. So, if you need to use the bathroom, do it now before the meeting begins. Unless you have any questions, that's all." Salah then sat down.

Several people excused themselves to use the facilities. Salah gave them only eight minutes to return. Promptly at 3:30 p.m. everyone was seated.

Abed stood up, faced the east, lowered his head, and prayed for a moment. Everyone else followed his example and then all sat down.

Addressing his team, Abed said, "Allah has asked that we deliver a second major blow to the American infidels - infidels who this very day occupy our holy lands, defy the writings of the Koran, and plunder and pillage our villages and holy places across the globe. We are all Allah's tools to avenge America's grievous acts of war. We must, and we will, succeed on this American battlefield." Taking a long and deep breath for emphasis, he said, "Our objective is to disrupt and obliterate as many Maryland businesses and Chesapeake Bay icons as possible. Essentially, we are here to hit America in its pocketbook. In doing so, we will kill as many Americans as possible. And, we are here to do it on the very day that America celebrates its Independence - this coming Sunday, the Fourth of July."

Electricity filled the room. Spontaneously, everyone got to their feet, clapped in unison, and shouted, "Allah Akbar! Allah Akbar! Allah Akbar!"

Once the clapping had ended and everyone had taken their seat, Abed said, "While for security reasons the specific targets are known to very few people, believe me when I tell you that when destroyed, these targets will kill many, disrupting American's way of life in a very dramatic way. Our plan for destruction in Maryland will be the first in a new series of attacks on the American infidels. If they think the World Trade Center was frightening, wait until they see how truly vulnerable they are - not just here in Maryland, which is close to their capital, but all across their country."

During Abed's introduction and presentation of their objectives, everyone who already knew what was planned, including Haamid, Maya, and Salah, were mesmerized by Abed's passion and the power of his words. They had been selected to be part of the deep thrust of the Koran's sword into the belly of the beast, America. They would live to tell their children of the glory that they had achieved. If killed, they would be the martyrs of their Islamic faith. They viewed it both as an honor and a privilege to avenge the atrocities that America had committed on their brothers and sisters across the world, especially in Iran, Afghanistan, and Iraq.

Rising again, Abed said, "You are the chosen ones. You are the apostles of your faith, and you are the future of Islam. Allah has blessed you with this opportunity. Do not undertake your tasks lightly. In your hands rests Allah's desired to crush the people of this land. You must avenge all that has been done to you and your families. You are the light and the hope. Do not fail me! Do not fail Allah!" Salah stood up just as Abed sat down.

There was a moment of silence as Salah let the impact of Abed's words sink into the souls of those in the room. Then he began to share with his team the logistics and the specific tasks that everyone was to undertake over the following three days.

With assistance from his communications director, Salah spent the next hour and fifteen minutes walking everyone through the detailed timetable and the plans concerning radio and phone procedures. He started with the time period from Tuesday, July 29, through Thursday, July 1. Most of those at the table made copious notes. From time to time, they asked pertinent questions. At the end of his presentation, Salah asked if there were any other questions. Silence prevailed and then the chief helicopter pilot, Bashir, sat up straight in his chair and said, "When do we get our specific instructions for the fourth?"

Salah dismissively replied, "When I am ready to share them with you."

"Yes, sir," Bashir replied respectfully, sinking back into his seat.

Salah turned to Abed and signaled with a nod. Abed stood up, making eye contact with each and every person in the room again, and said, "We are to meet again here at this farm at 3:30 p.m. sharp on Thursday, July 1st. Until then, each of you knows your assignments." Raising his voice, Abed said, "Failure in your duties is not an option. Go with Allah!"

As the meeting broke up, Haamid retrieved each person's notes and stapled them together. He also removed the remaining top three sheets on each of the notepads to secure any pages that might have pencil impressions on them that could divulge the notes that were made on the previous pages. Nothing was left to chance. Within five minutes, all but Haamid, Maya, Raffi, Kaleem, Omar, Salah, Bashir, and Abed had left the farmhouse to execute their duties.

Abed suggested that everyone take a five-minute break. At precisely 4:50 p.m. He then called the second meeting to order and began to discuss the agenda.

"Before we get to specific individual tasks and some security issues, I want to remind all of you of the macro view. You are here as instruments of Allah. You are here to wreak havoc on this state's businesses, transportation system, and energy supplies. Fear in America is our prime objective. We will this week instill fear on the Eastern Shore of Maryland where, in close proximity to the US Capital, no American citizen is beyond our reach. As always, the other target is to kill as many Americans as possible. By demonstrating how truly vulnerable all Americans are no matter where they live, we will strike fear into our enemies everyday lives, and we will weaken their political will. As you know, this is the first of many post-9/11 strikes that we will launch over the next few years. Because of your expertise and devotion to Islam, you have been handpicked to avenge the infidels' invasion of our homelands and their war upon Islam. You are holy warriors of Jihad. You must not fail!"

Abed cleared his throat and sipped from his glass of water before he continued. "As we all know, over the past few days there has been increased radio traffic between the Natural Resource Police and Homeland Security. While it may be typical for such an increase to occur prior to a major holiday, such as the Fourth of July, there are some aspects of this increased activity that may be directly related to us. Kaleem will fill you in on what he has uncovered, and he will offer some thoughts on how to minimize the problem. Kaleem."

Kaleem rose, sipped from his glass of water, and said, "As Abed noted, there has been a substantial increase in radio traffic concerning the activities of certain boats at the Kent Narrows Bridge and just off of Janes Island. NRP has reported sightings of a suspicious Bay-built boat at the Narrows during evening hours and one sighting of a Bay-built boat running speed trials just west of Janes Island. These boats are ours. While the radio transmissions do not indicate any illegal activity, they do refer to suspicious claims of fishing at night and to suspicious claims of testing of boat speeds. These communications have emphasized the need for NRP, Homeland Security, and the coast guard to keep their eyes out for our boats. We will need to put one of the two Hoopers' Island nameplates on the smaller boat and replace the plaque on the *Miss Gale* with the one marked the *Miss Martha* out of Stevensville. Jamil, you will be responsible for this. It must be done by tonight."

"Yes, sir," said Jamil. "But which plaque do you want on the smaller boat?"

"Put the plaque marked the *Lucy May* on first. We will change it to the *Miss Catherine James* later," said Abed. "Before you leave, I will give you the two smaller boat plaques. Be sure you store the *Miss Catherine James* plaque under the front portside bunk."

"Yes, sir."

"We will only have three more boat trips before we detonate. The first one will be to plant the pitons and clips at the Gas Docks. The second to plant the charges at the Gas Docks. The third trip will be to the Kent Narrows Bridges, where the pitons are set. The run up there will be to place the charges. After we set the charges, you will need to change the *Miss Gale* plaque to the *Miss Martha* plaque. Is that understood, Jamil?"

"Yes, sir."

"Good."

"Obviously, the key is for the boats to remain hidden at our home docks. To help camouflage both boats, Maya has two used crab-pot canvas stern bumpers that will cover the boat's names when it is docked. Jamil, see Maya after the meeting. She will give you the covers and a bunch of used crab pots to put on the canopy of each boat so that from the air they will look like they're rigged properly."

Abed took a deep breath and placed his hands on the table before him. He said, "Now, let me address a very serious issue. A team member, Carlos, who was sharing confidential information with a friend, is no longer on our team. Both Carlos and his friend have been dealt with, permanently. We also feel that there may be an additional traitor among us who is leaking information to the Natural Resource Police. The radio communications we are monitoring indicate that they know more than they should. While to date we don't believe that this information has been detrimental, we know that whoever is communicating with the NRP will in time start to tell them more information, ultimately endangering our mission. We do not know who the perpetrator is. Therefore, I have ordered Salah to undertake a housecleaning of all of the team members under your command who seem suspicious. To facilitate this cleansing, please take your notepad and write down the names of those people you feel might be possible traitors. Fold the paper and hand them to me. You have three minutes to write down the names. As you think about this, make sure you include both Islamic and non-Islamic personnel. No one is immune."

While several of the senior team members immediately wrote down a name or two and handed their notes in, several people carefully contemplated who on their team might be a possible leak. Haamid took the full three minutes, and he was the last one to turn in his piece of paper.

"Please tear off the next three sheets of paper from your pad and hand them to me."

As those around the table handed Abed their extra sheets of paper, he stood up and said, "There will be a security and planning meeting involving all of you at 6:30 p.m. tonight at the Chambers place. Be on time. This meeting is adjourned."

Within five minutes, everyone was gone.

Chapter 15

The Axe Falls. Monday, June 28 at 6:30 p.m.

At exactly 6:30 p.m. everyone was gathered around the kitchen table at the Chambers place. Abed distributed a sheet of paper containing the list of names that the senior team members had written down at the earlier meeting. There were only three names on the sheet. To the left of each name was the name of the person who had written the potential traitor's name.

Smitty's name appeared at the top of the list. All but one person had identified him as the number-one suspect.

The second person named was Mohammed Ahady, the bandolier packer who had worked next to Jamil placing explosives in the crab baskets at the weapons-cache barn. He had three votes out of the five.

The third person was Brady. His only vote had come from Kaleem Kahn, Abed's communications director.

Abed addressed Smitty first, "So, tell me why most of you think Smitty is the most likely candidate."

Kaleem immediately spoke up. "Smitty was very close to Carlos. They were friends and Smitty has local connections that would make him accessible to the NRP. Also, he is not of the Muslim faith."

Maya, Omar, and Raffi concurred with Kaleem's assessment, saying that they thought that he was the most likely of all of the team members to be a traitor. Haamid, however, said, "I disagree. Smitty was vetted very carefully. Don't forget, we wanted him on the team just because he was a local and had contacts on the shore. There is nothing in his past that indicates any interest in politics or current events, including the war in Afghanistan. Our background check revealed nothing that would lead us to believe that he was anything other than a hard worker whose only motivation was his paycheck."

Abed said, "OK, let's move onto your second choice: Mohammed Ahady. Omar, Maya, and Raffi, you chose Mohammed. Why?"

Omar spoke up. "Jamil has expressed real concern to me about Mohammed. We all thought that Mohammed didn't speak English, yet Jamil says he heard him speaking fluent English on his cell phone several times over the past two weeks."

Furious, Salah yelled, "What do you mean he spoke fluent English in the past two weeks? Why wasn't I told about this immediately?"

Omar flinched and said, "Well, I thought it was strange but I just didn't think it was important enough to report."

Still yelling, Salah said, "You didn't think it was important enough? You idiot. Everything is important!"

"I apologize, Salah. Please forgive me."

"No! I cannot! I will not forgive any security breach!"

Having been cowed into silence, Omar sat back in his chair and withdrew to a dark and fearful place. He knew retribution was just around the corner.

Salah sat down mumbling, "Stupid. Just plain stupid."

Abed slammed his fist on the kitchen table so hard that each person felt the reverberation. "This is not a game. This is life or death. This is success or failure. No one is to judge whether an event is important or not. Only I will determine that. You must, and you will, report any occurrence up the chain of command so that within a matter of minutes I'm aware of it. If there is another breach of this or any other rule, the persons responsible will be dealt with in the same manner as Carlos was. Is that understood?"

As if in one voice, everyone said, "Yes, sir."

Pausing to let Abed's words sink in, Salah said, "Now, Kaleem, what about Brady. You brought him up as a possible threat."

Kaleem stood up and addressed Salah, "Yes, sir. I'm worried about Brady. While we have yet to meet, I know he has been a hard worker and he has executed his tasks with competency and professionalism. But, I'm still concerned with his uncle's relationship with the Maryland DNR, especially the Natural Resource Police. Brady and his uncle, according to Maya, are very close. He's not a Muslim and lest we forget, he fought against our Islamic brothers in Afghanistan."

There was silence. As Haamid stood, all eyes focused on him. Haamid took a defensive posture and said, "As with everyone on the team, I vetted Brady thoroughly through his Islamic connections in Baltimore and through personal interviews. I believe that Salah will testify to this man's disdain for the American military and their poor treatment of both himself and the families of his friends who were killed in Iraq and Afghanistan. Brady has not exhibited any of the characteristics of a traitor. Sure, we should keep an eye on him, but we should do that with all of our team members.

No one responded.

Then Salah said, "Unless there are specifics that reflect a lack of commitment or treasonous actions, I agree with Haamid that Brady has given us no cause to worry. However, as Haamid noted, we should be aware of any actions or words that would give us cause for concern about Brady. Anyone else have a comment on Brady?"

Again, no one responded.

Abed rose from his chair and said, "Well then, I submit that Mohamed Ahardy and Smitty are too great of a risk, but Brady stays with us for now. We must be very vigilant of both Brady's actions and his words. Any further comment?"

"Abed, I agree with your assessment," said Salah, "but I'm also concerned that when Smitty vanishes like Carlos did, Brady will figure that he might be next."

"I understand, Salah, but right now we have no other choice. We need Brady to set the charges. We can take care of him once we don't need him anymore."

***

While loyal to Jihad and her Islamic faith, Maya flinched at the thought of Brady's death. She had developed such strong feelings for him, even though lately he seemed to have been distancing himself from her. At the beginning, she was sure that he cared for her as much as she did for him. She had entertained hopes for a possible long-term relationship, but now she watched those hopes begin to fade. With this discussion, it was clear that there would never be a long-term relationship. This meeting had dashed all of her hopes. She fell silent and felt the cloud of depression that overcomes people who know they are soon to lose someone they love.

"So, are we all agreed that Mohamed and Smitty go and Brady stays for now?"

Maya raised her hand along with everyone else and said, "Yes, sir."

"So be it," said Salah. "This meeting is over. We will meet again later this week. I will contact you on the date, the time, and the place."

As everybody was leaving, Abed pulled Salah aside and said, "How do you plan on disposing of Mohammed and Smitty?"

"The same way we disposed of Carlos," said Salah. "Unless you have a different idea."

"No," said Abed. "The same way's fine with me."

"Then - It is done."

✳✳✳

While Abed was talking to Salah, Brady was sitting up in bed reading more of the book called *The Soldier*.

He had not picked it up recently, since it brought back memories of friends he had lost in battle. However, it was not a book that was easy to put down or forget. Brady sipped from the glass of ice water that he kept on his bedside table. As he read about a firefight in the book, his mind drifted off to that horrible afternoon when the RPG round had exploded into the concrete wall that he and his fire team had been hiding behind. They had been popping up periodically to trade shots with the insurgents who were sheltered in the house directly across the alley. Then, a shell had hit the wall about ten feet away from their position.

Brady shivered as he recalled the exact moment when his friend Rick, the SEAL sniper attached to his marine unit, let out a muffled cry as shrapnel blew out the left side of his skull. His body slumped and his head came to rest on Brady's shoulder. Blood and brains were splattered across Brady's front. Brady remembered first calling to Rick, but there was no answer. Then he saw the devastation to Rick's head, and he immediately realized that Rick was gone. Easing Rick off of his shoulder and laying him on the ground next to him, anger and instinct propelled Brady to stand up and start firing across the alley as if he were possessed by demons. He did this in an attempt to kill the men who had just ravaged his friend. Brady fired wildly, not hitting anyone. He dropped down behind the wall and took a deep breath as he remembered his training. He had to make every bullet count.

When he popped up again, he spotted the guy with the RPG taking aim again at the wall to the left of him. He drew a bead on the center of this guy's mass, which was his chest. Brady squeezed off his round with precision and determination. The insurgent died before the RPG round ever left its tube.

154

Because he'd taken his time to aim and squeezed the trigger with great delibera-tion, Brady had stayed upright for a second too long. Brady heard the crack of a sniper's rifle. He even thought that he saw the puff of smoke at the window on the second floor of the building in front of him. Then everything went blank.

Brady's next recollection was of the white walls of the regional field hospital two days later, as he awoke from a medically induced coma. The surgery had gone well, but Brady had tossed and turned so much that for his own well-being, the doctors had kept him heavily sedated. They did this to keep him from tearing out his IVs and from doing harm to his neck, which was in a brace attached to the side of the bed's headrest.

As it turned out, Brady had received more than a bullet in his neck. Unbeknownst to him at the time, two pieces of the RPG shrapnel had entered his shoulder prior to the bullet hitting him. As often happens in war, soldiers receive wounds that are serious, but because of the adrenaline rush and the heat of the battle, sometimes they don't even know that they have been injured until minutes or hours later. In Brady's case, he awoke in the intensive care hospital bed two days after the sniper's bullet had torn through his neck and rendered him unconscious.

Still shivering from this flashback, Brady put the book down, got out of bed, and went to the bathroom for two pills of Excedrin PM. Hopefully they would help him get some sleep. He thought, *Perhaps tomorrow will be a better day.*

Chapter 16

The Day Run to the Gas Docks. Tuesday, June 29

At 5:30 a.m. sharp, Brady rolled out of bed, showered, dressed, and went down to the kitchen. There, he poured himself a glass of juice and dumped milk into a large bowl of cereal. Today he would be meeting with Maya, Smitty, and Jamil at the Chambers place to go up to the Gas Docks to place the pitons on the shelf of the most northerly pilings they had been contracted to demolish.

When Brady drove up to the Chamber's dock, he didn't realize that he was the last to arrive. As he parked his truck, he saw Maya standing next to one of Abed's Hummers and talking to a security guard who was looking at a map spread out on the hood of the vehicle.

Brady waved to Maya as he approached the Hummer. She didn't see his greeting, so she continued to focus on the map. Just before he came up to the vehicle, she folded up the map, told the security guard to get in, and turned to greet Brady. She was all business today.

"Let's get going," she said. "We're running a little late."

Opening the backdoor, Brady saw Jamil and Raffi but did not see Smitty. *Strange*, he thought. "Maya, where's Smitty?"

"He's been deployed to another job."

"What do you mean he's been deployed to another job?" asked Brady.

"I mean just that," said Maya. "He's gone to another job. He won't be working on this one anymore."

"Wasn't that kind of sudden?"

Maya didn't answer.

Brady stepped into the Hummer and said good morning to both Jamil and Raffi. As he shut the door, he leaned over the back of Maya's front seat and said, "Wasn't that short notice? No one told me."

"Brady, Salah organized it. You don't need to know everything, do you?"

"No. I guess not," said Brady, sitting back against his seat. *Man is she bitchy. I wonder what the real story is on Smitty? He seemed great yesterday. I know he would have told me if he were moving to another job - if he had known it himself*, Brady thought. *I don't like this at all. First Carlos and now Smitty. Wonder what the real answers are -Where are they and what are they doing? Something's wrong with this picture - very wrong*, pondered Brady.

On the way to the dock that housed the smaller boat they would use for the Gas Dock job, Raffi - not Maya - laid out the day's schedule and tasks. They would go to the Gas Docks to inspect the pilings, place the pitons, and set waypoints. Raffi handed Brady a copy of the map and began to explain to him where they were heading. Evidentially, the homeport for the smaller and faster Bay-built boat was a dock on a small farm just south of the Chambers place that had a rundown two-story cottage on it.

The farm was located between Wroten Island and Asquith on Parks Neck. It was just inside of Buoy R-6. The water was about seven feet deep there. According to Raffi, the boat had a three-foot draft, and because of this it would not be affected in case a low-tide departure was required.

To Brady, this safe-house seemed to have been strategically located in the middle of the Honga River for double access to the Chesapeake Bay and the Western Shore. One could either go under the Upper Hopper's Island Bridge at Tar Bay or around Lower Hooper's Island at the head of Hopper's Strait. Brady thought its location had been precisely calculated. Being midway between these locations, they would have access to the Bay from both the north and south if a storm came or the authorities pursued them.

In keeping with the strategy to reduce successful aerial surveillance, Abed had decided to locate both the workboats within easy reach of their targets so that they could escape quickly. The three cigarette boats were, however, all moored in a large boathouse at the Choptank River Farm. They were out of site and hopefully out of mind. Later on, two of them would be moved to Parks Neck to begin their final escape to Virginia.

When they arrived at the dock, Brady surveyed the boat as thoroughly as he had surveyed the *Miss Gale*. Again, he found what he believed to be a diving locker. Meanwhile, Raffi and Maya went to the farmhouse. Jamil stayed on the dock as security. Except for the large engine and some rubberized steel plates mounted on the deck at the stern, Brady found the two boats almost identical in terms of navigation aids, the communication equipment, and the onboard diving equipment. He also discovered that the stern bolts for the boat's plaque had already been installed. The plaque itself showed the boat to be the *Miss Lucy May*. Its homeport was Chesapeake Beach on the Western Shore.

During his walk-through of the boat, in the storage locker under the portside birth, he also found a second boat plaque. This one had the name *Miss Katherine James* on it and she was out of Deal Island, Maryland.

Everything seemed to be a duplicate of the *Miss Gale.*

After watching Raffi, who was both a demolition's and dive expert, it seemed to Brady that he was clearly one of Salah's top men. Maya also seemed to hold him in high esteem.

As they left the dock, heading out along the southern route via the Hooper Straight, Raffi sat behind Brady, as Salah had done, tracking the GPS course and monitoring the radio channels for the NRP, the coast guard, and Homeland Security. Before they arrived at the Gas Docks, they anchored outside of the restricted area and checked out the dive equipment. The dive equipment was found to be in perfect order. They then pulled anchor. Using the GPS, they re-anchored right at the edge of the five-hundred-yard restricted zone.

Raffi and Brady climbed into their wetsuits and checked out their tanks and regulators. Rolling off the port side, the two men began their journey to the pilings. Because of the substantial distance from the edge of the restricted area to the northeast pilings, it was a long and tiring swim. The weight of the pitons, clips, and Marine Goop caused them to move slowly. Since the trip would expose them to potential detection by those on the docks and the surveillance cameras on shore, they decided that they would have to perform all of their tasks beneath the surface of the water. This would include attaching the pitons, analyzing the current flows in and around the pilings, and determining the exact coordinates of the pilings themselves. As the dive was taking place, Maya and Jamil began to live-line for rockfish using spot that Jamil had brought from the Park's Neck Farm.

After putting the pitons and snaps on the pilings and noting the coordinates on their dive watches, the two men returned to the boat. Both of the men stepped out of their wet suits and replaced them with their fishing clothes. As Brady restarted the engine, Raffi directed him to move slowly northwest about two hundred yards. Raffi then took over the mid-station helm and maneuvered the boat to a place where they had an excellent view of both the dockmaster's office on the north end of the Gas Docks and the gas storage tanks that were a quarter of a mile inland. At that moment, Raffi pushed the MOB, or man-overboard, button. This permanently marked the spot and its coordinates on the GPS map. Satisfied that he had found the perfect spot, he turned the helm back over to Brady and told him to return to the Parks Neck Farm.

When they tied up at Parks Neck, Brady did his usual walk-through of the boat, making sure that everything was in good shape. He made sure that the electronics were off, the oil levels were right, and the dive tanks were recharged.

Maya had been pretty much silent since early morning. She opened the fish box. She and Jamil took out the three rockfish that they'd caught and transferred them to a large cooler, which the two guards hauled up onto land and placed in the Hummer.

Brady locked up the cabin and walk up to the Hummer. He took his earlier seat next to Jamil in the back. Over the next forty-five minutes, on the way back to the Chamber's place, no one said a word. Brady and Maya were still at odds over Brady's questions about Smitty, while each of the other three seemed to be in a stupor, staring out the windows to avoid any eye contact.

At 2:30 p.m. they arrived back at the Chamber's place.

Brady slid out of the backseat and said good-bye to Jamil and Raffi. As Maya got out of the Hummer, she pulled Brady to one side and told him that they were to meet with Salah the next day at 6:30 p.m. for a night run out to the Gas Docks.

Brady asked, "Why do we need a night run? We have set the pins and gotten all of the coordinates on the GPS?"

"Salah and Abed want to see what a night run to the docks is like. They are anal about being sure the job is done well."

"OK, but it seems a waste of time to me."

"It might be, Brady, but Abed's the boss. If he wants it, we do it."

"No shit."

"Now that's a poor attitude, Brady."

"Maybe," he replied. "But it's the truth."

Maya turned to go into the farmhouse with Raffi. "See you here tomorrow, Brady."

"See you tomorrow," replied Brady.

He got into his truck but before turning the key, Brady looked through his rearview mirror as Maya put her arm around Raffi and the two entered the farmhouse alone. Pressing his hands against the steering wheel and his back against his seat, Brady mumbled to himself, "You bitch!" Maya had started to take a haughty attitude toward him and treat him as though he were a disposable plaything, and now she seemed to have her eye on Raffi. Brady thought to himself, *The hell with her. It wasn't going to work out anyway. She had too much baggage. She lives in a different world - a world I no longer want to be a part of.* Brady turned the key, shook his head in disgust, and drove home.

On his way back to the house, he stopped at the diner in Cambridge and grabbed a meatloaf sandwich. Once home, he went directly to bed. He was relieved that his aunt and uncle were over at the fire hall helping out with the festivities for the Fourth of July. Thankfully, he was able to avoid any questions about his day. He just wasn't up to it.

✳✳✳

While Brady was driving home, Abed, Salah, Raffi, and Maya were meeting at the Chambers place. Salah had arrived there at about 2:00 p.m. to monitor Bay traffic and ship arrivals. Checking on freighter and tanker arrivals on the Internet, Abed confirmed that the *Mana Kia*, a Panamax container ship out of Argentina, would arrive at the Annapolis Anchorage on Saturday, July 3, 2010. Its timing had been part of the overall plan. He also learned that on July 3, 2010 an LNG tanker would be arriving at the Gas Docks to offload its cargo on Monday, July 5, 2010.

For security reasons, the coast guard normally did not post the arrival times of LNG tankers more than six hours ahead of their actual estimated times of arrival, but they had done so this time because of the need to be sure that adequate stevedores and other personnel were available over the Fourth of July weekend.

Another reason for posting her arrival was that the *Mana Kia* was to be the first Panamax Super Cargo Carrier to arrive at the new super-tanker terminal, and the mayor of Baltimore and the governor of Maryland were both set to make a big deal out of her arrival.

Abed and Salah believed that this LNG ship was a blessing that Allah had bestowed upon them. "Imagine the ferocity of this attack, Salah, when we blow up that tanker, along with the Gas Docks. It will be an even greater day than we had ever hoped for," said Abed.

As they uncovered further details, they realized that the *Mana Kia* would only be at the Annapolis Anchorage from Saturday afternoon until Sunday. She was scheduled to move to Baltimore and unload on the morning of Monday, July 5, 2010. The new super-cargo terminal where it would unload was the only Baltimore dock capable of handling the new Panamax Super Ships.

Only five more days, thought Abed. *Only five more days*.

Chapter 17
A Frightening Night Run To the Gas Docks.
Wednesday, June 30

The alarm went off at 6:30 a.m. Brady fumbled with the snooze button until he hit it square on, interrupting a Toby Keith song. Eight minutes later, the same thing happened. This time, Brady turned the alarm off returning his room to silence.

Two minutes later, he rose, showered, dressed, and went downstairs for a late breakfast with his Aunt Louise.

"Good morning, Brady," Louise greeted him in her normal cheery manner.

"Morning, Aunt Louise. Sorry I am a little late."

"Not to worry. I have your breakfast warming in the oven. Hopefully it'll be as good as Pete said it was."

"When was that?"

"About an hour ago."

"Where is he?"

"He's down on the *Miss Alice*, cleaning up for the weekend charter."

"It's a little early for that, isn't it?"

"Not for Pete. He's been polishing that boat seven days a week."

"Yeah, I know. I'll go down and help him when I'm finished. Wow, this is a great breakfast: eggs, biscuits, pork roll, and scrapple. You outdid yourself, Aunt Louise."

"Nothing's too good for my Brady."

"Thanks," he said. "But you and Captain Pete are too good to me. I'm one lucky guy."

"Oh, stuff," said Louise. "Listen, I have got to be off to the fire hall. Clean up, if you would, and I'll see you at lunch."

"Will do and thanks again," said Brady.

Aunt Louise eased back the porch door to avoid causing it to bang loudly. She had hoped, for way too long, that the men would get the clue to close the door like she did, but so far she had had no luck. Gently closing the door, she walked off to the fire hall with a to-do list that was nearly a mile long.

Brady cleaned up the dishes and left for the dock. "Morning, Uncle Pete."

"Hey, Brady. How are you?"

"I thought I'd come and help, since I don't need to be in Cambridge 'til six-thirty tonight."

"Thanks. I sure could use some help."

"Well, you've got it," said Brady, stepping off the dock and onto the *Miss Alice*.

After Brady washed down the *Miss Alice*, he started to work on all of the reels, checking the clamps that fastened them to the rods, lubricating the reels, and setting the drags. As he finished the last one, Pete called him into the cabin and handed him a cup of newly brewed coffee.

"Let's sit at the table, Brady. I'd like to get an update on the latest happenings with your job."

"Sure, Uncle Pete. Not much has changed, though. Let's see, we have now set all of the pitons at the Narrows and the Gas Docks. I don't know what the next move will be, but we are going to do a run to the Gas Docs tonight."

"Why?" asked Pete.

"I'm not sure, Uncle Pete. All I know is that the boss wants to do it, so I'll be doing that at six-thirty tonight. The only thing new that has come up is that Smitty, who I trust both as a person and as a professional dive expert, has been pulled off the job. Now both he and Carlos are gone and they won't say where. This troubles me."

"I thought Carlos was recuperating in a Baltimore hospital?"

"He has been, according to Maya. But now Smitty's also no longer on the job. When I asked where he was, they just said that he'd gone to another job site and he won't be returning. These two guys who were on my surface crew - two important dive safety experts - are now both gone."

"Do you have replacements?"

"Yes. Maya and a fellow named Raffi, who seems to be pretty high up in the chain-of- command."

"Are they any good?"

"Yes, both of them are more than qualified."

"Except for setting the explosives, all of the diving is complete. Doesn't it seem strange to you that these guys have vanished at this point in time?"

"Yeah. It seems strange. If you put yourself in Abed's shoes, though, it makes a lot of sense to relocate them to another job or get rid of them now that they are no longer needed. If it were me, I surely would dispose of them."

"Maybe. So, what else is going on?"

"I don't know much more, Uncle Pete. Everyone seems to be a little jumpier than they were a week ago. The atmosphere is much more electrified and tempers are running short."

Pete and Brady then went back to cleaning up the *Miss Alice*. Around 12:00 p.m. they returned to the house for lunch. After lunch, Brady told his aunt and uncle that he was going to take a nap, since he knew he'd be up late. Pete and Louise left the house around 1:30 p.m. to join the other watermen at the fire hall to prepare for the Fourth of July celebration on Sunday.

Brady lay in bed with his alarm set for 4:30 p.m. This would give him enough time to dress and be down at Cook's Point no later than 6:30 p.m.

✳✳✳

At 11:00 a.m. Jamil prepared the *Miss Martha* for departure. The plan was for Abed to captain the boat up to the Crab Alley Creek dock so that they could pick up some of the explosives that had been stored there - just the ones for the Gas Docks. Once the explosives had been loaded onto the boat, they would go back to the Chamber's place to await Brady's arrival.

The trip up was uneventful, as Abed, with Raffi standing by, maneuvered the *Miss Martha* along the GPS course to Crab Alley. Off of Poplar Island, Raffi helped guide Abed around the seine nets and crab pots by showing him the dotted course that Brady had taken to avoid them when he'd gone up to Kent Narrows earlier.

Everyone was surprised that Abed handled the boat as well as he did. However, when they got near Parsons Island, the tide was running fast. At the farm dock, Abed could not bring the boat in. His skills at docking and his experience with fast-moving tides were minimal. Finally, after three attempts, Abed turned to Raffi and said, "You take over and dock her."

"Yes, sir,' said Raffi. Taking the mid-station helm, he brought her in smoothly and barely kissed the dock. Jamil hopped up to secure the lines. Raffi shut down the boat. Jamil was told to stay put, as Abed, Salah, Kaleem, and Raffi met a security guard in a Hummer at the end of the dock.

After climbing in, not a word was spoken. They drove up to the tractor shed, where the crab baskets, which were full of the bandolier explosives, were hidden. The tops of the baskets were secured with zip ties. They loaded them into the back of the Hummer and onto a small ten-foot trailer that they had attached. After securing the trailer, they climbed back into the Hummer and headed for the dock. As they pulled up to the dock, Abed asked the security guard to get out. He and the other three remained in the vehicle. Abed turned to face the three men sitting in the back and said, "I think it best to keep Brady beyond tonight. I don't feel comfortable maneuvering in the Narrows when we set those charges on Friday, July 2, 2010. The tide will be running hard and rain is forecast to be heavy at times. Steady winds should be coming from the northeast."

There was silence.

Then Salah said, "I think that's a smart idea, boss. Besides, you will want to be free to listen to the radios and make instant command decisions without managing the boat at the same time."

"Well then, we agree that we will keep Brady on until the charges are placed at the Narrows. Salah, this means that you and I need to talk about exactly how to accomplish this. The surveillance of Brady will be paramount. Let's meet tomorrow to decide exactly how to handle it."

"Yes, sir," said Salah.

Abed opened the door. They all grabbed the bandolier baskets and carried them down to the boat.

Once everyone was onboard and the crab baskets had been stowed in the forward cabin, Abed, feeling secure with Raffi standing beside him, took the *Miss Martha* out of the creek and headed straight for the Chambers place.

Fog had settled in since they had docked at Crab Alley Creek. The clouds that were to produce heavy rains the next day had moved up the Bay. The overcast was complete. Even though it was only midafternoon, it felt and looked like early evening.

The boat had no running lights. A hood covered the glare of the GPS screen. Except for the phosphorescent wake, the *Miss Martha* was not visible to the naked eye. She was, however, visible on the large surveillance screen at the Baltimore Harbor shipping company, which Homeland Security relied on to monitor Bay traffic. Because she was such a small and insignificant blip on the screen, though, no one paid attention to her.

Though it was slow because of the fog and overcast skies, the run back to the Chambers dock had been smooth. On their run south, Kaleem had used the VHF with the new AIS system, which Brady had recommended, to monitor the larger ships that were either anchored off of Annapolis or plying the Bay toward Baltimore or Norfolk. Three ships that were awaiting Baltimore dockage were at anchor off of Annapolis. Only two other large ships were in the middle to upper Bay area. With only a twenty to thirty mile reach, the AIS Class-B VHF radio did not allow them to capture the signals from the numerous AIS-equipped vessels in the Hampton Roads Area. To plan for the assault on the Gas Docks and the arrival of the LNG tanker on Saturday, they had to be especially vigilant of the AIS screen, as well as the coast guard and Homeland security radios. If this significant yet diversionary attack was not perfectly timed, the major attack might be foiled. Thus, the expertise of Kaleem and his two communication technicians was crucial to the plot's success.

Raffi took over the helm from Abed as they entered Cooks Point Cove. With the same skill, they docked there without a hitch. It was now 5:30 p.m.

✳✳✳

Brady arrived at the Chamber's place at 6 p.m. He wanted to be sure that he wasn't late. At the very least, he did not want to be the last person to arrive, as he had been earlier that morning. Brady noticed that the lights were on in the manor house. One of the guards directed him to go directly to the back kitchen door. At the door, a second guard told him to wait outside while he announced Brady's arrival to Abed. The guard entered the kitchen. A minute later, he came out to escort Brady inside.

Abed, Salah, Jamil, Raffi, and a new person were seated at the kitchen table, poring over a map of the area around the Honga River. Abed stood up and introduced Brady to the new man, Kaleem, who was his director of communications. Brady was impressed by the man's stature. He was well over six-foot-three, and his eyes were steel blue. When they shook hands, however, Kaleem's grasp was like milk toast. It was certainly at odds with his bearing. *Strange,* thought Brady.

Abed then announced that they would be setting the Gas Dock charges that evening. Brady tensed up, as acid reflux crept up the back of his throat. He coughed and everyone turned to look at him.

Damn. I didn't hide that very well, he thought.

"Are you OK, Brady?" asked Salah.

"Yes. I've just been trying to survive the spicy crab sandwich I had for lunch. Seems to have gotten the better of me."

"Good. I'm glad that's all it is. All of us must be at our best tonight," said Salah.

"I will be," said Brady.

When the briefing was over, Abed asked, "Any questions?" No one responded.

"In that case, let's go," said Salah.

✳✳✳

At 6:30 p.m. everyone piled into the two waiting Hummers. Its engines were running and security guards were in the front seats. In addition to the two Hummers, the caravan contained a third refrigerated seafood truck that was carrying the crab baskets of explosives, which had been transferred from the *Miss Martha*. The side of the truck said, "Miller Seafood."

✳✳✳

At 7:30 p.m. sharp, Abed, Salah, Raffi, and Brady shoved off from the Parks Neck dock with twenty bandolier crab baskets aboard. In accordance with Abed's plan, Brady was to steer a course north, using the route through Tar Bay to get to the Gas Docks. Abed wanted to have a northern GPS course placed on the map that was similar to the earlier southern course they had taken to reach the Gas Docks when they had placed the pitons. This would give him two recorded escape routes if he or someone else had to captain the boat later on.

The sky was overcast and there was a light, steady rain. The wind was coming from the northeast at five to ten knots. It was perfect weather for them to set the explosives. The rain and the dark skies above hid them. Raffi sat behind Brady as they cut north to the bridge at Upper Hooper's Island.

Abed, Salah, and Kaleem went below deck into the front sleeping cabin and closed the door. Kaleem began to share with Abed and Salah the reports that he was hearing over the NRP and Homeland Security channels. Kaleem explained that in the last two hours, NRP's secure radio channel had been full of calls back and forth with Homeland Security about the sighting of a Bay-built dead rise with lots of antennas and no bottom paint on her. It seemed that the boat had been spotted in the Eastern Bay / Kent Island Area. Evidently, an unreliable drunk from one of the Narrows restaurants had said something about this to the security guard at an outdoor bar. The security guard was an NRP policeman who had been moonlighting to help pay for his son's medical bills, which had resulted from a motorcycle accident. The day the fellow recalled the incident was the same day that Brady was checking out the Narrows bridges. More disturbingly, two NRP police had confirmed the existence of that very boat at Kent Narrows that same evening. They claimed that the boat had been used for fishing at the bridge pilings. It too had no name. It too had a questionable port of call and a crewmember who spoke little English.

Abed and Salah were concerned about this discovery, but they were not surprised. They were both very familiar with these two incidents. They had hoped that these incidents would fade away before long, yet it seemed that this wouldn't be the case. So, they must now focus their attention on the radios. This meant that they were to monitor the radios in their cars, in their trucks, on the water, and in their safe house, twenty-four-seven.

In a serious tone, Abed said, "Before we arrive at the Gas Docks, I want to review the work that we must accomplish over the next two days. Since Kaleem's monitoring of the radios has revealed these two incidents, as well as conversations about two un-named dead rise boats that have been seen on the Bay with crew who were not native waterman, we must proceed with all caution. If our boats are boarded again, it may be the end of our mission. While it's true that they aren't sure about who we are or what we're doing, it's clear that we have raised some suspicions about our motives. So, I want everyone to be on high alert. With only four days left, I don't want any problems that might cause a change in our plans. Any questions?" No one responded. "OK then. Let's go outside and get this job done."

The *Miss Catherine James,* previously known as the *Lucy May*, reached the 500-yard security ring around the Gas Docks, slowed down, and began to move toward the three northernmost pilings at trolling speed. Once it was ten feet away from the Gas Dock's north side, Jamil quietly lowered the anchor.

Raffi and Brady donned their wetsuits, as Jamil and Salah hauled the crab baskets out onto the stern deck.

The rain continued to pound the canopy and the deck surfaces, making communication and hearing very difficult, especially for Raffi and Brady, whose skintight headcaps closed out normal sounds.

Just as Brady was preparing to roll off of the gunwale, he noticed that a light had gone on in the dock master's office right above where he was sitting. The door to the office opened, causing light to spill out onto the catwalk directly overhead. Immediately, he motioned to Raffi and the others, pointing out the light source. Seeing the light and the shoes of the man standing on the catwalk some fifty feet above them, everyone went silent and moved under the shadow of the boat's canopy.

The man's shoes shifted right, then left, and then right again, as he turned to see if he could identify the source of the noise he had heard from his desk inside. As the man turned each time, he looked outward and stayed in position, never thinking that the sounds had come from directly below him. Satisfied and tired of being pelted by the rain, he turned and went back into the office, slamming the door behind him.

No one moved for the next few minutes. They wanted to be sure that the man above them did not come out again. With hand signals, Abed indicated that Raffi and Brady should slide into the water instead of rolling off of the side. This would create less noise.

After slipping over the side, Raffi and Brady dove down to attach the bandoliers to the piling clips. The others on deck were readying the next group of explosives for when the two divers resurface. All the while, Kaleem monitored the airwaves, especially the VHF discussions between the guard above them and his watch commander onshore at the Gas Dock field offices.

"This is Night Watch 4. Come in Command Base. Over."

No answer.

"This is Night Watch 4. Come in Command Base. Over."

"This is Command Base. Over."

"Command Base, it's howling out here but I thought I heard voices. Is anyone out here working on the rig? Over."

"Night Watch 4, this is Command Base. No one is on the rig tonight. We have a tanker coming in on Saturday afternoon, but our prep crews and the coast guard won't be out there on station 'til midmorning, which is about six hours before she's due -------."

The message broke off into static.

"Command Base, say that last part again. You broke up on me. Over."

"No crew will be out there 'til mid-morning on Saturday. You must be hearing ghosts. Over."

"Command Base, maybe your right but it sure sounded real to me. Over."

"Night Watch 4, keep your ears tuned but I doubt it's anything more than the wind and your mind playing tricks on you. Over."

"Command Base, I'm sure you're right. Over."

"Night Watch 4, see you at the change of watch in about an hour. Out."

For the third time, Brady and Raffi surfaced to take the last set of bandoliers to the piling shelves below. Ten minutes later, they broke the surface and climbed up the ladder that Jamil had hooked to the gunwale. Tired and sore from the hour of strenuous work, both of the men sat on the gunwale to catch their breath.

"How's it look down there?" asked Abed.

"Everything is in place and ready for demolition," said Brady. "We're all set."

"Good. Let's get these tanks off of you and head back."

The door to the dockmaster's office swung open and banged against the catwalk railing. Light from the office again poured out and glistened onto the wind-driven rain. They all looked up.

Bellowing like a bullhorn, the man above them shouted out into the night, "Who's out there? Declare yourselves." As before, the watchman turned around on the catwalk above, looking in all directions to see what was out there. Seeing nothing and hearing nothing more, the man turned to return to the warmth of his tiny cubicle, which seemed precariously perched above them. As he did so, his wet flashlight slipped out of his hand and fell to the catwalk. As it hit the catwalk, it cast light on the boat canopy below. Everyone stood motionless as the night watchman reached down to pick up his flashlight. The beam swept across the boat's stern. But, they were fortunate. He hadn't seen them.

The door slammed shut, trapping the light back into the office. Everyone looked at Kaleem, who was monitoring the radios, to see if the night watchman would call his base commander again.

No call came.

Kaleem said, "My guess is that he doesn't want to look like a fool again."

Abed whispered, "Let's stay put for five minutes. Then we'll get out of here."

Brady and Jamil removed their wetsuits and stored the diving tanks and masks. Jamil went up to the bow to await Brady's signal to pull anchor.

Five minutes later, Abed whispered, "Let's go." Brady ordered them to pull the anchor and then he drifted south several pilings before starting the engine. He did this so that the dockmaster would not hear the engine starting up.

To make sure that they weren't seen, Brady headed south, under cover of the Gas Docks above. Once they were out from under the southern end of the Docks and far away from the night watchman's office, he gunned the boat and headed across the Bay to Barren Gap and the Hoopers' Island Bridge on his way back to Parks Neck via the southern route.

Kaleem motioned to Abed and Salah to come quickly into the cabin. Once they were inside, he turned up the volume on the overhead VHF, which was set to the dock master's frequency. "We've got a problem. I just heard the watchman trying to contact his boss. Let's see if he tries again."

"Night Watch 4, say again."

"I said I just saw a big Bay built leave the south end of the Docks and head out into the main stem of the Bay. Over."

"So? Over."

"Command One, I think that's where the voices came from. Over."

"No way. Not if they were at the south end, especially in this storm. Over."

"Command One, maybe they were at the north end and drifting to the south. Over."

"Maybe, but what would they be doing out here in this weather? Over."

"Command One, they were probably fishing for the big rockfish that have recently started schooling up around the pilings. They probably thought that no one would see them fishing in the restricted area at night. Over."

"Maybe, but they've gone now, so don't worry about it. Over."

"Yes, sir. Night Watch 4, out."

"Command One, out."

"Doesn't sound like a problem to me," said Salah.

"Perhaps not," said Abed. "Unless this info gets back to the NRP or Homeland Security and they start piecing everything together."

Kaleem shrugged his shoulders, thinking, 'If word gets out that we were here tonight, all hell could break loose.'

The boat continued to pitch up and down in the three-foot waves and the twenty-knot winds, pulling at the ribs and planks of the *Miss Catherine James*, but she was a well-built boat. She was a waterman's boat - a boat built to last.

Chapter 18

Murder on the River, Four Days to Go. Thursday, July 1

After a long and stressful day on Wednesday, Brady hit the snooze button on his alarm clock three times before Aunt Louise knocked on his door and said, "Breakfast is ready. Pete and Mack are downstairs waiting."

"Thanks Louise. I'll be right there."

Brady yawned, rolled out of bed, and went to the bathroom, where he threw cold water on his face. Deciding to skip the shower, he rolled on some deodorant, slid into a pair of shorts, grabbed his shirt and a pair of tennis shoes, and ran downstairs.

"Sorry I'm late. I got in late last night and had a hard time sleeping. I finally dozed off at about 3:00 a.m."

Brady pulled up a chair, and Louise placed the warmed breakfast before him. It was Brady's favorite: grits, scrapple, bacon, pancakes, eggs, juice, and coffee.

"Thanks, Aunt Louise. Are you trying to fatten me up?"

"Yes, Brady. Girls like guys with some meat on them, and you need a little more."

"I thought they liked lean guys with muscles."

"Some do, but not girls around here. Girls around here are used to waterman with meat on their bones, such as Captain Mack here."

"You saying I'm fat, Louise?"

"No, Mack. I'm just saying you're cute and portly."

"OK. I'll take that description," said Mack. "For a minute, I thought you were calling me somewhat tubby."

"She was, Mack," said Pete. "She was just trying to say it nicely."

"Huh. Y'all are confusing me, but that isn't anything new. By the way, Louise, this breakfast is delicious. Don't tell Beth I ate all of it. She'll have a fit."

"My lips are sealed."

Pete finished his breakfast, pushed his plate aside, and sipped at his coffee. "So, tell us the latest, Brady. I need to be brought up to date before I go see my friend, Lieutenant Price."

Mack said, "You're goin' to see Tommy Price with the NRP, Pete?"

"Well, that's what we discussed on Tuesday. We agreed that I was suppose to see him after Brady's trip to the Gas Docks."

"Oh yeah. Now I remember," Mack said.

After finishing the last pancake, Brady cleared his throat and said, "Why don't I start with what happened yesterday. Some of it was unexpected."

"Go ahead," said Pete.

"Well, let's see. So, the last time I saw you all was yesterday morning, when I told you about how we set pitons at Kent Narrows and how both Smitty and Carlos are, for some reason, no longer on the job. After I left you, I took a nap and met Abed and Salah at 6:00 p.m. at the Chambers place."

Brady walked his uncle and Captain Mack through a detailed description of that night. He also told them about the NRP and Homeland Security radio intercepts and about the *Miss Gale* being seen at Kent Narrows. Interestingly enough, there had been no mention in the radio intercepts of any NRP report concerning the boat's speed trial or his encounter with the NRP that afternoon.

Both Pete and Mack sat back and remained silent during Brady's story. Once he was finished talking, Pete leaned forward in his chair. With his forearms on the kitchen table, he said, "Jesus, Brady, you're lucky they didn't slit your throat and throw you overboard when you finished settin' the bandoliers!"

"Not yet, Uncle Pete," said Brady. "I was pretty sure they'd still need me to set the ones at the Narrows. I wasn't worried about last night, but if they ask me to do the Kent Narrows bridges, they'll get rid of me as soon as I finish setting those explosives."

"Brady, I have to go to DNR today. They absolutely need to get on this right away."

"You plan on telling them everything?" asked Mack.

"I'll just tell them the truth," said Pete. "If it's OK with you, Brady, I'd like to take your brown paper spreadsheet with all the events on it and show that to them."

"That's fine by me, Uncle Pete, but. I'll need to update it some before you do."

"That would be great, Brady."

Brady went up to his room to put the latest changes on his spreadsheet. Then he brought it down to Pete. The three of them agreed to meet on the *Miss Alice* over a six-pack after dinner so that Pete could give them feedback from his meeting with

Lieutenant Price. They settled on 8:00 p.m. since Mack was heading up with his son Mike at three o'clock to fish for rockfish off of Bloody Point in Eastern Bay. With Louise working at the fire hall on the Fourth of July preparations, this was a perfect time to meet. There was no need to have her overhear what was going on. If she did, she'd get all worried about Brady's safety. Pete himself was worried, but there was no need to have both of them fretting over him.

✳✳✳

Mack headed back to his boat to work on some crab traps, and Pete called his friend Tommy Price at DNR to see if he could meet him for lunch at Harrison's Chesapeake House. If one were in need of someone's help, there was no better place than Harrison's. Their atmosphere and great food were ideal. Besides, it was close and Tommy Price always stopped by every Thursday at Harrison's to check out what was going on at Tilghman Island. Lieutenant Price's NRP territory included both Talbot and Dorchester Counties, even though his base office was north at Matapeake. His budget had been slashed again that year, resulting in Lieutenant Price having to rotate his trips to places like Cambridge, Tilghman, Hoopers' Island, and St. Michael's so that he could get to each of these places at least once a week. However, since Lieutenant Price lived on Tilghman Island, Tilghman got the benefit - or as some watermen complained, the detriment - of more than one visit a week from Tommy Price.

The phone rang. "Tommy?"

"Yeah. This is Tommy Price."

"Hey, Tommy. Pete Creighton, here."

"Hey, Pete. How are you?"

"Well, I'm pretty good. But I got to see you on something. Are you able to join me for lunch at Harrison's around twelve-thirty today?"

"Yeah, sure. I got to be down there this afternoon anyway. What's the rush?"

"I can't say over the phone, Tommy. I need to see you in person."

"OK. I'll see you at twelve-thirty at Harrison's. You've piqued my interest, Pete."

"Wait 'til I tell you what's going on. It'll get your dander up. You won't like it, Tommy."

175

"What else is new? Most of what I have to deal with I don't like anyway, Pete. I'll see you at twelve-thirty."

"Thanks, Tommy. I promise it'll be worth your time."

✳✳✳

When Lieutenant Price arrived at Harrison's, Pete was already seated at a table at the far end of the dining room, where no one could overhear their conversation.

"Hey, Captain Pete."

"Hey, lieutenant."

"Wow, that's a formal greeting between old friends," said Tommy.

"Yeah, well this is going to be a serious meeting, even though it's between old friends."

The waitress brought two menus and asked what they wanted to drink. They both ordered tea. Knowing the menu well, they both ordered crab-cake sandwiches and a bowl of vegetable crab soup.

"So, what's so important that we had to meet today, Pete? Are the new regulations what this is all about?"

"No, Tommy. But the dam regulations are bad enough, and sometime soon we need to figure out how to make them palatable to us waterman. What we need to discuss today is far more serious and sinister."

"Sinister?"

"Yes, sir. It's sinister beyond your worst nightmare, Tommy."

Pete began to explain the saga that he, Mack, and Brady had been living since that foggy and prophetic day in February, when the rogue boat had first appeared off of Mack's bow. Tommy didn't interrupt him. Using Brady's brown crab-table spreadsheet, Pete started with that cold February morning and continued right up through Brady's most recent update earlier that morning. Pete finished his report, sat back in his chair, and waited for Tommy to respond.

Tommy leaned forward so that only Pete would hear him. "Pete, we are aware of some of what you've said. We've been trying to put the pieces together. In addition to the comments of the off-duty security guard at the Kent Narrows restaurant, two of our NRP officers also saw the boat as it fished off the bridge pilings that night. A few days later, those same two officers found that boat fishing again under the bridge. While none of the NRP encounters has shown any illegal or questionable behavior, we remain suspicious of this unnamed boat that's been hanging around the Narrows. We also have a report by two of our officers in Lower Dorchester County that a similar unnamed boat, also a Bay-built, was pulled over off of Janes Island after performing a speed trial. At least that's the way the captain of the boat described his outing. With the Narrow's boat, the report indicated that one crewmember was foreign. He was most likely Mexican or someone from the Far East. So, we know some of what you know, but. clearly your nephew's spreadsheet and your description of what you and Mack have seen and heard are brand-new revelations. And you are right. This appears to be far more sinister than we had previously thought. Brady's spreadsheet shows without a doubt that some plot is afoot and we have very little time left to thwart whatever is being planned."

Tommy then said, "The minute I leave here, I will contact the state police and request helicopter surveillance in the Kent Narrows vicinity and down around Hooper's and Janes Islands. I don't know when they can provide a chopper, though. Unfortunately, they cut the two helicopters out of our budget this year, so we have to rely on the state police to provide us the chopper surveillance. With all of the weekend preparations for the Fourth of July, the state police and we are under the gun to cover all of our bases in preparation for the huge crowds that they are expecting at the state parks and on the Eastern Shore. A lot of focus is on the Coastal Bays Area and Ocean City, where the crowds are expected to be more than last year. It seems that with gas prices where they are, most Marylanders will limit their travel to within the state. That puts extra pressure on our park system and on the state roads. If I had to guess, they won't be able to fill our request until Saturday. They will probably provide only one helicopter for a limited time period."

Tommy got up and placed a twenty-dollar bill on the table. He said, "Pete, I got to get going. I need to make that call to the state helicopter unit. I need to talk with the colonel in Annapolis, and I probably have to go to Annapolis to share all of this with the DNR Secretary. Do you mind if I take Brady's spreadsheet to help solicit the resources that I will need to run this to ground?"

"No, I don't mind. Take it. I'm sure Brady would agree if you think it will be helpful in your deliberations with the state police and with DNR's top brass. If I don't hear from you by tomorrow night, I'll assume you've got the chopper surveillance worked out".

"That works for me," said Tommy. "As soon as I get the report back from the state police and Homeland Security, I'll call you with an update. Hopefully all of this will turn out to be a huge misunderstanding. Please do not tell anyone what you all have seen or know. If this truly is a terrorist plot, we don't want the public panicking. Also, please tell Brady to be wired for any signs that restrict his inclusion in decisions or in his ability to communicate with you or Mack. I myself would keep the military Motorola phones on the special ops frequency all of the time, and I would have lots of backup batteries. Those walkie-talkies may be the only thing that saves you all and Brady if this thing blows up."

"Good suggestion. I'll tell Brady and Mack. Thanks for all your help Tommy, we really appreciate it."

"No problem, Pete. But the real thanks goes to you all for all that you're doing under very difficult circumstances. Right now, you guys are the ones who are at risk, especially Brady. That boy is a fine young man, Pete. You need to be sure he's going to be OK."

"Yeah, he paid his dues in Afghanistan, Tommy. We sure don't want him to have to pay again, especially here on his own soil."

"Take care, Pete. Be back at you."

"Thanks, Tommy. I look forward to hearing from you."

✳✳✳

Before lunch, Mack picked up his cell phone and called his son, Mike, to confirm that he'd be joining him late that afternoon to fish up north of Poplar Island. Word was that the rockfish had been running well up there. Mike had told his dad that he had to be in Cambridge at one o'clock anyway to pick up some crabbing gear, so that would work out fine for him.

At three o'clock, Mike met his dad and boarded the *Miss Patricia* for the trip to the Bloody Point fishing grounds. After Mike got onboard, Mack called Pete on his cell phone to tell him where he was heading to fish with Mike. He asked if Pete would like to join them, but Pete declined, reminding Mack about the Fourth of July work that he needed to do at the fire hall.

"Oh yeah, sorry I forgot about that, Pete."

"Mack, that was just this morning!"

"OK," said Mack. "But that's almost five hours ago, Pete. You know my brain's only capable of retaining shit for four hours, at most."

"You're forgiven, you old bastard," said Pete.

"Look, it's not really my fault. I just can't remember anything," replied Mack.

"You're right. I've got the same problem, Mack. I can't remember shit, including your first name: George."

Pete hung up before Mack could respond with another quip.

✳✳✳

With Raffi at the helm, Salah and Kaleem headed out from the Chambers Dock on the *Miss Martha*, which was originally the *Miss Gale*, to test their high-frequency military shortwave radio's reach, since the line of sight VHF could only project its signal about ten miles, at best. The key question revolved around whether or not the HF military radio could reach over a forty-mile distance from Parks Neck to Kent Narrows, or would they need a relay station at Walnut Point on Tilghman Island so that conversations could then be possible all of the way to Kent Narrows? While they didn't want the boat to be seen out on the Bay again before the attack commenced, there was no other way to test the radio's reach.

To perform the tests accurately, they headed out to Sharpes Island Light to see if they could contact the head security guard at the Parks Neck Farm. While not as strong as they would have liked, the signal that they received from Parks Neck, which was some twenty miles away, was acceptable. But would that signal be of sufficient strength to extend all the way to Kent Narrows? With its twelve-foot antenna, the military HF radio could reach much farther than the VHF with AIS-B or the standard VHF radio, which only had a one-to-ten-mile range, at most. It was unknown exactly how far the military unit could reach.

The *Miss Martha* continued north to Eastern Bay. Off of Parsons Island, Kaleem tested the system to see if he could reach the Parks Neck Farm. The reception was too weak to be of any help, so a relay at Black Walnut Point would have to be established. If for any reason they needed to lay up in Crab Alley Creek to avoid detection after they planted the explosives, Kaleem asked Raffi to pull into the mouth of the Creek to test the signal between there and the security guard at Black Walnut Point. At Crab Alley Creek, Kaleem found that the relay to Black Walnut Point was excellent, as was the relay from Black Walnut Point to Parks Neck.

After the communications tests were complete, Raffi navigated the boat back to Eastern Bay for the trip back to the Chambers dock. It was 4:30 p.m.

✱✱✱

Mack guided the *Miss Patricia* out through Knapp's Narrows and headed north toward Poplar Island and Eastern Bay. Mike prepared some light tackle for jigging and four trolling rods. Mack wanted to troll first off of Bloody Point, going from Buoy G-1 to Buoy R-4. If that didn't work, they would try the Lumps fishing spot near Buoy G-3.

Mack started trolling off of G-1 at about 3:45 p.m. On their second pass from R-4, they hooked two fish. Neither one was legal size, so they threw them back and resumed trolling back to Buoy G-1. Not a single fish hit on any of the four rods.

Disappointed and somewhat frustrated that the earlier fishing report had talked about a whole hassle of rockfish in the area, Mack continued to head back up the same line to Buoy R-4. This time, they got another hit on the line as they neared the steep drop-off just south of Buoy R-4. It was a nice twenty-six-inch keeper.

This dance between Buoy G-1 and R-4 continued for another half-hour. They had only one more hit, and it was a small sixteen-inch throwback. At four-thirty, Mack told Mike to pull in the lines. Mack had decided to go jigging off of Parsons Island first and then come back to the Lumps at Buoy G-3. While the drift jigging off of Parsons produced one more twenty-three-inch keeper and a few nice-sized croakers, it wasn't good enough for Mack. He wanted to get into them, so they headed to the Lumps at G-3, where he had always had good luck—not so much with rockfish as with croakers and Norfolk spot.

As they neared a location just north of Tilghman Point to begin a southwest drift to Buoy G-3, Mack scanned the horizon to look for birds that were flying low over the water. This was a telltale sign that fish were breaking. Then he stopped. He lowered his binoculars and stared back out toward Parsons Island. He put the binoculars back to his eyes and studied what he was seeing.

"Breaking fish, Dad?"

"No. It's a better catch than that, Mike," Mack said to himself.

There she was, coming out of Crab Alley Bay and into Eastern Bay, heading straight for him. It was the rogue boat. Her six antennas swayed in the wind, giving off quick,

180

brilliant flashes of light as the sun's intermittent rays reflected off of the smooth white surfaces of the antennas. The shape of her bow, the antennas, and the strictly white paint below the water line sealed her identity. There was no question. It was the rogue boat.

Mack called out, "Come into the cabin, Mike. Now."

Mike was surprised by the urgency in his dad's voice. He quickly stowed the rods in the gunwale holders and stepped inside. Mack handed him the binoculars, "Look out yonder, Mike. That's the rogue boat."

Mike took the glasses and zoomed in on the big boat. Sure enough, there was no bottom paint. There were six antennas and a Hoopers' Island flared bow.

"Looks like her, for sure, Dad."

"Yep. Take the rods out of the gunwale holders and put them in the overhead canopy racks. I don't want to lose them. We're going up there to intercept her." Mack took the *Miss Patricia* out of trolling gear and slammed the throttle all the way forward. While she didn't leap into the sea like the rogue boat could, she did steadily plow forward, gaining speed until she was on plane heading straight toward her nemesis.

"Mike, get my pistol and shotgun out from under the portside bunk and load 'em. Ammo for both is in the drawer under the forward dining seat."

"Dad, let's not confront them before we verify with DNR or the coast guard. We need their advice before we do anything on our own. It'd be better if you made the call first. Then we can stalk them 'til the cops arrived."

"No way, Mike. I'm not going to let those bastards get away this time."

"Dad, that's crazy. We aren't equipped to arrest or even overcome them. I'm sure they have automatic weapons and they're not afraid to use them."

As the two boats approached each other, the rogue boat, which was the *Miss Martha*, suddenly realized that the *Miss Patricia* was heading straight for her. Raffi turned her hard to port, as though he were going to head up the Miles River toward St. Michael's.

Seeing the rogue boat change course, Mack turned to cut right in front of her. Raffi had to slow his boat down. Again, he turned hard to port to avoid a head-on collision. Notwithstanding his efforts to avoid Mack's boat, the two boats clashed amidships, throwing everyone off-balance and causing a resounding crunch of wood and fiberglass.

Mack yelled to Mike to hook a line to their stern cleat. Mack grabbed his shotgun off of the engine box, where Mike had left both it and the pistol fully loaded. Pointing the gun directly at Raffi, Mack said, "I got you now, you bastards!"

Keeping a cool head, Salah came to the starboard gunwale and said, "What's the problem, captain? Is something wrong?"

Without Mack noticing, Kaleem slipped into the forward cabin to retrieve a sawed-off shotgun and his pistol. Raffi reached for the port canopy strut on Mack's boat. By doing so, Raffi was able to keep the two boats together at midships. It also allowed him to block Mack's view and if necessary, quickly jump onboard Mack's boat to gain control.

"Mike, get on the radio and tell the coast guard where we are."

In a commanding voice, Salah said, "I wouldn't do that, captain."

"Oh yeah? Well, you're not in control, sonny."

The sound of Kaleem's shotgun was like a giant explosion quickly followed by the suppressed sound of Kaleem's 9-mm silencer.

Mike was blown back. He fell on the engine box with blood spurting from the shotgun pattern on his chest and from the gaping 9-mm bullet hole in his forehead. By the time he slid off of the engine box and hit the floor with a horrific thud, Mike was already dead.

Before Mack could turn to see Mike fall, he pulled the trigger not once, but twice. Raffi's face exploded - first the left side and then the right side - as Mack spun to his left to follow Mike's fall.

Two more shots burst from Kaleem's pistol. Mack was hit twice, square in his back. He continued to spin, and then he staggered toward the spot where Mike lay. A final death rattle came from his son's blood-filled mouth.

Mack crumbled. The shotgun fell from his hands as he reached out for Mike. With a muffled report, two more shots hit Mack at the top of his spine and in the middle of the back of his head. Blood spurted everywhere. Mack hit the deck face-first, his arm reaching out to Mike. His body convulsed twice. Mack gasped one final time and then he became motionless.

The two boats gently rocked together as though in a final dance of death. Both of the watermen lay in an ever-widening pool of blood, gone from this earth forever.

***

Raffi lay disfigured and dead on *Miss Martha's* deck. His brain and facial features were strewed in bits and pieces all over the engine box, the deck, and the underside of the canopy.

Salah went into immediate action. There was no need to check on Raffi. He was clearly gone. Salah grabbed a line that was hanging neatly under the starboard gunwale and tied the canopy struts of the two boats together. Once secured, he jumped onboard the *Miss Patricia* and shut down all of her electronics. He then turned to look for her onboard saltwater hose. Finding it on the starboard side, he turned it on and began hosing the deck down with a gentle spray to avoid splattering the blood in a wider circle. Because he was so agile in responding to a crisis, Salah did all of this in under a minute.

"Kaleem, before you tend to Raffi and hose the deck down, put the anchor over and secure it good." By the time Kaleem had put the anchor over and set her, the winds had blown both boats around Buoy B-4, and they were slowly drifting toward Buoy G-3 along the marshy shoreline of Rich Neck.

We've got to move fast, thought Salah, *before we run both boats aground.*

Kaleem laid a hose on the deck so that its water would continue to merge with the blood oozing out of whatever was left of Raffi's mangled head. The pink mixture of saltwater and blood flowed to the scuppers and out into the mouth of the Miles River.

Kaleem retrieved three body bags from the storage locker in the forward cabin of the *Miss Martha*. He leaned over the gunwale and handed two bags to Salah as he continued to hose down *Miss Patricia's* deck. The boats were attached to each other without bumpers between them. As the waves gently rocked them together and then apart, Kaleem hooked two bumpers between them to avoid further damage to either boat. Some of the bumper railing on the *Miss Martha* was already busted and hanging over her side.

Now that the two men had some time, they stood, each on the deck of the opposing boat, discussing their next moves.

Salah said, "We need to get all three into body bags and then finish cleaning up. It's close to six-thirty now. With the bad weather moving in, we've only got about an hour of light left. Once we stow the two bodies in the bilge of this boat that I'm on, we can run her aground over there behind the marsh and that adjacent tree line. No one will see her there for at least a few days. That should keep us out of trouble 'til late Saturday night. That way, we'll be clear until Sunday morning. We need to fold the antennas down, break up her radios so that no one can call from here, and put anything on the deck that floats inside the cabin. Let's see. We'll also need to pull the plug in the bilge so that she sinks as low as possible in the marsh. Anything else you can think of?"

"Yeah, grab their money and IDs and take that one's watch. It's a beauty," said Kaleem.

"You know, you're still just a common thug, Kaleem. But you're a smart one."

"That's me," beamed Kaleem.

By 7:30 p.m. they had stuffed the two bodies into the bilge of the *Miss Patricia*, smashed all of the electronics, locked the forward cabin with Mack's keys, and separated the two boats. Salah started the *Miss Patricia* and maneuvered her into the marsh and up a small creek, driving the boat into the muddy bottom next to the tree line. Here, he tossed a small secondary anchor off of her stern. He turned off her engine, secured the bow anchor, lay the two antennas flat on the canopy roof, and took one final look around to be sure that he'd covered all of his bases.

Feeling like he had done all that was needed, he hopped overboard. He then pulled Raffi's body bag, which they had placed on the *Miss Patricia* to clear *Miss Martha's* deck for her final wash-down, over the gunwale and trudged through the muddy creek bottom. Pulling the body bag behind him, Salah emerged through the phragmites to the edge of the Miles River. There, he entered the water and swam out to the *Miss Martha*, pulling the body bag behind him. Salah arrived at the boat and Kaleem reached down to grab the body bag. Salah climbed onboard. Together, he and Kaleem pulled the body bag over the gunwale. The body thudded onto the deck. Exhausted, saddened by Raffi's death, and out of breath, Salah sat on the gunwale and collected his thoughts.

"Kaleem, we need to get back to Black Walnut Point before it's completely dark. I don't want us on any radio between now and when we reach the Chambers dock. There will be no communications 'til we see Abed."

Salah started the engine. Kaleem pulled anchor and secured Raffi's body below deck. They eased out from behind Tilghman Point. Luckily, there were no boats in the vicinity; hopefully, no one had seen them during the shootings, the last hour of cleanup, or the beaching of the *Miss Patricia*.

The weather began to deteriorate as the storm approached. Neither man spoke on their way back. Each of them quietly grieved over the loss of Raffi. He had been a faithful soldier and a trusted friend. This was the price of jihad. Losses were always part of the battle and the victory.

✳✳✳

By eight o'clock, Brady and Pete were having dessert on the porch, waiting for Mack to show up. The phone rang. Louise answered it and talked for a minute. She then put the phone down on the table. Louise opened the screen door to the porch and beckoned to Pete.

"Pete, its Beth. Mack and Mike aren't back yet and they haven't called in." Pete jumped up, ran to the kitchen, and grabbed the phone. "Alice, what's going on?"

Holding back her tears, Beth blurted out, "I don't know Pete. He always calls if he's going to be late, but he hasn't. He's overdue and I'm scared to death. It's not like him and it's not like Mike either. I called Mike's wife, Tonya, and she said she had not heard from them either. Something's wrong, Pete. I know it."

"OK, Beth. Take a deep breath. Relax. It's going to be OK. Maybe the fishing was too good to stop. Maybe his electronics went down or his engine quit. I'll call DNR and the coast guard, and I'll get right back to you. OK?"

"OK, Pete, but please hurry!"

"I will, Beth. I'll be back to you within twenty minutes."

"Thanks, Pete." Her quivering words could not betray the fear that she felt. She was desperate and it was clear that she felt that storm clouds were beginning to surround her.

"Shit," blurted Pete.

Brady could hear him from the porch. "What's wrong, Uncle Pete?" asked Brady, as he entered the kitchen.

"Mack and Mike haven't returned or called to say they'd be late. That's not like them. While I'm calling DNR, go down to the slip and get the boat fueled and ready. We'll be going out soon as I get ahold of DNR."

"Gotcha, Uncle Pete. I'll have her ready."

"When you get to the boat, call the *Chesapeake Flyer*, the *Miss Tyler*, and the *Hooper's Island Lady* and mobilize them to come out to meet us off of Popular Island."

Over the years, the community had mounted way too many of these search and rescues. Knowing exactly what this kind of search involved, Louise began to make crab soup, sandwiches, and cookies in case a full-blown search was needed.

"Tommy, this is Pete."

"Hey, Pete. I know what you're calling about, but I haven't gotten an answer on the chopper. The only thing I'm sure of is that it will not be before Saturday."

"Tommy, it's not about the chopper. It's Mack and his son Mike. They seem to be missing. They're overdue from a fishing trip up in Eastern Bay."

"Wow. Those are two experienced watermen. What do you think is going on?"

"I don't know, Tommy, but you guys need to get the NRP and coast guard on it ASAP. I'll get the Tilghman boys to start a search, but we'll need your guys to coordinate it."

"You got any idea, exactly, where they went?"

"Mack said they were going off to Bloody Point. If that didn't work, he said they'd move north to Eastern Bay."

"OK, Pete. You guys get your crews together. I'll send out the coast guard from Annapolis and Matapeake, and I'll send out my NRP guys from Kent Narrows for a northern search above Bloody Point. I'll also contact the coast guard at Solomon's Island for a Southern and Western Shoreline search. So that we get a clear channel, have your crews monitor both Channel 16 and Channel 48, which we'll set as the search channel."

"OK, Tommy. We'll probably get about four boats out, at least initially."

"That'll be good. If we need more, I'm sure you can get 'em."

"We'll get more if you need 'em, Tommy."

"Also, so we know who is part of search and rescue on the water, be sure to alert the guys to keep their deck lights and flood lights on, OK?"

"Sure thing, Tommy. Thanks a lot. We'll be out there by 9:00 p.m. I'll call you when we're on station."

"Good. See you then."

Pete raced down the dock and jumped onboard. Brady had the engine idling. Except for the mid-station line, all of the lines were undone and coiled. The *Miss Alice* was ready to go.

"Put on the deck lights and cast off, Brady."

Brady unhooked the mid-station line. They left Knapp's Narrows and headed out into the Bay. Pete reviewed the previous six hours of weather on the NOAA weather maps to see how the tides and winds had progressed since Mack had left his dock at midday. He figured that if anything had happened with Mack's engine, they would have drifted southwest to the Western Shore or perhaps more directly south toward Poplar Island.

✳✳✳

As Pete reached the lower end of Poplar Island, he headed over to check the western edge of the Island. He slowly moved north, surveying the west side. Nothing was there.

Fog was beginning to blow south from Eastern Bay. Reaching the northern end of the island, he slowed down the *Miss Alice*, turned on the canopy-mounted floodlights, and maneuvered the in-cabin spotlight handle in a slow arc to cast its beam into the fog across the entire northern edge of the island. There was no boat and no bodies, and he was having no luck.

The VHF came to life. *"Miss Alice, Miss Alice.* This is NRP Matapeake Command. Over."

Pete grabbed the microphone and said, "Matapeake Command, this is the *Miss Alice*. Over."

"Captain Pete, Lieutenant Price here. Where are you? Over."

"Lieutenant, I just finished searching the west side of Poplar. Right now I'm just north of the island. Where do you want me? Over."

"Captain Pete, based on our calculations, if Mack is adrift we think he might be west and south of you. He might even be as far away as Calvert Cliffs. Why don't you and one of the other Tilghman boats cover the western shore south to Calvert Cliffs and have the other two boats contact me? I'll have them join up with us at Bloody Point Light and organize a search from there to Kent Narrows. Over."

"OK. I'll take Captain Johns of the *Chesapeake Flyer* with me, and I'll call Captain Willis on the *Miss Tyler* and Captain Barnes on the *Hooper's Island Lady*. I'll have them head up to Bloody Point and call you directly. Over."

"Stay in touch, Pete. I've got the coast guard coming up from Solomon's to cover the southernmost part of the search area. My guys and the Annapolis coast guard will work the northern sector. We'll find them. Don't you worry. Over."

"God, I hope so, Tommy. *Miss Alice* out."

Pete called Captain Johns, who was just rounding the southern end of Poplar Island. Pete looked behind him. Just over the stern, he saw Captain Johns's deck lights and floodlights ablaze.

"Can you see me, Captain Johns? Over."

"Sure can, Pete. Over."

"OK. Follow me to the western shore. We should probably stay within one hundred yards or so of each other. Once we reach Chesapeake Beach, we'll work our way south to Calvert Cliffs. Over."

"Gotcha, Pete. I'm with you. *Chesapeake Flyer*, out."

For the next forty-five minutes, there was silence on channels sixteen and forty-eight. Pete called Louise on his cell phone and had her call Beth to relay that between six to eight boats were out scouting for Mack and Mike, including the coast guard, the NRP, and the watermen. He said that he would report every hour on their progress.

Pete, Brady, and Captain Johns scoured the western shore down to just below Calvert Cliffs. Then they worked their way north toward Bloody Point in a zigzag pattern, staying two hundred yards apart but within sight of each other's floodlit decks. Sadly, they saw nothing.

***

As soon as the *Miss Patricia* was aground and anchored in the marsh, Abed, Salah, and Kaleem moved out to the mouth of the Miles River. The right strategy was to get as far away as they could from the scene as quickly as possible. However, that meant taking the boat all the way south to Parks Neck, which would expose them to many other boats during the waning hours of daylight. Abed, therefore, made the decision to go to Black Walnut Point, which was much closer. The next night, they would set the explosives at Kent Narrows using the *Catherine James*. When they were finished, they'd move that boat under the veil of darkness back to Black Walnut Point. They had planned to dispose of Brady that evening, but the encounter with Captain Mack had changed all that. If a body were found that had a direct connection to Mack and Mike, the search to find Abed and the two Bay-built boats would intensify to a code red status. If this were to happen, their chances of success would be significantly diminished, if not made impossible. After docking at Black Walnut Point, Abed called Maya on his cell phone to alert her to their run-in with the *Miss Patricia,* the death of Raffi, and the resulting change of plans. Maya was stunned. After hanging up, she started to cry uncontrollably.

***

Lieutenant Price had rafted up with Captains Willis and Barnes off of the Bloody Point Light. They planned a zigzag pattern from there up to Kent Narrows. Each boat kept about a two-hundred-yard distance from the other. This was the maximum visible distance that they could maintain, as the night and fog closed in on the Bay.

The coast guard boat from Solomons Island met up with Captains Pete and Johns as they worked their search pattern north of Poplar Island. The coast guard decided to tie up at the Rip-Tide Restaurant's dock at Kent Narrows to plan the next phase of the search.

Colonel Wilson, the commander of the Solomons Island coast guard station, would take command of the search. On his way up from Solomons, he had ordered a unit out of Curtis Bay in Baltimore to join the Annapolis and Kent Narrows Team. Altogether, this search flotilla was comprised of thirty skilled personnel, including a recovery team of three divers. They were all to rendezvous at 9:30 p.m. at the Rip-Tide Restaurant.

By the time everyone arrived at the restaurant's dock, the weather had begun to rapidly deteriorate. Winds were blowing out of the northeast at fifteen to twenty knots and the waves were between two and three feet high. The storm was gathering strength.

NOAA had predicted this fast-moving front three days earlier. They were also reporting that just behind this front was a subtropical frontal system that was expected to gain additional strength as it rolled up the East Coast from Georgia. This front was projected to clash with a cold front that was moving across the country from Ohio. Maryland's Saturday weather forecast was not looking good, and the Independence Day forecast called for more cloudy skies, temperatures in the 80s, with a 70 percent chance of early morning showers.

✳✳✳

As the storm clouds and heavy rain moved in, Maya, Abed, and Salah gathered around the lunch table of the *Miss Martha*. Kaleem sat in the captain's chair, adjusting the radios in an attempt to listen in on the search. They knew from earlier calls on Channel 16 that the search was well underway. Finally, scanning the most likely channels, Kaleem found that the search-and-rescue team was using Channel 48 as its primary point of contact. Kaleem had the radios turned up loud enough for the other three to hear the transmissions but low enough to prevent the sound from traveling to the adjacent neighbors.

While there was some reporting back and forth between the Solomons Island team and the Annapolis and Kent Narrows teams, clearly very little progress was being made.

As the various teams concluded their initial searches and headed toward the Kent Narrows Bridge, Lieutenant Price hailed them all to meet, as Colonel Wilson had suggested, at the Rip-Tide Restaurant. It had more slips than the NRP dock, which was just north of the bridge. At 9:45 p.m. everyone was docked at the Rip-Tide Restaurant. Colonel Wilson called everybody into his boat's pilothouse. It was a tight fit but everyone squeezed in without too much trouble.

"Sorry for the tight quarters, gentlemen. If we met in the restaurant, someone might overhear us, and we'd no doubt have the press descending on us. First, I'd like a report from each of you on which areas you have covered so far."

As Lieutenant Price gave his account, Captains Willis and Barnes chimed in occasionally to verify the specifics of their search. Captain Pete did the same concerning his southern search with Captain Johns. The ship captain of the Solomons coast guard added additional details of his search from Solomons to Calvert Cliffs. As Colonel Wilson listened to each person's report, he traced as closely as possible each boat's coverage on the map before him. At the end of the reports, it was clear to everyone that the areas that they had covered had been covered well. The likelihood of their having missed something was very slim, and nothing should have slipped through the search net that they had cast.

"OK, so we're all in agreement that the areas we have already covered were thoroughly searched. Unless the *Miss Patricia* has sunk, we will most likely find her up a river creek or holed up at someone's dock. Since Solomons Station was the first to be contacted and I'm the senior officer, I will assume command of the search-and-rescue party. Anyone object to that?"

In unison, everyone said, "No sir." With unanimous consent, Colonel Wilson proceeded to outline the next search pattern and protocol.

Within fifteen minutes, all were back on their boats and at station. The radios came to life. "Gentlemen, we're good to go. I will see you back here no later than 11:00 p.m. Search Command, out."

The weather was worsening by the minute. For everyone to maintain visual contact, the distance between boats had now been reduced to one hundred yards. All deck and cabin lights were turned on to give each search group the best chance of seeing the other boats.

Pete, Brady, and Captain Johns were assigned to the coast guard lieutenant from Curtis Bay. They were responsible for searching Prospect Bay, including Marshy Creek and the Wye River area, as well as the Miles River up to St. Michael's Harbor. While it was questionable that Mack had gone into the Miles River or as far up as St. Michael's, Colonel Wilson had deemed that no stone be left unturned. Given that the weather conditions were worsening, time was of the essence. The longer it took to find them, the less likely there would be a good outcome.

Along with the Lieutenant and his crew from Annapolis, Captain Wilson, and Captain Barnes, Lieutenant Price was assigned to various creeks south and west of the Narrows, including Crab Alley, Cox Creek, Shipping Creek, and the Romancoke Area. There were two reasons for placing more boats along the western side of Eastern Bay and fewer boats on the eastern side: one, there were many smaller creeks on the western side, and two, if Mack's boat had drifted, the winds and tides would have taken him and the *Miss Patricia* in that direction.

At 10:30 p.m. after checking out Crab Alley Bay, Lieutenant Price was heading up Crab Alley Creek. Captain Willis was assigned to Cox Creek. Captain Barnes was assigned to Shipping Creek, and the new Lieutenant from Annapolis was assigned to the area south of Romancoke.

Lieutenant Price was about halfway up Crab Alley Creek when he thought he heard a marine radio. He could tell that it wasn't a weather channel because it did not contain the continuous verbal flow of NOAA's weather reports. There was little conversation but enough to know that it was a VHF radio. As Tommy Price reached depths that were rising toward four feet, he turned his boat around and headed back south to the mouth of the Creek.

The VHF radio got louder as he approached Hog Island. It was then that he recognized the voices. The sound he was hearing mimicked the sounds he was receiving on his own radio from the search teams on Channel 48. *Strange*, he thought. *It could be the radio waves bouncing off of the low ceiling overhead, but it sure feels like the noises are coming from the shore on my right.* Little did he know it was coming from the terrorists monitoring a VHF radio on the dock of the Crab Alley Creek Farm.

***

"Search Command to Search Party. This is Colonel Wilson. It's already a quarter to eleven, and the weather is getting a lot worst. NOAA predicts a strong storm with forty to fifty-knot winds approaching from the south. I am calling off the search for the night. Everyone is to return to his homeport. If for any reason you need to tie up rather than try for home, the Matapeake Station is prepared to take you in for the night. We will resume our search one half-hour before sunup at the Rip-Tide dock tomorrow morning. Any questions? Over."

Since no one responded, Wilson said, "Good. Then I will see you tomorrow a half-hour before sunup. Search Commander Out."

***

It was a rough trip back to Tilghman. The winds were mounting and the tide was running out fast as lightning. Pete and Brady remained silent, each of them controlling his emotions.

Back at the house, Pete called Beth to give her a rundown of the evening's search and to tell her that everyone would be back on-station at first light. Knowing that it was time to do so, Pete and Brady then sat down with Louise at the kitchen table and informed her of the events of the last five months. They told her about some of their suspicions. While amazed at the details of the story, Louise was not surprised to hear about the possible terrorist plot around the Bay. The subject had been a talking point in the watermen's community for years. After Louise expressed her thoughts and concerns about their involvement, Brady brought up the unthinkable. "Although none of us really knows what caused Mack and Mike to disappear without a trace, do you think it could be related to the rogue boat, Uncle Pete?"

"Don't know, Brady. Maybe it is, but I doubt it. Why would they encounter the rogue boat late in the day in Eastern Bay?"

"Well, I'm scheduled to place explosives tomorrow. I wonder if they've already placed them themselves ahead of time."

"I guess you'd have to ask them," said Pete.

Thinking on it, Brady said, "No. I guess that makes no sense. They need me to manage those tides in the Narrows, and they know it. They would not have done it without me, especially in this weather."

"On second thought, Brady, I don't think that *they* had anything to do with whatever happened to Mack. If Mack had been in trouble, he certainly would have used the Motorola walkie-talkie. Since neither of us got a call, I don't think that *they* were involved, but we'll know tomorrow. Speaking of tomorrow, we best get some rest. I'm going up to bed."

"I'll be along in a few minutes, Pete," said Louise. "I am frying up some chicken tonight for you to take along tomorrow. I want you all to have good food onboard for the search." As they turned to go upstairs to bed, Louise picked up a spatula. Waving it in Pete and Brady's direction, she said, "You two make darn sure that you watch your step and stay clear of any trouble. If things are as you suspect them to be, let the authorities take care of it - not you two! Oh and by the way, I should be mad as heck for your not bringing me in on this sooner. But also, thanks for not telling me. I would have worried myself sick for these past five months."

"We'll be careful, Louise. I promise," said, Pete.

"Night, Brady."

"Night, Uncle Pete. Thanks again, Aunt Louise."

"Night, you two," said Louise.

Chapter 19

The Gathering Storm. Friday, July 2

To make sure that their day began with pancakes, eggs, and bacon, Louise woke up at 3:30 a.m., after only three hours of sleep. The lunch bags were overflowing with sandwiches, fried chicken, and numerous treats. She had also fried up twenty additional chicken wings, legs, and breasts so that the others on the search team would have ample food for the long day ahead.

The winds howled through the masts and lanyards, resulting in a cacophony of sounds, as the sailboats at Knapp's Narrows rolled back and forth in the gale-force winds. It was 4:30 a.m. and the *Miss Alice* was plowing through Knapp's Narrows on her way to the Bay. As soon as she passed the last entrance buoy on the bayside, Pete turned north and followed the waves and winds that were blowing out of the southeast. It was an early warning. This new weather front was going to be a rough and headstrong opponent for the next twelve hours. However, Pete and Brady were determined to find their friends today, no matter what the weather was like and no matter how long it took.

When they arrived at the Rip-Tide dock at about 5:30 a.m. everyone was there, including several more NRP and coast guard boats. There were now twelve waterman boats there, seven of which were from Tilghman and Hoopers Island. The rest were from the Upper Bay Area. As Lieutenant Price had told Pete, according to the calls that Tommy had received from the Chesapeake Beach and Rock Hall watermen, by 8:30 a.m. there would be another seven or eight boats joining in the search.

Colonel Wilson reorganized the boats into three new search teams. Since the weather remained dark and overcast, he instructed the captains that all of the decks should be lit again so that they could easily gauge the distance between them.

This time, Pete and Brady were assigned the upper western shore from Shadyside south to Parker's Creek. Since the Solomon's coast guard Team had covered the western shore up to Parkers Creek in their early morning run, there was no need for Pete to go any farther south. Two NRP boats, the Solomon's coast guard team, and four other watermen boats joined Pete in the western shore search.

Colonel Wilson sent a small team north to the Chester River to search that area, in case Mack had decided to fish the mouth of the Chester River near Eastern Neck Island. The third team was comprised of three NRP boats, two coast guard boats, and six watermen boats. Led by Lieutenant Tommy Price, this team was spread out over Eastern Bay, Crab Alley Bay, and the lower portion of the Miles River. By 8:30 a.m. four more watermen had joined the search with Lieutenant Price's team. The weather was getting worse by the minute. Winds were now blowing twenty to thirty knots with gusts that were more than forty knots. Colonel Wilson called all of the boats under thirty-six feet in length to return to the Rip-Tide dock as soon as possible. Colonel Wilson also called the western shore search team to return to the restaurant dock. The tides were running high and most of the marshy areas of the Bay were now well under water. The storm and the moon's phase had collaborating to create a record-breaking high tide. It was now 11:30 a.m.

***

As Colonel Wilson began to turn his boat around and return to the restaurant dock, he picked up the VHF microphone to recall the Eastern Bay Team from their search. As he was about to push the talk button, one of the two officers out of Matapeake, Petty Officer Kurt Thomas, gave him the bad news. They had found a shot-up and beached

Miss Patricia. The tides had raised the *Miss Patricia* up above the marsh off of Rich Neck just north of Buoy G-3. Kurt Thomas and one of his men had boarded the boat, and they had just completed their initial search.

"Search Leader, this is Matapeake Four.

Petty Officer Thomas here. Over."

"Matapeake Four, this is Colonel Wilson. Go ahead, Kurt. Over."

As was inevitable during protracted search-and-rescue missions in which team members knew each other and the proper communications protocols were relaxed to speed up the discussions, that radio procedures were often shelved in favor of frank and to-the-point communications.

"Colonel, this is Kurt. We've found the *Miss Patricia.* The boat has been shot up pretty bad with what appears to be buckshot. One canopy strut looks like it was almost cut in half, and there are small bone and skin fragments embedded in a portion of it. So far, there are no signs of life or bodies. We'll call you back as soon as we have gone inside. Over."

"Thanks, Kurt. For God's sake, be careful. Search Leader, out."

The wait for a call back felt like a lifetime. After six minutes, though, the radio silence was finally broken.

"Colonel, this is Petty Officer Thomas requesting that we switch to our secure channel immediately. Over."

"Affirmative, Kurt. Out."

Both men switched to the secure coast guard channel, which eluded even Kaleem.

"Search Leader, this is coast guard Matapeake Four. Over."

"Back to you, Kurt. What's the story? Over."

"We've found them both. They were trussed up in body bags lying in the bilge, Over."

"Kurt, are you sure it's Mack and Mike? Over."

"I think so, but I believe Captain Pete or Brady will need to identify them, 'cause they're pretty well shot up, Colonel. Over."

Taking a deep breath and placing the microphone to his mouth, the Colonel said. "OK, Kurt. Don't touch a thing. I'll bring one of the two of them over to verify the bodies. Search Commander, out."

Colonel Wilson put the mike back in its cradle and switched back to Channel 48. Then he decided not to talk to Pete on the radio. Instead, he called Pete directly on his cell phone. Pete was watching the two boats on his port side and the one on his starboard, making sure that the distance between them and *Miss Alice* stayed at one hundred yards, as Colonel Wilson had requested.

Above the din of the winds, waves, and the old boat's motor, Pete heard his cell phone ring. He picked it up.

"Hello," said Pete.

"Pete, this is Colonel Wilson," he said, pausing and taking another deep breath. "We found them, Pete. Their boat came up with the flood tide, and Team Three spotted it marooned back in the marsh at the mouth of the Miles River."

"Are they OK?" asked Pete.

"No, Pete. They're both dead."

"Oh...Oh no! Oh God no!" Pete cried out. "It can't be!"

Then there was silence.

"Unfortunately, its true, Pete. Both of them were shot and placed in body bags. I need you or Brady to meet me at the restaurant so that we can identify them."

"Where are they, colonel?"

"The boat is beached in a small marshy area at Rich Neck off of Tilghman Point."

Overhearing the conversation, Brady asked Pete to hand him the phone. Pete, in a zombielike state of mind, handed it over to Brady without question.

"Colonel?"

"Yes."

"This is Brady. I'll be the one coming with you. Uncle Pete's too upset. I don't want him to have to deal with it." There was a pause. "Colonel, I've had lots of experience with identifying buddies in battles, so I can handle it better than Uncle Pete can. I'll meet you at the restaurant in ten minutes."

"OK. See you there," said the colonel.

At 12:10 a.m. Brady, Colonel Wilson, and Tommy boarded the lieutenant's boat. As they approached Rich Neck, they could see the canopy of the *Miss Patricia* tilted to port, as the water and rain continued to pound her.

To reach the *Miss Patricia* as Kurt and his men had done, the men anchored their boat, jumped into the marsh, and walked through the marshlands. While the tide had lifted her up onto the solid portion of the marsh, she was still leaning to port so that the portside was lying in a tidal pool. The starboard side was on fast marshland. To board her, they had to climb over her stern, using the rudder as a step to get high enough for Kurt and his men to lean over and help pull them onboard.

Once onboard, Kurt briefed the colonel, as Lieutenant Price and Brady looked on.

Pointing to a dark spot on the deck, Kurt said, "This is where we think Mike was standing when he was hit. From the damage to the engine box, it looks like one of them was blown back and crashed into the box cover before he hit the floor. You'll notice the blood on the floorboard just starboard of the engine box. The other, which we think was Mack, shot his gun from here, getting one of the guys as he stood across from him holding on to the canopy strut where parts of bone and brain matter are still embedded."

Brady was having flashbacks as he saw the rain drip off of the canopy and roll down the damaged strut, where skin and brain were solidly woven into the wood's grain.

"You OK, Brady?" asked Kurt, as he saw Brady's knees slightly buckle and his eyes take on a blank stare.

"Yeah, Kurt," said Brady. "I'm good."

Kurt led Brady into the steering cabin and then down into the forward sleeping area, where the two body bags lay on the floor between the bunk beds. Kurt warned Brady that the bodies were in poor shape due to the head injuries and the decomposition that had occurred over the last two days.

Brady stepped forward and unzipped the first bag. The stench of death rose into the air. It was Captain Mack. Brady put his hand over his nose and turned toward the other bunk bed. Kurt quickly zipped up Mack's body bag. When Brady unzipped the second bag, tears starting to roll down his cheeks. It was Mike. With one hand over his nose, he zipped the bag back up, turned around, and quickly exited the cabin.

Once he was back on deck, Brady reached for the canopy strut for balance. Then, realizing it was the strut that still contained embedded brain tissue and with shotgun pellets, he wiped his hands on his pants and sat down on the far gunwale.

Brady leaned forward with his elbows on his knees. He placed his head in his hands. The horror of the moment raised flashbacks from the firefights on those faraway Hindu Kush Mountains of Afghanistan. Pictures of his dying buddies mixed in like some gruesome slide show with the two images of Mack and Mike.

My God, he thought. *This war never ends. Now it's back on our soil, just like 9/11.*

At the moment, amid the pain of losing two more friends and fellow watermen, Brady resolved that he would make sure that whoever had done this would pay the price. The clarity of what had happened spoke to him. He was the only one who was close enough to the perpetrators to be able to stop them or at least help foil their plans.

Brady stood up, surrounded by the other men, and said, "We need to go back to the restaurant and decide what needs to be done. This is just the tip of the iceberg. This is just the beginning of the kind of terror these people are about to unleash. We've got to stop them or die trying."

Of the three, only Tommy Price knew what Brady was alluding to. He nodded and said, "You're right, Brady. Let's go back and talk about how to deal with this."

"Kurt, we're going to leave you with taking care of Mack and Mike. I'll have Captain Pete call Beth and Tonya to tell them what's happened. Get the fire company to meet you at Knapp Narrows and find out how the women want to take care of their husbands."

✳✳✳

Abed took the news about Raffi and the two watermen in stride. To him, it was the mission, rather than the men, that counted. Fearing more intensive searches as a result of hearing, over the coast guard channel, that the search team had found the two watermen and their boat, Abed decided to leave the *Miss Martha* in the boathouse at Black Walnut Point. There, they could clean her up, repair the canopy strut, and patch up the shotgun pellet holes in the gunwales, canopy, and sideboards.

✳✳✳

Salah called Maya and told her to meet Abed, Kaleem, Jamil, and Omar, the weapons expert, and himself at Black Walnut Point for a crucial meeting. The meeting began at exactly 3:00 a.m. Based on the facts as he knew them and the security calls that Kaleem had monitored, Abed brought everyone up to date on Raffi's death, the disposal of Captain Mack and his son Mike, and the coast guard and NRP search that was underway. He thanked Allah for the weather and prayed that Allah would continue the weather pattern for the next twenty-four hours to help hide their final preparations for the attack.

"We are so close to fulfilling our mission," said Abed. "We only need to remain undercover for another thirty-six hours. To guarantee our security, I want Salah, with Haamid's help, to dispose of all local team members, including those locals we hired as security. But no cell team members are to be disposed of. We will need a lot of their expertise to fade back into the woodwork after the attack is over."

During the meeting, Salah had required one of the security guards to monitor *Miss Martha*'s radios in case there were any pertinent communications from or between the coast guard and the NRP.

A knock came at the back kitchen door. The guard inside, with his AK-47 at the ready, opened the door and looked out to verify that it was one of their team members. When he saw that it was Miguel, he nodded for him to enter. Miguel quickly stepped into the dining room, approached Salah, and whispered in his ear, "Lots more chatter on the radios. Depending on the weather, they're planning to launch a crucial search at 6:30 a.m. from the NRP site at Kent Narrows. They'll be out looking for whoever was involved with the *Miss Patricia*."

"Any mention of our boats?"

"Yes. The search is focused on a large Bay-built dead rise with no bottom paint and lots of antennas."

"Let me know if there's anything new."

"Yes, sir." Miguel left to resume his radio monitoring.

Abed, after going over the schedule and the plans to dismantle the safe houses and cleanse the team of all non-essential members, started a discussion about the timing for setting the Kent Narrows detonation devices.

The encounter with Mack and Mike had thrown their timetable off. It was clear that they had to accelerate the setting of the Kent Narrows devices, regardless of the worsening weather. Raffi had been the backup captain. Except for Brady, they had no one else they could rely on to negotiate the Narrows and maneuver the boat safely to and through it.

Abed started off the discussion by saying, "I'm concerned that if we ask Brady to captain the boat, he will expose us to the coast guard and the NRP. He must be very upset with the loss of his friends, and I'm sure he has already connected the dots back to us. We also need to silence him as soon as possible, before they heighten the search for us. I don't believe we can afford to use our bay boats now, unless it's at night. And, we can't afford to use the cigarette boats until the attack is complete. So, what do we do?"

"Abed, I think we need to do three things," said Salah. "First, we must use Brady to captain the boat to the Narrows and help with the explosives. I believe that if we try to dispose of him now, they might soon discover him. As you said, that would only intensify the search for us. I think that Maya needs to call him and set up the Narrows trip, using the smaller and faster *Lucy May*. Second, after that trip is over, she can have him tied-up and sequestered. Then I believe the best place to initially hold him would be in the attic of the Black Walnut Point farmhouse. Once the *Miss Martha* is fixed up, we can transfer him to her dive chamber. The third thing is, we need to move the cigarette boats out of the Choptank Farm boathouse and down to the Parks Neck Farm, where we can put them in that larger boat house, out of view of any choppers."

Before anyone could react to Salah's suggested solution, Miguel returned to announce that a chopper had taken off to cover the upper and lower Hooper Islands, the Honga River, the Choptank River, and the area around Vienna on the Nanticoke River. Hearing this, Salah surmised that the Homeland Security search team was now looking in those areas. Not only were they looking for their boats but also for other bodies. He leaned over to Abed and expressed his opinion.

Abed nodded in agreement and told Miguel to return to his monitoring and immediately let him know of any further changes.

Salah said, "So, what do you want us to do now, Abed?"

Abed responded, "What we need to do now is to plant the Narrow's explosives and detonators. We need to verify the arrival time of the *Mana Kia*, as well as the arrival time of the LNG Tanker, *Queen of the Adriatic,* at the Gas Docks. We need to go over plans for the *Mana Kia* with both chopper pilots, Bashir and Haron. We need to keep a low profile and monitor the radios 24/7. If we only have personnel at Black Walnut Point and at the Choptank Farm, our footprint will be smaller and hopefully unnoticed."

Abed made the decision. Maya was sent off to call Brady. Even though they might never use the small Bay-built boat after that night, Jamil was sent to replace the original *Lucy May* name plaque with the new one, the *Miss Catherine James*, in case the NRP started to nose around the area between Tilghman and Eastern Bay. Abed announced that the meeting was adjourned, and everyone immediately dispersed to take care of the business at hand.

✳✳✳

"It was a trot-liner who found both of the bodies at about 5:00 a.m. They were floating along the shoreline north of the Nanticoke Bridge, over," said Lieutenant Price.

Colonel Wilson responded, "Do we know who they are? Over."

Lieutenant Price said, "No, Colonel. All we know is that they are Hispanic - probably Mexican - and they were shot execution style in back of the head with their hands tied behind their backs. Both of them have been in the water for some time. Over."

"Are you going to run forensics and DNA on them? Over."

"Yes, sir. Without any IDs, that's all we can do. Over."

"Thanks, Tommy. Keep me apprised of any changes. Over."

"Will do, Colonel. Lieutenant Price, out."

✳✳✳

"The word is out, Abed. Kaleem just heard that Carlos's body and his friend's body were found just north of the Nanticoke Bridge. Luckily, they're pretty well decomposed, so identifying them will be hard to do, and it will probably take some time," said Salah.

"What about Smitty and Mohammed?"

"I should hear back from Jamil about those two later this morning, before 12:00 p.m."

"Where are they dumping them?"

"I'm not sure exactly where they are dumping them, but it's some place in the marshes of the little Choptank River. It's somewhere around Dailville."

"Good, but make sure the tide won't take them out of there. We can't risk two more bodies being found before Monday."

"We've got them strapped to anchors, so they're not going anywhere anytime soon."

"Good," Abed said, hanging up. The discussion was over.

✳✳✳

Colonel Wilson gathered everyone around the Rip Tide Restaurant bar. To secure the area, he placed one of his men at the entrance to the bar. Everyone crowded around. Anguish and rage prevailed.

"Before we start, I want us all to bow our heads in silent prayer for Mack, Mike, and their families. This is both a tragedy and a warning of what might come. We need God's help on this. Please, bow your heads." For a minute, the only sound was the wind outside.

Finally, they all raised their heads and Colonel Wilson began to talk. "Kurt will be taking care of getting Mack and Mike back to Tilghman. Our search is over, but both the NRP and the coast guard personnel are to report to their respective stations as soon as possible. Rumors among us are rampant. Is what's happened here part of a bigger and more frightening prospect? The answer unfortunately is most likely - Yes.

I understand from those in charge that what we have seen with Mack and Mike is a small part of a larger plan to wreak havoc on the Bay over the coming weekend. I have contacted both Homeland Security and the governor's office. From now on, Homeland Security will lead whatever is going on in conjunction with the state police. Both the coast guard and NRP will be part of the response team, but they are no longer in charge. Our search-and-rescue task is over; our immediate mission is complete."

"Both the governor's communications office and Homeland Security are stressing that everyone in this room must maintain complete silence. Lives depended on this, as evidenced by these two heinous murders. No one - I repeat, no one - is to discuss what you have seen or heard here or out on the water today. This is now an issue for Homeland Security to manage. Any further action to be taken falls under the Homeland Security Act. Do not share what you've seen or heard today with either your family or friends. Homeland Security assures me that any leak will be prosecuted under the DHS Act, and that the consequences will be severe. On a different subject, our best guess is that arrangements for Mack and Mike will most likely occur next Wednesday, July 7, 2010.

"Any questions?"

"Yes," said one of the watermen. "How can this be kept quiet when everyone will know about Mack and Mike?"

"No one but us will know exactly what has happened. Homeland Security wants their deaths to be attributed to drowning as a result of the boat capsizing. This is to be described as an accident. Anyone with loose lips will be easy for DHS to identify, since we are the only ones who know the real story. For God's sake, keep your mouths shut. Is that clear?"

Everyone nodded and responded, "Yes."

"Any other questions?"

No one spoke.

"Thank you all for all of your hard work these last two days. Yes, we have had a sad ending, but we will find the perpetrators and justice will prevail. Have a safe trip home.

Again, if anyone wants to wait out the storm, Lieutenant Price says that you're welcome to tie up at Matapeake."

The meeting broke up. Pete and Brady climbed back aboard the *Miss Alice* and headed back home to tell Beth and Tanya about what had befallen their men. This was the saddest day of Pete's life. He'd lost his friend of sixty years - a friend who should have died from old age, rather than at the point of a terrorist's gun.

Brady took the helm, while Pete sat at the lunch table writing notes to himself concerning whom to call: the deacon at the church, the volunteer fire company, the undertaker, and other friends and family members. The list grew longer as they made their way south, plowing into the waves and the southeast winds.

Entering the calmer waters of Knapp's Narrows, Pete turned to Brady with tears in his eyes and said, "How am I going to tell Beth and Tonya about the details of the murders?"

"Uncle Pete, you're going to tell them that they died from drowning when the boat capsized, and that's all you're going to tell them. With these terrorist attacks, which are perhaps imminent, the rest of the story is not relevant. They're gone and right now security is far more important than the truth about how they died."

Pete sat up straight, leaned over, and touched Brady's arm. "Thanks, Brady. You're far wiser than I am. Your advice is absolutely correct."

"Thanks, Uncle Pete."

Later that afternoon, Pete, Brady, and Louise went over to Beth's home to tell her and Tonya about their men. It was very difficult.

$$* * *$$

The funeral arrangements were set for Wednesday the seventh. Both funerals would be held at the same time at the Methodist Church on Tilghman Island. Pete was to deliver the eulogy for Mack, and he and Brady would be part of a team of pallbearers that Beth and Tonya had chosen. Since the funerals would be held simultaneously, the church would need to provide additional space under a large party tent that Harrison's Chesapeake House would supply. The Harrisons were also supplying the electronic equipment and speakers that would be needed to provide those under the tent with a live relay of the funeral service that was taking place inside. They expected a huge crowd. Because of Mack's involvement in numerous watermen's associations and the greater waterman's community all along the Bay, they were expecting people to attend from Maryland, as well as Virginia and Delaware.

Pete and Brady left Mack's home as a continuous flow of others from the community filed through. As they climbed into Pete's truck, Brady said, "Uncle Pete, there's no question in my mind as to who killed them. Do you have any doubts?"

"No, Brady. There's no question about it. I only wish Mack and I had never pursued the bastards and their damn boat after our encounter last February. I'll regret that for as long as I live."

"Uncle Pete, you can't blame yourself for that. Considering the people we are dealing with and what we think they're all about, thank God you all did pursue it. At least we now know that they're plotting an attack and the authorities are on it."

"Yeah, but are they really on it, Brady? I still don't feel like they are following all of the leads and aggressively looking for either the terrorists or for the right answers."

"Well, after your meeting with Lieutenant Price, he went directly to his boss and they met with the DNR Secretary. So, the top brass knows what the story is."

"Yeah, but it seems to me that they aren't doing zilch," said Pete.

"Well, I am not defending them, Uncle Pete, but it is Fourth of July weekend.'

"That's no excuse, Brady. What I want to know is how to get the brass off dead center?"

Brady thought for a moment and then said, "I'll talk to the authorities about a time and place to ambush Abed and his Team."

"How?"

"Through my relationship with Maya."

"How so?" Pete asked.

"By setting up a meeting with her," said Brady. "She's supposed to call me anyway about placing the detonation devices at the two Narrows bridges."

"So, are you going to have Homeland Security show up tonight, or are you going to have them ambush them during one of their meetings?"

"I think I'll do the latter, Uncle Pete. It's best to get as many of them bagged at one time, and we need to do so as soon as possible. I should know tonight when they will have their next meeting, and I will alert Homeland Security to the time and place. Since we will be planting devices later this evening and into the early morning, they will probably stay over at the Crab Alley Farm. So, my guess is that their next meeting will be at the Crab Alley Farm early tomorrow morning, around 6:30 a.m."

As they arrived at Pete's driveway, Brady's phone rang. It was Maya. Brady put his finger to his lips to make sure that Pete knew to remain silent. He then mouthed her name and pointed to the phone. So that Pete could hear, he set the phone on speaker.

"Hello?"

"I'm so sorry to hear about your uncle and cousin," said Maya. "It sounds to me like they might have come across some armed drug traffickers who were afraid of being caught. Nasty business and nasty people."

"Thanks, Maya. That may have been the case. I just don't know. But the state police and Homeland Security are on it, and the perpetrators will be found. It's just a matter of time."

"Glad to hear they're on it, Brady. I'm so very sorry for your loss. You had enough of that in Afghanistan. You certainly don't need more of it here."

Curling his lip, Brady said, "No, you're right. We don't need any of it back here."

"If you feel up to it, let's set the Kent Narrows detonation devices this evening. Can you meet me at the Crab Alley Farm at 9:30 p.m.?"

Looking Pete straight in the face, Brady said, "Sure. I need a diversion right about now. I'll see you there at 9:30 p.m. Will the big boat be there at the dock?"

"No. We're going to use the smaller boat, the Miss *Catherine James*. It's there now. See you later, Brady."

"Gotcha," said Brady. "And thanks for your kind words about Mack and Mike."

"You're welcome," said Maya.

Brady ended the call and placed the phone in his pocket.

Pete asked, "Brady, how do you think she knew about Mack and Mike?"

In reply Brady said, "The fact that she already knew how they were killed tells me that her people did it. There's no way she could have known about it, unless they were the perpetrators.

Uncle Pete, did she sound convincing."

"Yeah, she sounded about as convincing as a liar can. It's a good thing she didn't see the disgust on your face. You sure are good at curling your lip, young man."

"Hopefully she will never know how I really feel. As long as they continue to need me, I guess I'm OK. Uncle Pete, I will be taking the walkie-talkie with me tonight. Please be sure to keep yours on. The battery should last about ten hours when it's turned on. I shouldn't have a problem getting a hold of you if I need to, but if you don't hear from me by 2:00 a.m. at the latest, start a search for me up near the Kent Narrows Bridge."

***

Kaleem called Abed on a secure line, "We've got another problem, Abed. I just heard over the NRP channel that a trot-liner working in the waters of the Nanticoke River above Vienna discovered two more bodies."

"Weren't they to be tied to anchors and dumped in the marsh way up the Choptank River?"

"Yes, they were," said Kaleem, "but obviously somebody got lazy and didn't carry out my orders."

"Find out who it was and take care of him immediately."

"Yes, sir."

Chapter 20

Final Preparations. Friday Night, July 2

Brady climbed into his truck and headed north to the Crab Alley Farm for his meeting with Maya. On his way, he called Lieutenant Price on his cell phone and told him what he was doing. He asked him to have Homeland Security raid the Crab Alley Farm early Saturday morning sometime between 4:00 a.m. and 6:00 a.m., which was when he believed Abed might hold the cell's next meeting. After parking behind the hedgerow at the head of the dock, he walked down to the boat where Maya, Omar, and Jamil were waiting.

The wind whistled through the six canopy antennas and buffed the boat against the dock's piling bumpers. The storm showed no signs of letting up. It would not be easy to maneuver and hold the boat steady under the Narrows bridges. Brady informed Maya that he would captain the boat to and from the Narrows, but he still did not feel comfortable enough to do the actual diving. She said, "I'll dive, no problem. Jamil will act as my backup and Omar will be our deck-safety backup."

On their way to the Narrows, Maya and Jamil donned their wetsuits, flippers, facemasks, and headlamps, preparing themselves for the cold water below. The boat arrived at the pilings twenty minutes later. Maya and Jamil backed up to the starboard gunwale and rolled over into the water, as Brady held the newly named *Miss Catherine James* against the rushing tide. While the propellers would still be in motion and thus a potential hazard, they had decided that it was far better to have Brady work the engines against the swift flowing tide, instead of using an anchor. In the event that they needed to depart quickly, it would take considerable time to haul in an anchor, which would expose them to possible detection.

It was pitch-black and the rain pelted the water, creating instant bubbles that floated off with the tide, popped, and then disappeared. No one in their right mind would be out in this downpour. Since the bandoliers and detonation boxes were identical to the ones at the Gas Docks, it was relatively easy for Maya to make the necessary connections, including the connections with the antenna.

After Maya hooked up the explosives, detonation boxes, and antennas at both bridges, Omar helped her and Jamil back onboard, while Brady maneuvered the boat around to the drawbridge pilings. Omar checked Maya's and Jamil's tanks and regulators. He gave them a thumbs-up to let them know that their equipment was ready. Dragging their flippers along the deck as they backed up to the gunwale, Maya and Jamil slipped over the side. Omar handed them the bandoliers and the detonation equipment. Diving down to the shelf on the pilings, they began to attach the detonation boxes and the ends of the bandoliers to the pitons that Brady had affixed to the pilings. When she had finished, she and Jamil broke the surface and tapped on the boat's port side. Within seconds, Omar reached over and pulled Maya and Jamil into the boat. The minute they were onboard, Brady pushed the throttle forward and spun the boat around into Eastern Bay, heading back to the Crab Alley Creek farm.

As they approached Crab Alley Creek, the winds increased, howling across the water. Waves rose two and a half to three feet high, and the swells ran thirty feet apart. Brady thought, *It sure would be easier if I had the big boat, but then again, it would've been a lot tougher to hold her steady up in the Narrows.*

Just as Brady pulled up to the dock, Maya ordered him to stay onboard with Omar while she and Jamil went up to the farmhouse. Brady thought, *That's a little strange. For some reason, she doesn't want me to be up there. She wants me to be onboard and under the watchful eye of Omar.* Brady, however, was getting used to Maya's aloofness and her obvious distrust of him. It was pretty clear that she was no longer romantically interested in him and that she no longer trusted him. Brady thought, *Now she knows how I feel.*

Maya proceeded to the farmhouse and instructed Jamil and the two security guards to check out the house, the sheds, and the barn, being sure to clear out everything. She didn't want anything left that was traceable back to them. Once all of the buildings were cleared, she instructed the two guards to drive back to Black Walnut Point, where she would meet them, as soon as she arrived by boat.

***

Because of the intensity of the storm, the ride back to Black Walnut Point took more than an hour and a half. Reaching the end of Black Walnut Point, Brady carefully pulled the *Miss Catherine James* into the east-side slip of the large boathouse. As he did so, he noticed that two of Abed's men were working on the canopy and the engine box of the *Miss Martha*.

Brady finished docking and hopped up on the walkway, when the two security guards who'd driven down from the Crab Alley Creek Farm suddenly came around the corner of the boathouse and overpowered him. They immediately whisked him up to the farmhouse.

Brady did not resist. He knew better. He realized, *This is it. The end is near. The* Miss Martha *was the boat that Mack and Mike had encountered, and it was now undergoing repairs. They were getting close to finishing him off.* Having been near death before, Brady knew that he should save his strength for that critical moment when he might have the advantage - the upper hand - just before they tried to kill him.

They patted him down and confiscated his walkie-talkie, his cell phone, and the fisherman's fillet knife that was hooked to his belt. They then dragged him up to the attic, where he was trussed up and left alone. The attic had no windows and no ventilation. It only contained a single army cot, a bucket to go to the bathroom in, and one bottle of spring water - that was it. Luckily, when they patted him down, they had failed to find the small penknife that had been his dad's. He always kept it inside a fold of the ball cap he wore.

Brady waited thirty minutes before making a move. Certain that the guards had left the floor below him, Brady knocked his cap off onto the cot. Twisting his trussed-up hands to access the fold in the ball cap, he removed his Dad's small penknife. He then sawed against the plastic ties that bound his hands. Finally, after about ten minutes, he was able to cut through the ties and free his hands.

Brady sat on the bed and took a few gulps of the bottled water. He was too tired and thirsty to notice that the bottle-cap's seal had been broken. In a few minutes, he started to feel drowsy. Too much was going on in his head, he thought. He lay down on the cot and closed his eyes for a few minutes to collect his thoughts.

✳✳✳

By hacking into the Baltimore-based private shipping company's computer system, which the DHS used to monitor ship movements on the Bay, Kaleem confirmed that the *Queen of the Adriatic* would be arriving at the Gas Docks on Saturday, July 3, 2010. On Tuesday, it was scheduled to unload its cargo to the land-based Liquid Natural Gas Terminal. Earlier, Kaleem had also confirmed that the *Mana Kia* was still anchored off of Annapolis. Constant radio monitoring revealed that, except for a skeleton crew of only six people, all of the crewmembers of the *Mana Kia* were on leave for the weekend.

✳✳✳

Late at night on July 2, 2010, Salah and one of his security guards loaded a small ten-foot Zodiac into the bed of one of the Black Walnut Point Farm's pick-up trucks and drove to the east side of the Bay Bridge.

At the base of the bridge apron, where it met the Kent Island shoreline, there was a small beach that was usually strewn with driftwood and abandoned crab pots. It was a place where kids came to play in the dirty sand and take a shallow swim.

Salah pulled the truck up onto the grassy area next to this small beach. They unloaded and finished inflating the Zodiac, attached a two-stroke, ten-horsepower camouflaged motor, and launch it from the beach. The security guard steered as Salah directed him out to the eastern edge of the channel, where he took soundings to confirm the depths shown on the Bay map, plotting the points on *Miss Martha's* GPS. Once the soundings were complete, they took the zodiac back to shore, deflated it, and loaded it onto the truck for their return to Black Walnut Point.

✳✳✳

By 10:00 p.m. when Pete usually went to bed, Brady still hadn't returned home. Pete set his alarm for 2:00 a.m., which was when Brady had said that Pete should start looking for him if he hadn't returned. At exactly 2:00 a.m. Pete's alarm went off. He rolled out of bed and checked the weather. The wind continued to blow like hell, and the rain had intensified. Not wanting to believe that Brady might be in trouble, Pete waited until 2:10 a.m. and then called the Natural Resource Police at the Narrows Office. Pete requested that the NRP office send out a couple of boats as soon as possible. He also told them that they should check out the Crab Alley Creek Farm. He thought that the terrorists might possibly be holding Brady there. All of this was consistent with Brady's belief that between 4:00 a.m. and 6:00 a.m. a terrorist cell meeting might be going on at that very farmhouse.

Within minutes of Pete's call, the NRP launched their largest boat. It was a twenty-five-foot boat from the Narrows Ramp. NRP immediately called the coast guard to send one of their patrol boats to meet them at the Crab Alley Creek dock. In addition, NRP contacted Homeland Security and the state police, who launched a pincer movement from the landslide to coincide with the arrival of the NRP and the coast guard boats.

***

Homeland Security, the state police, the coast guard, and NRP launched a coordinated assault on the Crab Alley Creek Farm at 3:30 a.m. The attack was two-pronged; they were attacking from the land and from the sea. NRP and the coast guard headed up the waterside attack, while Homeland Security and the state police launched the landside attack.

Based upon the call from Captain Pete and the information that Brady had shared with his uncle, they were hoping to find not only Brady but also Abed, Salah, and other key personnel in a meeting in the farmhouse kitchen. Instead, they found that the property was totally vacant.

The Maryland State Police and the DHS crime lab personnel did a thorough investigation, including fingerprint analysis. While they found numerous prints, none showed up on the national register. There was no trash. The refrigerator and freezer had been emptied and cleaned out. All toilet paper and paper towels had been taken from the farmhouse, and its contents had been left spotless. There was also evidence that security cameras around the property had been removed. Even the gravel in the barn and driveway had been raked to obliterate any tire tracks or footprints. Those who had occupied this safe house and outbuildings were real professionals; nothing had been left to chance.

The only piece of evidence that they found was in the dock area. In the parking area adjacent to the hedgerow at the head of the dock, they found tire tracks from a Hummer. The canine that they brought down to the dock area had sniffed for explosives and booby traps around the farmhouse and the outbuildings. The canine officer took his dog along the hedgerow to check out the undergrowth of multi-flora roses, bay berries, and switchgrass. In the thick of a large cluster of multi-flora, the dog found several crab baskets. The dog, Tucker, was one of the best bomb-sniffing canines of the DHS. He clawed at the baskets and announced his find with a succession of shrill barks.

Tucker's handler pulled him back and had him heel, while one of the crime lab techs pulled the baskets out into the open. The lab tech himself sniffed the inside of the baskets and said, "There's no question that these were used to transport C-4 or similar explosives."

They spent three hours scouring the entire farm, but other than the crab baskets they found no additional signs or clues about who had been there or what they had been doing. Most importantly, they had failed to find Brady.

With no leads and no conclusions, the raid had been a bust.

Chapter 21

Just One More Day. Saturday Morning, July 3

Three hours later, at 6:00 a.m. on Saturday morning, Brady woke up with the rain still pounding on the roof. He tried to stand up several times, but each time he fell back on the bed. After several attempts, his mind was finally sufficiently engaged for him to stand up, though he was very wobbly. Brady knew that he must escape or Abed's plot would become a reality. Still groggy, he looked at the bottle again and it dawned on him that they had spiked his water to knock him out.

Brady had no other choice but to overpower the guards. Without a window to escape through, his only route to freedom was to go back down the attic stairs. After shouting five times to get the guard to come up and empty the toilet bucket, Brady finally heard the lock on the attic trapdoor click open. Standing behind the hinge door, he waited for the guard to push it up and show himself. As soon as the guard stepped off the stairs and onto the attic floor, Brady overpowered him by throwing the bucket and its contents in his face. He wrestled the guard to the floor. Using the penknife, he sliced his neck several times. The guard died immediately.

Brady grabbed the guard's AK-47 and four clips from his ammo belt. Simultaneously, he lowered the trapdoor to await the second guard's response to all the commotion. Yelling out his fellow guard's name, the second guard came charging up the steps, AK-47 in hand. Brady stood behind the trapdoor again. As soon as the guard's head popped up, he slammed the door down hard on the guard's head. The guard slid down the steps. Brady, with the first guard's AK-47 hung over his shoulder, jumped down to the bottom of the stairs and sliced the fallen guard's throat four times, making sure that he was also dead.

Brady grabbed the other AK-47 and a few more clips from the second guard. With one gun slung over his left shoulder and the other in his right hand, Brady quickly checked out each room of the house as he raced toward the kitchen. When he reached the kitchen, he quickly grabbed a knife from the kitchen sink, in case he would need an extra weapon. He then went to the outside kitchen door, turned its handle, and opened the door just nine inches. Using the nine-inch clearance, he poked his head out to be sure that no one was guarding the rear of the house. He heard voices down at the boathouse - two voices. They seemed to be discussing the replacement of a canopy strut. More discussions occurred, but Brady couldn't make out the words or the subjects.

His objective was to reach one of the boats and hijack it for his escape. Remembering that the *Miss Martha* was being worked on, probably by the two men whose voices he had just heard, Brady set his sights on the smaller but faster *Miss Catherine James*. This was the boat that he had used just six hours earlier to help plant explosives at Kent Narrows.

Crouching into a special-forces assault position, he ran out at full speed to the east side of the boathouse. Upon reaching it, he quietly walked along the east side of the exterior cantilevered walkway and peered through the side window. There, directly in front of him, was the *Miss Catherine James*. Next to her in the far slip was the *Miss Martha*, which was undergoing major repairs on its canopy, canopy strut, and engine box. The engine box and underside of the canopy were peppered with shotgun pellets. The canopy strut, however, was almost severed in two.

Brady turned and squatted with his back to the wall just below the window. He thought, *Good! Mack and Mike must have gotten off some shots before they died. I hope they killed some of those bastards.* Shifting to the present, Brady thought to himself, *There have to be more guards than just the two in the house, but where are they?* Leaning against the wall, Brady thought, *Where would I put my men if I were Salah?* Suddenly, new voices jarred him out of this thought process. The voices were coming from the far end of the boathouse pier forty feet in front of him. Brady saw their backs just as they were turning to view the open water out front. Fearing that he would be seen, Brady slid off the catwalk and into the water. Where the catwalk was attached to the pier, the water was only about four feet deep. Brady hooked the AK-47's slings over some large nails that protruded from the cross braces under the catwalk. Rather than using his small penknife, he drew the kitchen knife from his belt. Standing frozen under the catwalk, he waited for the two guards. They were now approaching his position.

How the hell can I knife both of them without one of them firing his AK-47? . Just as the two guards reached the end of the pier, where it attached to the boathouse and the west-side catwalk, one of them stopped to call across to the two carpenters who were working on the *Miss Martha*. The other one continued to approach Brady's position. Just as he reached Brady's hiding place under the catwalk, Brady catapulted himself out of the water, grab the guard, and pulled him into the shallow water underneath the catwalk. He placed his left hand over the guard's mouth. Holding him under the water, Brady thrust the knife deep into the guard's chest. With an almost seamless motion, he withdrew the knife and cut the guard's throat from ear to ear. Within seconds, the combatant's resistance evaporated and Brady slid the body under the catwalk, pinning it between two double pilings.

The second guard continued his conversation with the carpenters. Finally, after a long and agonizing wait, the second guard reappeared from around the boathouse corner and began walking along the east-side catwalk. As before, Brady brought him down the same way that the had brought down the first guard. It took ten seconds to achieve his goal. Both guards were dead and securely wedged between the double pilings. 'Now,' he wondered, 'what's my next move?'

His mind raced through a number of scenarios. He considered swimming underwater to the stern of the *Miss Catherine James*, where he might be able to climb up on the inside boathouse catwalk. Moving forward in a crouch, he might be able to enter the cabin without being seen. As he mulled over this idea, his luck changed for the better. After the guards he had killed were no longer around, the carpenters turned up their radio, which was tuned into a Hispanic music station. Their boom box was just loud enough to mask the sound of Brady stepping onboard and entering the cabin of the *Miss Catherine James*. He slipped onboard and carefully undid the starboard stern line. He then crawled up to the starboard bowline and undid that too. Since the wind was coming out of the southwest, there was no need for port lines so the boat would stay put in its V-shaped catwalk berth.

Once he was inside the cabin, Brady stayed low until he was sure that they had not heard or seen him. He slowly moved over to the portside to take a look at the carpenters. The two men were hard at work repairing the *Miss Martha*, and they were completely oblivious to his presence. The clock above the console read 9:00 a.m. Brady desperately needed to get away and head up to Pete's dock at Knapp's Narrows.

Miguel called, "Salah, there is something very wrong at Black Walnut Point. I can't raise any of my four security guards on the phone down there."

"No answers at all?"

"None! Plus, the two carpenters working on the *Miss Martha* don't answer their phones."

"Where are you, Miguel?"

"I'm between St. Michael's and Tilghman, and I have Marco, with me."

"OK. When you get to the entrance to Black Walnut Point, stay put and wait for me. Marco and I will be there in ten minutes."

✳✳✳

Brady waited a few more minutes to see if the carpenters would take a break and go up to the farmhouse, allowing him to start the engine and quickly back out of the boat slip. The last thing he wanted was for them to hear him start the engine and have them call for reinforcements. They were repairing the *Miss Martha*, but this didn't mean that they weren't part of Salah's security detail. As with all of his security personnel, Salah made sure that each guard was well trained in all aspects of guerrilla warfare and had a least one or two additional skills, such as carpentry, engine maintenance, and communications.

✳✳✳

Miguel, Salah, and Marco arrived at the farmhouse simultaneously. Salah sent Marco into the house to check on the two guards, while he and Miguel checked on the perimeter around the house and the outbuildings between the house and the water. Fifteen seconds after entering the back door of the farmhouse, Marco came running out. Pointing to the kitchen door, he shouted to Salah, "Both guards are in here. They're

218

dead! One's on the second floor at the bottom of the attic stairs and the other one's in the attic. Both of them have been stabbed and their AK-47s have been taken."

Salah grabbed Miguel and said, "Brady would head for the boathouse to make his getaway by water. You take the right side of the boathouse. Marco and I will take the left. I don't want Brady to be killed until tomorrow, just before the attack, but I sure as hell don't want him to escape. If he's in there, we need to overpower him. Don't kill him. Marco, are you sure the guards' AK-47s are missing?"

"Yes, sir," he said. "I didn't see them and I didn't find any magazines."

"Damn. He's armed. He probably has both guns. If you need to shoot, go for his legs. We may need him later for his boating skills, or we might need to keep him as a hostage. You guys got that?"

Both Miguel and Marco nodded.

The men bolted off toward the boathouse. As instructed, Miguel ran to the west-side catwalk. Salah and Marco ran to the east-side catwalk. Stepping onto the catwalk, Salah noticed the smell of blood. Placing his hand behind him, he indicated for Marco to stop in his tracks. Sniffing the air, Salah scanned the shoreline first and then the water in front of him. Finally, he scanned the catwalk beneath his feet.

Barely visible between the catwalk boards, two large objects had been wedged between the corner pilings. Whatever they were, the incoming waves were moving them to and fro as the water rolled under the boathouse. Salah quietly slipped off of the catwalk and into the water. He crouched underneath the catwalk to view the wedged masses. They were bodies - his security guards' bodies. Blood flowed from their knife wounds and slowly mixed with the froth of the small waves, as the cold water gently lapped at their open wounds. Both men were clearly dead.

Marco reached down and helped pull Salah back onto the catwalk. Rather than risk looking through the boathouse window and perhaps being seen, Salah quietly walked to the end of the catwalk. Marco followed him. Here, the catwalk connected to the pier at the boathouse's open end. Salah peered around the corner and saw Brady crouched down in the cabin of the *Miss Catherine James*, and he looked over at the carpenters. Then he heard one of the carpenters call out to Miguel, whom he had spotted on their side of the boathouse, "Ola."

Miguel placed his finger over his lips and shook his head. The carpenters immediately went silent and looked to him for instructions. Miguel signaled with his arm for them to drop in their tracks. Both men dropped to the deck of the *Miss Martha*. Miguel entered the boathouse and crawled along the north-side catwalk toward the bow of the *Miss Catherine James*. As he did so, he saw Salah and Marco peer around the east-side catwalk at the open end of the boathouse. Miguel indicated with hand signals that he would distract Brady while they closed in on him from behind.

Miguel stood up once he had reached the bow of the *Miss Catherine James*. He called after Brady as he jumped up on her bow, and he lowered his AK-47 so that its laser beam was focused squarely on Brady's chest. Brady now stood straight up between the captain's chair and the dining bench. He held one of the AK-47s diagonally across his chest. The other AK-47 lay two feet away from him on the dining table to his left.

"Don't move, Brady. Take your hand off of the gun now."

Brady said nothing. He stayed absolutely still and smiled at Miguel, "So now what, Miguel?"

As Miguel's name rolled off of Brady's tongue, Salah and Marco quietly stepped onto the stern of the boat. Through the open cabin door, they charged Brady from behind, pinning him to the back of the captain's chair. Marco grabbed the AK-47 on the dining table and threw it out onto the rear deck. Then he grabbed the AK-47 that Brady had looped over his neck and threw that onto the rear deck as well.

Unarmed and under siege, Brady decided not to resist for fear of being incapacitated and thus unable to escape later on. Survival was critical. It was the only way he stood a chance of getting to Homeland Security in time to thwart the attacks.

"Your escape was costly, Brady. Those were four good men you killed," said Salah.

"Evidently not good enough," said Brady, smiling.

Salah smashed the butt of his 9-mm pistol into Brady's left cheek. Blood spurted from Brady's open facial wound as he fell to the floor. Instinctively, Brady started to grab Salah's leg to upend him, but he thought better of it. *This is no time to resist*, he thought. *I've pissed them off enough. I've got to save my strength for another escape, if they don't kill me here and now.*

Miguel shoved Brady flat on the cabin floor and then kneeled on his shoulders. Marco straddled Brady's legs and pulled out two thick plastic ties to secure Brady's wrists behind him. The two men yanked the ties tightly and then pulled Brady back to his feet. Blood continued to flow from his busted cheekbone, but luckily not fast enough to impair him.

✳✳✳

Salah and Miguel hopped off of the boat, leaving Marco to watch over Brady. They walked over to the *Miss Martha*, where the two carpenters stood on the west catwalk holding their weapons across their chests. Salah asked them when they would have the repairs finished. The head carpenter looked at the other carpenter and said, "About two more hours, including the repaint." The other man nodded in agreement.

Salah looked at his SEAL watch. "It's already eleven-thirty. I can't wait that long. Get it done in less than an hour."

"If Marco can help us, we can do that, sir," said the head carpenter.

"Good," said Salah. "I'll have him come over right away."

Salah and Miguel walked back to the *Miss Catherine James*. Salah stepped onboard and told Marco to tie up Brady, lock him in the cabin, and go over to the *Miss Martha* to help the carpenters finish their job.

"Marco, the three of you have less than one hour to complete the work. Do you understand?"

"Yes, sir!"

Salah and Miguel discussed the best way to confine Brady until the attack was underway, at which point they would shoot him and dump him into the Choptank River on their way out of Maryland. Miguel suggested, and Salah agreed, that the dive compartment on the *Miss Martha* was best. They felt that he couldn't escape from it. As opposed to the *Miss Catherine James*, they could shut off the duplicate hydraulic controls that were inside the chamber. Like a steel coffin, if a person were locked in the chamber, there was no way for anyone to hear him. His shouts would never be heard outside. "This will be perfect," said Salah. "As soon as the work on the *Miss Martha* is complete, we'll transfer him."

✳✳✳

At 12:30 p.m. one of the security guards walked up to the farmhouse to inform Salah that that the *Miss Martha* was ready. Salah and Miguel returned to the boathouse and transferred Brady to the cabin of the *Miss Martha*. While Marco and Miguel guarded Brady, Salah removed the dining table, rolled back the bench, and spun open the hatch to the dive tank.

To place Brady in the tank, they had to undo his plastic cuffs. As they hauled him in front of the stainless steel chamber, Brady said, "I thought this was a fuel tank?" He said this so that they would not know that he was familiar with how the tank operated, including the interior hydraulic controls.

Once they put him inside, they saw no reason to retie his wrists. The space was tight and secure.

Before closing the hatch, Salah said, "Too bad you're on the wrong side, Brady. You would have made a good jihadist."

Lying on the bottom of the steel chamber, Brady looked up through the opening and replied, "I'd rather die than fight alongside you."

Salah slammed the hatch down and spun the cover's lock, forcing it to have an airtight fit.

"Are we going to flood the chamber now?" Miguel asked.

"No, not yet. Let's let him stew in his coffin for a while. We'll flood it later when we dump him on our way south."

***

Louise and Pete were beside themselves with worry. The last word they had received was from Tommy Price. He'd said that the raid on the Crab Alley Farm was a bust. The farm was not inhabited and the only things that had been found were a few crab baskets that appeared to have held explosives of some kind.

With the deaths of Mack and Mike, Louise and Pete had been helping Beth and Tanya, who was Mack's daughter-in-law, with the never-ending list of funeral preparations. Wednesday, July 7, 2010 was rapidly approaching.

Luckily, the Creighton's received help and support from their son, Bo, and their grandson, Wes. Both of them had made calls to Mack and Mike's friends who lived outside of the close-knit waterman's community - people who had moved off of island, old customers, and others whose lives had been touched by the father and son.

Bo and Wes had also helped Pete and the other members on the search team replace the sea plug of the *Miss Patricia*, pumped her out, and pulled her from the marsh. Once afloat, they all went about cleaning her up, including scrubbing off dried blood and other human tissue, before they towed her back to Tilghman. Pete and Bo handled all of Mack's insurance claims, which dealt with the replacement of the electronics of the *Miss Patricia* and the much-needed overhaul of her engine, which had been totally flooded.

Rather than return Mack's boat to his slip, Pete had her moved to a friend's boathouse at the south end of the island.

Working on the *Miss Patricia* was the hardest thing that Pete had ever done. He was surrounded by the memories, as well as the blood and tissue, of his lifelong friend. The only solace he derived was in knowing that he was doing what Mack would have wanted. He was restoring the *Miss Patricia* to her former glory.

It was hard yet therapeutic. He wouldn't have wanted it any other way. Working with Mack and Mike's friends on the *Miss Patricia* was also a way to keep his mind off of his fears for Brady's safety. It was crushing and physically debilitating not to know where Brady was or whether he was injured or dead.

Three more bodies floated out of the Nanticoke marshes north of the town of Vienna. All of them were undocumented South Americans whom the police identified as having lived in Cambridge for the past twelve months. All of them had been shot execution-style in the back of the head. Though tied to concrete blocks, the ropes that had held them had been cut by the sharp edges of the concrete as the storm's waves and tides whipsawed the bodies back and forth.

The DHS and NRP figured that this was part of the terror cell's plan to rid their team of anyone who was not part of their core group before they fell into the authorities hands for interrogation. This was a standard operating procedure for the terrorists. They were committed to leaving a clean slate behind as they slipped away into another unsuspecting community to once again strike fear into American.

***

With Brady's disappearance and the discovery of more bodies in the Nanticoke River, the search for the leaders of the terrorist cell intensified. The DHS, Naval Intelligence out of Washington, and the coast guard began to throw every resource available into the hunt.

After substantial DHS and coast guard pressure, the governor of Maryland requested the use of one of the state police helicopters to assist Homeland Security in the search for Abed and his team. The duration of the state's helicopter assistance was, however, limited to only four hours of flying time. The governor's staff stated that no money was available for additional time.

While the public at large remained unaware of the terrorist threat, the NRP and the coast guard had alerted several members of the state legislature who represented the Eastern Shore of Maryland to the severity of the problem. Frustrated by the lack of serious response from the state and the governor's staff's obvious dismissal of their concerns, these elected officials had in an earlier letter demanded an immediate meeting with the House and Senate leadership to press for more state resources in the hunt for the terrorist cell. As with previous requests for Shore assistance, though, the delegation had received little response.

In a second hand-delivered letter on Friday July 2, 2010 that went to both the governor and the House and Senate leadership, the Eastern Shore representatives threatened to go to the press and expose the suspected terrorist threat and the state's unwillingness to provide the necessary financial and manpower resources to stop Abed and his team. Without the requested resources, there was a very good possibility that a terrorist attack, which the DHS, the coast guard, and Maryland's NRP knew was going to occur, could not be thwarted in time. As of 12:00 p.m., Saturday, July 3, 2010, no one on the Eastern Shore Delegation had received any response from the governor's office or from the House and Senate leadership.

Late on Saturday afternoon at 4:00 p.m., the head of Maryland's Eastern Shore Delegation finally received a phone call from one of the governor's aides, explaining that the governor and the House and Senate leadership were fully aware of the situation. They were in contact with the DHS, and they would bring to bear all of the appropriate resources necessary to assist the DHS in its efforts to deal with the potential attacks. However, upon contacting both the DHS and the coast guard, the head of the delegation learned that little assistance had actually been offered, and the state considered it to be a federal issue.

The truth about the state's lackluster response to this threat would finally come to light months later, during a thorough and revelatory congressional investigation of the terrorist attack. The state had transferred 87 percent of its Catastrophic Event Fund monies to the state's general funds for pet projects of the administration. Only one million dollars were left in the fund to cover the first seventy-two hours of any catastrophic event. The state had been caught with its hand in the cookie jar.

***

Lying on the bottom of the stainless steel dive chamber, Brady shivered. The cold metal became an irritant to his back, but, he knew that he must remain still for some time before initiating his escape. He feared that Salah had left one of his security guards onboard to be sure that Brady would not escape. Brady was most concerned that Salah, when he decided the time was right, would call upon this guard to flood the chamber and drown Brady in the process.

Time eluded Brady. He could not determine exactly how much time had passed since he had been placed in the chamber. All he knew was that he had heard no sounds or movement on the boat. Clearly, if someone were onboard or nearby, this person was alone and not talking. Finally, Brady decided that if someone were around, that person was not onboard. Most likely, that person was somewhere else in the boathouse. He felt that the time was right to initiate his escape.

Remembering that a duplicate set of flood and drain controls were on the inside of the chamber, Brady reached behind him. Using his fingers as his eyes, he felt for the four-way waterproof toggle switch that opened, closed, flooded, and drained the chamber. Brady was feeling once again in control. Then he remembered that the duplicate panel above him and behind the forward dining bench included another breaker armature, which was marked, "Unarm Interior Panel." His heart sank. Perhaps this chamber was to be his burial coffin after all.

Biting his lip, he tried to recall and visualize which way to move the toggle switch to flood the tank and which way to push it to the open position. If he didn't flood the chamber before opening the doors, there would be unequal pressure between the outside water and the air chamber. This perhaps would make it impossible for the doors to open. Drawing on his almost photographic memory, Brady was pretty sure that moving the toggle switch up would flood the chamber and that moving it straight down would open the doors. He thought to himself, *Shit. What if they disarmed the interior panel before they placed me in the chamber? I'd better try it now before they come back.*

Brady nervously bit his lip again and flipped the switch to the up position. Nothing happened.

***

All of the original cell members gathered at the Parks Neck Farm. Abed called the meeting to order at 4:00 p.m. Salah gave a report on the status of the safe houses.

"As you know, the Crab Alley Farm has been abandoned. We have closed the two downtown Cambridge safe houses. All six of the local maintenance and security personnel, except for the two security detail carpenters at the Black Walnut Point Farm, have been disposed of. While the main headquarters farm on the Choptank River has been abandoned and locked up, the munitions farm, though cleared of any signs of our occupancy, is still available if needed. The Chambers place has been cleared and all signs of the boat repairs, such as scrap metal and leftover wood scraps, have been taken to a dump in Somerset County. The only two remaining safe houses are Black Walnut Point and here, the Parks Neck Farm.

From what we can gather through monitoring the NRP and coast guard radios, the raid on the Crab Alley Farm was uneventful, and they found no signs of our occupancy. We have learned from our monitoring of the state police radios that the state police are in touch with authorities in New York City to find out about the LLCs that we used to sign the leases. That, however, will be a total dead end, since there is no way to trace the LLCs to us. We also know from the state police radios that they have found our two in-town safe houses and the bodies of the two maintenance workers that we executed but failed to remove for disposal. This was a sloppy mistake and those responsible have been dealt with.

When Salah finished his report, Abed rose from his seat at the head of the table.

"At nine o'clock tomorrow morning, we'll have our revenge. All explosives are in place and wired for electrical triggering. The two RPGs are hidden under the bunks on the *Miss Catherine James*, and the mortar pads have been bolted to her deck. She is gassed and ready to go.

All three of the cigarette boats are here in the boathouse. They are also gassed and ready to go. The *Miss Martha* is up at Black Walnut Point. She has been repaired and she is ready to go, if we should need her. We have locked Brady in her dive chamber and will dispose of him just before the attack

226

Maya shifted in her chair as Salah's last sentence hit home. Tears began to swell up in her eyes, but she remained in control of her emotions. While this attack was something that she had dreamed about for more than two years, Brady's demise was not what she had wanted. Raffi was gone and now Brady was only hours away from his death. Other than her father, who'd been killed by an American airstrike on his command post in the Hindu Kush Mountains of Pakistan, and her brother Haamid, these two men, Raffi and Brady, whom she had cared so much about, had been or were about to be casualties of jihad. Maya's life had had many ups and downs, but this was going to be the worst loss she had ever felt. Incongruently, this was going to be the best moment of her life.

Abed continued to share the events of the last two days, including the sea and air searches, which had escalated significantly since Brady's disappearance.

Then he switched gears. "This time tomorrow, we will be clear of Maryland and on our way to rendezvous at the West Virginia safe house. Suburbans, rather than Hummers, await us in Oanoake, Virginia, for the short ride to the airport. We will abandon the Suburbans at the airport and board a Cesena Caravan that we have rented. We will depart immediately upon arrival. Chief pilot Bashar will be in command, along with Haron. These men are very familiar with the caravan, and they will file an IFR flight plan to a small non-towered airport in Virginia. There, we will refuel and depart promptly under VFR flight rules for the private grass strip at our safe house in the West Virginia Mountains.

We will remain undercover in that safe house for the next three months. All necessary provisions have already been stored there for us, including radios, communications equipment, phones, assault weapons, ammunition, trucks, food, clothing, mortars, and RPGs. We have three Florida-based cell members who were all trained in Syria. They excel in weapons, flying, diving, and security, and they are already stationed in Miami for final assignment to our next target. The leader of this team is my nephew, Rahim.

When we leave here, Maya, Salah, Bashir, Haron, and I will depart in the larger of the two cigarette boats. The smaller one, with Omar onboard and Marco at the helm, will follow us just in case we need to create a diversion in the event that we're followed. They will provide backup if the larger boat has engine problems. Marco's boat will have an RPG onboard, in case it's needed. Starting at five-thirty this afternoon, we will load up the larger boat with the equipment that we need to take to West Virginia. In early evening, Salah and Haamid will drive up to Black Walnut Point to prepare the *Miss Martha* for her trip up to the mouth of the Miles River, where they will detonate the Narrows Bridges at nine o'clock tomorrow morning. Omar and Marco will mount the eighty-two-millimeter Russian mortar on the *Miss Catherine James* and load the Soviet-made RPGs and mortar rounds onboard. Our two pilots will head to the Bay Bridge

Airport and stay undercover in their Hummer until they meet the private helicopter service at 7:30 a.m. At that point, they will depart the Bay Bridge Airport, fly south to the grass strip just north of Knapps Narrows, dispose of the pilot, pick up myself, Salah, and Marco, and await orders to proceed to the *Mana Kia,* which is anchored off Annapolis. At 9:00 a.m., we will simultaneously execute the various bridge and Gas Dock attacks."

"Are there any questions?" asked Salah.

No one answered and no one moved.

Abed stood up and said, "Salah will now hand out the Navy SEAL watches. Each has been synced with the others and set to the local time. From here onward, we will execute all of our actions by the second hand."

Salah handed out new field radios with new channel crystals for internal communications within the cell team. He also established shoot-to-kill orders for any civilian or security personnel whom they suspected of spying on them.

"Our next and final meeting will be held at Black Walnut Point tomorrow at 1:00 a.m. That's all. Allah Go with you!"

In unison, the team responded by shouting, "Allah Akbar!"

✳✳✳

At 6:00 p.m. on Saturday, Homeland Security called an emergency meeting with all of its partners at the Bay Bridge Search Center. The meeting's objectives were to find the terrorist cell's hierarchy, interrogate them, and then stop them before they initiated the attacks. While they might be able to locate Abed and Salah in time, the chances of getting anything out of them were mighty slim, even if they resorted to torture.

The addition of a state helicopter to Homeland Security's two choppers was helpful, but the amount of time that the administration committed was only four hours, and none of it would include night searches. These limitations severely hampered a full and adequate air search.

The meeting's discussions revolved around the recently discovered bodies in the tributaries of the Bay, the land and air searches for cell members and their safe-houses, finding the boats they were using, and identifying the terrorist targets themselves.

The governor's team now consisted of twenty people. Homeland Security had requested another twenty men and technicians, but the state had turned them down. The Fourth of July holiday was the excuse that they gave for not providing the additional resources.

As the meeting was wrapping up, the Regional DHS Chief received a note from one of the state police team members that indicated that the state police had uncovered two downtown Cambridge safe houses that had been abandoned. Both hideouts were located in different parts of the Latino community. These two safe houses were first-floor condos with both front and rear exits for fast escape. With several bedrooms and an array of mattresses resting on the wooden floors in the living and dining areas, each condo had enough room to sleep six people. The places were thoroughly trashed. To the police teams, it looked like security workers, maintenance workers, and construction workers had occupied each condo. Various items were found on the kitchen tables and in several wall cabinets: 9-mm hollow-point ammunition boxes, small-bore cleaning supplies, carpenter tools, wire cutters, splicing sleeves, and five spools of different-sized electrical wire. At the bottom of the note, it stated that two bodies had been found in the basement of one of the condos. They were believed to be Hispanic illegal aliens and they had no forms of identification on them. Their best guess was that the bodies had been there for about twelve to eighteen hours. Their hands and feet had been tied together before they had been executed with a single 9-mm shot to the back of the head.

The discovery confirmed that the cell was substantially larger and more ruthless than they had first thought. Before dismissing those in attendance, the regional DHS chief called for another update meeting at 6:00 a.m. on Sunday morning.

✱✱✱

"Shit," said Brady, his words reverberating in the small stainless steel chamber. *They did throw that breaker armature. I have no electrical flow to the toggle.*

Brady lay quietly on the cold steel floor of the chamber, trying to sketch in his mind how the disconnect armature might work. Brady tried to picture in his own mind where the armature's plunger might actually create the disconnect. It could be at the top of the armature or at the bottom, near the inside toggle switch. Then he remembered. If it were at the top, it would just be a short battery-type connector switch. But if it were at the bottom, it would truly require plunging the connector rod down to engage and up to disengage. Recalling an image of what it looked like, he immediately knew that it was a plunger. Therefore, the disconnect should be directly behind the toggle switch just above his head.

Feeling confident with his analysis of the situation, he removed his belt buckle, turned over, and determined that he could use the metal buckle itself to pry open the toggle switch gasket, which would allow him to remove the switch and reach back through the hole to manually pull the rod down and make the all-important electrical connection.

Brady pulled off his belt. Then he heard voices coming from the deck above. He was no longer alone.

"Damn it," he whispered to himself. "I'll have to wait."

Lying back, Brady resigned himself to whatever amount of time it would take for whoever was onboard to leave. Tuning his ears to the sounds above, Brady realized that the carpenters were back to put a final coat of paint on the struts, engine box, and canopy of the *Miss Catherine James*. He guessed it wouldn't take them more than an hour or two. He estimated that he could begin his work to activate the steel chamber system at about 4:00 p.m.

✳✳✳

Pete was frustrated. He called Lieutenant Price two hours after his last chat with him, but Lieutenant Tommy Price had no new news to share, except for the fact that Homeland Security was now fully in charge. They had launched land, sea, and air surveillance. Additionally, three more Latino bodies had been discovered in the Nanticoke River, and the raid on the Crab Alley Creek hideaway was a complete bust.

He hung up with Tommy Price and turned to Louise, saying, "Honey, there's no new news on the search for Brady or the terrorists. A little while ago, before I called Tommy, I got a call from one of the members of the Eastern Shore Legislative Delegation who said they were putting pressure on the governor's office and the legislative leadership to add more resources and urgency to the search efforts."

"So," said Louise. "What did they say?"

"Well, they aren't getting much encouragement for more personnel for the search. They claim that with the Fourth of July coming tomorrow, their resources are stretched to the limit. It seems to me that they're more worried about the tourists going to state parks and our shore resorts than they are about a terrorist attack on the Bay or about our Brady."

"Pete, I keep holding out hope that Brady will show up and that they'll find these guys before it's too late. We just got to keep the faith and make sure that Beth and Tonya get through these next few days. The funerals on Wednesday are going to be really tough."

"You're right, Louise. We've got to keep hoping and saying our prayers. I don't think I could take the loss of Brady, so I'm just going to ask God to help return him to us, safe and sound. I know he'll hear our prayers, Louise. I just know he will."

***

By 3:30 p.m. the carpenters' voices were silent, and Brady thought he heard them packing up their paint cans and supplies. The boat had rocked back and forth twice in the last few minutes, indicating that they had both stepped off of the boat and onto the catwalk. Brady decided to wait another half hour or so before he'd start to work on the toggle switch.

***

Thirty minutes later, Brady had heard nothing and he believed that the workers had left for the day. He rolled back over and began working the belt buckle clasp under the gasket around the switch itself. He figured that the rubber gasket had an indentation in it that fit around the thickness of the stainless steel plate's hole. If he could pry it up and pop it out, he might then be able to work his fingers into the hole, find the armature rod, and pull it down, thus making the electrical connection.

Brady worked the buckle clasp between the rubber gasket and the side of the steel tank counterclockwise. After making a continuous circular prying motion all around the gasket, it finally popped free, exposing the boat's framing behind it. It was too dark to see much detail, but with some light filtering in between the cracks in the bench framing above, Brady was able to see the metal armature just to the right and above the hole. He reached with his middle finger and was just barely able to touch the armature.

"Damn. I need to find a way to get both middle fingers around it to pull it down," he said to himself. He reached in with both fingers, but he couldn't even touch the armature. There was not enough room for both fingers to get into the opening.

Brady rolled over on his back, feeling disappointed and exhausted. He'd been in the chamber for several hours now. It was clammy and cold, and the air was stagnant. Almost all of the original oxygen in the tank had been depleted. By removing the toggle switch, he had luckily accessed additional air from the areas below deck and the small airways that were under the dining bench above him. The smell of fuel from the bilge was difficult to take, but at least it was mixed with some oxygen. Brady continued to slow his breathing so that he could stretch the oxygen as far as possible. The environment he now found himself in reminded him of the close quarters he had experienced in the many mini-sub dives he had made off of the coasts of California and Virginia during his early training. It also brought back sharp and painful memories of the days he had spent hiding behind enemy lines in small caves in the mountains of Afghanistan. *No time for those thoughts*, he said to himself. *That was then and this is now. I've got a job to do and damn little time to do it in.*

Brady lay still for the next fifteen minutes, trying to figure out how he could reach the armature and pull it down. Searching for an answer, he thought that if he could place the metal loop of the belt buckle onto the armature and twist the belt so that the buckle turned and locked onto the rod itself, then by twisting it tighter the belt would bring enough pressure to lock the buckle tight against the armature. It would thus act like the grip of a pair of pliers. Then, if he could use that vise-like grip to pull down the armature, he would be able to make the electrical connection.

But how would he pull it down? The hole in the steel tank was at the same level as the buckle, and there was only an inch or two of rod left below the buckle. Therefore, he had no leverage to pull downward to connect the armature with the U-shaped electrical connection that was several inches below the hole.

Thinking, Brady remembered that the exterior of the tanks had hoist handles on each end for raising and lowering the gas tanks into the boat. Uncle Pete had mentioned seeing them when they were spying on the boatyard at the Chambers place.

He also recalled having seen a handle at the end of the tank on the *Miss Gale* when he discovered the tank while searching behind the steps in the forward berths. Brady turned back over on his stomach and slipped two fingers into the hole to find the handle that would allow him to thread the belt through it and then feed it back up and out of the hole.

He proceeded to initiate his plan. Brady dropped the belt-buckle end of the belt down through the handle. Stretching his index finger to a point where he was cutting it against the rough steel around the hole, he was able to wrap his finger through the buckle and pull it back up. At this point, he inserted it onto the bottom of the armature. About two inches from the bottom of the rod, Brady started twisting the belt to tighten the buckle around the armature. The buckle slipped down an inch as he quickly tried to tighten it against the rod. "Damn!" he said to himself. "I sure don't need that to slip off before I get it tight enough." Brady twisted the belt a few more times to establish a tighter hold on the armature. Feeling like he had pretty much achieved a vice-like grip between the buckle and the armature, he slowly began to pull up on the belt. By doing so, he pulled the armature down as the belt was simultaneously pulled up through the handle that was below it.

He figured that the fit between the armature and the U-shaped connector piece had to be tight for a solid electrical connection to exist. He also figured that securing the armature would take substantial downward pressure to lock it in. So, he decided to pull hard and fast as the end of the rod got close to the U-shaped connector.

As before, if the buckle were not tight enough, it would slip down and off of the bottom of the rod. He would have no opportunity to reattach it.

This was it. Brady twisted the belt two more times to be sure the buckle was tight against the rod. Then he twisted it twice more for good measure.

Catching his breath, Brady pulled with all of his might. The buckle held.

"Click." The armature engaged with the connector. *Finally. Success,* thought Brady.

Because the buckle was now locked around the armature above the U-shaped connector, he could not retrieve it, so he stuffed the rest of the belt through the hole. It fell out of sight, down into the interior bilge.

Brady placed the toggle switch back into the hole. Applying pressure with his fingers and his fist, he snapped the gasket back into place. He then decided to test the switch by pushing it down to see if he could hear the grind of the electric motor and the tightening of the gaskets along the chamber doors that he was lying on.

He pushed the switch down. Along with the tightening of the gaskets under his stomach, he heard the surge and strain of the electrical motor. It was working. "Thank God!"

Exhausted, sweaty, and mentally drained, Brady rolled over onto his back and allowed his muscles to relax. He took a few slow and deep breaths. He listened carefully for any sounds of activity or voices above. Then he began to execute his escape.

✳✳✳

"Hello."

"Captain Pete?"

"Yep, who's this?"

"It's Dan Howard with Philips Construction."

"Oh, hello Dan."

"Word has it, Captain Pete, that Brady's missing and that your friend Mack and his son were killed. Is that right?"

"I am afraid so, Dan. It's a mess down here - a real mess."

"Well, I need to come down. I think I can help find Brady or at least lend a hand in the search."

"We can use all the help we can get, Dan. If you come, let me know when you'll be coming. You sure can stay here with us."

"Thanks, Captain Pete. Sure glad it's OK with you that I come, 'cause I left work three hours ago and I am just about to Easton."

"Well good. You come on and stay with us. If I'm not here at the house when you arrive, I'll be back soon. Just come on in and grab the room upstairs next to Brady's."

"Thanks, Captain Pete. I need to do this for Brady. He's a marine brother to me, and I can't let him down."

"OK, Dan. We'll see you in a little bit."

✳✳✳

Brady lay still for five minutes. Then his breathing returned to normal. The boat abruptly rocked, as if someone had jumped onboard.

Crap, he thought to himself. *Damn it. They're back.*

Brady stayed motionless and focused all of his energy on listening. He heard no conversation, but he did hear someone moving around in the cabin. Whoever was there had turned on the radio that was set to monitor the NRP and DHS channels. The person listening tuned the radio back and forth between the two stations, obviously trying to listen for information concerning the search for both Abed's team and himself. This monitoring lasted for about thirty minutes. As abruptly as it had started, though, it ended. Whoever was in the cabin left. Brady could tell by the rocking of the boat that this person had stepped off of the boat and onto the catwalk. The sound of footsteps slowly faded. Brady figured that this person had left the boathouse. He strained to hear the start of a car or truck engine, but he was too far way to hear a thing.

He waited for twenty minutes, running through the sequence that he was going to follow after flipping the toggle switch. He hoped that this would initiate his escape. Brady figured that it would take about one to two minutes to complete the flooding of the chamber. Then it would take another minute or two for the doors to open enough for him to escape. This meant that he would need to hold his breath for more than three minutes, which was thirty seconds less than he needed to pass the dive test during his training. While he wasn't in the best of shape, Brady knew that he could and would pass this test also.

✳✳✳

As Salah had ordered him to do, Miguel had been monitoring the radios on the boat, but no new information was forthcoming. The only thing for sure was that the searches were continuing, but the chopper flights had been suspended at dusk and would not be restarted until dawn the next day, the Fourth of July.

Hearing nothing new, Miguel decided to slip up to the farmhouse for a quick dinner, after which he would return to monitor the radios throughout the night. He found a day-old pepperoni pizza in the refrigerator with three slices left. He heated up the old

Kenmore oven to 350 degrees and placed the three pieces on a sheet of aluminum foil. A few minutes later, he pulled out the reheated pizza and sat down to eat as he watched the eighteen-inch, black-and-white TV on the Formica counter. Knowing that Salah might show up at any time, Miguel decided to stay tuned to the news channels instead of watching something he would have preferred to see, such as sports or the military channel.

✳✳✳

It was 7:15 p.m. Brady took several deep breaths to expand his lungs. He reached back over his shoulder and found the toggle switch. Reassuring himself that pushing up on the toggle would flood the chamber, he wrapped his fingers around the toggle. Simultaneously, he took another deep breath and pushed the switch up .

As he flipped the switch, water started rushing in. Brady was surprised at the speed with which it entered the chamber. He also was glad it was filling up as quickly as it was. This meant that he would be able to open the double doors sooner than the four minutes he had allotted himself.

At the two-minute mark, the water had all but covered Brady. He took one last deep breath. When the chamber was full, Brady reached back again to locate the toggle switch. With his fingers holding the toggle switch, he thought through the various toggle switch positions. Still comfortable with his memory of the directional markers on the outside switches, he pulled the switch down to hopefully open the doors.

Brady had now been without air for close to two-and-a-half minutes. The electronic motor whirred and then stopped. He hit the switch a second time. Again, the motor whirred and then stopped.

Huh, he thought. *Maybe the doors are stuck.*

Brady had been without air for three minutes. There was not much time left. He lifted his feet and arms. Then he slammed them down onto the doors beneath him. The doors gave a little. He did it again and again. With the water resisting his attempt, it took a lot of effort to stomp down. His lungs, in response to this effort, started to burn. Finally, the doors gave way a little more.

With maybe thirty seconds of air left in his lungs, Brady flipped the open switch again in a final attempt to open the doors. He heard the whirring sound again, but this time the sound graduated into a steady hum, as the doors finally began to open. Brady's lungs were about to burst as he scrambled out of what could have been his stainless steel coffin.

Brady dropped out of the tank. The water was only about four feet deep in the boathouse, so he ended up scraping the bottom as he swam past the stern and popped up to get his first breath of fresh air since being locked in the chamber six and a half hours earlier. He had made it, but just barely.

After gulping down several breaths of air, Brady began to swim out past the end of the boathouse. He headed east along the shoreline, figuring he'd then swim across Black Walnut Cove to Bar Neck, where he could go ashore and walk back to his uncle's home.

Brady stopped along the shoreline at a spot that was parallel to the farmhouse. This was where he would cross the Cove to Bar Neck. He sat down at the water's edge to catch his breath. As he did so, he realized that going directly back to his Uncle Pete's was exactly what Salah would expect him to do, but he had no choice. He had to warn his Uncle Pete that the terrorists might come to the house looking for him. But, how could he get ahold of Pete? Then, he remembered that the walkie-talkie was back at the Black Walnut Point Farm house. When he'd been overpowered and taken up to the attic, they had patted him down and found the walkie-talkie hidden in his life vest. He remembered that they had placed it on the kitchen table before dragging him up to the attic. That was it. He had to go back and find that radio. It was the only way to alert his Uncle Pete to the potential run-in with the terrorists. Brady set off for the farmhouse, knowing that he very well might end up running into Salah, Miguel, and some of the guards. Slithering along in the tall switch-grass as he approached the farmhouse, he was reminded of similar days in Afghanistan, when he ever so slowly crept up on enemy strongholds. Flashbacks were part of the price one paid for service to one's country. Some things you just never forgot, especially when lives were at stake.

Peeking out of the tall switch-grass at the edge of the cornfield, Brady saw a Humvee leaving. No one but the driver and one front-seat passenger were in the vehicle. Cautiously fearing that one or more people might still be in the farmhouse, Brady belly-crawled through the corn stubble to the hedgerow next to the entrance road that was adjacent to the farmhouse.

In a low crouch, Brady got up and ran to the back door. He stayed motionless behind a small holly tree at the kitchen door. After four minutes of hearing no movement or any voices coming from the house, Brady quickly opened the rear kitchen door and slipped into the kitchen alcove. From here, he had a good view of the entire kitchen.

There it was, still sitting on the Formica counter: the Motorola walkie-talkie. Unfortunately, a guard had taken his cell phone to deliver to Salah. It was nowhere to be found.

Brady looked all around the kitchen and the adjacent dining room. He clearly was completely alone. He walked straight to the Formica table, retrieved his radio, and disappeared back into the shadows of the hedgerow.

Looking back at the house to be sure that no one was watching, Brady tore through the corn stalks and the switch-grass. Arriving at the water's edge, he sat down in the marsh, surrounded by tall phragmites. Brady took out the radio and called Pete on the frequency that they had agreed to use a few days ago. No answer. He tried again. Again, there was no answer.

Brady stuffed the radio back into the large pocket of his work pants and swam for the opposite shore. While the distance was less than a quarter of a mile, swimming wore him out. He had grown weak from staying in that chamber for close to seven hours and lying on that cold stainless steel.

Brady reached the other side and sat in the Bar Neck marsh to plan his next move. He looked at his watch. It was now 8:15 p.m. He tried to contact Pete, but again he had no luck. Then, he carefully walked north, remaining parallel to the road and staying as concealed as he could in the trees and the hedgerows.

Once he was at his Uncle Pete's, he'd be able to contact Lieutenant Tommy Price and get the ball rolling to stop these terrorists in their tracks. Brady pulled out the waterproof radio and pushed the talk button.

"Brady to Captain Pete. Over."

There was no reply.

"Brady to Captain Pete. Over."

Again, nobody replied.

Discouraged, Brady continued walking so that he could get to the house as quickly as possible. As he stuffed the walkie-talkie back into his pocket, a response crackled over the radio.

"Brady, is that you? This is Dan."

Brady pulled the radio out of his pocket and pushed the talk button.

"This is Brady. Is that you, Dan? Over."

"Sure is. Semper Fi, buddy. Over."

"Semper Fi back to ya. What the hell are you doing down here? Where is Uncle Pete? Over."

"I came down here to try to find you. I just got to your uncle's house. Captain Pete's out right now. He left me a note saying that he'd be back soon. Where the hell are you?"

"I just escaped from my captors and I'm heading up to Uncle Pete's. They are out looking for me, Dan. When and if they find me, I'll be a dead man. My best guess is that they are headed your way. They're armed with AK-47s and Glocks. You need to keep your eyes open, Dan. They won't hesitate to shoot. You also need to warn Uncle Pete."

"Pete's over at Mack's house. I'll call him there. Don't worry, Brady. I'll take care of those guys if they come up here. I wouldn't suggest you come here, though. Where do you think we ought to meet?"

"What about behind the Oyster House at the Narrows?"

"Sounds good to me."

Dan immediately called Pete on his cell phone to tell him about Brady and to warn them to stay away from the house until he gave the all-clear. Pete and Louise had left Mack's house, and they were now at the fire hall. Dan insisted that they stay away until they heard from him.

Dan closed his cell phone. He then moved his truck out of Pete's driveway and parked it down the street near the dock. There, he could keep an eye on the house to see if and when Salah and his men showed up.

Less than fifteen minutes later, a black Hummer drove by the house and turned around almost in front of Dan's truck. When Dan saw the Humvee coming, he slipped down in his seat.

The Humvee pulled up to Pete's driveway. The man in the front passenger seat got out and quickly ran to the rear of the house. Nothing happened for five minutes. Then, the man returned to the Humvee and they drove off.

Dan waited for five minutes. Then he pulled his Ruger 357 out of the glove box, stuffed it in his back pocket, and went up to Pete's house. A serrated knife had sliced the porch screen door. The door was unlocked and the back door was wide open. Dan took a quick tour of the house, but he saw nothing that looked as if it had been disturbed. It was clear that the person who'd broken into Pete's house was looking for one thing and one thing only: Brady.

***

At 7:45 p.m. Salah arrived back at Black Walnut Point just as Miguel was leaving the farmhouse to return to the boathouse. Seeing Miguel heading to the boathouse, Salah got out of his Humvee and walked over to Miguel.

"Miguel, why aren't you on the boat? Is anyone else covering for you?"

"No sir. I just went to the house to get some dinner."

"You're not serious?"

"Yes, sir. I was too busy to eat lunch today, so I wanted to be sure to get my dinner."

"You left your post to get dinner?"

"Yes, sir."

"Brady better be onboard! Follow me now!"

Salah took off at a run with Miguel close behind him. Salah jumped onboard the boat and Miguel followed him. Salah pulled back the bench and the dining table to expose the circular cover. He knocked on the stainless chamber but he heard nothing. He leaned down and set his ear against the stainless hatch. Silence. Salah took out his nine-millimeter Glock. Pointing it down at the chamber, he used his left hand to spin the hatch cover open.

As Salah pulled up the hatch, he pointed the cocked pistol into the blank space below. Bay water lapped at the opening. Brady was gone.

Salah stood up, pointed the gun at Miguel's face, and pulled the trigger. Once again, blood splashed and brains filled the air on the *Miss Martha* as the back of Miguel's head exploded. Miguel's lifeless body fell backwards against the cabin door. It swung open and Miguel hit the deck just outside the cabin.

Stepping over his most recent victim, Salah pulled out his cell phone and called Haamid. In a cold and unemotional voice, he told Haamid what had happened. He said that he needed to immediately send the carpenters back to clean up the mess and repair the damage to the cabin wall and the ceiling. He also instructed him to have Miguel's body taken to the farmhouse attic for hiding.

He then called Abed to alert him to what had just happened. Abed instructed Salah to get Marco and to start combing the area along the shore from Black Walnut Point back to the Knapp's Narrows Bridge. His guess was that Brady would work his way back to his uncle's house and then call for help from DHS and the NRP. This was exactly what they didn't need to happen. Abed thought, *This is not good. Things are not going the way I'd planned.*

✳✳✳

Dan drove over to the Oyster House at the base of the Knapp's Narrows Bridge. He pulled up along the east side of the building. He turned the truck so that it faced the island with his back to the water, and he waited for Brady.

All of a sudden, the right front passenger door opened. Brady hopped in and shut the door.

"Man, am I glad to see you, Brady. You scared the shit out of me. I never saw you coming."

Brady grabbed his friend's hand, shook it vigorously, and said, "Nowhere near as glad as I'm to see you! Let's get out of here."

"Not so fast. These guys just cased Pete's and I don't know where they went. They may still be on the island."

"You haven't seen them leave?" said Brady.

"No. When they left Pete's, I stayed put at the end of the street so that they wouldn't see me."

"Dan, they either left the island or they're driving around looking for me. I don't think they would have returned to Black Walnut Point for fear of being caught by DHS. Also, they wouldn't need the *Miss Martha* anymore. They only need the *Miss Catherine James*."

Just as Brady finished his sentence, Dan grabbed Brady's head and shoved it down below the dash, as he himself ducked down.

"They just went by the Tilghman Store heading to the bridge going like a bat out of hell."

As both men sat up, Brady jumped out and ran to the edge of the Oyster House. He peeked around the corner just in time to see the Humvee speed up the road toward St. Michael's.

Jumping back in the truck, he said, "Let's head back to Pete's. I need to get out of these wet clothes and get my gun. I've got to get ahold of Tommy Price and meet with him right away."

✳✳✳

Salah was livid. Brady had escaped and his plans for the next day were in serious jeopardy. He knew that he should not stay at Black Walnut Point, for fear of another raid like the one at the Crab Alley Creek farm. Besides, they still had the Parks Neck Farm and access to the munitions farm. As he sped north on Route 33 toward St. Michael's, Salah called Abed to give him an update.

Abed's phone rang. "Go ahead, Salah."

"Brady has escaped. I had to kill Miguel. He screwed up badly, which is why Brady's on the loose."

"Where are you?"

"I'm on my way to the munitions farm."

"Good. I want everyone to meet there at 10:30 p.m. I'll have Maya make the calls."

***

Promptly at 10:30 p.m. Abed started the meeting. Salah, Haamid, Maya, Marco, the two pilots, Omar, Kaleem and Jamil were all there. Having quickly repaired and cleaned up the *Miss Martha,* the two carpenters were repositioned outside for a second time, in case the authorities had figured out where the munitions cache farm was located.

"In twelve more hours, our work here will be done. This is the final stretch. The enemy is closing in, so we must be alert and ready to move at a moment's notice. I want everyone to synchronize their watches to 10:05 p.m. exactly at the count of three. One, two, three - synchronize. At the end of this meeting, I also want each of you to go with Jamil to the munitions shed and have him check your weapons. He will replace any weapons he deems necessary, hand out additional ammunition, and disperse the C-4, RPGs, the mortar, and the mortar rounds to Omar and Marco. Now, Kaleem will bring you up to date on the monitoring of the enemies' communications."

Kaleem stood up and said, "As best we can tell, Maryland has added one of its choppers to the two that Homeland Security has, but Maryland has limited Homeland Security's use of their chopper to just four hours of flight time. They have further limited DHS's use of their chopper to daytime flights only. DHS and the NRP have raided the Crab Alley Creek farm, but since we had already vacated it, they found nothing that would lead them to our other hideouts or to the team. DHS has accelerated both its air and ground searches, focusing most of the search in the Eastern Bay Area and on the Nanticoke River, which is north of the town of Vienna. That's it for now." Kaleem nodded to Abed and sat back down.

Salah and Abed, who were sitting adjacent to each other, tilted their heads toward each other and whispered a few words. Salah then asked, "Any other reports or information to share?"

Maya stood up and said, "I'm worried about the explosives at both bridges in the Narrows. I need to go back and dive on them to be sure the recent high tides and unusually swift currents have not disturbed the pitons that Brady set. Haamid and I will drive up there. I will enter the water from the landside rather than by boat. It will be less obvious and safer."

Salah said, "Be careful, you two. We can't afford to have anyone see you there."

"We will be fine, uncle. The way the weather is now, I doubt anyone could see ten feet in front of them, and surely no boats will be passing through there at this late hour and in this rainstorm."

When Maya had finished talking, Abed stood up straight and raised his chin slightly. Assuming a military bearing that spoke volumes about his command presence, he said, "We are about to embark on a holy journey for Allah. The souls of our Islamic brothers who have gone before us will be at our side as we strike another blow against the infidels who wish to enslave us. Tomorrow, some of us will see our departed brothers face-to-face, while others shall survive to strike again at the heart of America. I wish each of you a safe journey and a successful day. Each of you knows your job. I expect you to execute your tasks with determination and precision. You must not fail. Any questions?"

"No, sir," everyone responded in unison.

"Allah is counting on you!" said Abed. "Destiny awaits you."

"Allah Akbar. Allah Akbar."

"Lieutenant Tommy Price, please."

"Who's calling?"

"This is Brady Wilson. Get him on the phone right now!"

Five seconds later, Tommy asked, "Brady, is that you?"

"Yes, sir. It's me all right. If we stand a chance of stopping the terrorists, we need to meet right now!"

"Where are you, Brady?"

"I'm on my way to my Uncle Pete's house."

"Brady, I'm at the command post at Kent Narrows, but I can be there on Tilghman in fifteen minutes. I've got a chopper here at the post. I will meet you at the Chesapeake House ball field."

"OK, Lieutenant. I'll see you there."

Eighteen minutes later, the chopper arrived at the ball field.

Heavy rain, low cloud cover, and thirty-knot winds hampered the flight from Kent Narrows. As they approached Tilghman, Lieutenant Price thought to himself, *If it weren't for these navy pilots with lots of combat hours under their belts, I doubt we could find the island, let alone the ball field.*

As the chopper touched down hard on the grass field, Brady and Dan jumped out of Brady's truck. They ran to meet Tommy Price and what turned out to be the DHS's Maryland regional director and a state police colonel.

Over the howling wind, Tommy Price yelled, "Let's get out of this weather and go inside."

The five men ducked under the chopper blade and ran to the restaurant. They found a quiet corner in the dining area and sat down. Without delay, Brady relayed his experiences over the last twenty-four hours. After a fifteen-minute intense delivery of his day's experience, the DHS Regional Director asked Brady, "Would you mind, once more, diving on those bridge pilings at Kent Narrows? We need you to disarm the explosives that were set."

"Sure," said Brady.

"Once they are deactivated, we are in the clear."

"No. There are others at the gas docks."

"At the Gas Docks? Where at the Gas Docks?"

"On the two northernmost pilings."

"Is that all you're aware of?"

"Yes, sir. However, as I mentioned to Tommy at our last meeting, they also have heavy weapons, RPGs, and mortars. The only problem is, I have no idea where they are planning to use them."

Brady's voice could not hide his disappointment at not being able to tell them where or how those weapons would be used.

"Brady, Lieutenant Price told me about that. Don't worry. We'll figure it out. Hell, if it weren't for you, we wouldn't know a damn thing about their plans. You've done a terrific job, son," said the regional director. "A terrific job!"

"The job's not over, sir. I need to disconnect whatever explosives are connected, and I need to find out where they intend to use those weapons."

The director looked over at Tommy Price and said, "Lieutenant, we need to get to the Eastern Shore command post on Kent Island as soon as possible. Do you have the required diving equipment there?"

"Yes, sir. We do."

"We'll need two sets of gear. I want someone to dive with Brady."

"Yes, sir. Actually, we have three sets of dive equipment, extra tanks, and two back-up generators. I'll call back to my office and have a boat and all the equipment ready when we arrive."

"Good. Now Brady, are you sure you can handle this, especially in this weather and with the tide changing?" asked the director.

"Yes, sir. I'm sure, and besides no one knows the setup the way I do. So, I have to go, no matter what."

"Not if you're not physically able," said the director.

"I'm fine, sir," said Brady. "I am just fine."

"All right. Let's get to the chopper and head for Kent Island."

The two navy pilots, who were sitting at a nearby table drinking coffee and eating some homemade Chesapeake House apple pie, overheard the director's order to leave. The chief pilot got up and came over to the director's table.

"Sir, if you want to leave right now, I don't advise it. The wind has picked up with gusts at thirty-five to forty miles an hour, and visibility is less than an eighth of a mile. I suggest we wait until the storm abates. When we came in here, sir, we were below the minimums for this aircraft, and now it's substantially worse."

"We can't wait, captain. We must get back to the Narrows immediately, no matter what."

"Yes sir, but I need to contact my flight center to alert them and get their approval."

"You can contact them, captain, but we are going regardless. This is a national security emergency. When that occurs, DHS is in command. Now let's go."

"Yes, sir."

✳✳✳

At 10:15 p.m. they arrived at the Kent Narrows Command Post. During their trip from Tilghman, they had encountered blinding rain and wind gusts that buffeted the helicopter around in such gyrations that both rear doors had come unlocked. Brady and the director had been forced to grab ahold of the handles and re-secure them. If they had not had three-point harnesses on, both of them would've been sucked out into the storm's fury. As they landed, the two NRP officers who manned the Narrows office, Ken and Marty, met them. Ken was already in his wetsuit to back up Brady if needed.

"Director, follow me to our boat dock," said Marty. "The Whaler is ready to go. To save time, whoever your diver is, he will have to put on his wetsuit there."

While Brady had never seen the two NRP officers before, he instantly recognized their voices from the encounter that Maya had had with them earlier in the week.

Brady donned a wet suit as Ken started to move the whaler across the Narrows to the bridge pilings. Brady gave the instructions for where the boat was to be anchored. Once it was in place and anchored, he grabbed a pair of wire snips and rolled off the boat into the rapidly moving waters. The safety line he had around his waist was forty feet long in case he lost his hold on the piling in the swift tide that swirled around them.

Because Brady knew exactly where the bandoliers and detonation boxes were on each of the two Narrows Bridge pilings, he dove without an oxygen tank and with only a snorkel facemask. Within two minutes, Brady was back along the Whaler's portside.

"One down, one to go," he said.

"Need any help down there?" asked Ken.

"No. I think I am fine, but thanks."

As Brady treaded water, he took in three deep breaths and dove down once more for the other piling. In two minutes, he again resurfaced, having cut the wires on the adjacent piling.

They then moved the boat over to the drawbridge to take care of those explosives. For a third time, Brady dove down to cut wires.

In the boat, they waited for him to resurface. Two minutes went by, but still Brady had not come back up. Suddenly, the safety line started to play out rapidly. With a jerk, it went taut. Ken and Marty immediately grabbed the line and began hauling it in. The weight on the line was made much more difficult to pull in because of the fast-moving tide.

Within a minute, they had pulled a breathless Brady up to the gunwale.

"You OK, Brady? asked Ken. What happened?"

Choking on a mouthful of saltwater, Brady pulled his mask off and said, "I lost my hold just as I cut the last wire, but she's disarmed and that's all that matters."

They hauled Brady into the whaler and headed back toward the ramp. With these two bridges now secure, the Director switched his focus back to the Gas Dock pilings and the search for the terrorist cell.

✳✳✳

Maya and Haamid sat motionless in the black Hummer. They were parked under the bridge on the east side of the Narrows. The wind howled around them and the rain blew horizontally across the Hummer. Every few minutes, Maya hit the windshield wipers and did a single swipe across the glass in front of them. They saw fairly clearly through their camouflage binoculars, keeping watch on the NRP boat as it moved from the NRP ramp to the bridge pilings.

They had arrived under the bridge almost at the same time the helicopter had landed on the pad in front of the DNR office. They were about to exit the Humvee when they heard the chopper overhead and watched it drop out of the storm. Allah was clearly with them. If they had exited the vehicle and headed to the water - or worse yet, if Maya had been in the water - they would have been seen and either shot or captured.

Maya was sure they were disarming the explosives. As she strained to see who was in the boat, Haamid, using his binoculars, was sure he'd spotted Brady in a wetsuit seated on the bow platform.

"Damn. That's exactly what they've done! They've disarmed the detonators," said Haamid.

"So what," said Maya. "We'll just go back and reconnect the detonators. That's what we came to check on anyway. I wonder if they did the same thing with the drawbridge?"

"Well, Maya, we'll soon find that out too."

"Haamid, we need to wait until they've secured the whaler and either gone back to the office or taken off in the chopper. At that point, I doubt they will give the explosives at these bridges another thought. They will be convinced that they've solved the problem."

"I agree," said Haamid.

Within fifteen minutes, the NRP boat was secured at the ramp and all five men had retreated to the safety of the DNR office. If they, however, were to leave by helicopter before Maya had reached the other side of the Narrows, she would surely be spotted.

So, Maya decided to wait ten minutes, in case they came back out to the helicopter and took off.

After fifteen minutes, Maya felt comfortable that the weather would keep the chopper grounded for at least an hour. She got out of the Humvee, donned her wetsuit, strapped on the tank, and slid the mask over her head.

"I must go now, Haamid, before they return to the chopper. I've decided to leave from the boat ramp, instead of swimming directly across to the pilings. Based on how hard the whaler was having to work against the tide before it turned west and crossed the Narrows, I need to launch myself further north so that I can cut diagonally across, allowing the tide to take me downstream to the pilings. If I don't do that, the tide will force me south of the pilings toward the restaurant on the other side of the bridge. If I end up there, I won't be able to successfully swim back against the tide and reach the pilings. I know this will expose me to possible detection, since I will be much closer to the DNR office when I move out, but I have to risk this to successfully reach the other side."

"I don't like it but I do agree, Maya. It's the only way."

"Don't you need me to hold the security rope?"

"No. I'm not going to use it. It's too risky."

"Maya, that's crazy! If you run into trouble, there's no way I can pull you back to safety."

"Haamid, it will be much easier for them to spot two of us instead of just one. It's just way too risky. It's my decision. I'm going without the safety rope. All you need to do after I enter the water is to drive over to the drawbridge and park on the west side, jump down below the bridge, and wait there. When I see your flashlight signal, I'll swim toward it and you can pull me out. I will need another small tank before I dive on the drawbridge pilings. OK?"

"I still don't like it, Maya. It's too dangerous without the safety rope, but you're in charge, so I guess I've got to go along."

"Yes you do, Haamid," said Maya, as she lumbered with her flippers across the pavement to the water's edge.

"Allah is with you, sister. I'll see you at the drawbridge."

Maya waved back at him, slipped down the ramp, and disappeared into the stormy waters.

✳✳✳

The winds whistled through the bridge's steel understructure. The halyards on the boats in the cradles at the marina produced a cacophony of sound as the cold night air played them like the strings of a harp. The wind's rhythm was erratic and the rain pierced the air like needles. Maya fought through the fierce and unrelenting onslaught of the elements in her struggle to reach the first set of pilings. She had misjudged the ferocity of the tide and the winds just enough. They swept her past the first piling and into the second one. There, she was able to hold her ground by attaching her tether rope with its snap to a piton clip that was embedded into the piling shelf. Once attached, she maneuvered around the shelf and discovered that the detonator and the antenna wiring had been cut. She repaired the wiring with the pliers and with Marine Goop. She also confirmed that the pitons were still in place.

Now, her concern was with how to swim against an eight-knot tide to reach the first piling twenty feet in front of her. Maya looked over at the rock-strewn shoreline ten feet away, and she decided that her best bet was to reach the shore and walk north along the rocks to a point thirty feet beyond the first piling. Once there, she could dive off of the rocks. Fighting the tide, she could swim in a northerly direction. The tide would force her south. Hopefully, it would bring her to the first piling, where she could then grab a piton and attach her tether rope. Once secure, she could locate the wires and check out the connections.

Maya took several deep breaths and dove north into the dark waters. Using every ounce of muscle and know-how, she swam hard against the tide. In less than five seconds, she bumped into the first piling and reached out for the shelf with the embedded pitons. She missed the first set of shelf pitons and barely secured her hand around the last set on the piling, thus avoiding being swept away toward the piers that were south of the bridge.

Maya found that Brady had sabotaged this piling the same way. Again, she fixed the wiring and connections in a similar manner to the other piling. Thank goodness she had decided to take this dive. Holding onto the last piton, she turned around and faced the drawbridge, which was about a hundred feet away and diagonally south from where she was. She held onto the tether rope to get her strength and her wits back. Then she launched herself across to the drawbridge pilings. If her calculations were right, she would swim against the tide until she was halfway across the Narrows. Then she would turn south and swim hard for the drawbridge. If she missed, she would be blown south into Eastern Bay, where she would most likely drown.

This is it, she thought as she launched herself into the swift waters of the Narrows. Maya used her flippers to speed across the water. She saw Haamid's small flashlight off in the distance beckoning her to reach it as quickly as possible. Maya pointed her lighted headlamp toward Haamid and flashed it three times to confirm her identity.

Just south of the next set of bridge pilings, she encountered an eddy that slowed her southerly movement and helped her correct her course toward the western shore.

Haamid's flashlight quickly grew larger as Maya fought to reach her brother's hand, which she knew lay just above the water and directly below the flashlight. Maya hit the rocks just below the drawbridge bulkhead. The impact knocked the breath out of her. She rolled along the rocks until she felt Haamid's strong hand grab her wetsuit just below her arm. He had her. Maya crawled up onto the rocks and slowly climbed to the top of the bulkhead, where Haamid was now crouched just below the drawbridge's understructure.

"You OK, Maya?"

Breathless she replied haltingly, "Ye…Yes. I'm OK. But that was too close for comfort."

"Now what?" he asked.

"Let me catch my breath, brother. As soon as you change my tank, Haamid, I'll swim out to check those," she said, pointing to the drawbridge pilings. "I'll also need the long safety rope, just in case I get swept away. The water is running much faster than I thought it was."

After attaching the rope to her safety belt and the other end around her brother's waist, Maya set off to check the explosives. This time, with the aid of the safety rope, it took her far less time to check all of the connections. As she was about to return to where Haamid was crouched on the bulkhead, her eyes caught a silver flash between two bandoliers. Something was amiss. She moved closer to the bandolier where she had seen the silver flash. The silver flash turned out to be the end of a wire that had been cut. She repaired it, as she had done with the others. She then checked all of the bandoliers to be sure that they didn't have the same problem. Thanks be to Allah, she had noticed the silver reflection of that wire. Otherwise, these pilings would never have blown.

Surfacing, Maya tugged on the safety rope, signaling for Haamid to pull her in. Reaching the bulkhead under the drawbridge, Maya quickly removed her flippers and climbed up to the roadbed. With the help of her brother, she slid into the front passenger seat of the Hummer. With the headlights turned off, Haamid took off for the munitions cache farm.

Just as they drove off the drawbridge, the NRP chopper ascended and crossed their path not more than forty feet above them. Then the sound of its propellers faded into the storm sounds around them. In the blink of an eye, the chopper was gone. It was 12:30 a.m. as they sped down the road toward safety.

Chapter 22

The Day of Reckoning. Sunday Morning, July 4, 2010

At 12:45 am, due to the severity of the storm, the Regional Director had ordered the helicopter back to the landing pad in front of the search and rescue headquarters at the base of the Bay Bridge. Again, the chopper pilots had called their superiors, and they were reluctantly given permission to fly in the below minimum conditions.

In consultation with the state police, the NRP, and his boss in DC, the Director suspended the land and sea search until 6:30 a.m., when the weather was predicted to start breaking up and the morning's first light would allow them to renew their quest.

Knowing that they needed to disarm the explosives at the Gas Docks as soon as possible, and given that no one knew the terrorists' timetable for the attack, the Regional Director ordered a cutter from the coast guard to meet him at the search headquarters at the base of the Bay Bridge on the western shore.

The coast guard immediately contacted the Gas Docks dockmaster, the LNG tank farm manager, and the captain of the *Queen of the Adriatic* to alert them to the cutter's arrival and the mission that they were on to deactivate the charges that had been set at the Gas Dock pilings.

For fear of somehow setting off the explosives by moving the LNG tanker from her berth, the *Queen of the Adriatic* was ordered by the coast guard to remain secured to the Gas Docks. This was in direct conflict with the ship's owners, who had immediately contacted the coast guard and DHS Headquarters in Washington D.C. In the hope of saving the ship, its cargo, and crew from going up in flames, the ship's owners requested that they be given clearance to depart the Docks, but. DHS invoked their powers under the National Security Act and denied this request.

At 2:30 a.m. the cutter arrived at the search headquarters, and the Regional Director, Brady, Dan, and the rest of the dive team boarded. The cutter set off for the Gas Docks. By this time, the wind had shifted again and was coming directly out of the south, making the trip to the Gas Docks both unpleasant and unsafe. The waves rose four feet high. The swells were at eight-second intervals, and the wind was blowing at more than forty knots. Brady had made sure that Dan was approved to join him on his dive at the Docks. Since he held a master diver's certificate and was still in Special Forces Reserves, it was an easy authorization to obtain from the coast guard. In addition, another coast guard diver and two dive-support personnel were also onboard the eighty-seven-foot cutter as it made its way through the fog bank and the stormy weather that had now settled over the midsection of the Chesapeake Bay.

The skills of the captain of the *Barracuda Class Cutter* were being tested to their fullest. While seaworthy, the ship carried a fairly narrow beam. The beam was only nineteen feet wide, yet the boat was almost ninety feet long. Thus, she tended to pitch and roll in weather of this kind, especially with the Bay's swells starting to reach forty feet in separation.

To be heard over the roar of the two diesels and the high-pitched sounds of the wind as it tore across the bridge, Brady had to lean close to the Director as they stood at the open door of the bridge.

"Brady, the captain says he won't be able to bring the cutter up next to the pilings. He says he will have to launch the twenty-two-foot, short-range *Prosecutor*. The captain says that if it doesn't let up, that's the only way to get you, Dan, and their diver, Timmy, close enough to do the job and do it safely."

"That's fine," said Brady, "as long as the inflatable sides keep the water out."

"Not to worry. The entire boat can be full of water and the damn thing won't sink."

"Yeah, that's what they said about the Titanic."

"No problem, Brady. We got your back."

"I'm just kidding you, Director. The only thing I'm worried about is capturing those guys before they strike. Time is in their favor - not ours."

✳✳✳

The *Prosecutor* was under the command of the cutter's chief petty officer. Another petty officer and two seamen were also onboard. The two seamen slid her off the stern ramp and into the choppy waters forty feet from the two northernmost Gas Dock pilings. Before the boat hit the water and just prior to slipping off the stern platform, the chief onboard had started the water jets. Using the vector thrust control he quickly maneuvered to the port side, where Brady and Dan hopped onto the boat. Brady, Dan, and Timmy pulled on their dive tanks, zipped up their wetsuits, and strapped on their flippers. The *Prosecutor* moved off toward the pilings.

Maneuvering to within ten feet of the pilings, the captain of the *Prosecutor* gave the order to roll off the inflated gunwales. All three men hit the water at the same time and held onto the three thirty-foot safety ropes that were attached to the inflatable's side. Each man turned on his safety light, which was attached to his chest strap, and his headlamp. Without these lights, it would be impossible to locate the others and to see the explosives that were attached to the pilings below.

With a thumbs-up and a hand gesture that said, "Follow me," Brady dove for the pilings, trailing behind him one of the three safety lines that was attached to the *Prosecutor*. Dan and Timmy, with their own safety lines flowing behind them, followed Brady down ten feet to the piling's ledge. Similar to Brady, they attached their short ten-foot safety lines to one of the piton clips. The tide was running so strong that Brady swam to the south side of the first piling, where the piling helped block him from the tide's full force. Within thirty seconds, Brady located the detonation box and the antenna. Dan and Timmy held onto several of the piton clips and watched Brady work the piling ledge. Dan and Timmy were impressed with the way that the bandoliers had been secured and with the professional way that the charges had been laid out and linked in sequence. They were there to assist Brady in case he needed help. More importantly, they were there to make sure that Brady would be safe if anything went wrong or if he suffered oxygen deprivation, as he had earlier at the Narrows Bridge.

Once the first pilings' explosives were deactivated, Brady turned to his fellow divers and indicated the direction he would be moving in to reach the second piling. Brady unhooked his short safety line from the piling and headed off into the muddy waters to the second piling. Dan followed behind him, dragging along his safety lines. Thinking that Dan's safety lines were still connected to him, Timmy grabbed one to pull himself toward Dan. As he did so, he yanked both safety ropes out of Dan's hand, sending Dan off into the slipstream of the fast-moving tide, as he and Brady cleared the corner of the piling.

The rapidly moving tide swept Dan from the relative safety of the south side of the piling into the riptide-like current. Instantly, Dan disappeared into the dark waters under the pier and out of sight from Brady and Timmy. Brady motioned to Timmy to immediately surface for help, and he indicated that he would go after Dan. Brady calculated the tide's direction and made allowances for the deflection of the current around the pilings. With his safety line tied to his wetsuit, he headed off in the direction he believed Dan had gone. If he were lucky, he figured that Dan would be swept into the next piling. If luck was with him, he'd grab onto that pilings' pitons and bandoliers until Brady reached him. Brady adjusted his headlamp so that its light shone straight ahead. In order not to float past the next piling, he pulled his safety rope all of the way out from the dive boat above and carefully played out the line, as the swift waters accelerated him forward.

Brady's headlamp caught the flash of something bright just as it cut across his right peripheral vision. It was a large rockfish, he guessed. Then he realized that it was his light's reflection off of the reflective silver safety tape on Dan's wetsuit. Using all of the strength he could muster, Brady swam off to his right in the direction of the flash of light. Three seconds later, he reached Dan, who was clinging to the bandoliers that were attached to the second piling.

Thank God, Brady thought. *If Dan hadn't lucked out as he was being swept away from the first piling, we probably never would have found him.* Brady figured that Dan would have been pulled under the hull of the *Queen of the Adriatic,* the LNG tanker that had recently arrived at the Gas Docks. Since her bow was only thirty yards away, the current would have swept Dan underneath the ship's steel plates. He would have then had an inevitable rendezvous with her rudder or propellers. Dan would not have made it.

As Brady grabbed Dan and attached him to his safety rope, Dan gave Brady a high-five. Once he was secure, Brady made his way along the piling. He found the detonation wires and the antenna and pulled both of them, thereby disarming the explosives on the second piling.

As he turned back to Dan, Timmy emerged from the murky waters in front of them with an extra safety line. Brady attached Dan to the new safety line, snapped his own line off of the piton clip, and reattached it too his belt. The three began to slowly pull themselves along toward the *Prosecutor*.

Brady focused his attention on his teammates and made sure that Timmy and Dan were safely aboard before he began to move toward the rescue tender. Suddenly, Brady began to feel very lightheaded and weak. He lost his grip on the line and passed out. Brady quickly floated off to the end of his safety rope. The rope held but by the time it had fully played out, Brady was unconscious.

Right after Dan and Timmy were hauled over the side of the inflatable, Dan turned back to help Brady come aboard. Dan expected Brady to pop up above the surface, but he didn't. Dan shouted above the rain and wind, telling two of the seamen to assist him and Timmy in retrieving Brady. The men grabbed Brady's safety line and struggled to drag him back to the boat. At this time, Brady was sinking like a dead weight.

As soon as Brady was pulled out of the water and over the gunwale, the chief petty officer directed the captain of the *Prosecutor* to plow full-speed ahead to reach the *Barracuda Class Cutter*, which was now anchored a hundred yards to the north. Dan started mouth-to-mouth resuscitation but to no avail. In three minutes, the *Prosecutor*, running full-speed against the gale forced winds, slid up onto the stern platform of the *Barracuda*. Two navy medics were waiting with oxygen and a defibrillation machine. Fearful that any lapse in continuous resuscitation might cause a major problem, the medics started their work in earnest the minute the crew laid Brady down on the deck.

Knowing that a quick airlift to Anne Arundel Medical Center would be Brady's best chance, the captain of the *Barracuda Class Cutter* called in the DHS's helicopter from the Bay Bridge Search Headquarters.

The chopper arrived at the Gas Docks within ten minutes. Brady was immediately lifted off of the *Cutter*. It took another fifteen minutes to get Brady to the Arundel Medical Center. All the while, the medics continued to work on his vital signs. Although they had finally restarted his breathing, he remained unconscious. His vital signs were barely apparent.

Dan remained at Brady's side throughout his evacuation. From time to time, he would lean over him and say, "You made it through Afghanistan and Walter Reed, Brady. You will make it through this too. I'm right here, buddy. I won't leave you. I promise."

***

Arriving at Anne Arundel Medical Center, Brady had been rushed to intensive care. At this point, Dan had a chance to call Captain Pete and Louise to fill them in on what was going on.

"Louise, this is Dan."

"Thank God, Dan. What's going on? Where are you? Is Brady OK?"

"Miss Louise, everything is under control and Brady is in good hands at Anne Arundel Medical Center."

"Why the medical center?" interrupted Pete. "What's going on, Dan?"

For the next five minutes, Dan relayed all that had transpired since he had last called Pete just after Brady had escaped.

At the end of the call, Pete said, "We'll leave here as soon as we can, Dan."

"Good," said Dan. "I'm sure your being here will be a real help to Brady. When you arrive I'll probably be gone. Since I know all of the background that Brady has shared with me, DHS has asked me to help them. I doubt I can really help, but I'll do my best."

"Stay in touch, Dan," said Louise.

"I will," said Dan. "And you all call me if there's any change in Brady's condition."

"We will," said Pete. "By the way, how have they listed him?"

Dan hesitated to relay Brady's official status. Convinced that they needed to know, though, he responded, "Critical, Captain Pete. They say he's in critical condition."

"Thanks for your honesty, Dan. Now go find those bastards and take care of 'em."

"Will do, Captain Pete. Talk to you later."

It was 6:00 a.m. when Dan hung up. He checked one more time with the doctors and learned there had been no change in Brady's status.

***

Dan's cell phone rang.

"Hello?"

"Dan, this is Lieutenant Price. If you're willing, I need your help figuring out if there are more targets than just the Gas Docks and the two Narrows Bridges. The State Police uncovered a small handwritten note at the terrorist headquarters farm that refers to various ship arrivals in early July. I don't know if it's of significance or not, but. I do know that they should've gotten on it hours ago, right after they raided that farm. God, I hate bureaucratic incompetency!"

"Me too, Lieutenant, but there's nothing we can do about it now. Where should I meet you?"

"I will pick you up outside the ER entrance in fifteen minutes, Dan."

"OK, see you then," said Dan.

As Dan waited for Lieutenant Price, he called his boss, Mr. Duncan, to tell him what was going on and to say that he probably would not be coming back to work before Thursday, after Mack and Mike's funerals.

Dan got ahold of Mr. Duncan on his cell phone, knowing that he would be on vacation at his place in Bethany Beach, Delaware. After apologizing for the early call, he relayed the details of the diving accident and gave him a rundown on Brady's condition, making sure that he did not mention the terrorist issue. Dan also told Mr. Duncan about how Mack and Mike had died in a boating accident.

Mr. Duncan listened without interruption. Just before the call was completed, he requested that Dan keep him in the loop, and he also suggested that he call Michelle directly about Brady. He knew that she was soft on Brady and that she was to have dinner with him the next week.

"She'd be upset if you didn't call her to let her know about Brady's condition, Dan."

"Yes, sir. I think she would. So, I will call her as soon as I hang up."

Dan hung up and immediately called Michelle. He hated to call her so early, but if he didn't call while he had the time, he might not be able to get to her for several days.

"Hello," said Michelle groggily.

"Hey, Michelle. It's Dan."

Michelle said, "Dan, its six-fifteen in the morning. What's so darn important? You know I need my beauty sleep."

Dan smiled at her quip and then said, "Yes you do - more than most people I know - but this is important. Otherwise I wouldn't have disturbed you so early."

"OK, go ahead. I'm all ears."

"Michelle, Brady's in the hospital suffering from a series of diving mishaps. While I think he'll pull through, he's in critical condition. Mr. Duncan wanted me to let you know."

Immediately, Michelle's attention became focused and she said, "What does *critical* really mean, Dan?"

"Well, his vital signs are fair but not great. We've got him back breathing on his own, but he's still very groggy and his blood pressure is still way too low."

"How did this happen?"

"It's a long story, Michelle - too long to go into now. But suffice to say, he's been involved in rooting out a terrorist plot on the Chesapeake Bay. The guys he's come up against are really a tough bunch. In fact, they have already killed Captain Pete's friend, Mack, and his son, Mike. They were about to kill Brady when he escaped."

"Jesus, Dan. How long's this been going on?"

"Well, Pete and Mack became suspicious of a rogue boat they encountered in February. Pete then told Brady about it. So, I guess Brady's been involved for about four months now."

"He never said a word to me about it."

"I wouldn't think he would, Michelle. He's a very private person and he wouldn't want to alarm anyone unnecessarily."

"Yeah, I guess you're right."

"Hopefully he'll recover fully in the next twenty-four hours. I'll let you know."

"Do you think it would be all right if I came down to see him in the hospital? We were supposed to have dinner down there this coming week."

"I don't know but I'll call you in a day or two. Say a prayer for him."

"I will Dan, and thanks for your call. I sure hope he's OK."

"Oh, also, Michelle, please do not say a word to anyone, including Mr. Duncan, about the terrorists' involvement. If it gets out that I leaked this information, I will be subject to harsh legal action from Homeland Security."

"I promise I will not say a word to anyone, Dan."

I'll call you later, Michelle. Take care."

"You too, Dan. Thanks again."

It was 6:30 a.m. when they hung up.

✳✳✳

Louise packed a small suitcase for Captain Pete and herself in case they had to stay by Brady's side. Before leaving the house, they called Beth North, Mack's wife, to tell her where they were heading and to assure her that they'd be back well before the funerals.

When Pete and Louise arrived in Chester, Maryland at the Medical Center, and they were immediately ushered into the ICU to see Brady. In the short amount of time he had been at the center, he'd made amazing progress. He was now fully conscious, very alert, and ready to leave so that he could continue to track down Abed and his men. The doctors refused to release him, knowing that the effects of the lack of oxygen required continued rest, IVs, and monitoring. They were especially concerned he had been deprived of oxygen several times within the last few days. However, Pete, in his inimitable way, negotiated a deal between the doctors and Brady that resulted in an agreement that he could leave at 8:30 a.m. if all of his vital signs were good and the IV that they were administering to him was completed.

At 8:30 a.m. the IV was finished and the ER doctor declared that his vital signs were normal. To leave right away, though, the doctor demanded that Brady sign a release absolving the Center of any liability. Brady signed the release form, dressed in a flash, and headed out into the parking lot with Captain Pete and Louise. Captain Pete drove Brady to the NRP office at the Narrows and dropped him off. He and Louise then headed home to Tilghman.

Before she left, Louise stuffed a chicken sandwich, some homemade cookies, and a soda into Brady's Sou'wester raincoat. She then wished him Godspeed. Pete gave him a big hug. He told him how proud he was of him, and he said to take care to watch his back. He also promised Brady that he'd call his mom, Judy, to give her an update on everything that had been happening and to assure her that Brady was OK. Brady gave them hugs and told them not to worry, as he scrambled into officer Marty's truck for the drive to Matapeake, where he hoped to catch up with Lieutenant Price and Dan before they shoved off for the Gas Docks.

Pete and Louise headed home to help Beth and Tanya prepare for a day that Pete was dreading: the Wednesday funerals. His mind traveled back to that bitter February morning when the rogue boat had come so close to ramming into Mack's *Miss Patricia*. He never imagined that six months later he would be giving a eulogy for his faithful friend of more than half a century.

Aboard the *Mana Kia,* the day, like so many before it, began for Captain Jurgensen at 5:00 a.m. The Captain began his daily mustering of the ship's crew. He received a headcount and some reports from the night watchmen and the ship's engineer. Thirty-two crewmen and all officers were accounted for. No anomalies were reported during the watch between 11:00 p.m. to 5:00 a.m. The captain completed the muster, called out the names of the twenty-six crewmen who had passes to go ashore for the day, and ordered the first mate to organize their departure. He then released the remaining six crewmembers and his officers to perform their daily duties. Along with his chief engineer and the ship's loadmaster, he started a forty-five-minute tour of the ship's engine room, communications shack, and cargo.

Returning to the bridge at 6:30 a.m., the captain reviewed the ships manifest, and signed one-day-leave, Fourth of July, passes for twenty-six crewmembers. The *Mana Kia's* tender was sent into Annapolis to deposit the twenty-six at dockside. Unbeknownst to them, this group was lucky enough to get a new lease on life. For the next twenty-four hours, the captain would await the call from the Baltimore Port Administration, clearing him to proceed into the Baltimore Harbor on the morning of July fifth. Next would come the second call from the Bay Pilot assigned to the *Mana Kia*, announcing his means of arrival, either by pilot boat or by helicopter, and his ETA.

The *Mana Kia* had been anchored off of the south end of the Annapolis Anchorage, awaiting a berth in Baltimore Harbor. Captain Jurgensen didn't expect to get a call to enter the harbor until July fifth, since most dockworkers and stevedores would have a longshoremen's day off for the Fourth of July.

So, it was quite a surprise when he received a call after breakfast from a Bay pilot, informing him that a berth was available and that he should expect him to arrive by a R-44 Raven II Robinson helicopter Number 106XC at 8:15 a.m. He told Captain Jurgensen that he was also bringing two Bay pilots in-training with him as part of their pilot program's in-the-field classroom curriculum. While surprised that the Bay pilot was delivering the notice of berth availability, Captain Jurgensen took it in stride. The Bay pilot had explained that because of the holiday the Port Authority was short of staff. He had asked him to convey the berth's availability when he called to confirm his arrival by chopper.

During the conversation with the Bay pilot, Captain Jurgensen asked if the Port Authority had notified his company. Normally, he would have received a call from his company authorizing the ship's movement prior to a Bay pilot's arrival. In response, the Bay pilot confirmed an earlier phone conversation that had occurred between Captain Jurgensen's company and the Port Authority. He explained that evidently the company's Philadelphia-based marine communication system was undergoing modifications. It was therefore unable to contact the captain directly. The Bay pilot said that he understood that the company would e-mail instructions within the next thirty minutes to verify their authorization.

Although not critical to the docking, since this would be handled by the Bay pilot and the skeleton crew, Captain Jurgensen had the first mate call the twenty-six crewmen who had just left for shore, ordering them to meet the ship at day's end at the Baltimore Harbor berth.

Within fifteen minutes, the captain received an e-mail authorizing him to prepare the ship for the Bay pilot's arrival and the ship's subsequent move to the container berth that had been opened up for the *Mana Kia* in Baltimore Harbor.

Kaleem finished sending the e-mail from the Parks Neck Farm by hacking into the shipping company's e-mail program. In both content and structure, the e-mail was a perfect counterfeit of the standard notice-to-proceed letter. In the e-mail cover letter, Kaleem asked for the captain's cell phone number so that he could call him the minute the berth was ready for the *Mana Kia*'s arrival.

As Captain Jurgensen ran through his checklist and reviewed the GPS and the hard charts, the R-44 Raven II was lifting off from the Bay Bridge Airport.

Because of his expertise in handling oil tankers off of the coast of Somalia and container ships in the Middle East, Salah would take the helm of the *Mana Kia*. Instead of piloting the Raven II, he would guide the *Mana Kia* to its encounter with the largest icon on the Chesapeake Bay. It had taken all of his persuasive powers to get Abed and their headquarters in Kabal to agree to his hands-on involvement in piloting the *Mana Kia* to her destiny. If he were successful in doing so, he was sure that it would lead to the approval of other similar hands-on opportunities for him in future attacks on America. Although he was a good leader and manager of men, he still loved to be on the front lines and in the thick of the battle. The trenches were where he had been born and where he would ultimately die.

✳✳✳

At 7:30 a.m. Omar and Marco took the *Miss Martha* from Black Walnut Point to the Miles River to prepare for the 9:00 a.m. detonation of the two Narrows bridges. Once the detonation transmitter switch was thrown and the explosions had occurred, the two men would immediately proceed to St. Michael's, and dock at the in-town waterfront restaurant adjacent to the public boat ramp. There, they would abandon the boat. Maya would meet them at the ramp and take them straight back to Parks Neck, and they would then escape to Onnoake, Virginia.

At 7:30 am, as Omar and Marco headed for the Miles River, the two pilots, Bashir and Haron, met with the helicopter service at the Bay Bridge Airport. After completing the necessary paperwork, the helicopter pilot, as instructed by Bashir, took the two pilots on a short hop to a private grass strip that was just north of Knapps Narrows. Upon landing, Bashir asked the helicopter pilot to walk with him to the small aero-maintenance support shed at the end of the runway. They were there to ostensibly pick up some instruments to deliver to Norfolk, Virginia. Upon reaching the hedgerow adjacent to the shed, Bashir turned to face the pilot, pulled out his nine-millimeter Glock, and shot him straight between the eyes. Bashir dragged the dead pilot into a hedgerow, hid him under a pile of branches, and returned to the helicopter.

Salah and Abed showed up fifteen minutes later in a Humvee and boarded the Raven II. At exactly 8:15 a.m. Bashir applied power and lifted off. Within a few minutes, they were hovering over the helicopter pad of the *Mana Kia,* as she lay at anchor opposite Annapolis. Below them, the first officer of the *Mana Kia* raised his hands and crossed them to indicate that they were now directly over the bull's-eye mark on the pad. Bashir gently lowered the Raven II to the deck. He remained in his seat with the engine idling, as the others exited the helicopter. Bashir had to be prepared to lift off with full power just before 9:00 a.m.

As Abed stepped from the helicopter, he handed his counterfeit captain's license to the first officer. In return, the first officer handed him the pilot card. As required by maritime law, the card contained all of the ship's relevant information, such as its maneuvering characteristics, draft, speed, the number of containers it held, and electronics. Abed stood on the deck next to the chopper and quickly scanned the pilot card, which said, "Statistics: Panamax Container Ship. 951 feet long. 105 foot beam. Draft, sixty feet. 5,000 containers onboard. Maximum speed, twenty-seven knots. Location: Anchored seven miles south of the Chesapeake Bay Bridge, and one-and-a-half miles north of Buoy R-8."

The first officer stood next to Abed and checked his Bay pilot license and qualifications, before escorting the four men to the bridge.

At 7:40 a.m. Kaleem called Captain Jurgensen's cell phone from Parks Neck to inform him that the Baltimore Container Pier was ready to receive his ship. He further stated that since the Port was understaffed and the window for docking and unloading was very tight, he should bring his ship's engines up to full power. At 8:15 a.m. sharp, when the Bay pilot arrived, they must be prepared to pull anchor and immediately depart for the harbor at precisely 8:45 a.m. He also requested that the first officer, chief engineer, load master, and security director be with him in the pilothouse on the bridge when the Bay pilot arrived to take command.

✳✳✳

At 8:15 a.m. Jamil, Haamid, and Kaleem left Parks Neck on the *Miss Catherine James* and headed across the fog-bound Bay to the Gas Docks. As they neared the Gas Docks, like some prehistoric monster rising from the sea floor, the superstructure of the Gas Docks and the hull of the *Queen of the Adriatic* emerged from the fog and rain that still dominated the Middle Bay.

Jamil steered the *Miss Catherine James* to the MOB point on the GPS screen. Once they were there, they anchored her so that the mortar's baseplates were directly under the MOB coordinates.

The team was concerned about their ability to deliver the kind of accuracy that was demanded. They were severely hampered by the lack of sight lines, which had been lost due to the heavy mist and rain. The shifting winds and waves also compounded the visibility issue.

But Jamil was an expert at calculating elevations and windage. He would wait until the *Miss Catherine James* was fairly steady at the bottom of a swell before he commenced shooting. Jamil set the mortar up and brought two cases of shells out on deck. He also pulled the RPG out from under the forward bunk, and he brought it and two cases of RPG shells to the stern of the boat. One box contained anti-personnel rounds and the other contained armor piercing rounds. He then pulled the four Ricin mortar canisters out of the locked ammo drawers in the forward cabin.

Kaleem, who continued to monitor the radios, discovered that there was an LCS-class coast guard cutter out of Matapeake who was now in the Middle Bay area. Its prime mission was to protect the LNG tanker, the *Queen of the Adriatic*. It was also obvious from the transmissions that their secondary mission was to try to find their boat, the *Miss Catherine James*.

With his AIS radio connected to the Garmin GPS screen, Kaleem learned exactly where the cutter was, and he determined the critical information about her speed and direction. Because of the fog and the winds, the cutter was moving at only about eight knots toward the Gas Docks from across the Bay. Luckily, the weather made the discovery of the *Miss Catherine James* very difficult. Since the AIS B program was installed on one of the *Miss Catherine James*'s VHS radios, they were able to receive AIS signals, while the transmission of their own position remained silent. Thus, they saw the cutter approaching on their GPS screen, but it couldn't see them. The cutter's radar, because of the weather conditions and the fact that Kaleem had initiated a radar-jamming program, was of little help. With multiple echoes bouncing off of the LNG tanker and the Gas Dock's superstructure, the radar returns were indecipherable and ineffective. Nevertheless, the cutter was clearly heading their way. Kaleem estimated its arrival at their position to be, at most, thirty minutes away.

At 8:50 a.m. they were in place and ready to launch their portion of the attack from the deck of the *Miss Catherine James*. It was the day of reckoning: July 4, 2010.

✳✳✳

At 4:00 a.m. Abed unlocked the munitions cache farm, which was north of Cambridge. While he had abandoned this farm earlier, he had decided to have his team's last meeting there, since most of the team was already in the Cambridge area.

Abed started the meeting at 4:45 a.m. by reiterating the attack plans, the schedule, and the evacuation plan. He also shared with everyone that the DHS net was tightening and that he expected that they would be invaded within a matter of hours at both the farm where they were and at the headquarters farm, which was just five miles away. He also told them that he had gotten a call from a friend who was an Islamic real estate agent about how members of the Eastern Shore Legislative Delegation had been calling around looking for leased properties with armed security and restrictive quiet-enjoyment clauses. Luckily, they had limited their search to Talbot, Caroline, Queen Anne's County, and parts of Dorchester County. No one, however, had been searching the lease records in lower Dorchester County, considering its distance from what appeared to be the hub of the terrorist activities. Therefore, everyone who was not on either the detonation or helicopter teams was instructed to immediately head to the Parks Neck Farm.

Before breaking up the meeting, Salah instructed Omar and Jamil to take any additional ammunition in the cache that they might need, such as hand grenades, RPG rounds, the balance of the mortar rounds, and all of the extra Ricin canisters.

Salah was concerned that if the authorities had heard through Brady about the explosives at the Narrows Bridges, they certainly would know about the ones at the Gas Docks. He figured that if they had found and deactivated the explosives at the Docks, they could still wreak havoc on the Gas Docks and the inland storage tanks with mortar and RPG rounds.

✳✳✳

At 6:30 a.m. on the dot, the three search helicopters, under DHS's command, returned to the sky. The land search resumed along the Eastern Shore, from Queen Anne's County to Somerset County. Feeling confident that the two bridges at the Narrows and the Gas Docks had finally been taken care of, the Director began searching for the two Bay-built boats, their crews, and any remaining safe houses that the terrorists were still occupying.

Through its realtor contacts, the Director had instructed the Eastern Shore Delegation to attempt to uncover any leases that had been made with a New York City LLC in the last twenty-four months. They were looking for leases that contained "quiet enjoyment" provisions that precluded any agent or owner from entering the property. Especially important, were leases on properties that were protected by security guards with heavy weapons. They were looking for guards from nonstandard local or regional firms - guards of Hispanic or Arabic origin.

After many early wake-up calls to realtors, they discovered two such places along the Choptank River above Cambridge. One was on a creek leading to the river and the other was farther inland. By 7:00 a.m. the state police, along with DHS personnel, had entered the inland headquarters farm, but they had found absolutely nothing other than a handwritten note about ship arrivals in the Chesapeake Bay in early July. They found five beds and two additional mattresses on the floor in the living room. They also found empty containers of Mexican food from a restaurant in Easton. DHS personnel made a note to have their people go to the restaurant to see if their employees could identify anyone from the DHS terrorist file photos..

✳✳✳

As soon as Abed and his men entered the bridge of the *Mana Kia*, Abed took charge. On cue, all four men pulled out their nine-millimeter Glocks and handcuffed the officers - all but the captain. Abed stood next to Captain Jurgensen and announced, "This is a hijacking. You are to obey our instructions *to the letter*. If you disobey you will be immediately shot."

Abed confirmed with the chief engineer that the engines had been warmed up and were prepared to go to full-speed at a moment's notice. Abed grabbed the captain's arm, and looking directly into his eyes said. "Captain have the engine room proceed: *All Ahead. Slow* and order the anchor to be pulled, now!" Captain Jurgensen immediately carried out Abed's orders. The ship slowly moved forward, extracting the anchor from the grip of the muddy bottom. Once the anchor broke the surface, Abed's flight officer, Haron, handcuffed the captain to the rear bulkhead, and Salah took over the joystick. He would steer the ship from its present location just south of Price Creek, which was approximately one nautical mile off Kent Island's western shore, up to Buoy R-88. Then, he would take it on a course of thirty-three degrees north to the pilings that supported the first eastern suspension span of the Chesapeake Bay Bridge. Since Salah had done the depth-soundings from the Zodiac on Friday night, he knew that he must steer slightly to the west a degree or two to avoid any depths less than seventy feet. Should he fail to do so, there was a distinct possibility that they would run aground.

Salah pushed the joystick to full speed. The giant turbines roared to life. The hull began to vibrate, as though alive. Before they reached the two-mile mark of this, the Mana Kia's, final journey, they found themselves one half-mile from Buoy R-88 and three thousand meters from the ship's initial Annapolis Anchorage. The *Mana Kia* was already at sixteen knots. She was well on her way to her top speed of twenty-seven knots, which she would reach just before crashing into the bridge.

After pushing the *Mana Kia* to its full capacity, the captain received several calls from his assistant engineer in the engine room. He kept asking why full power was needed when regulations called for no more than quarter-speed when nearing a major bridge. Finally, Abed pointed a gun at Captain Jorgensen's head and handed him a note instructing him to advise the engine room that he, Captain Jurgensen, was confirming his earlier order to proceed at full speed.

"This is Captain Jurgensen. You are to immediately proceed to *"All Ahead Full"*. Is that understood?"

"Aye, aye, sir," the assistant engineer responded. *"All Ahead Full."*

The ship continued to gather speed. Salah concentrated on steering the ship to its rendezvous with the bridge. With his AK-47 slung over his shoulder, Abed ordered Haron to have the loadmaster take him to the bow of the ship so that he could inspect the top three layers of the deck containers. He had to be sure that they were numbered in accordance with the explosives plan. Two months earlier, the jihadist loadmaster at the departing port had made sure that the top three layers of containers were the ones that housed over forty thousand pounds of high explosives. Each trailer contained five thousand pounds of explosives. For identity purposes, they had been specially marked with an Arabic number in the lower right-hand corner, just above each container's base.

✳✳✳

"Mana Kia. Mana Kia. This is the watch commander, US Coast Guard command, Curtis Bay. Over."

No Answer.

"Mana Kia. Mana Kia. This is the watch commander, US Coast Guard command, Curtis Bay. Do you read me? Over."

No Answer.

"Mana Kia. Mana Kia. This is the watch commander, US Coast Guard command, Curtis Bay. Do you read me? Over."

Again, no answer.

Three minutes later, after receiving orders from the DHS headquarters in Washington, D.C., the watch commander resumed the transmission.

"Mana Kia. Mana Kia. This is the watch commander, US Coast Guard command, Curtis Bay. You are hereby ordered to stop all engines immediately. You have failed

to contact Baltimore Vessel Traffic Service for approval to leave your anchorage and proceed.

You are hereby put on notice that you are in violation of US Coast Guard regulations, Maryland Port Authority regulations, and Bay Pilot directives. You are hereby ordered to place your engines in full reverse. Once forward progress has ceased, you are to anchor immediately and await US Coast Guard boarding. Is that understood, *Mana Kia?*"

No Answer.

Mana Kia. Mana Kia. Be on notice, *Mana Kia*, we have dispatched a coast guard NSC cutter from our Curtis Bay / Baltimore station and a coast guard littoral combat ship from Annapolis, Maryland, to intercept you. Unless we hear from you immediately, we will consider you an enemy combatant, and under the Homeland Security Act, we will take whatever action we deem necessary to halt your movement and to secure both your cargo and crew. *Mana Kia. Mana Kia.* Do you read me? Over."

Again, no Answer.

The tension level at the coast guard station in Curtis Bay increased with every passing minute. Numerous calls were made, but the *Mana Kia* failed to respond. The coast guard station in Curtis Bay was now convinced that the *Mana Kia* was a Homeland Security threat. This nine-hundred-and-fifty-foot-long Panamax super-container ship was not racing toward the Bay Bridge's middle-span in the main channel. Instead, it was heading toward the first small span on the east side, which was way too low to allow the ship to pass underneath it.

All hell was about to break loose.

At 8:15 a.m. due to the fog and low overcast, Omar and Marco could barely make out the glow of the lights emanating from the restaurants, hotels, and Marinas along Kent Narrows. They knew that in less than an hour, that typical warm glow would grow into a huge orange and red fireball. People would see it in papers and on TV around the world. As they simultaneously unleashed the fury of their explosives across the Bay, the sound of more devastating explosions would reverberate down to Washington, DC and up to Baltimore, MD. On July 4, 2010, the next 9/11 will have been unleashed and a new era of terror in America will have been launched.

Omar and Marco both checked their watches. Only fifteen minutes were left until the detonation. They sat quietly in the cabin. Only the eerie glow of the GPS and the AIS-equipped VHS radio showed any sign of life onboard. It was a waiting game aboard the *Miss Martha*, as the final countdown to detonation began.

Chapter 23
The Attack!

It was exactly 9:00 a.m. on the Fourth of July, 2010.

Omar pushed the button. The handheld transmitter sent its signal from the *Miss Martha* on the Miles River. In less than a second, the charges erupted at the pilings of the Narrows Bridges. The sky exploded as though a volcano had erupted from beneath the Narrows.

The walls of Ken and Marty's offices rattled with such force that the shock wave broke or imploded all of the windows. All of the restaurants along the Narrows experienced the same ferocious shaking and concussion. Large chunks of concrete, rebar, and wood, as well as parts of vehicles, boats, and bodies, erupted in all directions. Boats at

271

the marinas and on land were lifted and hurled into bulkheads or smashed against other boats. Many boats sitting on land were blown off of their blocks and hurled across parking lots. All of them suffered either major damage or total destruction. The watermen's boats that were docked along the drawbridge were completely engulfed in flames. They all exploded like firecrackers as the gas-filled waters erupted in flames. Cars and trucks on both bridges were lifted into the air. Their fuel tanks broke open, pouring thousands of gallons of gas and oil onto what was left of the bridge's twisted and tortured roadway. As tanks exploded and fire erupted, the three restaurants and the oyster house along the east side of the Narrows became engulfed in all-consuming flames. Ken and Marty emerged from their office to see the havoc that was now the Narrows. Literally a hundred separate explosions and fires had started within a quarter of a mile of the bridges. Fireballs launched from the explosions of multiple cars, trucks, and propane tanks, lighting up the stormy morning.

These two experienced police officers could never have imagined the incredible fireworks that were erupting before their eyes.

✳✳✳

Like 9/11, the results far exceeded the terrorist's expectations. Marco took his Nikon camera out of its waterproof bag and began to film. Zooming in, he was able to record the destructive details before him.

Omar said, "It's been six minutes, Marco. You've gotten plenty of film. Let's go. We need to meet Maya at the dock at 9:18 p.m. I'll pull the anchor. You start her up."

Marco put down the camera and turned on the engine blower to clear the fumes. Thirty seconds later, he turned the key. The engine clicked but didn't turn over. He turned the key again - *Click-Click-Click-* again no response. The anchor was up and the *Miss Martha* was drifting with the tides and the winds toward the mouth of the Miles River. This was not good. This was not part of the plan.

The world of leisure and entertainment at the Narrows contained restaurants, hotels, bars, and marinas, along with a working waterfront of workboats, docks, and seafood industries. In the blink of an eye, it ceased to exist as a place. Kent Island was now cut off from the east. Its connection to the Eastern Shore of Maryland was no more. As it had in the early 1800s, Kent Island stood alone in the waters of the Chesapeake Bay. Fires and secondary explosions would continue to plague the Narrows for the next thirty-six hours. Recovery and reconstruction would take years. Al Qaeda had struck a severe blow to the State of Maryland and to the United States of America - a blow that would never be forgotten.

AT ST. MICHAEL'S HARBOR

It was 9:16 a.m. There was no sign of the boat. Maya was wondered, 'Where are they?' Maya was parked at the far edge of a public parking lot that was adjacent to a large boatyard. Though the Hummer had tinted glass windows, she kept her head down to avoid being seen.

People were beginning to show up at the St. Michael's docks, hoping that there would be a break in the weather so that they could get out on the water to enjoy the holiday. This mixture of locals and tourists were greeted by the sounds of jihadist fireworks. The sounds were like a staccato drum roll. Intermittent bass-drum accents came every few seconds. Blasts of eerie light reflected off of the low cloud cover. Flashes of orange, green, and red punctuated the sky. Everyone in the parking lot began to talk to one another.

"What was that?"

"What's going on?"

"Those couldn't be fireworks this early, could they?"

"No," said one young man in marine pants and a bright Orioles T-shirt. "Those are explosions - big explosions."

"Wow. You really think so?" replied one young woman.

"Yes, ma'am," said the young man. "I know those sounds well, miss. I heard them every day in Iraq - every damn day."

"What the hell's wrong, Marco?"

"I don't know, but it could be that the batteries are too low. I'm going to check them right now."

"Well, you better hurry or we'll miss Maya."

Two minutes later, Marco emerged from the cabin. "The boat's two batteries are completely drained, so I jerry-rigged the bank of communication batteries to the engine. Hopefully that'll work."

He turned the key and the *Miss Martha's* engines roared to life. At full speed, with the sky still erupting in brilliant explosive reds and oranges, they headed for their rendezvous with Maya.

✳✳✳

At 9:28 a.m., Maya saw the *Miss Martha* emerge from the mist that lay over St. Michael's Harbor. The boat was moving at full speed in a six-miles-per-hour zone. Dark smoke spewed out of the *Miss Martha's* two stacks. Somewhere in the process of starting her, they had blown out the suppression mufflers. The deep guttural sounds, which only six-hundred-horsepower diesels can produce, rolled across the water. She was loud - very loud. People began to turn their heads to see who it was.

The minute the *Miss Martha* pulled up to the restaurant dock, several people came over to ask if they knew what was going on over where the fireworks were lighting up the sky. Both of the men threw up their hands and replied, "I don't know."

While this might have satisfied a few of the inquisitive folks on the dock, it didn't satisfy the young marine. He knew that the sounds were explosives and that whatever was causing them was out of the ordinary. Noting that they were of middle-eastern origin, he continued to question Marco and Omar, but they remained unresponsive. After tying up the boat, the men moved off toward Maya's Hummer. The young marine was close on their heels. Maya started the Hummer and drove toward her team members. Sensing that the guy following them was up to no good, she steered the vehicle directly toward him.

Marco and Omar jumped into the backseat. Maya continued to drive straight toward the young man, slamming her foot to the floor. Swerving just before she would have hit him, she tore out of the parking lot. The young man jumped aside, narrowly missing being hit, and fired off a fusillade of descriptive words at the Hummer as it streaked up the road.

All the way down to Parks Neck, Maya silently monitored the crackling coast guard and NRP radio channels that she had installed in her vehicle. From the distress calls she was hearing and from the police scanner that was abuzz with speculation and panic, she knew that the plan, so far, was a howling success.

AT THE GAS DOCKS

The *Miss Catherine James* had left the dock at Parks Neck at exactly 8:15 a.m. Jamil used the GPS to plot a straight course to the man-overboard waypoint, from which they'd launch their attack. On their way out, Kaleem intercepted a coast guard transmission that stated that the *Barracuda Cutter* was on its way to intercept them. Time was of the essence.

By 8:55 a.m. they were anchored directly over the waypoint.

At exactly 9:00 a.m. Kaleem pushed the piling detonation button. No response. The only sound that he, Jamil, and Haamid heard was the click of the detonator switch. He pushed it repeatedly. No response.

Jamil called out to Kaleem, "They must have found the piling explosives and cut the wires."

"Must have," yelled Kaleem.

Throwing the detonator to the deck in disgust, Kaleem shouted, "Start the mortar and RPG attack now."

With Jamil manning the eighy-millimeter mortar and Kaleem passing him the shells, the attack on the LNG field farm immediately got underway. By the time the third shell had left the tube, Jamil had zeroed in directly on the coordinates of the large cluster of LNG tanks he was targeting. Regardless of the weather and his inability to see the target, he was an expert in field weapons. He was considered one of Al Qaeda's top artillery officers. His ability to zero in that quickly attested to his extraordinary abilities.

Starting with the third shell, the devastating barrage continued until both mortar shell boxes were empty. Only five minutes had passed since the first shell had been launched. The sky over the tank farm was nothing but billowing black clouds. Punctuating this dark sky were continuous orange fireballs erupting from the tanks and gas lines that traversed the field. The winds fanned the fires as they started to spread west into the adjacent neighborhoods.

At the same time that the mortar attack was launched, Haamid began his RPG attack on the dock master's office, which they had anchored beneath when setting the piling explosives. Using a combination of armor-piercing and anti-personnel shells, Haamid began the barrage. He first sent five shells into the dock master's office. The metal siding structure exploded. The roof lifted thirty feet into the air. The windows blew out, and the doors shot off of their hinges, skittering sixty feet down to the deck of the *Queen of the Adriatic.*

Haamid then focused on the bridge of the *Queen,* launching ten more shells into the ship's superstructure and tearing all of her antennas, radar pods, cranes, and twin smokestacks from their anchored bases. Metal flew in all directions. Secondary fires and explosions occurred all along the front and the sides of the ship's massive bridge.

The dock and the ship's bridge were both ablaze. Heat from the fires and the secondary explosions shot across the waters, rattling the *Miss Catherine James* some hundred yards away. Haamid aimed the RPG at a spot three feet above the *Queen's* water line on her starboard side. At that spot, he placed the crosshairs of the RPG over a steel plate that was thirty feet from the ship's bow.

Kaleem loaded an armor-piercing shell, tapped Haamid on the shoulder, and backed away from the RPGs blast.

Whoosh! The shell shot out of the tube, heading straight for its target.

The RPG ripped into the side of the *Queen of the Adriatic.* The metal curled inward, as the shell dove deep into the hull and exploded. Flames shot out of the ship's wound, and the follow-up concussion exploded out of the only exit available—the huge new hole in her side. Engulfed in flames, two men were blown through the hole and into the water. Within minutes, after flailing about and screaming for help as their skin began to peel from their faces and arms, both of the men disappeared below the surface.

The next shell entered the same hole. Without the need to pierce the hull, this round bore even deeper into the center of the ship and exploded into the pump and the electrical center, which monitored and managed the liquid gas compartments. The flashpoint for the liquid gas was reduced significantly, as the compartments erupted and the gas, mixing with the warm air, turned the liquid into a volatile vapor.

When the third shell hit, the gas vapors had reached a flashpoint, and the great ship, with a thunderous roar, lifted out of the water and began to heal to starboard. Water cascaded into the twelve-foot-wide gash in her side.

Haamid switched to personnel rounds and focused on the ship's crew, who had begun to gather along the starboard rail. Three shells later, no one was left standing along the rail, and the bridge was engulfed in flames and smoke. Bodies and body parts lay splattered on the ship's tilted deck and in the rough Bay waters below.

Haamid had one more thing left to do. He had to create another large hole amidships. Three more rounds penetrated the hull of the *Queen of the Adriatic*. The result, however, was far more devastating than the previous rounds, since these shells penetrated deep into the fuel compartment of the tanker. Once again, the ship lifted out of the water and into the air. Then she slowly rolled over onto her starboard side. In a matter of minutes, her angle of list went from eight degrees to twenty-two degrees. Men began to dive over her side, seeking relief from the inferno on deck. Explosion after explosion ripped through the ship's interior, as she began her dying spiral to the bottom of the Bay.

Kaleem launched three eight-millimeter Ricin shells in a triangular pattern toward the LNG tank fields that he had decimated with mortar rounds eight minutes earlier. These shells would render the first responders totally incapable of assisting those in need. Depending on the wind conditions, the effect would last between twenty-four and thirty-six hours. The Ricin would render those in its path helpless, and many of them would die from its deadly vapors.

Kaleem shouted out from the cabin, "Dump the mortar, the RPG, the shell boxes, and casings! A coast guard cutter is right off our port side and closing in fast!"

Jamil quickly shoved all of the weapons, shells, and boxes overboard. He then started the engine, while Haamid pulled anchor.

During the attack, Kaleem had sporadically used a video camera to memorialize their success. Now, as the *Miss Catherine James* headed south, Kaleem recorded the *Queen*'s death rattle, as successive explosions continued to wreak havoc on her structure and cargo. Onshore, the tank farm was fully ablaze. Black smoke and orange flames licked at the low cloud ceiling above. The winds were now coming from the southeast, driving the burning gas and Ricin clouds inland, creating even more devastation in the surrounding neighborhoods on shore.

They had accomplished their goal: complete destruction of the LNG tank farm, the Gas Docks, and the *Queen of the Adriatic*.

***

AT THE BAY BRIDGE

It was 8:50 a.m. and the *Mana Kia* had already reached a speed of twenty-five knots. By the time she impacted the Bridge, she would be at her top speed of twenty-seven knots.

Watching the large GPS screen before him, Salah slightly adjusted the joystick. To avoid running aground, he made sure he progressed along the map's depth contour of eighty to eighty five feet.

Abed cast his eyes upon the handcuffed captain, the loadmaster, chief engineer, and the ship's head of security, all of whom were seated together on the floor in the far corner of the bridge. He removed his 9mm Glock, walked over to the crew in the corner, and summarily shot each of them in the head. Two of the crewmembers died immediately upon impact, while two others remained writhing on the deck. Pointing his nine-millimeter at each of their hearts, Abed delivered the coup de grâce.

Abed replaced the partially spent clip and stood next to Salah at the helm again.

Abed called Bashir in the chopper to let them know that takeoff would be in seven minutes.

Calls from the coast guard continued to demand that they put the *Mana Kia* in full reverse. They could now see the NSA cutter from Annapolis moving at full speed toward them. The littoral combat ship cutter from Curtis Bay in Baltimore was steaming south. It was just passing the Eight-Foot Knoll Light House, also closing on them at full speed.

Because the bridge's structure was between them and the LSC cutter, the possibility of the coast guard accurately shelling the *Mana Kia* or successfully launching ship-to-ship missiles was moot. Too much bridge structure and metal was in the way.

At exactly 8:50 a.m. Abed told Salah to lock the joystick. He ordered his team to run for the helicopter. All three of the terrorists jumped into the chopper, and Bashir lifted off at exactly 8:57 a.m. It was just three minutes until the impact.

The helicopter hovered at about two hundred feet above and behind the *Mana Kia* as her bow drove into and through the eastbound span on its way to collide with the westbound span.

Using a handheld transmitter, Salah detonated the explosives that had been placed in the forward six on-deck containers. The ship's impact and the container explosions had a devastating effect on the eastbound span of the Bay Bridge. For three hundred feet in each direction, the bridges superstructure and pilings dissolved. The ships inertia propelled her into the westbound span with added force. Here again, the westbound span seemed to evaporate before one's eyes.

With a second transmitter, Salah set off the heavy explosives that his foreign agents had planted deep in the crew's quarters on the third deck of the ship. In each direction, both of the spans and several hundred feet of the bridge crumbled into the waters of Chesapeake Bay.

Abed ordered Bashir to fly low over the bridge so that Salah could drop the Ricin canisters on the roadways between Kent Island's western shore and the destroyed spans. This would keep the closest first responders away from the carnage of cars, buses, and trucks for at least eighteen hours.

As Bashir put on full power and lifted up above the bridge's central span, fifty-caliber machinegun fire rocketed skyward from the gun turrets on the LSC. Since the bridge's superstructure was between the LSC and the Raven II helicopter, most of the shells ricocheted off of the steel girders and superstructure or exploded on contact, causing additional structural damage. To make sure he kept the bridge between his chopper and the LSC, Bashir moved directly east along Route 50, staying low - only one hundred feet off of the deck. In a matter of minutes, he was able to maneuver the Raven II out of sight of both of the coast guard cutters. Just before turning south, Bashir flew over the Narrows Bridges and dropped four Ricin canisters amid the death and destruction below. By dropping the canisters on both sides of the Narrows itself, Bashir could keep first responders from both directions at bay for at least another eighteen hours.

By 9:05 a.m. the *Mana Kia* had plowed through both bridges. It had exploded and started to sink. The Panamax container ship listed to starboard and then slowly settled on the bottom, leaving much of her structure and the remaining containers above the water line, exposed to view, and engulfed in flames.

Upon impact with the eastbound span, fifteen cars and two trucks plunged off of the bridge and bounced off of the containers, landing on the deck of the *Mama Kia*. Others careened into the rough waters of the Bay below. Two trucks, each forty-two foot rigs, shot into the newly created gap of the eastbound span, crashing on top of the containers that had exploded. Secondary explosions resulted from this mayhem of twisted steel, pulverized concrete, crushed vehicles, and the carnage of mutilated bodies. Worst of all were the screams of the innocent and the screeching of the metal as it twisted and contorted into unbelievably grotesque forms. Many people were squashed between the metal, the plastic, and the airbags of their vehicles as they rode them to the bottom of the Bay.

For thirty miles in all directions, the shock waves from this inferno rippled across the land. Black smoke enveloped the rainy skies, adding to the funereal smell of this senseless tragedy. Flames shot out of the ship's structure and the parts of the *Mana Kia* that remained above water.

At 9:20 a.m. the entire bridge of the *Mana Kia* lifted off of its base as the fuel cells amidships erupted into a volcano of molten flames and searing heat.

By 9:30 a.m. both spans of the Chesapeake Bay Bridge were fully engulfed in the conflagration. The smell of burning flesh and melting steel mixed with the Ricin to create a sickening and pungent blend of death and destruction.

Haron, who had filmed the entire Bay Bridge attack, placed the camera back in its crush-proof case and handed it back to Salah for safekeeping.

As they sped south to their rendezvous at the Parks Neck Farm, portions of one of the great icons of the Northeast, The Chesapeake Bay Bridge, stood amputated from both the mainland and the Eastern Shore of Maryland. The destruction was immense. The lives of those who perished would be remembered and memorialized in an annual Fourth of July ceremony starting in 2011.

The commercial impact on Maryland and its adjacent states would be felt for years to come. Most importantly, America's sense of security and self-preservation would be lost forever. From this day forth, Fourth of July 2010 would be an American Day remembered for its vulnerability, rather than celebrated for its independence.

***

AT KENT NARROWS

As Ken and Marty stood just outside what had once been the front of their building, which had collapsed when the office roof had lifted into the air and sailed into the adjacent marsh, they were struck by the blast of superheated wind that cut across the water from the newly created void in the Narrows Bridge. Ken and Marty found themselves in the vortex of a *hell on earth*. Kent Narrows was ablaze - totally ablaze.

Both men instinctively ran toward the main bridge, as cars and trucks continued to fly off of the jagged and twisted ends of the structure, falling end over end into the swift waters below. By the time drivers realized that the middle of the bridge had ceased to exist, more than thirty-five cars, trucks, and forty-foot trailer rigs had plunged into the Narrows. The low overcast and rain had contributed significantly to the driver's inability to see the missing portions of the bridges. On the drawbridge, because it carried far less traffic, only ten vehicles had slipped over the edge and into the void.

As Marty reached the drawbridge, he realized that the drawbridge blast had demolished many of the watermen's workboats that were moored along the drawbridge bulkhead. The shock wave from the blast had destroyed most of the seventy boats that were moored there. Those that had not flipped onto their sides and sunk had been set ablaze by the flames and the burning debris from the many explosions. Marty gasped at the destruction he was witnessing. In the mist and smoke, the wind whipped a hundred small fires into a crescendo of orange, red, and yellow flames. The water was on fire. A holocaust surrounded them.

It looked like the hellfire and damnation that traveling preachers from the 1920s use to talk about under the great evangelical tents as they crisscrossed the Eastern Shore of Maryland, bringing old-time religion to the watermen and farmers.

Marty thought, *If this isn't hell on earth, I don't know what is.*

Ken called Marty on his handheld radio and told him to immediately return to the ramp alongside the Narrows Bridge. They needed to launch the old Jon-boat. It had been the only NRP boat that had survived the explosions. Luckily, it had been flipped over several months ago and tied to some pilings along the bulkhead. The three other NRP boats were either upside down in the water or ablaze in the firestorm.

Ken and Marty pulled a pair of oars out from underneath the boat. They flipped her over and dragged her thirty feet to the ramp. They launched the Jon-boat and began to row out to the sixty-foot wide gap in the main bridge.

Marty rowed toward the bridge in hopes of saving those still alive. Ken, sitting in the stern, guided Marty in the direction of the people screaming for help. The heat from the restaurant fires along the bulkhead made it feel like they had entered a sauna. Rather than turning around every few seconds to see where he was going, Marty with his back to the bow, asked Ken to give him directions for navigating through the burning oil slicks and debris that now covered most of the waters around them. Marty felt the searing heat at the back of his neck, and he could see the reflection of the restaurant flames on Ken's face. Ken shouted out calls to starboard or port, as they maneuvered through the pieces of bridge structure and debris that poked- up through the dark waters.

The underwater shock waves had stunned and killed thousands of fish, which were floating everywhere. Approaching the wreckage, Marty suddenly let go of the oars and clutched his throat. Ken did the same. They couldn't breathe. The Ricin fumes began to fill their lungs. The doses they were receiving were far more than anyone's lungs could endure. They slumped forward and fell to the bottom of the boat, gasping for air. The Jon-boat floated free with the outgoing tide, bouncing off of bridge structures, floating debris, bodies, and vehicles that were partially submerged in the swiftly flowing waters of the Narrows. Their journey through the Narrows and out into Eastern Bay was the last boat ride they'd ever take.

Thirty-six hours later, their small boat, with its precious cargo of selfless heroes, would be found on the deserted beach of Parsons Island. Two more brave and committed police officers had paid the ultimate price for a lack of preparedness on the part of the country and the state.

By 9:45 a.m. the Narrows was fully engulfed in flames, smoke, sirens, and screams. The winds continued to blow at fifteen to twenty knots, but the rain had slowed to a steady pace, and the fog and overcast had just starting to lift. Thirty-five cars and trucks lay on top of one another at the bottom of the bridge's gaping hole. Three more vehicles hung precariously over the edge of the bridge. Two were on the west side and one was on the east side. Several people were trapped in their vehicles, while many had fallen out on impact. Numerous accidents, some of which were quite serious, had occurred on the two bridges as drivers wrestled to avoid going off into the water.

The steady sounds of sirens filled the air. Worst of all were the screams and cries for help from those injured and dying. Gradually, these sounds began to dissipate from the overriding effects of the Ricin and the deadly smoke that choked the air out of those desperately trying to cling to life and hope.

By 10 p.m. the screams and moans had almost stopped. The Narrows was no longer a place of joy and frivolity. It was now a cemetery for hundreds of people who had died, entangled in the nightmare of the attack.

✳✳✳

AT THE GAS DOCKS

Kaleem, knowing that the coast guard cutter was closing in fast, jammed their radar with a naval program he had lifted off of the US Navy's secure warfare site.

Suddenly, the cutter's radar screen shifted to a snowflake-like image, rendering useless their radar's capacity to locate the *Miss Catherine James.*

Haamid tried pulling up the anchor, but she was stuck fast in the bottom muck. Knowing that time was precious, he decided to use the box cutter on his belt instead. With two swipes, Haamid sliced through the anchor line, cutting the boat free.

Haamid called out to Jamil, "She's free."

Jamil shoved the throttle forward and the *Miss Catherine James* charged off into the pea soup. Onboard the cutter, the captain got word from the forward-bow observer that he had glimpsed the *Miss Catherine James.* She seemed to be heading for Solomon's Island. The observer also relayed to the bridge that she seemed to be moving extremely fast. He estimated her speed at thirty knots or more.

During her speed trial the *Miss Catherine James* reached a top speed of forty-two knots. Remembering this, Brady immediately asked the captain to launch the *Prosecutor.* Unlike the cutter, it was capable of going close to this speed.

Taking Brady's advice, the captain had his first officer launch the *Prosecutor* with two seamen. A chief petty officer would be the captain. Brady, Dan, and General Bob Whitfield, the director of Homeland Security, requested and got an RPG with a half-case of antipersonnel shells and two armor-piercing shells. With this weapon, they would pursue the *Miss Catherine James.*

Just before they launched the *Prosecutor,* the radar officer notified the captain that he had managed to circumvent the terrorist's radar-jamming signals. He said that the *Miss Catherine James* was not headed, as they had thought, to Solomon's Island, but rather toward Barren Island.

The Captain's decision to honor Brady's request for the *Prosecutor* turned out to be a very good one. It had allowed the cutter to stay at the Gas Docks and lower several life-boats to recover many of the crewmembers who had jumped or been blown overboard from the *Queen of the Adriatic.* The task of retrieving the bodies of the seamen, some of whom were burned beyond recognition and some of whom were barely clinging to life, was a gruesome one.

Brady stood next to the chief petty officer, as he steered the *Prosecutor* toward Barren Island. As with the cutter, after clearing Kaleem's jamming signal, the *Prosecutor's* radar finally picked up the *Miss Catherine James.* It was flying across the Bay, but it was not far ahead. Proceeding at full throttle, the *Prosecutor* started to close in on the terrorist's boat.

"There she is," yelled Brady, "Dead ahead!" The fog had begun to lift as they neared the Eastern Shore.

Jamil suddenly saw them coming up behind him. He jammed the throttle all the way forward. The *Catherine James* quickly gathered speed as she raced across the waves, slowly lengthening the distance between the two boats.

Realizing that the *Miss Catherine James* was slightly faster and that they would soon lose sight of her, Brady picked up the RPG and ordered one of the seamen to load an armor-piercing shell. Brady adjusted the site and yelled, "Clear." He then slowly squeezed the trigger.

Seconds later, the shell hit the stern of the *Miss Catherine James*. She erupted into a mass of flames, flying wood, and the cries of those onboard.

Wanting to be sure that the *Miss Catherine James* would go dead in the water,

Brady fired another RPG shell into the cabin. Once more, the *Miss Catherine James* exploded into a rain of splintered wood, ignited fuel, shattered electronics, and burning flesh.

The *Miss Catherine James* listed to port, taking on water faster than her pumps could bail. Brady could now see that she was not only dead in the water, but also slowly and inevitably on her way to her grave in the dark waters of the Bay's ship channel. She would eventually come to rest fifty-one feet below the surface.

The *Prosecutor* pulled up to the *Miss Catherine James*, keeping thirty feet between them. The searing heat of the burning hull was almost unbearable. Even thirty feet away, their eyes were burning and the hair on their arms was being singed.

Brady saw that Jamil's body was draped over the steering wheel and smoldering. Jamil had a six- to eight-inch gash in his skull. Blood ran down the side of his face, pooling on the deck. He was clearly dead. Haamid, who had been blown from the stern of the boat when the first shell had hit, was lying face down in the water ten feet from the *Prosecutor*. His legs were both missing.

Kaleem, however, was floating off of the bow of the *Miss Catherine James*, clinging to a portion of the cabin's roof. His face was black. The skin on his head and hands was peeling off. He was seriously injured but still alive.

The chief petty officer carefully guided the *Prosecutor* alongside Kaleem. As he screamed in pain, the two seamen pulled him up into the boat and laid him on the deck. Five minutes later, Kaleem died.

Chapter 24

The Escape

Unbeknownst to Brady and the crew of the *Prosecutor*, just before Brady had launched the first RPG shell, Kaleem had called Abed on the secure military radio. As Kaleem was describing the chase scene to Abed, Brady's first RPG round and the ensuing explosion cut the conversation short.

Abed heard the first explosion, which was closely followed by the screams of his men. Haamid's voice was the only one he clearly heard. Haamid screamed, "They've killed Jamil. We're not going to make it!" Then the line went dead.

***

Aboard the Raven II, there were only the sounds of the high-pitched engine and the wind, as the helicopter streaked toward the Parks Neck Farm. In the cabin, the mood was solemn. No one dared to speak. They knew that Abed was deep in thought. He clearly suspected the worst. The *Miss Catherine James* and three of his best men were never going to see the dawn of the next day.

As they touched down on the farm, Abed gave orders to Bashir to roll the chopper into the barn and lock the doors, sealing the Raven II from aerial view.

Haron, Salah, and Abed quickly walked to the farmhouse to meet Maya, Omar, and Marco. When Bashir arrived, Abed gathered everyone around the kitchen table to announce the fate of the *Miss Catherine James* and three of their brothers-in-arms. Having no time for emotions, Abed ordered Salah, Haron, Maya, and Bashir to gather their duffel bags and board the larger of the cigarette boats, which Maya and Marco had pulled out of the boathouse and tied up at the farm's dock. Everyone grabbed his or her bags and the remaining RPG, which had been stored in the farm's attic. They then ran for the dock. Prior to everyone's arrival, Maya had placed two RPG shell cases, each with ten rounds per case, in the smaller boat.

No need to lock the house or clean it, thought Abed. *Homeland Security and the police will be here within an hour or so.*

At the dock, Abed instructed the team about which military radio channel crystals they were to use. Again, he gave them a brief overview of the escape plan. Abed then signaled everyone to board. Salah and he, along with Maya, Bashir, and Haron, would take the lead in the larger boat. Marco and Omar would follow them a half-mile behind.

Only one question had been left unanswered. Would the coast guard and Homeland Security figure out their escape route? The hope was that they'd discover the Parks Neck Farm first, rather than the cigarette boats, as they headed for Onancock, Virginia. Hopefully by the time the coast guard and Homeland Security realized that they had escaped by boat, they'd be at the airport in Melfa, Virginia, heading off in the Caravan to their safe house in West Virginia.

✳✳✳

Brady had the chief petty officer mark the coordinates of the *Miss Catherine James* on the *Prosecutor's* GPS. The *Miss Catherine James* began to go from a thirty-degree port list to vertical, as she started her final ride to the bottom of the Bay. The water was about fifty-one feet deep. Brady's thinking was that DHS would want to dive down to the *Miss Catherine James* later or perhaps even raise her to discover as much as possible about the terrorist cell. As he looked at the waypoint on the chart, Brady said to the chief, "At least we got her here in fifty feet of water, rather than the middle of the channel, which is one hundred and fourteen feet."

"Yes, sir. Better here than there," said the chief, pointing to the one-hundred-and-fourteen-foot mark on the chart.

After arriving alongside the *Miss Catherine James*, it took a mere eight minutes before she slipped beneath the waves and the fog that surrounded her. The chief called back to the cutter for further instructions. He was told to return to the cutter to have the *Prosecutor* hauled onboard. The only survivors the cutter had found were eight men and one woman whom the lifeboat crew had picked out of the water. These people were either onboard in sickbay or they were waiting to be transported by helicopter to the burn unit at Harbor Hospital in Baltimore. It was estimated that it would take another hour or two for the fog to lift enough for the choppers to be able to land on the cutter's aft deck. Unfortunately, by then most of those in sickbay would be dead. The *Prosecutor* returned to the ship and was secured to the stern platform.

Many more bodies were still floating in the water when the gas vapor hit its flash point and erupted into an almost atomic fireball. The captain of the cutter immediately ordered the ship to turn to port and head away from the gas explosion at full speed. The cutter went to general quarters and all personnel on deck were ordered below. As chance would have it, the fireball erupted skyward and spread out horizontally. The winds blew it toward the land and not toward the cutter. Even though the winds kept the fire from destroying the cutter, the fierce heat singed the exterior gray paint on the ship's hull, the lifeboats, the *Prosecutor* and any non-metallic materials on the exterior of the ship.

***

Back at the DHS search headquarters at the west end of the Bay Bridge, there was an overwhelming sense of despair and mass confusion. Three major attacks had been launched within a five-minute period. The first had started at 9 a.m. Would there be a fourth? And if so, would there be further attacks after that? Fear hung heavily on the shoulders of the DHS and the state police. Quick and decisive action had been hard to come by. No one had been prepared for such a devastating attack.

During the attack, there had been little communication between the various search organizations and no real command structure. Now, DHS finally assumed the overall responsibility. It was the best organization for the job. Egos and politics, however, remained the prime ingredients in these early decision-making processes. This meant that most leadership time was spent on posturing, laying blame, and on trying to figure out how to avoid being tagged as the person or organization that was responsible for the bad security, the poor intelligence, and the slow response to the attack. The fact was, everyone was culpable. Those living on the Eastern Shore, however, squarely placed the blame on state leaders. They felt they had been ill prepared to handle a disaster of this magnitude, and that they had given this type of threat a low priority. With only one million dollars of reserves in the state's catastrophic event fund, that money would last less than one day. Since federal funds would not be available for thirty-six hours, the state would be facing additional deficits that it was ill prepared to handle.

The political maneuvering was in full swing, but the rescue efforts were not. The Ricin, as well as the ill-conceived centralization in Baltimore of major first-responder equipment and resources, created significant delays in the abilities of local first responders to efficiently and effectively respond to the attack. To leaders like Lieutenant Price, the regional DHS director, the head of the state police, the NRP, and other savvy war-tested veterans, it was clear that rescue and recovery was not going to be counted in hours, days, or weeks, but rather in months and years.

Maryland was in for a prolonged period of cleanup, recovery, and mourning. It would be years before the Eastern Shore would be whole again. It was possible that a sense of security and tranquility might never return. When the dust finally settled, there would be hell to pay.

✳✳✳

At 4:00 p.m. Salah and Marco tied the boats up at a private pier on Onancock Creek in Virginia. The trip had been uneventful. They monitored the heightened chatter on the channels for the coast guard, the NRP, and the state police. They listened to anxious citizens relay false sightings on Channel 16. Other than this, nothing interrupted their ride to Virginia.

The individuals who had left two Suburbans, some new passports, some photo IDs, and three large bundles of cash at the drop-off point were gone. They were well on their way to Miami by the time Abed's team got in their vehicles and drove off to the Accomack County Airport.

At the Fixed Base Operation at the Accomack County Airport in Melfa, Virginia, Bashir met with the owner of the Cesena Caravan to exchange papers and deliver the plane's $15,000 two-day rental fee. The owner was under the impression that the plane would be returned to Melfa before dark on the following day, July 5, 2010. Little did he know that the next time he saw his plane would be eighteen months later. It would be on the front page of a Florida newspaper. Only its tail section would be visible. It would be sticking out of the blue-green waters of the Florida Keys.

At exactly 4:45 p.m. the Caravan containing Abed and the six surviving members of his team lifted off from the Melfa, Virginia, runway and headed toward West Virginia. Once they had cleared the area around the Chesapeake Bay, their visual flight rule trip was clear and smooth. As they headed northwest, Bashir spoke into the headphone-intercom, "Look out to your right and you can see the effects of our attack."

Darkness moved across the skies of the Maryland portion of the Chesapeake Bay. Billowing black clouds of smoke and the yellow glow of continuing fires dotted the horizon. Flashes of orange and red from secondary explosions would momentarily appear in the plane's windows.

Everyone was quiet yet personally thrilled to see the destruction that they had wrought. Finally, Abed said, "Allah and our martyred brothers surely are pleased with these results. Now, my friends, we can devote all of our efforts to our next target, Allah Akbar!"

Bashir had not requested *flight following*, where the traffic controllers keep *tabs* on your location, so only a small blip showed up on various flight-center radars along their route. Otherwise, they were not seen or heard during the entire flight. An hour and a half after taking off, they landed at a private strip of grass on a farm in West Virginia. Rahim, Abed's nephew, met them there.

The Caravan was stored in a large barn on the farm to provide quick access and security for a getaway in the event that their safe house was discovered. Abed split up the group. Half of them stayed in the main house, and the other half stayed in the farm's guest cottage. To maximize their ability to communicate, both dwellings had been connected via a two-way intercom system.

Housed on a secluded farm, the jihadist team, which DHS now referred to as the *Independence Day Cell*, planned to wait out the next three to six months before moving to their next target. Twelve months from this day, they would resurface to execute their second major attack on America.

***

At 6:15 p.m. the last helicopter carried the dead and the dying off of the cutter's aft deck for their last ride to the temporary morgue, which had been set up at DHS's search-and-rescue headquarters. The cutter itself arrived there at the west end of the Bay Bridge forty minutes later. Her exterior paint was still smoking from the fireball that had scorched her hull.

At 7:00 p.m. Brady, Dan, and the regional director of the DHS went directly to the search-and-rescue headquarters to find out the latest news. The news was not good.

Six hundred people were dead. Thousands were injured and thousands more remained unaccounted for. Two regional bridges had been destroyed. The iconic Bay Bridge had been cut in two. A critically important LNG tank field, which held tens of millions of gallons of LNG, had been destroyed. The accompanying burning cloud of gas had annihilated all neighborhoods and businesses within half a mile. The Gas Docks were destroyed and the resulting burning clouds of gas had come within a mile of affecting the Calvert Cliffs Nuclear Plant. One LNG super tanker, the *Queen of the Adriatic*, and one Panamax container ship, the *Mana Kia*, now rested on the bottom of the Bay. They were now nothing more than scrap.

Because of the public's concerns about reestablishing an LNG terminal and tank farm, there would be no hope for rebuilding either the Gas Docks or the tank farm. The Bay Bridge would be out of commission for at least thirty months, due to structural issues, lengthy security approvals, and a lack of funding. The two Narrows bridges would not be rebuilt for at least twenty-four months, due to security and design approvals, a lack of funding, and the required re-engineering.

Though their ranks had been cut almost in half, the perpetrators were still free and on the run to god-knows-where.

Chapter 25

The Aftermath

The funeral for Mack and his son, Mike, was held at the Tilghman Island Methodist Church at 10 a.m. on July 7, 2010.

All over the mid-Bay area, the smell of the burning and smoldering remnants of the attack lingered in the air to remind everyone of the devastation. Those inside the church and in the open tents outside were reminded with each breath they took of the death and the heroism that had taken place on the Bay just two days earlier.

Pete gave a eulogy for his dear friend Mack and his son Mike. It was worthy of comparison to Bobby Kennedy's eulogy for his brother, President John F. Kennedy.

Among other things, Pete said, "From the common beginnings of a shipwright's only son, Mack had risen to become one of the best watermen to have ever plied the Chesapeake Bay. He was a man of great integrity - a passionate advocate of the waterman's way of life, of uncompromised work ethic, and of strong family values. Because of his unconditional devotion to both family and friends, he became a leader in the Tilghman Community and the father of a son worthy of the same praise."

Simple folks and state leaders alike also rendered numerous tributes to Mack and Mike, but none were as beautiful or as true as Pete's praise.

Brady sat in the front pew with Michelle, who had finally arrived at Pete's home on the evening of the Fourth of July. She had spent the last day and a half helping Louise prepare for the reception that was going to be held after the funeral at Harrison's Chesapeake House. It was clear to all who knew them that something was going on between the two. The way they looked at each other for support and comfort was perhaps a harbinger of things to come.

Judy Wilson, Brady's mom, sat next to Michelle. After only one day in her company, Judy had already realized just how special Michelle was. She could see that Brady liked her, and she could tell how well she might fit into Brady's life if something more were to come of their relationship.

Without exception, all of Mack's and Mike's relatives and friends had come to pay their respects. Some had come from as far away as Maine, Florida, and California. All sorts of people showed up to see Mack and Mike off: Mr. Duncan, Dan Howard, Mr. Phillips, Lieutenant Price, Colonel Wilson, Captain Johns, Captain Willis, and Captain Barnes, the head of NRP, the colonel of the Maryland State Police, the Eastern Shore's Legislative Delegation, and the regional director of Homeland Security, General Whitfield. Also present was the national head of Homeland Security, Secretary William Michaels, as well as five hundred other people.

When the funeral and internment were over, everyone gathered at Harrison's to greet the families and share in the camaraderie of a healthy, family-style, Eastern Shore meal. Over 450 people joined Beth and Tonya North to rejoice and give thanks for the lives of their waterman, whom they had been privileged enough to known and love.

Once the reception line had been reduced to just a few people, Pete took to the microphone that had been set up in the middle of the room. Acting as MC, Pete introduced those who wished to speak. Numerous people stood up to tell tales and share various experiences they had enjoyed as friends, co-workers, and neighbors of these two special men.

The last to speak was the regional director of Homeland Security, General Richard Whitfield. Prior to his present position, he had been a chaplain and a general in the marine corps special forces. He first thanked everyone who had assisted with the search for Mack and Mike. He especially thanked those who had responded to the crisis as true neighbors, friends, and Americans. Lastly, he singled out Pete's efforts and his unconditional commitment to Mack and Mike.

Taking a deep breath, tears formed in his eyes. He began to share how very blessed Maryland had been to have a young marine named Brady Wilson as part its watermen's community.

"Most of you - and certainly the vast majority of Americans - have no idea of the courage and sacrifice that one of our own had to endure before and during this devastating attack. Imagine a wounded warrior returning from the horrors of Afghanistan to spend two years in therapy at Walter Reed, trying to regain his senses, physical strength, and his life's purpose. Imagine him coming here to recuperate on the Eastern Shore of Maryland with his aunt and uncle. Imagine this young man, suffering from shrapnel wounds and posttraumatic stress disorder. Imagine him dealing with flashbacks that were constant reminders of his dying buddies and of the radical Islamic hatred he had endured on the battlefields of the Hindu Kush Mountains. Finally, imagine his unselfish commitment to his country and this community as he was drawn back onto a new battlefield - his homeland, American soil - where he had to face some of the most difficult decisions of his life.

Most men would have turned their back on the trouble that knocked at Brady's door. Of those who answered this call to duty, no one - I repeat, no one - responded with more passion and commitment to the task at hand than he did."

The audience remained silent.

Whitfield continued, "On this sad yet triumphant day, I ask that you keep Matt, Mike, and their families in your prayers. Know that The Lord has opened his arms and embraced these men as the wonderful, God-fearing men they are. I ask that you bless the thousands who have lost their lives in this attack. I ask that you pray for the first responders who have sacrificed so much to recover and save the innocent victims of this dreadful attack. May those who have perished rest in peace. Lastly, I ask that you pray for Pete and Brady, whose actions and bravery saved so many lives. We ask all these things, in God's name, Amen."

✳✳✳

Brady found it hard to embrace the General's kind words. He did not feel worthy of the praise. In his mind he, had failed to stop the attack. To him, that was all that mattered.

✳✳✳

For the next three days, Brady and Michelle helped Pete and Louise clean up Beth and Tanya's homes. They helped them with the paperwork that funerals always generate, including the death certificates, the transferring of bank funds, the funeral payments, and the grim task of going through personal belongings. Because he had dealt with losing many of his buddies before, Brady was well equipped to help handle the issues that Beth and Tonya encountered. Because of his age, Pete, who had dealt with the aftermath of many funerals, was also a true blessing to Beth and Tonya. Between them, they got a lot done. Their help made things much easier for the two widows.

✳✳✳

On July 8th, 2010, Brady, Pete, Lieutenant Price, and other experts in the field of state and national security met with General Richard Whitfield. The meeting was held in a lecture hall at the Naval Academy. It began at 8:00 a.m. and concluded at 4:00 p.m. The purpose was to obtain a historic timeline of everything before, after, and during the event, which was now known as the *Independence Day Attack*, or IDA. Later, there would be many more follow-up meetings to gather more detail on the terrorists themselves, their cell network, their operating procedures, and any thoughts on locations that they might attack in the future.

At the end of this first meeting, General Whitfield and the Secretary of Homeland Security, William Michaels, approached Brady with an offer to join Whitfield's Regional Team. General Whitfield had recommended Brady to the position of Assistant Director, and the Secretary had approved this recommendation. He would be responsible for regional field operations. His first job would be to locate and apprehend the six remaining members of the *Independence Day Cell*. While his duties would most likely take him outside of the Northeast, he would be given the authority to operate in any other territory with autonomy, as long as it related directly to fulfilling his primary mission of tracking down and capturing the remaining IDA cell members.

Brady was stunned by the offer. He asked how much time he had to make a decision. General Whitfield gave him until the following Monday, July 12th, to decide. After that, they would have to find someone else, since the hunt for the six remaining cell members had to be launched right away. Their concern was that if they didn't follow up immediately, the cell's trail would grow cold, and they might lose the terrorists without a trace. Brady thanked the men, took cards from them, and promised to get back to them by Monday.

***

Pete and Louise were so happy to have Michelle and Brady staying with them. They had wanted Brady's mom, Judy, to stay for the week. However, due to work commitments, Judy had to return home to Pennsylvania.

Each evening Pete, Louise, Brady, and Michelle, sat on the screened-in porch and shared their day's events. They talked about cleaning up the *Miss Alice*, finishing up the renovations on Mack's *Miss Patricia*, and helping Tanya and Beth get through those tough days following the funeral. Tonight, Brady was anxious to discuss DHS's offer. Before making his final decision, he wanted input from all of them, especially Pete.

After explaining the offer he had received, Brady asked, "Uncle Pete, what do you think? Should I take the job or turn it down?"

"Brady, it's just not that simple, son. If you accept, it will be a life-changing event for you. You'd be traveling a fair amount. You'd probably have to move to wherever the cell might be, you'd miss fishing with me and eating Louise's famous pot roast. All kidding aside, though, you'd also have a career and a steady job. You would avoid the highs and lows of being a waterman. You'd have a great pension. Most importantly, you'd be stopping terrorists from repeating another Independence Day Attack." Pete paused. "Brady, it seems to me that you've got to weigh all of the pros and cons. Then you can decide on your own what course of action is in your best interest."

"Uncle Pete, you're right. I just need some time to evaluate both sides of the equation. What about you, Aunt Louise? What do you think?

"Well, Brady, that's hard for me to say. Of course I want you to stay on Tilghman, but that's selfish on my part. When I think about you and you alone, I know this is the opportunity of a lifetime. There's no question about that. I think you should take it."

"Wow, Louise," said Pete. "I haven't heard you be that decisive since you agreed to marry me forty-two years ago!"

"Pete, it was forty-three years ago, you old goat!"

"OK, so I can't count, Louise," said Pete. "But they've been a damn good forty-two -oops, I mean forty-three - years, haven't they?"

"Yes they have, Pete," said Louis. "They've been a blessed forty-three years."

"Hum. Now that's more like my old girlfriend."

"Oh yeah," said Louis. "Who's your old girlfriend?"

"Damn it, Louise. You are! How come you always seem to get the last word?"

"Because I'm quicker than you. I'm not as smart, mind you. I'm just quicker."

"So, Michelle, what do you think?" asked Pete.

Wiping a tear from her eye, Michelle said, "As you know, I'm somewhat prejudiced. I don't want Brady to leave or undertake the kind of dangerous work this job will demand. You can see from my tears that I don't ever want him to get hurt again."

Brady got up from his chair and slipped beside Michelle on the rattan couch. He put his arm around her. She nestled her head onto his shoulder. He dried her eyes with his handkerchief.

"Michelle, I don't plan on dying, even though I've come close a couple of times. If I take this job, I will have my own team of professionals to rely on for security and to deal with any conflicts that arise. Let's put it this way: I'll be far safer than I have been for the past month, that's for sure."

"Brady, can we talk about this later," said Michelle. "I'm too upset to discuss it rationally right now. It's all a shock to me. Is that OK?"

"Sure," said Brady. "We'll talk about it whenever you like."

"Thanks."

Michelle took Brady's face in her hands and kissed him sweetly on the lips.

Ten minutes later, they all retired to their rooms. It'd been a long day, and they were all in need of a good night's sleep.

***

The next morning, as they sat on Brady's bed holding hands, Michelle told Brady that he should absolutely take the job, as long as she could visit him.

Brady responded, "Of course I want you to visit as often as possible. Who knows, maybe if I am transferred to a place you like, we might even consider moving in together."

If they decided to do so, there would be many things to resolve, including figuring out where to live. Michelle would also have to figure out what to do for work. Brady was happy with Michelle's openness and her positive attitude. He wanted the new job and he also wanted Michelle to join him in this new venture. He gently kissed Michelle and thanked her for her support.

***

The kitchen table was piled with bacon, sausage, scrapple, toast, biscuits, and the delicious tiny sugar donuts that Michelle had made. The breadbasket was overflowing with goodies. There were also eggs, various juices, and hot cups of coffee.

At breakfast, Pete and Louise agreed with Michelle that Brady should take the DHS job. They felt that it was a wonderful opportunity. However, they would miss him terribly.

Pete reached across the table and speared two slices of bacon. Then he scooped two eggs onto his plate.

They heard a knock at the door.

Louise got up. She walked over to the screen door and opened it. It was the island's postman, Alan Todd.

"Hi Alan," said Louise. "You're a little early, aren't you?"

"Just a little, Miss Louise," said Alan. "I'm trying to finish early so that I can do a little afternoon fishing."

"Alan, you men are all the same. Fishing comes first. The job comes second and family comes third."

"No, ma'am. That ain't true," said Alan, as he stuck his head in the door, directing his comments more to Pete than Louise. He was looking for support.

"No. You're right, Alan," said Pete. "Fishing comes second and family comes third. The job always comes first."

"You men," said Louise. "Always smart-mouthing the ones you depend on the most."

Everyone lightly applauded Louise for her sharp and valid response. Alan handed a letter to Louise and continued on his postal rounds.

"It's for you, Brady." Louise said, handing the envelope to him.

Brady looked at the address. It was written in beautiful calligraphy and it had been postmarked in Onancock, Virginia. He knew immediately whom the letter was from. Brady took out his pocketknife and slit open the envelope. It was a short letter, but it packed a frightening punch.

Dear Brady,
I can't express how disappointed I am in you.
I believed you would have made an excellent jihadist.
But you fooled me.
You turned out to be nothing more than another self-centered American, and a true enemy of Islam.
Now, you are my enemy.
Enjoy the pictures of our work.
This is only the beginning.
Always watch your back, Brady.
I owe you one, for the brothers I've lost—especially for Haamid.
Your time on this earth is short.
You are a marked man.
Allah Akbar. Allah Akbar. Allah Akbar
—Maya

Accompanying the letter were photos of the attack. The images would be burned into Brady's mind forever. Brady excused himself. He got up and walked onto the porch. Immediately, he called General Whitfield. Two days later, he reported for duty.

The die was cast.

Brady would seek revenge for the terrorist attack on Independence Day, 2010.

In the year to come the terrorists, especially Maya, would also seek their revenge on Brady.

--- The End ---

Made in the USA
Charleston, SC
19 May 2014